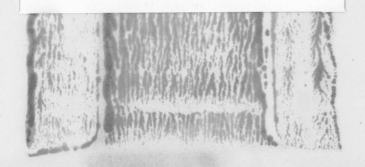

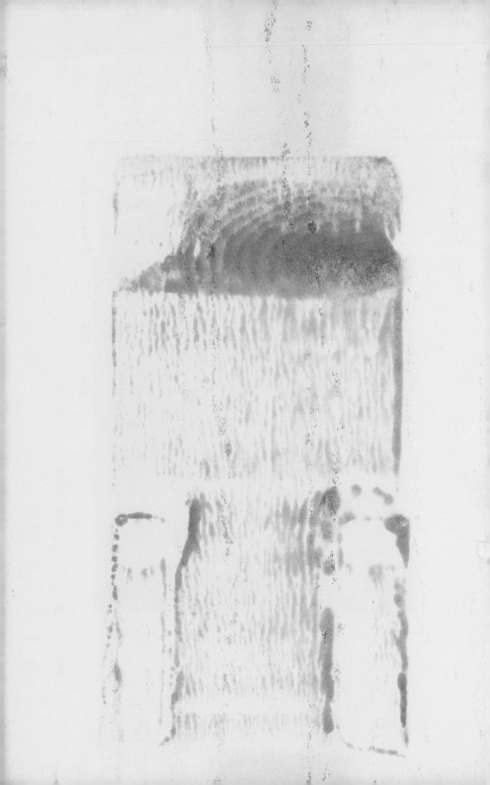

THE SMILE ON THE FACE
OF THE LION

BOOKS BY

P. M. Pasinetti

✵

VENETIAN RED

THE SMILE ON THE FACE
OF THE LION

The SMILE
on the FACE
of the LION

P. M. Pasinetti

Random House   New York

TO *L. B.* MORE THAN ONCE

*My return confronts me with the facts of over twenty years past,
years that seem very close, but not because time is quick (in
relation to what?) or life short, but rather because facts, actions,
once they have entered time, are never exhausted; the telling of a
story is never finished; everything is alive around me, and full of
questions; writing this I stir the ground, but I don't pretend that
I am settling anything.*

—MARCO PARTIBON in *Venetian Red*

THE SMILE ON THE FACE OF THE LION

CHAPTER ONE

✳

After crossing a vestibule crowded with raincoats, Genziana Horst had only to enter the Solmis' living room and
look around a moment to realize that the evening would be
wasted. There was no one there of any importance, and it
was improbable that the situation would be saved by the
arrival of new guests; nothing by now could change what
Tranquillo Massenti, a journalist friend long ago discarded
but whose manner of speaking had stuck with her, would
have called "the composition" or "the blend" of the reception.

She saw first of all the Solmis themselves, in full force:
Orlando, the father, more and more pretentiously taciturn
with the passing of years and of failures, his head lowered
and his shiny, questioning eyes looking at you above the
glasses that slipped down his nose—an expression that was
intended to be sly, and betrayed instead uncertainty and
visions of bankruptcy. And she saw Aurora, his wife, who
in contrast to her husband looked self-assured and expan-
sive, although in her expansiveness one suspected streaks of
folly; she was now talking, with stubborn intensity, to
"good" D'Abbate, who was, like Orlando Solmi, a labori-
ous and minor journalist. And there were the three sons,

(3)

Duilio, Amerigo, and Sebastiano ("The young Solmis," Tranquillo Massenti had said once, "have patriotically been named after battleships"), who by the very fact of looking so much like one another, seemed forever excluded from any possibility of distinction. Two of the daughters-in-law were insignificant, but the third, from Milan, was very attractive, spoke with a nasal unfriendly accent, "came from a much nicer family," and therefore maintained an attitude of challenging impatience.

Finally there was also a peripheral Solmi, not literary or artistic and suspicious like the others, but in fact looking rather provincial, round, rosy-cheeked, and disinterestedly happy to be there. Genziana could place this last Solmi too, with his shiny silk shirt, Tito by name: his home was in Bologna, and, even according to her very demanding standards, he was very rich; when he came down to Rome he went to all of the previews at the theaters, and made it clear that he had been to all of those in Milan as well; he was also very well informed about recent literature and films—all of which, in Genziana's eyes, was the infallible sign of provincialism.

Then she noticed all of the D'Abbates, all of the Merlos, people whom she hadn't seen in years. A Russian theatrical pair, of the second or third order. The "little" Asteggiano girl, who was, all things considered, a perennial acting-school student. And an isolated and inexplicable Navy officer. The rest were friends of the young Solmis': young men now stuck in the background, holding tall glasses of a fruit beverage up to their chests.

"I was right," Genziana whispered to her escort, Quarto Martelli, who from the height of his basketball tallness was looking around delightedly. "I told you that it would be deadly." Genziana could immediately catalogue the young men in the background as belonging to the peripheries of the cinema. One of the Solmis was an architect and had dreams of branching out into set designing. Was it possible that they had invited her to see people of that caliber?

Quarto Martelli did not understand her. Quarto was originally from the Northern and Central Italian countryside, and did not always behave in such a way as to make one forget this and other points against him. But rather than saying "points against him," talking to herself Genziana would say, using the English word, "liabilities." Especially after her months in America, she had taken to mentally listing people with two columns, as in banking accounts. However, in the end Quarto's assets won over his liabilities, his stock was solid: very evidently handsome; very rich; very devoted to her.

Among the people present at the Solmi party, Genziana gave the largest assets to the Milanese daughter-in-law: she was practically the only hope of the house. Genziana now saw her cross the living room with the usual impatient tension on her beautiful lips, and move toward the next room, the "small" living room. Therefore Genziana, after exchanging conventional greetings with the Solmis, took Quarto's arm and followed the Milanese daughter-in-law, who crossed the "small" living room with determination, disappeared through a back door toward the bedrooms, and perhaps one would never see her again.

But in a far corner of this darker room, three isolated people were sitting: two women and a man. All three turned their faces to look at Genziana and Quarto, who therefore saw themselves suddenly trapped. Genziana's irritation grew because Quarto, grasping the situation with the sly quickness which in docile characters occasionally erupts like the unexpected, jumpy agility in the fat, left her side and retreated toward the larger living room, murmuring that he thought he had recognized an old friend there.

Of the three people who now stared at Genziana from their comfortable chairs, she could recognize only one: the Fassola girl; the man with them looked like a blond and curly prize fighter and was absolutely new to her. At first Genziana tried to tell herself that Dora Fassola was decidedly "much better" than any of the guests in the next room; but almost immediately, recalling past encounters at exhibitions or shows or perhaps at some embassy, she concluded that they must all have been "cultural" occasions, of a film-club type. Again she felt the bite of anger. She remembered the insistent voice of Aurora Solmi on the telephone: "We know how busy you are, but Tuesday evening, really . . ."

At some point Genziana had even thought that the Solmis might want to cultivate her in view of the prestige of her father. She no longer lived in his house on Via Po, since for some time now she had been living by herself on Via Archimede, but she maintained tender relations with him, and the custom of attending Mass and dining together on Sundays. She had always been amused and "a little bit moved" by the idea that being the daughter of Senator Horst could represent a large asset in people's eyes; it was like remembering herself seated on her father's lap, or standing in a picture, a very thin girl, her mother in a Red Cross uniform holding her by the hand. Her father's assets, even when he was Undersecretary for Foreign Affairs, a post which had a sort of superficial elegance, to her had always seemed "frankly a bit funny"; however, she knew how to accept her father, along with the memory of her mother, now dead twenty years, and of the Church, and of that vibration of colors, uniforms, and words that was the fatherland, the *patria;* and if other people had use for values of that kind, and therefore saw in her, above all, the daughter of Senator Mario Horst, she was ready to make

(6)

them happy by assuming the proper attitude.

But it was evident that this had not been the case with the Solmis this evening. The "themes" of the evening (even that word "themes," she realized, could be traced back to Tranquillo Massenti) were, if any, Art, Cinema, and perhaps even Society. And then Genziana asked herself: Was it possible that the Solmis did not know *her* caliber? A more serious feeling of rancor overtook her: *Nobody has the right to impose upon me a single hour that is not either amusing or useful.*

"Good evening, Dora," she said, answering the little Fassola girl, who had got up to greet her. Her dark hair was parted in the middle in a slightly antiquated style; her reddened cheeks shone against the whiteness, also somehow old-fashioned, of her skin; her eyes followed Genziana's every gesture as though she were ready to copy them. Genziana recalled that Dora Fassola was reputed to be a sensual and easy girl, and with a cutting smile she observed her breasts: at the right point of roundness, clearly desirable. She did not allow her time to make any introductions: "I am Genziana Horst," she said, offering her hand to the other lady, who was small, looked thirty, and was seated with her legs drawn under her in the armchair; she registered that introduction without opening her mouth, maintaining an expression of sweet and disarming curiosity in her large, light-colored eyes; for a long moment she held Genziana's thin, athletic hand in her own left, which was heavily ringed, extremely small, soft, and warm. Irritated by that behavior, Genziana turned abruptly to the huge blond man, and offering him her hand she said with determination: "Good evening, and who can you be? I don't believe I have ever seen you."

Bernardo Partibon nodded as he raised himself, huge and corpulent, mumbling his own name, shaking Genziana's hand. He made room for her near himself, and when they were seated he kept staring at her in silence. After a few moments he said in a deep, slow voice: "The Boschinettis were telling me about you."

"Umberto?"

He nodded by lowering his eyelids slowly: "Umberto."

"So you know Umberto Boschinetti. We are very old friends. I adore Umberto."

Again he nodded with his eyelids; after a silence he added: "He is my agent here in Rome."

"What an extraordinary thing. I find this is really rather an extraordinary thing."

He looked at her uneasily. "For that matter," he went on with a deep, secure voice and yet as if every word cost him considerable effort, "so many others, too, not only Umberto and Teresa." Suddenly he lit up: "But of course. From a distance, you are tremendously admired by Clement Blumenfeld." He paused. "The sculptor, you know." He turned to the other two women: "Clement's show opens next week on Friday," he told them.

"Did you think I didn't know?" Dora Fassola said.

"Next week on Friday?" the other lady said with surprise.

"Well, I knew it, didn't I?"

"Clement admires you very much, and so do several little girl friends of his," Partibon resumed, turning to Genziana. "They all admire you madly."

Dora Fassola was following this talk with clear embarrassment.

"How amusing," Genziana cried out, "tell me all." Her eyes were fixed on Bernardo but they did not seem to see him. They were green, still eyes.

"But Bernardo, just now when you were going to reveal to us the anguishing mysteries of Maria," the little lady crouching on the chair said with disappointment. She had a

(8)

northern accent and a leisurely, yet hard way of talking. "Go on, don't let the lady interrupt you." And to Genziana: "Bernardo here was telling us things that you can't even imagine."

"Really? May one listen?"

There was a tense silence; Dora Fassola broke it: "I guess it's you, Genziana, that stopped him dead."

"I had nothing to say anyhow," Partibon mumbled, "nothing to reveal, especially concerning Maria."

"What a pity," Genziana cried, "and who is Maria?" She obtained no reply, so she asked Partibon in a lower voice: "And you, where are you from? You don't live in Rome, do you?" From Bernardo's mumbling at the introduction she had grasped the name Partibon, which she could place on account of the fame of other members of that family, but she thought she wouldn't concede this point.

"No. No," Partibon said, "no. I'm a Venetian."

"Yes, of course, you are from Venice," Genziana said quickly.

"No. Or, at least, not I. I'm a countryside Partibon."

"What an amusing way to say it. Have you been in Rome a long time?"

"I am in Rome now."

"Are you going back to Venetia later on?"

A shadow went through Bernardo's eyes. He turned in confusion to the little lady: "Yes, after all, that's what we were talking about, *after all?* And yet, Cecilia, you don't really know anything at all."

Dora Fassola, while she stared at Bernardo, was so tense that she clutched the arms of her chair and bit her lower lip.

Bernardo remembered Genziana and tried to answer her naturally: "No, I don't live there, I don't live in Venetia."

The little lady moved her eyes a couple of times from

(9)

Bernardo to Genziana; then she shrugged: "You know what I am thinking? I am thinking that I would like to leave. I don't think anybody would notice. Dora brought us here, but I don't know anybody here, and besides, I got it all wrong—I thought it was an invitation to dinner and I'm famished."

From the next room came a short, unconvinced clapping of hands, then somebody at the piano started playing California jazz. Bernardo cocked his ear.

"Oh, God, this is Gianni Merlo starting," Dora said.

"I am asking myself too," Genziana said, "how I happen to be here, and I won't deny that an unobserved escape appeals to me considerably."

Nobody bothered with her. Then she looked fixedly at the little lady and adopted a tone which could be taken, at one's choice, for either camaraderie or aggressiveness: "When we introduced ourselves I did not quite get your name. Are you a Venetian too?"

"No, I am not. I came from Lombardy originally, but we are often here in Rome or in other places. However, I love to stay in Rome, even more than in Paris, I don't mind telling you. I'm here more often than in the Brianza or in Switzerland, no matter where my husband is, you know? As a matter of fact, he too likes to be in Rome as often as possible."

"The Ghezzi-Walthers," Dora Fassola said with mechanical good manners, "have a house here in Rome too, so Mrs. Ghezzi-Walther lives a little bit everywhere."

"That's it, I live a little bit everywhere, and in spite of the fact that he has his business and I, generally speaking, have not, in the long run I travel even more than my husband does. This year I took my little trip to New York all alone, and it was in New York that I discovered Bernardo"—she laid her small hand on Bernardo's forearm, shaking it gently—"so that now he has come to Italy to see us; in fact, he and I flew across together."

"To see *you?* Really, Cecilia . . ." But as though there were too many things to be said, Bernardo Partibon limited himself to a deep sigh.

Mrs. Ghezzi-Walther's explanations made Genziana feel completely at ease: she had placed these people, she had regained her bearings. She looked at the little lady expertly, measuring her; she postponed her until later; she turned authoritatively to Partibon: "So you live in New York? And how come we didn't see each other? I spent six months there last year and I met everybody; where were you?"

Partibon opened his arms wide, shaking his head, and at that point Genziana abandoned him; she turned to Mrs. Ghezzi-Walther: "The trip to New York has become for everybody a little bit what the trip to Paris used to be." Even this phrase, she recalled, was a relic from Tranquillo Massenti; it could be traced back to a few years earlier, when Tranquillo had managed to have his newspaper send him to America for a couple of months to write some articles which, as a matter of fact, had turned out to be rather brilliant; at that time the phrase had been an exaggeration, and therefore acceptable; but now, Genziana felt, one had to distinguish oneself from the already numerous Italian tourists in America.

Bernardo Partibon's natural question: "And what were you doing in New York?" offered her the useful cue.

She drew from the world of fashion a couple of personalities which she considered key names and let them drop into her speech; as for the cinema, she hinted at one or two eminent figures in the industry; she smiled, ready to turn the whole thing into irony if it should appear that Partibon despised the cinema; she mentioned actresses for whom she had designed costumes, and the titles of the pictures; when

(11)

she mentioned *Appointment at Taormina* everybody made a sign of recognition, so that, feeling safer, she concluded with a phrase she had already launched a few evenings earlier, trying to be elegantly modest: "And now I have been signed as the wardrobe mistress for *Caligula*."

"Is that so?" Partibon said. "Do you also accept roles as an actress?"

The girl's eyes, lit with surprise, looked like the glass windows in an aquarium.

"No"—and she laughed in a dry, forced manner—"I say wardrobe mistress meaning costume designer; I design costumes."

"Oh, I know you do that"—but it wasn't clear whether Bernardo had really understood—"in fact, as a matter of fact, what's his name, Umberto Boschinetti was telling me about you . . . And then, as I was saying, Clement Blumenfeld. Clement reads the papers a lot, and all that you . . . and then . . . " His voice was lost in a mumble.

"They have asked me to design some costumes for *Caligula,* the mammoth production, the supercolossus, the horror that Harry Berger is coming to Italy to produce . . ."

At that name, Partibon had a brief glimmer of recognition, immediately extinguished; he limited himself to smiling wistfully.

"But I wonder," Genziana cried, "what Umberto Boschinetti may have told you about me."

"Umberto? He goes fox hunting here in Rome, pink coat and all; he is really a funny fellow." Bernardo lowered his voice: "Some of his friends, on account of his monarchist bit, call him Umberto the Third."

"Is that so?" It didn't seem as though Genziana had been listening. Then, as if she were memorizing a telephone number, she repeated: "I adore Umberto."

"I wonder," said Cecilia Ghezzi-Walther, "whether you have realized that we don't give a damn about your Umberto? Do you know him, Dora? I think I've seen him perhaps once or twice. Why don't we talk about people that we all know well? I like tremendously to talk about people, but to really like it, it has to be people I know well. Then really . . ."

"You were saying that Umberto is your agent here in Rome," Genziana said to Bernardo, "does that mean that you too have something to do with art?"

"Why, yes"—and Partibon lowered his huge head—"yes. In fact, I always had to do with art. I know about it," he said sadly. "From the time when I was a boy, I have been buying, selling, and then I have redesigned houses, many in California, several also in Texas."

Now the little Ghezzi-Walther lady was following him with delight. "Wait and see what he is going to do next!" she inserted. "He'll fix up whole cities."

Bernardo went on without listening to her: "One can make a lot of money," he announced with astonishment, as if he were discovering at that point the money he had made, "you have no idea the amount of money you can make. Now," he concluded hastily, "I am sort of associated with an extraordinary architect, of Bulgarian origin."

"Lucky you," said Genziana, who found it elegant to refer to herself as a pauper, "you should teach me the secret."

Bernardo looked at her straight in the face: "At this point," he said, "the whole thing leaves me completely cold." He turned, in confusion, to the two other women; Mrs. Ghezzi-Walther extended her short arms toward him, took his hand, and kept it softly in her own.

Dora was watching Partibon as if he had been a patient;

(13)

now it was as if she had recognized a predictable symptom. "Listen," she said with determination, "what would you think if we left this place?"

"We would think that that's what I said a moment ago," said Mrs. Ghezzi-Walther, "the problem is how to do it."

"Do you want us all to go?" Genziana asked, rising abruptly. All looks were on her. "Do you know what I'm going to do? I'm going to the next room, I'll see how things are and I'll prepare the way, then I'll come back and report to you."

"Really?" Partibon asked as if hypnotized by her practicality, yet with an air so somnolent and confused that it was not clear whether he had really grasped the scheme. "Let's do this," he mumbled, "let's all go to . . ." He mentioned a bar. "There we'll talk, we'll sit down and talk. Let's go there, let's sit down and talk."

"That's exactly why the lady is going there to study the situation," Mrs. Ghezzi-Walther said, "then she'll come back here and tell us the best way for us to leave and go somewhere. Not to drink but *to eat*."

"We'll go to that place there . . . "—Bernardo insisted on his bar—"we'll sit down and be quiet."

"In a moment I'll be back with a definite plan." Genziana left the room rapidly.

In the larger living room she found most people assembled around a piano that Gianni Merlo was playing. Strategically that suited her very well.

Genziana Horst enjoyed at this point a feeling of voluptuousness which was no less exhilarating for being restrained, a feeling she always had when she was on the verge of taking hold of a situation and conquering a new world. The appearance of Bernardo Partibon, somewhere between a Northern Italian country gentleman and an American athlete, the big industrial name of Ghezzi-Walther, the curiosity, or, to be frank, the violent attraction that those people had aroused in her were increased by the fact that the reception at the Solmis' had appeared at first so hopeless. Moreover, there was now the amusement of going back to Quarto, a young man who was sufficiently attractive and well fixed in his own right to make her find pleasure in any demonstration of her social superiority to him, and announcing her project to leave the place together with those people who were by far the best there, possibly to go to more brilliant gatherings.

She became aware of difficulties as soon as she found Quarto engaged in conversation with the Solmi from Bologna. Quarto turned to her with a reddened face, got up from his seat to make room for her, and announced with a wide, festive smile: "Genziana, you don't know anything yet. You can't even imagine what I have found here." Solmi listened to these words with his mouth open, looking at Genziana with his blue, round, shiny eyes, and with a beatific smile which was like an inner illumination.

"You don't know who this man is?" Quarto asked, his left arm around Tito Solmi's shoulders, holding him close to himself, and with his right hand giving little pats on the man's rubicund cheek. "This is Tito! You don't know. Just think of this: all of our secondary school together, and do you think that's all? Oh, no. When he was at the University of Bologna, and I was at Ferrara, we played together on the national basketball team. And now I find him here, I see him all of a sudden in front of me, a thousand years later. It's been at least a thousand years, hasn't it?" He looked delightedly at Solmi's full red cheek, as if ready to stamp a kiss on it. Then suddenly: "And the Bertuetti girls, Pia and Malvina, do you remember them?" Tito nodded energetically, without words, choked with joy.

"How curious," Genziana said without looking at them.

(15)

"By the way," Quarto asked Solmi, "you know Genziana, don't you?"

"What . . . what a question, we're very old friends, aren't we?"

Genziana observed with some disgust that while Tito exaggerated rather heavily, he did not do so in order to show off in front of Quarto but rather out of exuberant affection toward his rediscovered comrade; in other words, this was their triumph, the males' triumph. "Damn them," she said to herself, looking at the two men, "they are from Bologna." They were not exactly, but to Genziana the name of that city epitomized a mixture of rich greasy food, wines, warm voices, expansiveness, deep sensual satisfaction, which she found singularly detestable.

"Listen, Quarto," she said, managing not to alter her voice, "there are some extraordinarily charming people in the next room, and we said we would all leave together."

Quarto's voice became thin and lamenting: "You are joking, aren't you? And for that matter"—he returned to his usual robust and friendly tone—"there are some nice, wonderful people here, you know. Not to mention Tito, who is like a brother. And then he knows everything about the sort of things that interest you. Art exhibits, actresses. Sit down here with us for a while."

Quarto's speech, putting her on the same level as that man, was wildly embarrassing to Genziana.

Meanwhile the jazz at the piano was finished, and the people who had gathered around it were dispersing. Most of them knew about the reunion of Quarto Martelli and Tito Solmi, and they came to admire them. The host, Orlando Solmi, dismissed his usual expression of suspicious slyness, and said with suddenly childish eyes: "Our world is very small, isn't it?" He was sincerely curious to discover on those two red faces the secret of such a festive meeting.

From a distance the "little" Asteggiano girl was devouring the two huge comrades with her eyes. Small and
shapely, with shiny black hair slicked down on her egg-
shaped head, and sensual dark eyes, she had a way of hatch-
ing other people's feelings as though they belonged to her
too: she claimed a kind of bonus on them. She kept apart
from the others and looked at Quarto and Tito with an expression of marvel, abandoned languor, and greedy possession, which she had perfected in acting schools; and she
seemed to be saying: "Yes, yes, everybody is gathering
around you to celebrate, but the only one in this room that
really vibrates along with you is myself." The two young
men felt the girl's eyes on them and were subconsciously
perplexed.

"In school he was already tall as a lamppost; playing
basketball he didn't even have to jump. He could make a
basket without moving, as you throw something into the
trash can." Standing at his side, Tito threw proud glances at
Quarto as if he were offering him for sale in the market
place. "And then he left and went to Ferrara, because with
his brains he would never have been able to get his degree
at Bologna."

"Well, well, if *you* managed . . . and besides, Ferrara is
a little jewel of a university," Quarto said, finding that
phrase between his teeth like the taste of fruit; he looked at
Tito with gratitude; he had visions of light clear mornings,
perfect for cutting school and going on bicycle rides; he saw
the sun hitting the river bank, he heard summer songs in the
country, far away, thin as the buzzing of insects.

Everybody understood the two men's state of ecstasy.
Even the young Solmis seemed to bask in the heat of that
encounter; the habitual tension on the pale, pointed faces of
those unsuccessful young men was being loosened.

"Not to mention the women," somebody murmured,

(17)

"Ferrara is famous all over the world for its women, isn't it?" Then Merlo started to play a waltz, which erupted triumphantly and spread around the room on its wide waves full of ceremony and tenderness.

Genziana had remained straight, near Quarto, looking questioningly at him; she whispered through clenched teeth: "I wouldn't want to let those people wait. What about coming to the next room with me, Quarto?"

He looked at Tito, who smiled back. He said: "What people? And at any rate, why don't you go with them? Take my car if you want," and he offered her the keys.

Genziana looked at him with open antipathy. She had never looked at him that way, nor had Quarto ever addressed her in that tone; there was in the man a dark sense of sarcasm and of retaliation. For the first time in the almost six months since they had started going together, Genziana suspected that her refusal to yield herself completely could turn out to be a serious danger. She felt that she had enjoyed over him the superiority of the self-controlled person—that she had, after all, preferred to exploit the possibilities for sadism that were offered by his face when he took the ardent and abject expressions of the repelled sensualist; she felt she was being abandoned now, and understood that this was the first fruit of the encounter between those two, of that "Bologna" alliance; she also realized that she had been physically afraid of Quarto. With a streak of anger she whispered: "I'm really going, you know? I'll leave you here and I won't come back."

"If that's what you want . . . But of course"—and his friendly, conciliatory tone gave her a vague feeling of vertigo—"I'll leave you my car, you may go with these people you've found, we'll meet later if you want, or perhaps tomorrow."

"Naturally, of course," Tito confirmed, "I have my

Oldsmobile. And by the way, do you know who else should be coming here tonight? Semenzato. Ovidio Semenzato. He is making a tremendously successful career, Ovidio is. Chair of Modern History practically assured. You do read his articles in *Roma Sabato* magazine, don't you? First-rate stuff." Solmi oozed the joy of feeling well fed, well dressed, generous, a subscriber to the right magazines, in touch with people who wrote in them, people in whose successes he proudly participated. "Ovidio studied at Padua," he explained to Genziana, "but he played basketball too."

Genziana looked at him icily. She raised her eyebrows and switched on a light of astonishment. For that matter, neither politics nor the university were particularly elegant things on the whole, and at any rate one should treat all friends of these two men as rather curious and marginal figures, thereby always confirming one's authority over Quarto. "Perhaps I'll come back later," she told him, as if Solmi's talk about this man Ovidio Semenzato had not existed, "meanwhile you stay here. And I doubt that we'll have any use for your car." She left them abruptly without giving him time to reply.

But the talk between the two went on in back of her, and the words that reached her made her unexpectedly shudder: with gravity and almost with a tremor of emotion in his voice, Tito Solmi was telling Quarto: "And you will see, perhaps Ovidio will bring Tranquillo Massenti."

"If Tranquillo isn't drunk," Quarto said immediately, not with the peremptory and silly tone of one wanting to show his familiarity with the habits of well-known people, but rather as if wanting to share at once a sorrowful thought with a friend.

Genziana felt short of breath. What was happening? Suddenly she was living in a nightmare of uncertainty and abandonment. With Tranquillo the alliance of the males would be concluded; the incomprehensible solidarity among men whom she thought she had possessed would be horribly complete.

Little Asteggiano, suddenly bored at having cast so many unrequited looks of sentimental complicity, decided somehow to prevent Quarto and Tito from remaining at the center of attention. "But," she cried, "wasn't Michelino D'Abbate going to show us his documentary?"

Genziana, already at the door, had a feeling of relief: the whole atmosphere of the larger room was clearly painful. D'Abbate was a dilettante who made sixteen-millimeter films; in a moment they would place a silver-paper screen at the far end of the room and the lights would be turned out. That darkness would offer the right moment for escape, perhaps without farewells to anybody. That also seemed the best way to give Quarto and the Bologna Solmi a slap in the face.

But she hadn't really ever done things of that sort. Standing on the threshold, she realized that she was trembling. Discourtesy, lack of form, put a feeling of void under her feet. The world was turning upside down. And who was making her do this? There were three people in the next room, about whom she knew little or nothing; two of them she had known only in the last hour. And yet wasn't it their presence, after all, that induced her to escape? Who were they? What force did they possess?

She tried to fight these questions and to regain her balance. At one point she thought that she would just say a few graceful words to those people and would not join them in the escape, after all. She would remain in the larger living room, stay on at the Solmis' a short while yet, then leave with Quarto. There was still time. It would be easy, alone in the car, to erase even the memory of that Tito Solmi. All would be normal again, under control.

Yet as soon as she entered the smaller room and saw in the faint light those three lonely figures whom she had left a moment ago, and who already seemed to be part of her life, she understood that the escape with them was inevitable. She had started it as a game, but now she realized that the game had come to an end.

In the larger living room, Tito Solmi was saying with a glorious smile: "I'll bet you this is Ovidio Semenzato."

And in fact, in spite of Genziana Horst's contrary predictions, guests even less punctual than herself were standing in front of the shiny old door of the Solmis' apartment, pressing the brass button of the bell.

CHAPTER TWO

✿

Ovidio Semenzato:

When I came in at the Solmis', all was dark. "Here we are," I told myself, "movies again." I may add that I did not like the Solmis. Besides, I was going through a period which I suppose exists in every man's life, when you discover that you are stuck with friendships that don't interest you, and you feel the rage of never having been able to say clearly to yourself: "I'll be impolite, they'll say I am not civilized, but I am not interested in seeing those people, and I shall never see them again." Instead, here I was again, with the lame music from the little piano, and the improvised screen on which there undoubtedly appeared landscapes and figures equally lame and useless. And I would again have to listen to the endless talks about the beautiful shots, magnificent sequences, etc., all things for which, frankly, I had no taste.

The friends with whom I had come were, however, interested in the cinema and its problems; they rushed immediately toward the, shall we say, projection room; they themselves, for that matter, were improvised—I mean, they were no particular friends of mine, rather people I had fallen back on; unfortunately I had not managed to locate Tranquillo Massenti and bring him along. I stood there a while, alone and disheartened, in that dark vestibule, airless, stuffed with overcoats.

And then, there we were. A huge man came in from the living room. He seemed to be feeling his way, both because the light was dim and because he was somewhat clumsy and uncertain in his motions; he went to look for the telephone on a chest in a corner.

I don't know what there was about the man, but the fact is that from the moment I saw him come in I could not take my eyes away from him while he sat heavily on the chest, disentangled the telephone from the overcoats that buried it, grabbed the receiver, dialed a number. He did not see me as I spied on his every gesture.

Then he started to talk and I almost jumped: I recognized something in the voice. This was rather odd, because I did not understand very much of what he was saying. I know little English and he was speaking English. He talked slowly and at length. Then he remained listening, punctuating the silence with several "all rights," always stressing the first of those two words: "*all* right, *all* right." After the last of these "*all* rights," he got away from the telephone, raised himself to the fullness of his enormous size, and came toward me. He had seen me. He stopped in front of me, looking. He said nothing, just looked. He had by no means the stupidly challenging aspect of a drunk; he was looking at me with huge, oval, still eyes, set unusually far apart in a wide face, well planted on the robust neck, which emerged freely from a comfortable collar. In spite of his somewhat strange expression, he managed to exude an air of such frank friendliness that I smiled and tried my English:

"How do you do?"

"How do *you* do?" he said expressively, as if to make me

understand that he attributed a precise significance to that otherwise conventional formula of greeting; then he took me by the arm and said in Italian: "Listen, you must do me a great favor."

His voice now gave me an even more vexing sense of recognition. Where had I heard it? And where had I seen eyes like those? Curiosity must have confused me because when we introduced ourselves, to his simple "Bernardo Partibon" I replied, "Professor Semenzato," whereas like every civilized person I hate introductions preceded by a title. Anyhow, his name gave me the clue.

"There is undoubtedly a family resemblance," I said. "You have no idea how your voice . . . something here between your eyes and your forehead . . . it all reminds me of your cousin Giorgio."

He had a curious way of receiving my words; as though I had spoken not of him and of a relative of his, but of my own affairs, and he was listening out of courtesy, without much curiosity. The fact that I knew his cousin did not surprise him at all—which was natural, I told myself, with people much used to fame. His casualness did not irritate me, I only wondered whether he had listened to me at all; therefore, as a scholar accustomed to ascertaining facts, I insisted: "Your cousin Giorgio and I took our degree in history at Padua. I saw him a few months ago in Paris; he gave some splendid lectures at the Sorbonne. Then he was going to England, to Oxford, and of course to see his sister."

As I was providing him with these data he was nodding rhythmically, but his abstracted smile convinced me that he was not listening. For that matter, the name of Bernardo Partibon, who I think was called Dino by the family, had been mentioned only rarely in our circle of Venetian university friends, as that of a person who had left Italy before the war and whose tracks had practically been lost. How could he be at all interested in our little local relationships, in old Europe?

It was at that point that his face brightened and he said in a slightly breathless manner: "Of course you took your degree together, you and Giorgio, but then you left for Vienna, for your studies in nineteenth-century history."

"But then," I stammered in astonishment, "you and I must have met before?"

"I don't believe so. I was away long before then. Left long before the war. Only, you see, I read, I read . . . But I wanted to ask you for a favor. There are some people in the living room"—and with his huge thumb over his shoulder he pointed to the room where they were showing the picture—"and they are waiting for me to come back so that we can leave together. Would you mind telling them that I had to leave and that they may go eat in peace and then join me at . . . " and he mentioned a bar. He evidently made a great effort to be casual as he gave me those instructions, but his preoccupied air of a moment earlier must actually have hidden some serious worry. I grew up in the house of a doctor, my uncle, and some of his gestures have remained with me: instinctively I extended my hand to take Partibon's pulse or to feel whether he had a temperature. But I limited myself to saying: "What's the matter? Did something happen?"

"Forgive me, I wouldn't ask you to do me this favor if there weren't reasons . . . " He was panting too. Then he took a deep, sportsman's breath. And he asked: "Do you know a lady called Cecilia Ghezzi-Walther?"

Firmino Ghezzi-Walther's wife; of course, I said, I knew who she was.

"Good. You'll find her in there. Talk to her and make my excuses. Thank you. And I hope we'll meet again." I nodded. He seemed a bit relieved. I realized that keeping calm must have cost him considerable effort.

He started looking around the room, on the chests and chairs. Finally, from a bunch of raincoats he extracted his own and put it on; it was short, tight, wrinkled. He came near me and offered his hand. He had very thick wrists coming out of the tight sleeves of his raincoat, and rather powerful hands with nails clipped very short. A peasant from the North, that's what he was, moving and acting like a gentleman. "Thank you," he repeated, "you do me a really big favor."

"You can't even call it a favor." I continued to look at him questioningly, a bit perplexed by his mysterious hurry. I would have been even more perplexed had I known that there was no really urgent reason for him to leave so abruptly. At any rate, not a practical one.

He was already opening the door to leave the apartment when somebody coming from the living room made him stop on the threshold. A girl I knew *vaguely;* Dora Fassola. So that was it.

I am trying to reconstruct what hit me particularly at that first moment. The name Fassola perhaps? And why? Because it was, so to speak, one of the historical names in the Italy of fifteen or twenty years ago? Or because as a scholar, or let us say as an observer of society and customs, I am interested in the history of families that were powerful? No, no. Dora's aspect, the way she walked, moved, looked—those are the things that matter. A radiance. A sudden and absolute revelation. So much so that I could not have put it into words. If I had been able to do that, I would have come out with a phrase of this kind: "Either I take advantage of this moment or my life will be extinguished in grayness." How about that?

"What are you doing?" she asked Bernardo Partibon in a low voice. She was not scolding him for attempting a secret escape; rather, she seemed to be protecting him. "Where do you want to go? Alone like that?" She was holding him under her gaze, but with devotion.

He told her: "You know? Now I am sure that Maria has been in Rome."

"And has she already gone back to Venice? Who told you that she has been here?"

I don't know why, but his answer at that moment seemed awfully curious to me: "People from the Vatican." And he specified: "That English Monsignor, you know, that friend of Debaldè's."

"So," Dora said. "And what about Clement?"

"The Monsignor told me that he called our house but only Clement was there, who in such cases sometimes pretends he doesn't know English, he pretends he is German, or Russian, you know how he is. Now, it seems that Clement too wanted to go to Venice. He said so to this English Monsignor, in German, a language that the Monsignor hardly understands."

"And did you look for Ugo Debaldè?" Dora asked. That name, Debaldè, rang a bell with me, although I couldn't quite place it.

Bernardo said: "No, I saw only that journalist, Massenti." At the mention of that great friend of mine I stepped forward, but the Fassola girl seemed to postpone further explanations with Bernardo Partibon. She was already aware of my presence but had done nothing about it until then; now she shook hands with me: "Good evening, Professor," she said. With her flushed face and her very black eyes wide open in the dim light of that room, she had an air somewhere between a woman and a child. At that moment I had

(2 7)

my first unmistakable feeling of tenderness. Let us put it simply: I could have taken her in my arms right there, squeezed her, kissed her.

"So, you see, I am sure that Maria has been here in Rome," Bernardo resumed gravely, "but I am sure of something else too—namely, that she hasn't wanted to see me."

Dora took him by the hand: "You have been asking yourself the same question for days. Well, find her somehow, and just turn up suddenly in front of her. I am saying this because obviously you don't feel like leaving for America again without having talked to her."

"It isn't simply a matter of seeing Maria and talking to her, there is much more than that. I mean, finding a sense of reality." A rather cryptic phrase.

And yet I felt no annoyance. I found him absolutely *simpatico*; it's an old word but there isn't a better one. "Listen," I told him, "you still want me to tell Mrs. Ghezzi-Walther that you've left, or are you going to stay on, or is . . . Dora going to deliver your message? What are you going to do? If I can be useful in any way . . ."

He had that way of looking at you as though he absolutely did not listen. Curiously, such behavior did not make you angry but rather gave you a desire to help him. I turned to Dora to create between the two of us the solidarity of adults contemplating a child in danger. But instead of a child we had a man, and of that size.

That was not all. On the one side there was the fact that Dora, although jealously guarding Partibon, did not want to asphyxiate him with sympathy and affection, and she let him make decisions, simply and naturally keeping informed; on the other side there was the fact that Partibon, in spite of his lost air, was capable at some point of a practicality which I shall describe as American, just to make myself clear, not because Americans seem to me more prac-

(28)

tical than others. Well, anyway, he took little Fassola by the wrists, and looking into her eyes he said: "You go back in, stay as long as you want, then you all go to the . . ."—and he mentioned a restaurant—"sit down and eat quietly, Cecilia is dying of hunger." He turned to me: "Thank you. It's all set."

Dora said in her sweet, well-educated voice: "Very well, I'll tell the others. We'll watch a little piece of the picture and then we'll go. Good-bye, Bernardo." She turned around and went into the living room, perfectly proper and composed, her small solid shoulders slightly stooped.

Bernardo shook hands with me: "I hope we'll meet again." I said I hoped so too, and I was being sincere. We exchanged a few more amenities. His hand was already on the doorknob.

But evidently fate was not going to let him go in peace. From the living room another person came in, a very recognizable figure, none other than Genziana Horst. I have always considered her one of the most attractive women in Rome. She is splendidly built, deceptively thin (*falsa magra,* I think), and she moves and addresses people always with the air of a lady asking for road directions from behind the wheel of an extremely classy automobile. And on the other hand she always knows how to find the familiarity and casualness of a person possessing two virtues: extremely good manners, and the sense of really counting for something. I frankly welcomed the idea of knowing her a little better. This was a totally disinterested desire on my part. My world is a different one, and the wide reputation of Miss Horst in some circles is not quite the sort of thing that makes a tremendous impression on me. However, even from a distance, in my own way I had admired her for a long time, because, although the daughter of Senator Mario Horst, i.e., of a rather prominent politician, she had not followed the routine of comforts and a good marriage but had opened a fashion shop in association with a friend; first with that, and later with theater and cinema work about which I do not know very much, she had made quite a name for herself; in other words, she had acquired a distinct personality. Well, this business of personality, and the difficulty that Italian women have in creating one for themselves, is a fixed idea of my colleague in journalism and cherished friend, Tranquillo Massenti, as well as of my own; in our way of life, women are really the victims, or as Tranquillo, who has a talent for the right phrase, would say even better, they are "not contemplated"; therefore we have a tendency to admire, perhaps with exaggeration, those among them who manage to break the chains of the system and to show their independence, even, coming back to Miss Horst, in the way they have of entering a room. What with her and with the Fassola girl (the latter, compared to Miss Horst, had the embryonic air of an apprentice), I was beginning to feel happy after all that I had come to the deprecated Solmis' to end my evening. I was again beginning to warm up to the idea that Massenti and I have had for some time, of a great journalistic reportage on "women as victims"—a project which could have been under way already a long time ago if it hadn't been delayed by the uncertainties of Perineschi, the superficially self-assured but basically indecisive editor of *Roma Sabato;* meanwhile, incidentally, the theme will become outdated.

It seemed as though the vision of Genziana Horst was paralyzing Partibon at the door, his hand still on the knob. He was, purely and simply, mesmerized by those eyes.

Miss Horst went toward him with the social air of cordiality: "And what are you doing?" she asked him. It was a perfect question. At that point I did not even know that they had just met: considering this and what happened later, the question seems even more perfect. "And what are you . . . " Casual detachment, and yet, actually, taking possession of him and of the situation. She did know her way around.

Partibon mumbled something about engagements that had turned up: "Dora knows . . . I'll join you later . . ." but she was paying him back with currency that was usually his own—that is, she just stared at him as if she did not hear him. Then, quickly but very distinctly she said: "If you go away, are you going to take me with you?" Even more perfect than the first phrase. Regal and submissive: commanding her own rape. Partibon, in fact, did not even answer: now that she had told him, he realized he had not expected anything else.

They hardly said good-bye as they went out. I did not resent that at all: in fact I had witnessed what is referred to as a happy encounter. Here I was again, alone in the room full of raincoats. I thought at once of little Fassola, and with a smile on my lips I finally joined the company in the living room.

Here, darkness. Darkness and a sixteen-millimeter film (on Sicily, or something). By instinct I found Dora at once and went to sit near her. She was with Mrs. Ghezzi-Walther. I had been introduced to the latter a couple of times by Tranquillo Massenti, who knew people of that kind in Milan, because in that city they maintain contacts between industry and culture; but I wasn't counting on her remembering me. Nor could I ascertain this, because Mrs. Ghezzi-Walther is one of those ladies all sweetness and light who always act as if they know everybody, and are generally, as the saying goes, adored. A billionaire and, to my way of thinking, slightly dreadful, because under the surface of gentleness, there is always, in people like that, the stupendous capacity always to have their own way and to get

(31)

everybody to do things for them. I am not necessarily saying that there is conscious calculation in this, but the results
are the same. And for all practical purposes there can be, in
people like that, a huge fund of cruelty.

"There, you see?" Mrs. Ghezzi-Walther told me at once,
evidently very far from bothering with the little film, and
taking me somewhat embarrassingly into her confidence.
"You see? Our protégé has left us. And what were you telling each other, all the time you were away?"

"Partibon had told me . . ." I mumbled, "but there is
Dora here, who . . ."

"I see, you don't want to tell me what you were saying to
each other. Now really! What's Bernardo up to now? Actually it's one of his endearing sides—the fact that he is always in trouble. He is also a little bit of a maniac." She
looked at Dora as though encouraging her to assent. "He is
making phone calls, trying like mad to see his famous
Maria, I'll swear."

This kind of talk, understandable only up to a point, irritated me. I said: "Partibon left a moment ago with Miss
Horst."

They didn't know that. They hadn't imagined that. "With
Miss Horst? But this is wonderful," Mrs. Ghezzi-Walther
said, taking my hand in her own soft ones, with a slightly
expert and therefore basically indifferent touch, "this is
really incredible, tell me more."

"What can I tell you? I already told you everything."

"Everything? Such an incredible thing and you treat it
like that? Sit down, let's talk about it." And turning to Dora
Fassola: "Don't you think?"

I was simply astounded. That is, I was beginning to rearrange my ideas about these people's identities, and it had
occurred to me that the Fassola girl and Bernardo Partibon
were, in a quite singular manner, relatives. I could sense

something serious and delicate in their relationship. But Mrs. Ghezzi-Walther apparently wanted to turn everything into frivolity and vulgarity. I wanted somehow to save Dora from feeling ill at ease, but even before I could open my mouth, there she was, talking in the tone of the well-bred Venetian girl, skipping all allusions to Miss Horst: "Perhaps Bernardo had to meet with Clement too . . . Clement's exhibition opens next week and I know that before that, Clement wanted to take a short trip to Venice; perhaps I'll go myself a couple of days to Mother's."

"Yes, but meanwhile," Mrs. Ghezzi-Walther asked relentlessly, "what do you think Bernardo and Miss Horst will be doing? Don't you realize, Dora, what a funny story this is?" With my usual slowness in getting the message, I finally understood: in certain circles there was a notion abroad that Miss Horst was a lesbian. "Think," Mrs. Ghezzi-Walther resumed, "poor Bernardo, how funny."

"I seem to have understood," Dora resumed with her simple, practical good manners which I found more admirable every minute, "that Genziana had come here with that friend of hers, Quarto Martelli. We should look for Martelli and ask him to come with us to the place where Bernardo will join us later." She added that she had seen Quarto Martelli quietly disappear from the projection room to go to the smaller living room with Tito Solmi.

The two men she mentioned, Quarto Martelli and Tito Solmi, were known to me too. I had lost track of Martelli long ago, but I saw Tito relatively often when he came to Rome. I remembered that a few days earlier, having met him in Piazza di Spagna, he had told me: "We'll see each other Wednesday evening," but at that moment I had not understood what he meant. There are people who specialize in "seeing people" and "maintaining contacts"—extremely well informed about all shows, conventions, etc., in the city.

(33)

Tito Solmi is one of those people. Since the time when we knew each other as students, I had always considered him an imbecile. What I am going to add may indicate that I entertain a rather reproachable idea of the world and of men, but the fact is that my judgment of Tito changed and I started to find him even a tolerable and nice person when I saw that, without any great fuss, he was making an extraordinary amount of money.

Mainly in order to avoid both the little film and the silly and malevolent conversation of Mrs. Ghezzi-Walther, I said that I would go myself to look for Quarto Martelli in the next room; and I left. There, both Quarto and Tito welcomed me with extraordinary cheerfulness. I hadn't seen Martelli in years; he hadn't changed at all. The two of them behaved as though they hadn't been waiting for anything but me in order to feel completely exultant. Something like that embarrasses me. There may enter into this my rather solitary childhood and a thousand other things: by nature I am reluctant to recognize some of the simple manifestations of friendship. To an affectionate pat on the shoulder I react with an evasiveness which, I admit, must look like haughtiness rather than timidity. I work a lot and I live very much alone: that may be a reason too. But there are moments when, confronted with such a limpid cordiality as that of Tito Solmi, I should like to be able to reply with equal naturalness.

I made an effort in that direction. I smiled like a "good companion." I must say that it took very little: they were like dry straw, a spark sufficed for them to burst into flames. They looked rather drunk too. But they were not. They were meeting for the first time after I don't know how many years, and that's what they were—drunk with memories.

Then Tito Solmi, out of a blue sky, started to talk about

my writing. He mentioned particular articles and he seemed to remember them better than I did; he spoke of my newly announced book, seeming to await its publication with sincere anxiousness. Strange man, I thought: where did he find the time to read? But perhaps we have an erroneous idea of businessmen, thinking that they are necessarily very busy people.

They suggested that I go with them "to conclude the evening in a worthy manner." It was clear that meanwhile the little film in the next room was finished. Dora appeared on the threshold, as though looking for us; Quarto's and Tito's eyes were questioning me.

At first I did not reply. I did not reply because I was looking at Dora Fassola. This is what was happening to me: in order to decide how to behave, I was depending on her. Just simply that. Solmi was watching the direction of my look. Then he said in a low voice: "Are you coming away with us?"

Curious, but what really decided me to agree was the smile that in that very instant was addressed to me by another of the persons who were suddenly crowding this room, until then neglected, thus revealing the basic characteristics of parties of that kind, namely, the boredom and anxious search for diversion. ("Thanks to us, this room has become the latest in fashion," Tranquillo Massenti would have said, seeing so many new heads emerge.) The smile I was mentioning was thrown at me by a little actress by the name of Asteggiano: a girl who, I deeply suspect, also writes poems. It was a possessive and curiously conspiratorial smile. It is already difficult enough for me to adhere to a justifiable cordiality such as that of Quarto and Tito; imagine how I react if somebody wants to force me to a kind of histrionics of feelings.

Thinking aloud, I told myself: "That girl's look is an exhortation to mendacity. If I stay on here, I'll be sick."

I turned around as though I were waking up. And this is what happened: Tito Solmi, who had listened to my last words, seemed struck by a revelation; he looked at me in a way that is typical of him, somewhere between admiration and astonishment, studying me, scanning my face with his quick, searching gaze. He took me by the arm and said: "You are absolutely wonderful." At that moment the kind of mutual understanding was created between the two of us which you no longer need to put into words: you are all instinct, and you start believing again in the reality of life. I was aware that I had always been wrong about Tito, and that he was, for example, more intelligent than Martelli. But perhaps intelligence is not the word. Our contact at that point was created by something which, with a trite but useful word, I'd rather call his goodness. Still looking at my face and as if reading it, he said: "Shall we bring that girl along with us?"

He was referring to Dora Fassola and expressing the very quintessence of a desire that I had not admitted even to myself. "She won't come. Besides, she is with Mrs. Ghezzi-Walther—imagine." I was saying this, and yet I felt absolutely certain that Tito would arrange everything. It turned out that he and Mrs. Ghezzi-Walther knew each other, and he was betting on the right card: the lady's great hunger. She was ecstatic at the idea of finally going to eat.

I don't know whether these pages will manage, even for my own purposes, to express the atmosphere of that moment. My joy. The sense that everything would be all right. And at the same time, the sense of moving toward the unknown: but not a frightening unknown, rather an exhilarating one. I can't express it, I can't find the right terms; at any rate, I want these pages to commemorate for me forever the hour of my first true discovery of Dora Fassola.

I don't remember taking leave of anybody, while I remember very well that there was a full moon. So we went, as if at least some of us had found the reason for our evening, and we did not care about anything else on earth.

CHAPTER THREE

☼

Neither too big nor too conspicuous, but made solidly of metal, wood, and leather, English and clearly very much used, Bernardo Partibon's automobile was "undoubtedly the right thing"; Genziana, for that matter, no longer had any doubts about the fact that Partibon possessed "a style." She studied him in silence during the first part of the ride through the center of the city.

"You, Partibon," she observed then in a calm, conclusive tone, "drive like a madman."

In driving, Partibon did not use his right hand except for shifting gears; he dedicated his left hand to the wheel, in fact leaning on it with his entire forearm, while with his right he went on gesticulating. He hardly looked at the streets, and had a casual way of turning into them as one puts his arm into the sleeve of an old jacket. "I can slow up, if you want," he said, accelerating. "The thing is that I want to get there before Clement . . . "

"Get where? And who is Clement?"

Bernardo drew a deep and almost anguished sigh, curiously accompanied by a sly smile: "Clement Blumenfeld; I already told you about him, but you have forgotten. Among other things, he is a great admirer of yours. But later on," he finished, "we'll sit down and I'll tell you everything."

"We are already sitting, my dear, and at any rate I don't want to know all of your secrets, which must be quite a few, I only want to know approximately where you intend to take me." She laughed with a sound, a warmth of such quality as to make Bernardo turn and look at her, as though that laughter had been a spectacle not to be missed. She guessed that, and turning to him, she let him comfortably watch that laughing mouth, exposed, as if she had been in front of a photographer. She repeated with a raucous voice: "Where? And who is Clement?"

"Clement is not at all a bad sculptor, you know," Partibon warned.

"Is that so? But this, at any rate . . ."

"Remember, however," Bernardo interrupted her, "that I want to hear you talk, I want you to tell me all about you. And if Clement should still be at home, don't let him get hold of you. If he catches you, he won't let go, he'll submerge you with words. I'd rather talk to you myself, and listen to you. I want you to tell me what you do, everything." He ended confusedly: "Your eyes! And I am curious as an old concierge." He went on driving in silence.

Suddenly, as he was driving at great speed through a narrow cobbled street, followed by and dodging all sorts of little motor vehicles, he took a violent turn to the right and threw himself with the automobile into a dark courtyard; here he stopped abruptly, with the front of the car a few inches from the concierge's booth.

"Here we are," he announced.

Their eyes met. They remained still a few moments, observing each other, as if following a previous agreement, fixed in the car surrounded by the columns of the old courtyard, the automobile, in its turn, immobilized on the uneven cobbled pavement, in the complicated lights and shadows which ancient lamps formed on their whitened,

(39)

moonlike faces, creating sparks in their intent and still mutually strange eyes. Then they lowered their eyelids a moment, as if to capture and hold the image of the other.

They got out of the car in silence. They crossed the courtyard to an old yellowish stone staircase.

They went up many flights of stairs to the top floor: here they stopped on the landing, on the uneven terrazzo. Bernardo rang the bell and waited a few moments; then he said with a sigh: "Let's look for the key." And without changing tone: "I wouldn't want you to believe that Clement is a protégé of mine," he said while he was locating the key and opening the door. "I don't believe in the possibility of being artists by proxy, so to speak. I can't really stand the so-called patrons of the arts. I can only tell you this: I organize exhibitions, and that's all; I'll bring something of Clement's to New York, to Los Angeles; that's it; we shall see." For Genziana the most impressive thing about these words was the way he uttered them: as he went on, Partibon seemed to find in them a charge, an intensity which bordered on a kind of grave anger. "Perhaps you know that Partibon is, among other things, a name of artists. The family . . ."

"I know very well."

"Anyway, the artists, the intellectuals, have always been the Venice Partibons. We from the countryside . . . Although actually we too . . ." Bernardo raised his head in a way peculiar to him, he seemed to thrust it toward Genziana as he talked; the extraordinary friendliness of his face divested that act of any arrogance. "I was going to say: strange people, we too. Aren't we?"

As they entered the silence confirmed to him that Clement was not there; he threw himself heavily in a chair. But he didn't take his eyes away from her while she sat in front of him. After a pause he started mumbling: "Always away

. . . such a long time . . . every now and then in Italy I meet a person like you and I must talk and talk . . . "

Genziana shrugged and laughed in her dry manner: "And how are you so sure that I want to sit and listen to you, Partibon?"

"No one is sure about anything, ever. Not even I, with my desire to hear you talk, and to talk to you, a desire that I manage to feel even in the midst of all my, of my . . ." —finally he had the word—"of my confusions," he went on with a tenuous smile, "not even I can assure you that I shall always listen to you." He changed his tone: "Horst," he said. "Horst. It's your father, isn't it, who . . ."

Genziana nodded quickly.

"Your father is a remarkable man," he went on as if Genziana had asked him for information on the subject, "and believe me, it isn't at all improbable that in one of the next coalitions they may offer him a post of some importance in the government."

Genziana looked at him as if asking whether he was joking.

"That speech I heard him make a couple of weeks ago . . . " Bernardo stopped abruptly, and, smiling, he thrust his head toward Genziana with an almost triumphant spark in his eye. "Am I right?" he asked, to make her participate in his approval of Senator Horst. "One of the few that made any sense, wasn't it?"

Genziana knew nothing about it. "Are you interested in that sort of thing?"

"Not particularly, it's rather Clement who talks about things like that continuously, and for that matter"—Bernardo spread his arms as if asking for tolerance—"I read too, I read, I read." Again he fixed Genziana with eyes full of sweetness—a sweetness, Genziana thought, that could imply vague shadows of insanity. "You have no idea, the amount of reading I do. My reading is like drinking."

Genziana badly wanted to avoid her quick, practical manner of speech, but she realized that she had no other kind ready on hand. "Have you ever met my father?"

Bernardo shook his huge head: "Not at all, my dear. Not at all. I saw only one or two government characters on business, and also out of curiosity. Italy . . . I wanted to see . . . But as I was telling you, the one who follows everything, including politics, society, scandals, new books, that's Clement, because among his other various incarnations he is also the American resident exile, who wants to go to the bottom of situations, diligent, pedantic . . ."

"Didn't you tell me he was a sculptor?"

"But of course; as a matter of fact, let me show you something."

They got up and crossed the dark living room, going from there into an asymmetrical room with wood-paneled walls; it looked like the prow of a huge boat, full of little closets and built-in furniture, including leather benches.

"Clement Blumenfeld," Genziana repeated to herself. "Maybe an announcement did come . . ."

"For the time being, Clement doesn't quite belong yet," Bernardo said, "and perhaps it's better that way."

"What do you mean?" But Genziana didn't wait for an answer, because in the meantime her attention had been drawn to various little pieces of sculpture in clay, mounted on perpendicular sticks that rose from wooden disks functioning as pedestals. Suspended like that, the sculptures looked to her like hats in a shop window. And the manner in which the clay was treated made it look like melting wax. Or simply like pieces of bundled-up cloth, pinned on those sticks as on huge needles.

(4 2)

"Are these your friend Clement's sculptures?"

"This is a small series. The larger things are already at the gallery."

"The two of you live together?" Out of pure habit, she had formed the supposition that the two might be lovers, although Bernardo's manner did not suggest the idea at all.

"He has been living here for quite a while. I stay at his place as long as I'm in Rome. Among other things, imagine, he is my brother-in-law."

"Is there something strange in that?"

Bernardo looked at her with the lost air that came upon him when he had to render exact account of something he had been saying.

"They look like melting wax," Genziana said, pointing her finger around at sculptures. "And why don't you put on more light in here?"

"If Clement heard you, he would agree: melting wax. He says himself that the initial image came to him from a huge candle, consumed almost entirely and with the melted wax hanging onto it. You know the way? A huge pyramid of wax? Extraordinary variety of forms, he says, as in rocks, or as if you could transfix fire, or the sea, or things like that. You know?" He put a light on, a single low lamp, violent as a flashlight, which immediately multiplied those sculptures into fascinating and obsessive shadows. Genziana pressed the palms of her hands on her eyes; Bernardo said: "Excuse me, but you told me to put some light on. And do you know the title Clement has for this series? *The World after the Great Ball*. There is that idea of candles at the end, of figures after a sleepless night. Not nightmares, but rather mutations of forms . . . the morning after . . . the dawn . . . " Bernardo shrugged: words were of no use.

"Don't they look like nightmares to you? With those needles piercing through them, I assure you . . . "

(43)

"Phoebe and Corinne," Bernardo said, smiling to himself. He raised a finger in the air: "Little American girl friends of Clement. They maintain that Clement, with those needles, is symbolically piercing through the Countess."

"Which countess?"

"Sometimes he calls his mother the Countess. In fact, she was born a Venetian, you know?"

"Really?"

"She went to America when she was very young. Her family name was Benzon; in fact, Benzon is Clement's middle name, he is called Clement Benzon Blumenfeld."

"So?"

"By her second husband she had twins, Clement and Ilse. But later she remarried her first husband."

These confidential details were more than she had bargained for. Now she seemed embarrassed; she turned her back; she observed the sculptures as though they might reveal the secret of such complex family situations. "Do you like these sculptures?" she asked. There was no answer; she turned around and saw that Bernardo had disappeared.

He reappeared reading a letter: "A message from Clement. He went to Venice," he said, handing the sheet to Genziana. "Read it, read it," but Genziana seemed reluctant; she shrugged. "Clement would be happy if you did read it," he said gently.

Genziana took both the letter and the envelope. On the envelope she read: *Herrn Baron von and zu Partibon, Kunsthändler* and the letter said: *Bernhard, I am abandoning you for a few instants. The Countess has arrived, and her program, I feel, is to put order in your life and in that of my (so to speak) sister Clare who, I believe, is with her. The news reached me by telephone through the Ghezzi-Walther business offices: the Countess had landed undamaged at Milan, immediately transferring herself to Venice,*

(44)

*longing for her Clement, who is running to join her within
the bosom of the Queen of the Adriatic, Hotel D.*

*Watch out, Bernardo: I believe that she has put into ac-
tion whatever she could of her original plan, and that for
example: a) she has not arrived from America alone (cf.
above); b) she has Milanese and Venetian meetings on her
schedule (Ghezzi-Walther; your sister Maria). Therefore,
your presence in Venice will bring confusion to an extraordinary degree, so that, even though it is obvious that
the Countess awaits and demands your coming, you must
come nevertheless. Clement.*

Genziana handed him back the sheet. She was annoyed
that the whole situation should continue to draw her. She
attempted a neutral question: "How does it happen that
Clement writes Italian so well?"

"He is insufferably bilingual. Trilingual. Quadrilingual.
His mother's first husband was also a diplomat for a while;
then, they have always traveled like mad. Schools in Switzerland, that sort of thing; a part of his childhood in Venice.
Clement and I once calculated that at a certain period we
were both in Venice. But we didn't know about each other.
Different worlds."

And now, Genziana thought, he would start telling her
everything about Clement's family, and she felt irritation
because she knew that at first she would follow him without
resistance. And then she would find herself confronted with
the odious thing, the faint revulsion, the sickness, the
nausea of danger: the danger of docile abandonment to the
will of a man. Suddenly a memory bit her. One of those
memories that were always there, in a corner of her mind—
reference points, customary faces. "My God, even physically," she said to herself, looking at Bernardo, "this man
reminds me of Ignazio."

She saw herself with Laura, her sister; the two of them

(45)

children, in front of the thirteen-year-old Ignazio: one of those little boys in whose company their mother liked to see them grow up; he was thick-set, curly-haired, his face wearing the color of generations brought up in the country; with a family name adorned with papal nobility; with a manner at once clumsy and authoritative: "Come, come, Genzianella. What are you waiting for? Look at Lauretta, how willing she is." And as a matter of fact, when Ignazio had expressed the desire that the two little girls take off all of their clothes in his presence, Laura had looked at Genziana as if consulting with her, slowly shrugging her shoulders, with a tranquillity ever so slightly enlivened by flippancy: these, she evidently was thinking, were things that had to be done at some point; and she had undressed herself, with occasional little outbursts of laughter and an expression of curiosity on her face. Laura and Ignazio had gone on looking into each other's eyes while the light, clean little bits of clothing were falling on the carpet. Then Ignazio stopped laughing, he lowered his bovine eyes to the already feminine breasts, on the little belly: "The stockings too," he said gloomily. Then, taking in the whole vision with his eyes, he drew a deep sigh, trembling. "And what about you?" He turned to Genziana, who started then to unbutton her dress and take it off with small, hard motions. "And what about you?" he repeated, as if Genziana were doing nothing. "You see how agreeable your sister has been?" But finally he said: "Well, you may stop, Genziana, that's enough," with embarrassment rather than with anger, seeing her rigid in her underwear. "Right, Ignazio," she had said, "I do think it's quite enough."

And after that one, how many Ignazios had there been in her life? Quarto Martelli the most recent; shortly before him, there had been the two American experiences; and, far back in time, Tranquillo Massenti himself, the journalist left behind . . . All of them, each in his way, with the same imperative, the same invitation; and in her, when she started really to give in, to feel the tremor of yielding, there it was, the malaise, the slight nausea, and the final recapture of herself in the controlled gesture, in the right phrase.

"Listen, carissimo, my dearest," she said now, "why exactly did you bring me here? Don't you think that perhaps we've had enough for today of your Clement and his artistic nightmares?" But she read on Bernardo's face such authentic and naïve disappointment that she regretted having spoken that way. She also had a curious feeling of remorse toward Clement, this unknown boy who admired her from the distance. She whispered apologetically: "I escaped with you to let you make a charming, entertaining evening of it."

The telephone rang. Bernardo let it ring three or four times.

"Don't you usually answer the phone?"

Bernardo turned his large head toward the telephone as though it had been a person coming to surprise him. "It's always a gamble," he said. "You have no idea . . . " The phone rang again, Bernardo looked at it for a moment, then went on: "You have no idea how I have waited for certain news that never came, certain contacts that I haven't yet managed to make. And yet, I hear the phone ring and I am paralyzed." It rang again. "I have had too many disappointments answering the phone. Not only now, you know, all of my life . . . that damned waiting for phone calls, for the mail. So that I often say . . ." He raised his huge hands, placing them as a protecting roof over the telephone, which was ringing again: "So many times I tell myself, better leave it there, leave it quietly there, nothing good can come from it anyway." But when it rang again, he shrugged and suddenly raised the receiver to his ear. "It stopped," he said. "Who do you suppose it was?"

"It will remain forever a mystery."

Bernardo looked at her worriedly. "Maybe it was Phoebe and Corinne," he murmured to himself reassuringly.

"Who are Phoebe and Corinne?"

"Little friends of Clement's."

"Think," she went on, "years will pass and your curiosity will remain unsatisfied. 'Who was it, on the telephone, that evening?' you will still be asking yourself, years and years from now. Perhaps it was this contact you are so anxiously trying to make . . ." She interrupted herself and measured Bernardo with her eyes; then in a low, practical voice: "What contact? Whom are you trying to see?" It was a businesswoman's tone. She modified it a little: "Some beautiful woman, I'm sure."

"As far as that's concerned, yes, she has always been beautiful."

Since Bernardo was not offering any further explanations, Genziana asked: "And who is the mysterious beauty?"

"Nothing mysterious. Maria. My sister."

"Do you mean to say you can't make contact with your sister?"

"That's right."

"Why?"

"I don't know." After a pause he added: "I haven't seen her in twenty years."

"But you see her husband?"

"What do you mean?"

"Isn't Clement . . ."

"Oh, no, Clement is my brother-in-law, but the other way around. Clement's sister, or rather, his half sister, is, so to speak, my wife."

"So to speak?"

Bernardo spread his arms: "I can't explain the whole situation to you at once."

"Carissimo, I have never asked you to explain anything at all, although I'll admit that all I can gather about your life sounds like a maddening puzzle."

Bernardo shrugged, as if he meant: "Don't you think I know that?" Then, high and overpowering above her, putting his huge hand forward in a gesture that seemed to request calm, clarity, and was at the same time almost a gesture of prayer, he said: "I warned you, I told you that right away, I am caught by this need to talk, to hear myself talk, and when I saw you, I . . . I did . . . I attached myself to you."

"You saw the victim in me."

Bernardo took her by the wrists, he squeezed them. They looked into each other's eyes for a moment, as they had done in the dark courtyard. Then Genziana lowered her eyes, looked at her wrists held tightly in his hands, she freed herself slowly and turned her back. She saw cigarettes on a coffee table, took one, lit it.

"So you don't manage to see your sister?"

"Except in photographs in the newspapers."

"Who is she? Somebody one knows?"

Bernardo sighed and began with some effort: "Maria Gervasutti. This is the name they gave her in some of the papers. Which is right, since she had married somebody called Gervasutti." Genziana was looking at him with a kind of exaggerated astonishment which confused him. He insisted: "But her little girl's family name should more correctly have been Fassola." He looked at Genziana's face to read on it whether she had recognized the story.

"What a mess," she said offhandedly. But then: "Of course—now I know what you are talking about. So that's

(49)

your sister? The mother of the girl who was a kind of little saint? They also gave her one of the Caritas awards because she used to pay visits to an old teacher in the hospital, or something like that."

"In the lunatic asylum."

"I didn't remember that the mother of the little girl was a Partibon, and frankly, I recall only now the connection with the Fassolas, perhaps because, after all, I detest stories with a religious-mystical background."

"Well, there are these charity awards now in Italy, and what happened in this case is that the child later died, and that some newspapers went ahead and tried to reconstruct . . . Isn't that how it was? What else is there?"

"Oh, that's more than enough; really, I find stories of that kind slightly asphyxiating, but now that I know that they were relatives of yours . . . Curious thing—a journalist I know, Tranquillo Massenti, covered the story for one of the magazines. He looked for the little girl's mother and all that, he even went to Corniano, if I remember correctly; that's the name of the place, isn't it?"

"That's the place where I was born."

"Curious to think that that was your sister. And now you don't see each other."

"I am forced to believe that she doesn't want to see me."

"All of this, after all, turns out to be rather fascinating, I find." She looked at Bernardo, that huge head full of worries: "And may I ask," she said, smiling, "why you don't stop thinking about it for a while?"

"That's exactly the same thing Massenti told me."

Genziana's smile disappeared: "I recognize Tranquillo, that's just what he would say," she whispered. "So you've talked to him? How is he?" Bernardo did not answer. "He is not a bad journalist. I knew him rather well, years ago."

And now, inevitably, there had come to her the memory

(5 0)

of Tranquillo Massenti's face and voice as he stood leaning over her. She was in bed with her usual interminable bronchitis, with that little flame of fever which seemed forever inextinguishable, with that faint, stubborn cough, like long despair attenuated by habit. *Why do you want to be alone, Genziana? Let me stay near you, why not? If you sleep, I only want to stay and look at you. Then you'll wake up, and we'll talk if you feel like it: I can calm you, Genziana.* And she would say: *Go now, carissimo, you know that I have never been able to rest with somebody near me,* hoping that instead he would remain, that he would allow her to go on pushing him away, with that faint breath of a voice, to feel that she was, however weak and unresponsive, still living. And through the years, Tranquillo continued to come back to her memory, with his weighty turns of thought, the phrases, the definitions, which in a select circle of friends had become epoch-making, but made her only feel that it was right to have pushed him away, left him behind: he had been his own judge, he had placed himself, on his own, among the unsuccessful, the outcast; as a matter of fact, there was something obsessive about him, about his supposedly brilliant phrases; and then, all things considered, as a person he was not really too presentable . . . Yes, of course, an important reason for Tranquillo's failure had been there, a matter of style, of tone, so that sometimes she would tell him, between annoyance and exasperation: "You are a Venetian but you've acquired the worst from the Southerners, their typical complexes, that lamenting quality—you know, that continuously apologetic attitude . . . " And he would correct her, smiling patiently, sticking to the useless detail: "No, not Venetian, we are originally from Parma, but of course we traveled a lot, in the Venetion region too, on account of my father," insisting on making her recall that his father had been moved through

(51)

various places in Italy for that curious reason, that he was a *carabinieri* officer, so that Genziana, studying Tranquillo's face, square as a chest of drawers, and that brushlike military hair, would repeat to him, with a smile that in the very early days had perhaps contained a bit of tenderness but had later become simply tired: "That's what you have, a *carabiniere* head: the character of the *carabiniere* in puppet shows."

Now she studied Partibon, whose head, she concluded, was big too but of a decidedly spherical shape. She had already decided that the talk about his sister Maria was substantially tedious; on the other hand she had no doubt that Bernardo should be used, and by no means allowed to get lost. In her relations with men she was accustomed to keeping things easily under control in the period before the rise of the enervating—and sometimes anguishing—erotic demands. Partibon now, this kind of huge bear she had accidentally discovered at a useless party, seemed generally trustworthy in spite of an occasional strangeness: with him, perhaps, the easy rapport of a preliminary kind could be protracted indefinitely. Why not do something about that? She needed rest; she had already planned a long weekend before the arrival of Harry Berger next Monday and the beginning of conferences on the costumes for *Caligula;* she was thinking of going to the country, to the Piglioli-Spadas', even this early in the week, and somehow bringing Partibon along. She was not in the habit of considering men's occupations as grave obstacles to her own schemes on them; and for that matter, an invitation to the Piglioli-Spadas' could look attractive to a man like this, who was used to the informal, American type of hospitality, and who was perfectly presentable, but not widely introduced here in Italy.

Bernardo went on talking. Planning her very long weekend, she looked at him as if she were taking measurements, without following his talk. Finally it was as though he woke her up with a phrase that Genziana suddenly heard: "Why don't you come to Venice too?"

"To Venice," she pondered. "When and by what means do you intend to go to Venice?"

"As I was saying, by car, tonight."

"Is it so urgent for you to get to Venice? Is that the place where you are going to find your famous sister?"

"Well, yes, perhaps . . . but not only that . . . at any rate, I like the idea of crossing a large piece of Italy at night."

"And what about sleep? You know, if I don't get my eight hours . . . "

"You can sleep while I drive. Don't be afraid, I won't fall asleep behind the wheel, it hasn't ever happened to me."

"Why are you in such a hurry to get to Venice?"

He turned to her with urgency: "Well, sooner or later I'll have to go there, won't I?"

"Certainly, but Venice will still be there, you know, even if they say that every century it sinks a little bit."

"And I shall have to go to Corniano."

"Of course," she recalled, "you are a Partibon from the countryside."

Bernardo smiled with a sudden opening of jovial serenity: coming as it did, over a totally opposite expression, to her it looked vaguely like insanity.

"Do you still have a family . . . relatives . . . up there?" Meanwhile Genziana was telling herself: "True, that's the way men act: suddenly, when they look most anguished, they smile as if they were telling themselves a joke. Perhaps they are all mad?"

"Think," Bernardo said, still with his smile, "think: I have not seen my mother in twenty years." He opened his arms wide: "Just about that long," he added.

(53)

"Where is your mother?"

"At Corniano. My father died last year, Maria is always between Venice and Rome, as far as I know, so my mother must be alone, I suppose?" He seemed to wait for a confirmation from her.

Genziana would have liked to say: "What do I have to do with your mother?" But instead, she produced only a brief whisper: "Did you at least write to each other?"

Bernardo looked around as if seeking a reply in the air: "Well, my mother . . ." There was a long silence.

Again she saw that seraphic smile on his face and she decided to cut it, to keep her feet on the ground: "Doesn't your mother know how to write? Is she illiterate?" she asked.

"She doesn't feel like writing," Bernardo answered at once, reassuringly. "Every now and then a friend of hers would write. And mind you, this aversion of my mother's to writing," he went on, brightening up, "or rather, not even aversion, this total strangeness to the idea of writing letters, is doubly curious in the case of my mother." He paused and explained: "Because as a young woman my mother was both a schoolteacher and a post office employee. In different periods."

Again Genziana felt the bite of irritation and worry. Why did she go on talking about this man's affairs? Why get involved? Who was this man? But her questions came out anyway: "So, one way or another, you did communicate. And what kind of messages did your mother send you? Did she want you to come back? You've been in America for many years, haven't you?"

"Her friend," Bernardo replied at once, "her friend would write. Well, she asked for money. I'm quite sure my mother would tell her not to do that, she wouldn't forbid it, she would just say no. But the friend would do it anyway, you know?"

(54)

"And did you help her?"

"What do you mean?"

"Did you send money?"

"Who? Me? Well, you know, through the banks . . ." It was as though Genziana's question had been concerning only the technical side of the payment.

Genziana would have liked to say that the whole business lacked even the remotest glimmer of interest; but in the last phrase, under Bernardo's usually neutral Italian accent, she had suddenly detected the countryside Venetian. Somehow she associated those sounds with the vision of that round head, and that gave her an odd feeling of restfulness. Even that madly serene smile of Bernardo's did not trouble her any longer. And that restful feeling, she thought, as if she had discovered a new tranquilizer, should be exploited.

"Listen, carissimo, why don't we do something? Let's keep Venice as our maximum program, but meanwhile, why don't we go to my sister's in the country? Her husband is Rodolfo Piglioli-Spada, a very amusing man, and then, for a man like you who is interested in art, the house . . . you'll see some beautiful furniture."

"I should have been a cabinetmaker. Born centuries ago, however."

"There, you see? At Laura and Rodolfo's you'll see things that will make your mouth water."

"But I usually *buy* furniture."

"Maybe you'll do some business too. From the way Rodolfo runs things, I have the impression that if you took away some table or cabinet, you'd beat the creditors' agents by only a few lengths." She laughed very happily.

Bernardo's face darkened. "But I have to go to Venice, don't I? And then"—he pointed his finger toward Genziana—"I wanted to talk to you."

"Is there a better place to talk than an old country house? And then, my sister is a gem, you'll see. If you don't feel like staying, you can come back to Rome tonight or we can ride on to Venice, as you wish. But you'll see, we'll stay at my sister's."

" . . . talk to you . . . " Bernardo mumbled. Now Genziana was standing in front of him, her beautiful body firm and erect, her breasts the right size, her eyes green and self-assured. They held each other by the hands and kept looking into each other's eyes; then he brought her hands to his chest, pressing them tightly.

She lowered her eyes and said: "Now, listen, be patient. Oh, dear, what violence," she added, freeing herself, "and how your heart is pounding."

They stood a few moments without looking at each other. Genziana suggested: "Well, then, shall we go?"

They went out of the city through sumptuous and deserted Vatican sections, then coasting past old houses, storehouses and depots with rusty fronts; then sections with new buildings, very tall apartment houses recently emerged from grounds whose countryside quality had been subverted and devastated without a city harmony's taking its place. She explained the way to Bernardo and then, silent, let him drive. She was dozing off. His voice was a restful murmur. After perhaps half an hour, or an hour, a higher pitch brought her back to the surface.

"You are sleeping, aren't you? I'm sorry, but I wouldn't want to miss the left turn . . . "

"Oh, my God, really . . . "

"I was talking to you, and I went on talking even though I realized that you were sleeping," Bernardo explained with a reapparition of his beatific smile.

"Oh, dear, God knows what marvelous things I have been missing . . . " It was one of her usual conventional phrases, but this time it had come out in the lingering and tender tone of an awakening in bed. She begged sweetly:

(56)

"Why don't you repeat the essential points for me, Bernardo?"

"I have been boring you while you weren't aware of it. At least I made you sleep."

"No, I want you to repeat. Were you talking about somebody? About your mother? Your sister?" The brief, unforeseen sleep had relaxed her defenses, her fears. Since Bernardo was shaking his head in denial, she insisted: "What were you talking about, then?"

"I wasn't talking about my sister, I was talking about Clement's sister, at this point—Ilse Blumenfeld. They are twins, you know, I have already told you about them—I just happened to be telling you that as a child he would look up gynecology books to see the position of twins in their mother's womb."

"What an extraordinary thing." It was another one of her useless phrases. And this time it had been uttered by the usual Genziana, fully awake, in a high, flat voice, like a quotation. "I find this quite extraordinary, really rather incredible. And how did that happen?" She did not wait for an answer: "Oh, dear, where are we now? In a moment you'll have to take that left turn, you know." Shadows of pine trees ran along their left side, and something in the air, temperature, glimmers of light, scents, made them feel the not too distant presence of the sea. "Open the window. Let me breathe." They went on a while in silence, breathing that new air.

"Here we are. Turn here."

Advancing into the pine wood, there was no longer any doubt—coming here had been the right idea. "Stop. Stop here a moment."

They listened to the swishing noises of the night, high tremors in the trees; they breathed that pine-scented air in which a feeling of moist sand was mixed.

(57)

"Do you like it? Do you understand now why I wanted to come here?" She felt reassured. She belonged to herself; she almost had no use for him any longer. But looking at that huge head, those large astonished eyes above her, she felt gratitude: "You are not sorry that I brought you here, are you?"

She even added: "With some people, very few, the moment I see them I want to bring them to a place that is particularly dear to me."

At this, Bernardo took her hands and squeezed them hard. Genziana let him do it; she had a feeling this was a sort of payment for his having driven her here. Bernardo put his right arm around her shoulders, drawing her to himself, while with his other hand he caressed her face, watching it, his eyes moving happily all over it.

She reacted with a kind of bland curiosity: "What do you think you are going to discover? I'm ugly, you know, especially so close up, my skin these last few days has been looking dreadful." Only when he tried to kiss her on the mouth did she turn her head to one side, and the kiss fell on her cheek. Actually, her skin was a little rough.

Bernardo started to talk slowly, clumsily: "It isn't only from Boschinetti that I had heard about you. And from Clement, who doesn't know you, but has a tremendous admiration for you. There was that journalist too, the one we talked about and who was your friend, Tranquillo Massenti. You have no idea, I am fantastically curious and Clement must be even worse than I. That Massenti is an exceptional man, I understand him when he talks. And as far as I could gather, he had the misfortune of being in love with you. But then, why misfortune? I think I can quote his exact words: 'Genziana Horst, with her coldness, with her desire not to feel, holds all of the cards, while one loves her desperately.' But if a man can define a situation with such

(58)

lucidity, he has already won, hasn't he?"

She shrugged: "Phrases. Men made up of phrases. And not very brilliant or very true ones, at that." She lowered her eyes, her mouth tense, as if in pain.

"What does that mean, for example," she asked, " 'desire not to feel'? Can you tell me what that means?"

Then, seriously, quietly: "You must also realize that I am never really well. I am not a woman that enjoys good health. In fact I'll tell you more—I am convinced that women are never really in good health. We need at least five times the strength you need, in order to endure."

"I know that. I've been married twice. Especially my first wife . . ."

She caressed his check rapidly: "Married twice"—and she laughed—"you really must be a big mess. But I find you restful," she finished and sighed deeply.

"Why don't you come to Venice? Do you really have to go to your sister's?"

"You'll like Laura very much, she is completely different from me, and Rodolfo too is quite a person. They'll be crazy about you; for that matter, you are incredibly attractive." Her tone changed, she looked pensive: "In New York," she said, "I lived for a while with a friend of mine. Sometimes after a cocktail party or an evening at somebody's house, she wouldn't come back home with me, she would go with some boy she had met at the party and spend the night with him. Well, those are things I don't do; I wouldn't know how to do them even if I wanted to. But if it were at all conceivable in my case, it could be with you." She looked at him with a new expression, genuinely amused: "Look," she said, touching him with her elbow, "I gave you a terrific compliment."

"Let's go to Venice."

Genziana took Bernardo's forearm, which was lying on

the wheel; she pressed on it, producing a honk. "Let's wake up the birds." She laughed, "No, let's go to Laura's. I adore the house, and you'll see, you too . . . " Their eyes met: "You'll be happy. It's a large house and we'll be alone as much as you want. We'll spend a few days there."

"But I must go to Venice."

"In things of that kind, there is never anything one *must* do. Aren't you on a vacation?"

"No, I'm in Italy to do certain things."

"What things?"

"To . . . to understand," he said rather lamely.

"Americans especially, you know, are like maniacs in such matters—to understand, to get information. Are you an American?"

"I was in the war too for a while, in the Pacific."

"Really? Think of that. I find this . . . " She hadn't the right phrase; she changed directions: "You must talk about it with Rodolfo; he was a Navy officer for a while." Bernardo started the car again.

At the far end of the pine wood where the sandy road ended, they came across something like the walls of a little castle. They rode along them for a brief stretch until they came to a gate. It was half open; Bernardo stopped the car, and before he realized it, Genziana had jumped out to open the gate wide. Raising and moving her arms ghostlike in the light of the car, she gave him directions. Within the walls, there was a large courtyard; on the left there appeared a tall dark building like an apartment house buried in sleep; on the right, at the far end, the villa stood, two stories high, long and flat, terminated on the wall side by a very small chapel. On the upper floor a couple of windows, rather far apart, were lit. Genziana walked backward ahead of the car and made Bernardo stop near the entrance door to the villa.

She put her arm into the car window and honked three times.

Bernardo got out of the car; they waited a few moments, holding hands. Very soon the door opened and against the background of the vestibule Laura appeared, blond, small and round, barefoot, evidently naked under her robe.

"Darling, how perfectly wonderful," she said. She sounded exactly like Genziana: identical voice and high flat tones, like a quotation, while in appearance they were entirely opposite. "Think," Laura went on, "the whole evening Rodolfo kept saying: 'I feel Genziana coming, I have the Genziana buzz in my ears.'"

"Rodolfo has his own odd way of talking, as you will hear," Genziana told Bernardo; and without interruption, in passing, she introduced him: "This is Bernardo Partibon."

"Good evening," Laura said immediately, "how are you?" Without waiting for a reply she turned again to her sister: "Did you see Father today?"

"No, we talked over the telephone, he is working. He was going to the Senate library, imagine that; I'll have dinner with him next Sunday unless we go to Venice."

"Are you going to Venice?" Laura asked, and again without waiting for an answer: "Why do we stand out here? Don't you want a drink? Listen," she said to her sister in a more languid and drawling intonation, taking her by the arm and walking with her into the large living room while Partibon, as if forgotten, followed them, "listen. Funny, isn't it, that you arrived just when we were waiting for you."

From the little wheel cart the girls took some whiskey, filling the bottoms of two extremely tall crystal glasses. They sank into two soft old armchairs and crossed their legs; they looked at each other. "Listen . . . " Genziana said, but nothing followed; they smiled at each other happily.

Partibon was walking around the room, looking appraisingly at the furniture. It was clear that the sisters thought they were doing him a favor, leaving him by himself like a pasturing animal.

"Listen . . ." Laura said in her turn. It was like an announcement they gave before thinking of what to say. There was another pause. Bernardo turned to Laura as if she had spoken to him. Laura extended her arm, showing her whiskey glass. "You too? Do you want to pour your own?" she asked.

"Well . . . " Bernardo nodded. He went and poured himself some whiskey.

"Listen . . . " Laura resumed. And finally: "What an angelic face the gentleman has."

"Hasn't he? He knows Teresa and Umberto, you know, the Boschinettis. Curious, isn't it? We were at an obsessively boring party, and Quarto met an incredible old friend of his, so I left them there; in fact, Bernardo here was really my savior, you know."

"Cheers," Laura said in English, raising her glass in the direction of Bernardo, who returned her toast and then suddenly turned to his right, discovering close to him a new apparition, the host himself, also wearing simply a robe—and barefoot, so that he had entered the room noiselessly.

He was bald, with only a trace of delicate, curly blond hair above his ears; he was minutely built but well set on his slightly crooked legs, as though he were always on horseback. Genziana, sunk in her armchair, felt him standing behind her back; she raised her arms offering her hands backward; he took them in his own, leaning down to kiss his sister-in-law on the head; before raising himself he freed his left hand to offer it to Bernardo like a wing: "Piglioli-Spada," he said with a slightly conspiratorial smile.

"Partibon," Bernardo said.

"Partibon," Piglioli-Spada registered; he went to sit near his wife; it looked as though he had chosen that spot in order to observe Bernardo from the right distance. "Partibon. Your grandfather," he announced with the evident intention of surprising him, "was a great gentleman."

"Which grandfather?"

"My father paid a visit to him once in his studio in Venice, before World War One. The painter, of course."

"There has been more than one painter in the Venetian branch of the family."

"Bernardo calls himself a countryside Partibon, which I find very amusing," Genziana said.

"I imagine," Bernardo said, "that you are referring to the old one, Taddeo, not exactly my grandfather—I suppose one would say great-uncle. He used to paint some incredible still lifes that looked like needlework." He burst out in a brief laughter, soon echoed by Piglioli-Spada, who intensified the degree of his attention toward Bernardo.

Then Piglioli-Spada said: "There was a whole civilization in Venice, once upon a time."

"If you are referring to Taddeo Partibon, you are talking about the late nineteenth century and the beginning of the twentieth. It's a period that you certainly cannot have known directly."

"I know that," Piglioli-Spada said gravely. "Don't you expect me to know that?"

"Bernardo arrived from America recently; usually he lives in America; he had been away from Italy a very long time."

"So I am sure you have realized," Piglioli-Spada asked, "in what kind of hands Italy is now?" It was as though he had asked for the observation of a physical phenomenon.

Bernardo made a few evasive gestures.

Piglioli-Spada went on in the courteous, pleased tone of one showing a guest around the house or the garden: "I shall have to admit, out of a sense of equanimity and fair play, that in various cases and at first sight they may even offer some perfectly plausible imitations of well-bred people."

"I told you he had an amusing way of talking," Genziana said.

"Even when I used to buy the weekly magazines," Piglioli-Spada went on, "which I ceased to do some time ago, I could observe that although the gentlemen in question were normally presented with the faces of monsters in a neon light, still one could be deceived into distinguishing within their texture a few thin threads of civilization and manners. As a visitor, be on the lookout against hastily optimistic judgments on that score. Yes—you will see cleaned-up, motorized people. But do you know," he said, pointing his finger toward Bernardo, pleased to offer him a curious statistical datum, "that in this period, measuring the thing in lire and centesimi, or as you would say, in terms of dollars and cents, Italy is producing more and bigger crooks than the country has ever known in the entire course of its history?" For a few moments he looked cheerfully at Bernardo: "Did you know that? If not, I am happy to have provided you with the information. You see, you cross the ocean and you stop in Rome, and then from Rome you have to come up here to get the right picture from a silly ass retired in the country like myself."

"I find Rodolfo very amusing," Genziana said.

Laura said: "He is always here in the country and that's how he has arranged this way of talking, all by himself."

"Then you should never move him from here," Genziana said.

"Here in the country I feel perfectly well. And I may be a silly ass but I am not a boor; in fact I consider my good disposition one of my prize assets. You shouldn't believe, Partibon, that I am one of those people who make long sermons on the corruption of the times and the end of noble traditions. Please. I was mentioning your grandfather, or rather great-uncle, and that whole world—precisely because I have never known it, as you wisely made me observe. Traditions? On careful inspection, there has never been in history a period or a milieu that really functioned, and thank God we've become aware of that. By now the only country that can permit itself any traditions is America; a friend of mine who, don't ask me why, went there to teach at a university, told me that students had a committee for the establishment of local traditions—do I make myself clear? Obviously America is the ideal country, but it is equally obvious that we can't live there. How can *you* live there?" While Bernardo was looking for an answer, Piglioli-Spada resumed: "Once upon a time, one was an Anglomaniac, but now England too . . . It hasn't changed much, you know; in fact, basically it hasn't changed at all; only, we have opened our eyes."

While his wife was saying: "I am just crazy about London," Piglioli-Spada lowered his voice to a more confidential tone: "But now I want you to do me a favor, to satisfy the frivolous curiosity of a former reader of the magazines. Am I wrong, or did the Partibon family have something to do with the story of that little girl from the Venetian countryside who, according to some people, died in the odor of sanctity?"

"According to whom?" Bernardo asked a little aggressively. Then, swallowing: "Yes, the mother of the little girl is my sister."

"You see that I guessed right? I didn't follow the story through, since it was exactly in that period that I stopped buying the weeklies. But if I remember correctly, I had been able to form some opinion. In the development of, shall we say, the thing, the person to watch was that man Debaldè. A kind of manager. Perhaps I remember him also because I have rarely encountered a more curious name —more difficult to place, I mean. Correct me if I'm wrong. What is he? Of French origin? With that spelling?"

Bernardo said: "I used to know Debaldè when we were boys in Venice; his mother was a baroness, or at any rate, they called her Baroness Debaldè, and she was the proprietor of a *pensione* on the Zattere. I had been sent to Venice to study, but later I gave up, and I have never seen Debaldè since."

Laura and Genziana also followed Bernardo's talk intensely; they looked at him, smiling tenderly.

"That would be the little man to find and approach," Piglioli-Spada said, "if anybody had any interest in the problem, and, I might add, any faith in people of that sort. Very fashionable type, these last few years. A cultural organizer. An active man. Am I wrong?"

Bernardo spoke, seriously now, slowly, as if seeking the words in the deepest funds of his memory: "All things considered, I understand more and more clearly that one should try to find without searching, even as far as Maria, my sister, is concerned."

Piglioli-Spada stood close under Bernardo, to drink in his every word. The two women looked at Bernardo without understanding, but with an almost openly amorous expression.

"For that matter, it seems that Maria doesn't want to see me. Her sisterly ear seems to be deaf."

With a shiver of surprise, Genziana saw the sly, angelic smile reappear on Bernardo's face. Slightly confused, she turned to her brother-in-law, but she realized that an in-

(66)

creasingly pleasant harmony existed between him and Bernardo.

"When we were children, you see," Bernardo continued, "I loved my sister very much."

"Situations like that are very rare," Piglioli-Spada said, "and you are certainly right if you want . . . " He interrupted himself, obviously not because he was uncertain but rather because everything by now seemed too clear for him to waste any more words on it. He turned to his wife: "Where are we going to put him up? Your father's room?" And to Bernardo: "You are going to stay with us at least until tomorrow night, aren't you? Or until next Monday."

No one seemed really interested in Bernardo's reaction to this suggestion; Genziana and Laura realized that it was almost two o'clock, and they started to go upstairs, chatting away.

"Tomorrow has been today for a couple of hours already," Laura said. On the landing she waited for Bernardo, and as if to tell him that he was trapped with them for the new day, she hung onto his arm, looking up at him. "I am madly happy he is going to stay with us, and I think father's room is the right thing. One feels one has always known him," she said, craning her neck toward Genziana on the other side of the guest.

Genziana confirmed: "I told you that he was a marvelous acquisition." Piglioli-Spada, in evident agreement with these favorable opinions, led the way, so that Bernardo found the door of his room already wide open when they all came to the upstairs corridor.

Suddenly, after confused good-nights followed by laughter, steps in the corridor, doors being shut, Bernardo found himself alone in front of a canopied bed. He stood like that for a while, face to face with that bed, massive and motionless like himself.

It was a Russian bed, Piglioli-Spada had told him; and along with this, other words came back, first only phrases from their recent quick parting and then, as the silence grew wider, phrases from the whole evening since the by now prehistorical reception at the Solmis' started crowding Partibon's mind and soon seemed destined to remain there forever. He realized that Genziana a moment ago had taken him to one side and had whispered to him: "You see, you big idiot, that it was a good idea to come here," and these words, the way they had been uttered, Genziana's inviting and conspiratorial look, all of this was melting within him, like music, or like a general feeling of tenderness spreading through his vast limbs. He looked at the wardrobe, at the chairs, at the night table, and again at the Russian bed: second-rate furniture, he evaluated, a little bit odd, somewhat bric-à-brac; perhaps it came from heterogeneous sources, distant, wide-traveling ancestors—there must have been some diplomats among the Piglioli-Spadas—and the Horsts themselves, with that name, where did they originate? But finally even questions of that kind seemed empty and insignificant, because there hovered above all the image of Genziana, her voice, her eyes. He looked around the room, and it seemed to him that her absence was a concrete, tangible feeling: in the same way as she had shown him the pine grove, so she should have been here now, surrounded by this furniture, or in that bed. What eyes, he thought, what a body. And always that same peremptory and chic tone of voice to utter both her touching and her inane phrases. "But of course," he murmured, "Clement always has the right idea."

He felt an intolerable heat, entirely out of season. He laughed aloud. He went to the window and opened it. He put his elbows on the window sill, stared for a long while at the pavement of the vast courtyard in the moonlight. Finally he heard a swishing noise in a bush, then the light, neat noise of dogs' nails ticking on the hard stones. Two enormous mastiffs, one behind the other, crossed the courtyard diagonally, and lost themselves silently in the dark, as if marching toward a night expedition.

"They go to the sea," Bernardo murmured, "how marvelous." Then again, Genziana's words and gestures came to him, starting from that very distant prelude in the Solmi vestibule: "If you leave here, will you take me with you?" to her "you big idiot, what a mess you are," of a more recent time. He started walking aimlessly around the room, repeating phrases aloud, mimicking gestures and accents.

He realized that at some point he had automatically undressed; he discovered himself fully naked in the mirror: "What bulk . . . what horror!" Piglioli-Spada had left one of his larger robes on a sofa; Bernardo put it on, still talking to himself: "Now I'll lie quietly on the bed, and keep awake, cocking my ears; if I hear the noise of doors being opened, I'll get up, and if she appears at her door, I'll appear at mine." These very thoughts, once he lay on the bed, became entangled with sleep. When he heard doors being opened and shut, it seemed faint and improbable; there also were, it seemed to him, hurried steps down the staircase. After a period which could have been one hour or one second, he even heard the noise of an automobile being started in the courtyard. "They are taking my car away and leaving me stranded here. But, no, I'm dreaming. Or perhaps it's those dogs. Dogs that drive a car?" In his sleep he laughed aloud.

CHAPTER FOUR

✵

Editor Perineschi's windows at the *Roma Sabato* office were still lit. Tito Solmi was driving with Quarto Martelli and Ovidio Semenzato, and when he found himself riding along the massive building, where on the second floor those solitary windows were shining, he slowed down and turned his round eyes toward them; they literally made his mouth water. "Perineschi used to work on a daily paper and he has maintained his nocturnal habits," he said tentatively; then, decidedly, he put the brake on: "Let's go up and see him."

Only Quarto was reluctant. As they were going up the marble staircase with brass and cast-iron banisters, in the faint light, he kept saying: "Why are we going?" He occasionally read *Roma Sabato,* but he had no friends among journalists; going to meet, in the middle of the night, no less than an editor-in-chief worried him, disturbed him profoundly; however athletic and healthy, he was subject to nervous stomach upsets.

When he received them in his office, the editor of *Roma Sabato* was in an ambiguous mood. He remained standing behind his desk. He was small, compact, self-assured; he had a triangular face with quick blue eyes. When he put a question to somebody, he craned his neck forward with a sly smile and a glimmer of curiosity on his face, not in anticipation of the answer, which he evidently already possessed, but to see how the other person would get out of the predicament.

"Where have you been?" he asked. The Solmis had invited him too, and according to custom, he had accepted the invitation and neglected to go. When the three told him that they had been there, he raised his eyebrows in surprise, as if they had confessed to a curious, secret vice.

"I must find Tranquillo Massenti," he said. "Do you happen to know where he may be? He didn't go to the Solmis', I imagine."

"No," said Ovidio glumly.

"Why do you need Tranquillo?" Tito asked, ready to start a search that would pivot around his Oldsmobile.

"Senator Horst just died, and I want Tranquillo to write a beautiful article for me. Don't you think it's a good idea?" He waved his hand in a gesture that signified inspiration, inventiveness. "Something lively, brilliant . . . Why—do you think Horst wasn't interesting enough?" He felt, with uneasiness, Quarto Martelli's look fixed on him. Turning to him, Perineschi repeated: "Senator Mario Horst is dead," also because he wanted to create a bridge between Quarto and himself: people to whom he was not safely known made him suspicious. "Mario Horst," he went on. "After the war he was also Undersecretary for Foreign Affairs for a while. But he was a rather peculiar figure. Tranquillo Massenti knew him quite well, besides knowing the two daughters, Laura and Genziana." He observed Quarto Martelli's intense interest and even heard a whisper: "Dead? Are you really serious?" Pleased with that, Perineschi went on more eloquently: "I want a kind of capsule biography, something really elegant, that may trace Horst back to the period of the First World War, not only the politician but the scholar as

(71)

well, all that sort of thing; well, in other words, what I want is the cultural background."

"Listen," Quarto said, stooping toward Perineschi as he would at a post office window, "there is this thing, you see—I too am very friendly with Miss Horst, Genziana Horst. As a matter of fact, her sister Laura and I are almost relatives, because she married a distant cousin of mine, the younger brother of Ambassador Piglioli-Spada. So please, I should like to have some details."

"Coronary thrombosis," Perineschi said quickly, snapping two fingers. "Just like that. He was at the Senate library. It simply looked as though he had lowered his head over the page to read some small type. One of the librarians, Arista, sees him, from an angle as from here to that door, goes to him, feels his pulse, realizes it's already finished. A few minutes before ten." Perineschi professed "dry facts" as an ideal, which he considered American. "Shortly before ten," he repeated. "So, you knew him?" he asked without interest.

"We must find Genziana, see where she is . . . " Quarto turned to Ovidio and Tito to engage their interest while he dismissed Perineschi with a gesture of the hand. "I must look for Genziana. What are you going to do? I've got to look for her, haven't I?" He was surprised and slightly frightened by the general indifference, especially since he felt indifferent himself; he had little desire to go and start looking for Genziana. From all this he derived a sense of confusion, of universal error. He had left Genziana to come away with two friends from pre-Roman days; Mrs. Ghezzi-Walther and the little Fassola girl had joined them; they had taken them to dinner, then one of them had said: "Let's go to a night club," and they had descended into a cardboard grotto with little holy-image lamps, from which they had re-emerged almost immediately; they had brought the two ladies home and then he had prepared himself for a night of recollections with his friends, to drink the sweet potion of memories in huge gulps. And now this thing had happened. Abandoned, Genziana found a way to present herself to him again—the plaintive child was once more disturbing the virile game.

"I only need Massenti," Perineschi was saying.

Tito Solmi nodded; Perineschi was right, his choice of the obituarist could not have been more brilliant. Tito could already see himself in his Bologna house, next week after lunch, with his good-looking and authoritative maid bringing him his coffee in the living room, he lying on the bulky pillows of the chintz sofa reading Tranquillo Massenti commemorating Senator Horst. "In certain things, Tranquillo is incomparable."

"I tried his house a thousand times," Perineschi said, "but apparently neither he nor Ingrid is in. Where is he? Can you find him for me?" he asked Ovidio.

"He may be somewhere drinking," Ovidio said, immediately regretting his words.

Quarto Martelli followed his thought aloud: "We were out together all evening, Genziana and I, and meanwhile, this thing was happening. Probably they tried to reach her from her house, but they didn't know where. Before going to the Solmis', we had dinner on the Appian Way," he said apologetically, turning to Tito.

"Do you mean to say that you were with the daughter of Senator Horst tonight?" Perineschi asked.

Quarto did not answer. He measured Perineschi with a look, and had a frightening vision—that the man might be thinking of going to look for Genziana together with a photographer duly armed with flash bulbs in order to catch the moment when Genziana received the news of her father's death. High like a statue above Perineschi, Quarto contracted his muscles, in a preparatory pugilist's act. He was no longer shy in front of an editor; in fact an old schoolmate of his came to mind, one whom he had been in the habit of beating frequently, Romolo Bevioni by name. He was sure that if he had mentioned it, Tito Solmi would have recognized the phrase with a joyful howl: *Twelve-fifteen, end of class; twelve-twenty, preventive beating of Bevioni.* During one of these violent ceremonies, Quarto had been stopped by the professor of natural science, who had asked him for an explanation. Curiously, the teacher had let him go with the simple justification: "Because *I don't like* Bevioni." It was one of the few school recollections that made him proud. He felt his own body traversed by a voluptuous shiver of anger. If Perineschi were to suggest that he would himself start looking for Genziana, Quarto would hit him on his left cheek with a blow, of which he could already see the trajectory in the air. As young students they used to say: *There are people who should be recognized by their odor, and beaten up at once, without wasting time to explain to them why.* Things like that could no longer be done, but this man Perineschi was evidently capable of anything, he should be watched and, if necessary, stopped by violent means. Suddenly, in Quarto's thoughts, Genziana reappeared. He obscurely felt that his anger against Perineschi was an excuse to feel chivalrous, upright, her protector and her master. Genziana was no longer the plaintive little girl ruining the males' game by her intrusion; he could just see her when he kissed her and she assumed that air of annoyed docility, as if she meant: "Well, hurry up, what is this to you? Why do you want more?" That very image gave him now a burning tension.

Perineschi's words came to him through a fog: "I am sure somebody must have told her. The family. The radio. TV."

Then Ovidio Semenzato spoke through that fog: "There is one thing I haven't told you. As a matter of fact I didn't think it could matter to you. Now, here it is. I was coming into the Solmis' apartment, and in the entrance I met a guest who was leaving, Bernardo Partibon, he is a cousin of Giorgio Partibon, he has lived in America many years . . ."

Visibly the others were losing the thread of this talk. Ovidio went on, inspired; he had a full face, but with high cheekbones; his flushed cheeks were like two new and larger freckles joining the others that were spread over his red-haired-boy's skin; he too was a countryside Venetian. "That Bernardo Partibon, I feel I've always known him. One of those people you are always happy to help if they ask a favor of you. The Partibons, in more than one case, have aroused either great attraction or great antipathy. And now, here was this new character, just arrived from America. I want to find him again. Why has he come back? And he always seems so worried; what is he looking for? I'd like to know him better." He looked around, smiling: "You made a mistake, you know," he said to Perineschi, "snubbing the evening at the Solmis'. Actually it was an evening full of revelations. I'll never forget it."

There was a suspended silence, then Perineschi said: "Forgive me, but weren't you talking to us about Miss Horst?"

"What?" Ovidio said as if awakened.

"All of this that you've been saying about Bernardo Partibon, what does it have to do with Miss Horst?"

"What it has to do with Miss Horst? Why, of course, Bernardo Partibon left with her, didn't he?" Then, almost to himself, in a very low voice: "He left with Miss Horst, so the little Fassola girl stayed with us. God, what a significant evening."

"I told you," Solmi inserted rapidly, "that if you wanted

we could have stayed longer with those two women, perhaps have tried another night club."

"No, you see," Ovidio said to him dreamily, "actually, I am timid. What there was, was enough. For one evening."

Already at dinner, close to Dora Fassola, to her warmth, to her breathing, to her rosy cheek, he had imagined the moment when he, at home alone, would start going over that whole evening in his mind, without the embarrassment and tension of actually living it.

Solmi looked at him with affection: "I see," he murmured, "I see."

"You see?" Ovidio said with intensity, brightening up. "You see?"

Now Solmi looked at him with some alarm: "See what?" he asked.

Ovidio was not listening any longer. "When I think that I didn't even want to go to the Solmis'. It's always like that. The day after tomorrow I'll meet Dora Fassola again."

Meanwhile Perineschi kept mumbling: "Bernardo Partibon, Bernardo Partibon," looking at his hands as though he were holding that name and weighing it. Then he raised his head abruptly, pointed his blue eyes at Ovidio: "I know him," he said. "He was here in my office. You know who he is, don't you?" He was the examiner placing a question on the table and looking at the student in silence. He let a few moments pass and then resumed: "His sister's name is Maria. Maria Gervasutti, née Partibon; does that ring any bell?"

"But of course, Massenti covered the story for you," Solmi said.

Now Perineschi's blue eyes lingered on Ovidio: "And what were you saying?" he asked. "Who did you say you were going to meet the day after tomorrow?"

"This girl who was at the Solmis' too, Dora Fassola."

"And does the name Fassola suggest anything to you?"

"Of course it does."

"Who was the Fassola girl with? In whose company had she come?"

Ovidio shrugged. He did not dislike Perineschi but considered him ignorant and weak. He allowed himself to be considered less strong and capable than he; his sense of superiority fed on secrecy. He looked Perineschi straight in the eyes, and spoke as if lecturing: "We may suppose that Dora Fassola had gone to the Solmis' with two people: Mrs. Ghezzi-Walther and Bernardo Partibon. Mrs. Ghezzi-Walther is the wife of the industrialist, Firmino Ghezzi-Walther, a man whom I too met in Milan—through Tranquillo Massenti, to be sure. Tranquillo knows *also* people of that type, especially in Milan, where they maintain certain relationships between industry and culture."

"Get to the point."

"Don't you want me to talk to you about the Partibon family?"

Perineschi shook his head: "Now, the fact that Partibon and the Fassola girl were together, does it mean anything to you?"

Tito Solmi interrupted: "Perineschi, just tell us what it means to you."

"I shall put"—Perineschi opened his arms wide—"a simple question to you all. As you know, if for no other reason than because you read my magazine, the reputation of Maria Gervasutti, née Partibon, is connected with the story of her little girl, Massimina."

Tito sighed with boredom.

"You also know," Perineschi went on, "that the little girl was not the daughter of her husband. He had married an already pregnant Maria." He made a rather long pause; he looked around; he asked peremptorily: "Who had made her pregnant?"

Ovidio now spoke, in a low voice, not answering, rather ruminating to himself: "Massimo Fassola. Crashed in flames testing a plane. 1938 or '39. The lives of those years. The biographies of the period. It was natural that Dora Fassola and Bernardo should be together, there must have remained some links between the two families, don't you see? Perfectly natural," he repeated, for Perineschi's benefit but mentally telling himself: "It isn't as simple as that. What did lead Bernardo Partibon here, what makes him tick, what makes him almost look persecuted?"

"Bernardo Partibon," Perineschi resumed. "He came here to see me. About ten days ago." He corrected himself: "In fact a bit more: a couple of weeks, perhaps. He wanted to talk to Massenti. A very tall man, very much Americanized."

The Americanized man had appeared in front of him so simply, armed with the sole authority of his bulk, entering and standing still: "My name is Bernardo Partibon. Maria Partibon is my sister. Who is Tranquillo Massenti? I would so much like to talk to him. Would you give me the address?"

"I don't believe, you know, that Massenti can tell you much more than what he has already written in my magazine, which, as a matter of fact, he did rather brilliantly."

And Bernardo, thunderstruck with astonishment: "Brilliantly? What does this word have to do with it?" And then, with a look both anguished and naïve, and a firm, disarming courtesy: "You see, I would be interested in trying to understand."

This was easy: all that Perineschi had to do was to place a generic record on the plate: "My dear Partibon, with things of that kind, there are those who accept them, and those who do not accept them; as for understanding . . ." And then, self-assured, professional: "When I sent Massenti up to Corniano, where I gather you were born, I gave him my usual instructions: 'You talk to people, get impressions, opinions; and then report: "I've talked to this person who has told me this, to that other person who has told me that."' Reporting exactly on what one hears—is that, or is it not, a way of presenting *facts?* The objective picture of a certain climate of opinion?" The blue look had now stopped on Bernardo: "Tell me if I'm wrong. Actually, I don't remember the details, but I seem to recall that Massenti did very well . . ."

The description of the Corniano milieu, he did remember, had been very competent; that of Maria and Bernardo's father, Odo Partibon, had been quite subtle and picturesque; and then, rather by a stroke of luck, Odo Partibon had died in those very days, so that Tranquillo had gathered, one might say, his last breath, later dedicating a particularly lively piece to the funeral.

Perineschi was turning now to Tito Solmi in a defiant tone: "Do you realize why I like Massenti? Because he never lets anything slip away from him. Even if in an alcoholic stupor, he sees clearly, he grabs every opportunity. Does he need to drink? Does he have to have that? Well, all right, if that's what he needs, I'll send him a case of whiskey every day . . ."

Tito Solmi kept his head lowered and interrupted him, speaking through clenched teeth: "Why whiskey? I never saw him drink anything but wine or grappa."

"Wine, eh?" Perineschi said as if that information contained some recondite and ambiguous significance. He laughed sourly: "Then let's send him a nice case of Valpolicella. In fact, bring it to him in my name, all I want is to get this Horst obituary from him, pronto."

A heavy silence followed. Quarto Martelli broke it: "Listen," he said to Tito and Ovidio, "we've got to get out of here." Solmi was opening his mouth to reply but Quarto prevented him with a gesture: "First of all, let's get away from here." His face was red and he started to perspire and tremble; precisely because his body was so athletic, with a solid stance, and he had that handsome, well-shaped head with hair parted in an old-fashioned style on one side and brilliantined, those signs of nervous ebulliency gave an even stronger impression of disorder and upheaval. "We must do something about Genziana, mustn't we?" he insisted, trying to convince himself.

Perineschi let him finish, then asked calmly: "Tell me one thing: where do you want to go? In what direction?" Then, addressing himself to all of them with a bright smile: "I have a problem for you. Where is the body of Senator Horst?"

There was a new, heavy silence while they all looked at him with surprise.

Perineschi shook his head: "After all, it *is* a rather interesting question: where is the Senator? As a matter of fact, if you want to find the daughter, the first logical place to look for her is near her dead father." He had won a point. He paused and looked them in the eyes, one by one: "Do you suppose they brought him to his house? Or to the morgue? Or did they perhaps keep him at the Senate? To have him lie in state there? Or—this is a possibility too—to the Foreign Office?" The three remained silent, suspicious. "In America, the thing would be simple," Perineschi went on, genuinely interested in the problem, "they would bring him to a de luxe mortuary, I'll bet you; but what about here in Italy?" He looked at all three in turn, waiting, with a half smile.

It was at this point that Quarto Martelli leaned over toward him, again as at a post office window, this time, however, scrutinizing him with histrionic intensity: "Listen," he said, "your questions are out of order. We must go back to the starting point. The question to be posed is a different one, namely: is Senator Horst dead?"

Only Tito Solmi understood immediately; he felt he was going back twenty years. He recognized the tone, the strategy: this was what as students they had referred to as "the idiotization" of a person.

"How do you know that Senator Horst is dead? You live here within these four walls and you receive telephone calls from all over Italy from people telling you silly lies. Only every now and then people like Tito and myself come in bringing a wave of truth. Your paper? All falsifications. It's not their fault"—and Quarto pointed to Ovidio—"they write what you ask them to write; to them it is strictly a technical procedure." He pointed his finger toward Perineschi: "Try. Try and go to the private residence of the Senator, on Via Po. Go up the stairs. Stop at the door of the apartment. A tall walnut door. You will find it ajar, as is traditional in the house of the dead. And through that narrow opening, *you will hear the clatter of a typewriter*. The Senator is the author of thick volumes on history, and that clatter is the typical sound of the Senator *at work*. Let's push the door open, let's enter." Quarto paused in the general silence; Tito was watching him with intense delight. "We find all that one finds in similar circumstances: quantities of flowers, people with gloomy faces, stern or weeping relatives. But, all of this, in complete silence: a motion picture without the sound track. You, a journalistic maniac, nevertheless do not dare ask anything, not even your prize question, *where is the dead man*. You go out through the same door, leaving it ajar as you found it. And already while you are going out, there it is . . . again that clatter of the Senator's typewriter following you while you descend the staircase. Try"—and he protruded his finger far enough to poke Perineschi's nose—"try. Go there. You'll see."

For an instant Tito Solmi was afraid that those two would start a fist fight. But instead, Perineschi kept watching Quarto with an expression that could have been either fear or humiliation: his whole face seemed to contract and wrinkle, his eyes darkened. When he talked he had the same sincerely inquisitive tone as a while earlier: "Excuse me," he asked, "could you tell me why you came here? Who are you? What do you do?"

Quarto raised his finger in a gesture of admonishment: "Olympic basketball team," he said. "And I came to see you because *they* came—my friends and teammates."

"A moment ago you seemed desperate at the news that the father of one of your dear friends had died, and now you start acting like a buffoon. You are really a strange person."

Quarto seemed hit by these words, he brooded over them a while; then he asked with curiosity: "Really? You find that what I say is just buffoonery?" He lowered his head; then he spoke in a convincing, humble tone: "Believe me, Mr. Perineschi: the death of the prominent man, the arrival of the daughters for the funeral, the speeches—well, all of this, deep underneath, has a definite comic streak."

Perineschi did not allow himself to seem surprised: "I see," he said at once. "I see. And listen, do you perhaps find"—Perineschi sounded like an interviewer—"that in this sense, Rome, the Roman spirit . . ."

Quarto interrupted him: "Rome? Rome?" he repeated as if it were a new name he couldn't quite place. He shrugged, produced a short dry laugh: "And do you think I know Rome? I've been living here I don't know how many years . . . and do you think I am, as they say, acclimated? That I have a real rapport with people? Do you know what my entry, my bridge into Rome has been?" Perineschi shook his head imperceptibly, in order not to interrupt him. Quarto went on: "Women. I am—well, there is no other way to put it—I am very good-looking. But do you believe, Mr. Perineschi, that I know these women who have been with me? Very important people too, you know, wives also of people—well, very very important, with splendid new houses."

He stopped dreamily, because as usual there came by contrast to mind the images, sounds, scents of the world in which he had been born and raised. He was from the Bologna region, but his family was a matriarchy and a good deal of his mother's estates were in Venetia, so that Padua had for many years been their center, an old house in the Padua of long ago, not "the Milan of Venetia" as it was now, but rather a city of porticoed piazzas and irregularly cobbled streets, with breaths of countryside smell, with primitive tramways crowding medieval streets.

"We Martellis are counts, imagine that. I absolutely must add that in our house this fact never had any significance at all, and do you want to know why I believe it didn't? Because we really had the land, the money. That's something other than titles and coronets. But as soon as I started growing up a little, I realized that being a count could be used to great advantage. You do remember, don't you?" he said, turning to Solmi, who nodded by closing his eyelids over his round eyes. "Calling cards, a crown embroidered on my shirt front, with nine points, above my initials." Solmi burst out laughing. "But you see"—he turned to Perineschi again —"all of this, after all, was still a joke, one of the many ways we had to make a burlesque of everything. Wasn't it?" Again by lowering his eyelids Tito underlined everything. "But later, instead, when I started living here in Rome, the thing got confused . . . I'll never forget the first times I went out with Genziana, how she occasionally would get it into her head to introduce me with my title: I am still asking myself whether she was joking." He mimicked her accent, exaggerating it, but without sarcasm, rather with a kind of painful languor: " 'You know the count, don't you? Or don't you? Then I'd like you to meet Count Martelli . . .' Once or twice she 'liked me to meet' people of royal blood, relatives of the former king here or of foreign ones, I never could quite understand whether Genziana really cares that much to keep up acquaintances with people like that. With Genziana you never can understand, and that's also because she keeps so busy, but deep underneath she always feels so very unwell. But mind you, she has a drive, oh, such drive . . . They say she has no pity for anybody, but the first person she feels no pity for is herself." He sighed deeply, as if Genziana's energies were overpowering him.

Perineschi, rather than simply curious, now seemed fascinated: "Martelli," he murmured, "you are a strange character, you guessed certain things . . . You know what? *You* should write that piece for me, on Genziana Horst's father."

"You have no idea how illiterate I am," Quarto said rather cheerfully. "Misspellings, things like that." It appeared that his own talk had given him relief; now he spoke with gusto, caught in the situation, heeded. He breathed deeply, expanding his chest: "And this is not the complete picture, yet. Society people, with titles, et cetera—all of this, shall we say, is *one* of Genziana's fields. Then there is art and all that sort of thing. She knows the painters, the writers, and so on. We've been to all imaginable art shows, all presented by friends of hers. She designs costumes, and she is very good, you know. When the big shots come from America, for instance, first thing they do they go to her; now she will dress Chet Marshall in the part of Emperor

Caligula and you can bet the costumes will be beauties." He took another deep breath: "I liked her immediately, the very first moment I set eyes on her. God, how I liked her."

"*Caligula,* eh?" Perineschi asked, intrigued.

"Yes, it will be a big historical picture but the character of Caligula apparently will be treated—well, psychoanalytically, sort of," said Quarto with a certain pride.

"I've always maintained," Tito Solmi inserted, "that Genziana is one of the most desirable women in Italy." He was obviously delighted that his old companion was putting up such a splendid show in front of the editor of *Roma Sabato.*

Quarto looked at him with a sigh, as if to convey that Tito's words gave only a very pale idea of the situation. "Genziana is a woman who could have everything," he said slowly, "and yet . . ."

"Yet what?" Ovidio cut in with intense curiosity.

"She is an impossible and hopeless woman. They say she is without pity—no, I say she is without hope. Here I am, saying this, and I don't understand very well myself what I mean. And I'll tell you something else too: in the final analysis, if she wanted me, I would marry her." Then, as if to complete the explanation: "There are times when I feel that the greatest happiness would be never to see her again. You noticed earlier tonight, didn't you"—he turned to Tito and Ovidio—"when she said that she wanted to leave by herself, how relieved I felt."

Without malevolence, simply because he wanted Quarto to go on talking, Perineschi said: "But I seem to have understood that you let her go with somebody else, with the famous Bernardo Partibon."

There was a silence: both Tito and Ovidio looked at Quarto apprehensively.

Quarto remained still, with bowed head. Then, as if con-

(8 5)

cluding a train of thought, he said: "I'm not jealous, you know." And to Perineschi: "You see—for example, about Genziana's past life, her relationship with men, et cetera, I know everything, even the most precise physical details. So, as you can imagine," he went on with unexpected sadness, "I know everything of her relationship to her father, even if I never did meet him. Genziana will shed very few tears; she'll keep it all inside herself. Her sister will do the weeping. Laura is quite a different person from Genziana, even physically. She too, however, in her small way . . . " and Quarto produced a greedy smile, with a winking of the eye and clicking of the tongue, all of which seemed rather inappropriate. "That's where I met Genziana, at Laura's . . ." He stopped as if caught in the vision of his first meeting with Genziana; but when he resumed he said: "Laura is a pretty little woman, soft and round, and she lives in the country in a kind of small castle, but she often comes to Rome for visits. Rodolfo stays in the country and she comes to Rome to have terrific affairs with other men."

Tito Solmi tried to recapitulate in his mind how much wine Martelli had been drinking at dinner; from their distant student years he remembered what he used to refer to as time-bomb drunkenness; he knew that Quarto could continue to talk on like that uninterruptedly until morning. Therefore he suggested: "Didn't you want to begin a search for Genziana?"

"It's impossible," Quarto replied immediately with the lucid and inventive self-assurance of the inebriated: "Genziana has disappeared." Tito was opening his lips to try a different approach to the question, but Quarto cut him off at once. "I'm telling you. I know Genziana, don't I?"

"Actually," Ovidio said, "Bernardo Partibon did seem to have the best of intentions to go and sit alone with her

(86)

somewhere. We looked for them at a restaurant and a bar he had mentioned, but they weren't at either place."

"She has disappeared," Martelli repeated. "I know her intuitively. I couldn't describe to you the reasons for what she does; perhaps you literate people could and you'd probably get it all wrong; but I feel, I feel everything." Unexpectedly, he started to laugh. "When I say that she has disappeared I mean she has gone somewhere to sit all by herself. Even if she is with a man"—he stopped laughing and became grave—"Genziana is all by herself."

Rome, Tito thought, had been good for his friend; he had found him in splendid form, capable of silencing a man like Perineschi. However, both be and Ovidio were perplexed for a moment, and looked at Quarto with apprehension when they heard Perineschi ask: "Excuse me, but since you are so frank about it . . . Am I wrong, or haven't people been saying that Miss Horst is a lesbian?"

Quarto said quickly, quietly: "That's not true, you know." After a silence: "People," he added, "tend to simplify matters."

"Simplify?"

"Certainly. You hear them say: this one is a lesbian, that one is a fagot, this one sleeps with everybody, that one is terrifically good in bed. I know this thing about being good in bed, because they say it about me. And it's really not always true." There was a second of absolute silence, then the four of them burst out laughing.

"Lesbian," Martelli resumed as if announcing the title of a new paragraph. "Mr. Perineschi, just to give you an idea how things are, I'll tell you this: it was I myself who suggested to Genziana, more than once, to try to have a lesbian experience. I even pointed out to her a couple of prospects who seemed suitable, among girls I knew. I have a friend who is a specialist, he has a kind of collection. He gets them up to his house in pairs to arrange them on his bed and watch them."

Perineschi tightened his lips as for a nervous shock, but then he managed to transform that contraction into a smile: "Nice things," he said suggestively. He knew very well that nowadays there was a certain vogue for irregularity and so-called orgies, and he wanted to show himself adequately casual.

"I recommended it to her but she didn't do it," Quarto went on, unaware of the interruption, "and who knows, if I had seriously thought that she would do it, perhaps I wouldn't have encouraged her, while instead"—he laughed briefly—"I encouraged her even rather insistently. What a mess. Oh, God, the truth of the matter is that a thing like this, that Genziana should go to bed with a woman—there seems to be no reason for doing it, and there seems to be no reason for not doing it."

"Hmmm," Perineschi said, nodding. He scrutinized Quarto with increasing attention: "Of course," he murmured, "undoubtedly, as a general pattern, obviously, more or less . . ." His eyes wandered among the three. "And what do *you* think?" he asked Ovidio, his friend and colleague. But Ovidio remained impassive. "You know what?" Perineschi then said, getting up. He walked around his desk and stopped behind Solmi's chair, putting his hands on the man's shoulders. "You know what? I am really happy you came to see me." He patted Solmi's shoulders a couple of times, then left him to start walking up and down the room. "I feel good in your company," he went on in a higher voice, not so much as if he were addressing a large audience, but as if he had decided on a public confession, "and there aren't many people in whose company I feel good. In the same way as I am sure there are few people who feel good in *my*

(88)

company . . ." The three men were silent; Perineschi shrugged briefly. Then, including them all in his look: "You people," he said, in a tone of irritated perplexity, "seem to get along so well together."

"And think that Martelli and I met this evening for the first time in I don't know how many years," Tito said quickly, without elaborating. There was no need for that. He knew that the three of them, that evening, were producing sparks; just as at the Solmis'—other people's admiration did not surprise him. Instead, he said: "You, Perineschi, work too much."

Again the man shrugged: "I was here wasting time. I stayed on because even if I go home I can't sleep."

Solmi raised his eyebrows, ready to offer advice; he was a splendid sleeper himself but by cultivating friendships among intellectuals and artists he had become a specialist on insomnia. "I'll give you something that will make you sleep like an angel, even physiologically; Leo Gerolami has put thousands of people to sleep with that product. He literally changed their lives."

"Do you think I haven't tried that one?" Gerolami was a doctor à la mode, with a wide clientele encompassing the artistic and the fashionable. "You know the only thing that sometimes makes me sleep like a baby?" Both Tito and Ovidio had heard him tell it many times, but they let him repeat it: "A bottle of champagne."

They also anticipated what he immediately suggested: "Why don't we go and continue our chat at my house?" He did not wait for an answer, went back behind his desk to gather his papers, and put them in his briefcase. "Before we go I want to see again if Tranquillo by any chance . . ." He grabbed the receiver, dialed the number.

The three men stood up. Perineschi let Massenti's telephone ring about ten times; from the place they were standing, the three heard in the silence the very distant muffled sound of the futile call.

"He must have unplugged it," Ovidio said.

"He never does," Perineschi replied, looking at him dejectedly. Then he seemed to want to correct the impression and smiled.

Through Ovidio's mind there floated by now monotonous thoughts: "Here we are, Perineschi can't be alone. He needs us. It's the hour of capitulation."

"Are you going to give us a champagne sleeping potion too if we come to your house?" Quarto Martelli asked. He had guessed Perineschi's panic at the idea of being alone, and he came to his rescue; he saw no contradiction between this impulse and the one that not long ago had almost moved him to beat Perineschi; it was as if both sprang from the same source.

Going down the marble staircase, Perineschi took Quarto by the arm: "You come in my car; they know the way."

In Perineschi's apartment on Salita del Grillo they found excellent champagne in abundance. They went on talking till dawn, drinking champagne; their nerves relaxed, they were all calm, without further needs; a deep sense of repose and friendship pervaded them and tied them together; for hours, with the same words repeated an infinite number of times, they kept going around in circles over two or three themes; the sun was already up when Perineschi enunciated once more the last of those:

"By now," he said, "one dies only of a heart attack or cancer, and even with those, it's a matter of time. For example, now they make nylon arteries. The question is rather, why go on living?" These problems were far removed from them, since now they all felt very well.

Tito opened a window—the sky was clear, the fresh air wafted over Roman ruins and walls, bringing a smell of damp earth. "Talking of thrombosis," he said, "we have completely forgotten Senator Horst."

With a jump, Perineschi went to the telephone; this time Tranquillo Massenti answered immediately; Perineschi listened to him a long while with an ecstatic smile on his face.

After he put down the receiver and joined the others again, he announced: "He was the first to talk to the daughter, Genziana. I believe he used to be very fond of her. He'll write the piece for me. Tranquillo is insuperable."

After two hours of dreamless sleep, Bernardo Partibon was awakened by the silence around him. He felt that the house was empty. He rushed out of the room, looked for a bathroom, washed and dressed himself in a hurry. Now he was sure that all rooms off the large corridor were empty.

When he came down, he found Rodolfo Piglioli-Spada at the foot of the stairs, dressed like a jockey. He looked smaller and drier than ever. His wrinkles too, and his tanned skin, showed up more sharply than the night before.

He waited for Bernardo to address him before shaking hands.

"Am I late?" Bernardo asked. "Did something happen?"

"Why late? Late for what?" Piglioli-Spada asked. "We have been left here alone, the two of us. The house is empty. We let you sleep on. I'll join my wife and my sister-in-law in Rome later."

Taking him by the arm, he accompanied Bernardo through the large living room, and from there into the dining room, with two places ready for breakfast at the table.

"Sit down, sit down, let's eat something."

When they were seated near each other at a corner of the immense table, Piglioli-Spada drank the orange juice that they had found already poured into the glasses; Bernardo did the same. Then Piglioli-Spada put one of his small hands, hard as iron, on Bernardo's forearm, and said: "Last night, around ten to be exact, Horst died, my wife's father. The news didn't get to us until several hours later—nothing really functions around here; at any rate, she and Genziana left immediately." Bernardo mumbled something incomprehensible. "And he wasn't in bad health at all," the man went on. "Once upon a time, when I still adored England, I would have turned this scene into a masterpiece of restraint and stiff-upper-lip, apologizing to you because circumstances compelled us to offer you such confused and unpleasant hospitality. Now I'll tell you that the death of my father-in-law causes me considerable sorrow, although there is an abundance of redeeming features: he was old; dead of a stroke, probably without realizing it, et cetera." He sighed deeply, which seemed to re-establish his strength and his voice. "It looks as though the maids have left too, or perhaps they have gone to their rooms to weep; they were deeply devoted to the Senator. So, let's pour our own café au lait."

They drank their coffee and ate for a while in silence.

"But I must add that I am really sorry to offer you such paltry hospitality," Piglioli-Spada then resumed, "and for such a brief time. I hope there will be other occasions." After another silence: "As I was telling you last night, I don't buy the magazines any more, since they have nauseated me slightly, always photographing exactly the same, extremely limited number of people—people who were rather insignificant to begin with. But if you find out something about that little Venetian girl, remember to tell me. I'm not interested in this story in itself. Are you surprised? I'll try to elucidate my point of view. Let us start from the premise that actual information no longer exists—I'm not talking

(92)

about absolutes, which we gave up long ago if ever we had any—I mean news, information, the simple reproduction, journalistic or otherwise, of things said or heard. Therefore, on the very rare occasions when we find ourselves close to authorized sources—as you could be, or become, in this case—we want to take advantage of it. It's a little bit like when during the war you would buy a more or less useless object for the simple reason that it just happened to be there, not rationed."

Bernardo produced a questioning sound, of which Piglioli-Spada remained clearly aware, going on practically without taking a breath:

"It is not improbable that in the case of that little girl, the story may have been rather publicized by people like that man Debaldè, whose name—you'll call me a maniac— I'll never be able to forget, being one of the most 'unplaceable' names I have ever encountered. It was he who spoke, I am almost sure, of 'odor of sanctity.' Or am I dreaming?"

"I do hope you are dreaming."

The man had a rather unconvinced smile, raising his quiet, clear eyes toward Bernardo—eyes that could be convinced only by their own visions; and he went on meditatingly:

"Beatification is a very long and complicated procedure—this is proverbial. A Monsignor friend of mine was talking to me about that; he happened to be working in the specialized office at the Vatican, and he was telling me that right then there were about a thousand cases being processed. That many, if I remember correctly. About problems of that kind, I assure you, I know very little. My brother, who is an ambassador, is a very pious man; I do things a little bit my own way. For that matter, you know, problems of that kind . . . it's a world in itself. The whole organization of the Church—terrific as it is, of course. Do you want more milk? But each of us, I believe, does things a little bit his own way; Italians have no Protestantism perhaps because each has his own particular protest—homemade, as it were. His own particular form of communication with God. A handy little God, actually. Would you like another brioche?" Without changing his tone he proceeded to ask: "Do you know Genziana well? I hope so. She hasn't had much luck since the time of her first love at sixteen—he was a forty-year-old officer, who lived in Africa and wrote her letters which I remember distinctly: from the point of view of handwriting, and of grammar as well, they looked like letters from a maid."

"No," Bernardo said with a quick, silly laugh, "imagine, we just met last night, your sister-in-law and I. We were out together, so evidently they couldn't reach her to give her the sad news about her father."

Now it seemed that Piglioli-Spada had decided to stop talking; after listening to Bernardo's explanation he went on staring at him with a satisfied expression and a subtle smile.

"The Senator," Bernardo said to fill the embarrassing silence, "was a very remarkable man as far as I could . . ."

"Really? No, no," Piglioli-Spada interrupted him affably, "believe me, Horst was a silly ass." Without pausing he went on: "Where will you go now? Will you go back to Rome?" He lowered his voice: "Or will you go up to Venice?"

"I'm thinking of going to Venice and to Corniano."

"In search of authentic information?" Piglioli-Spada whispered.

"I haven't seen any of my family yet. My mother is still living. To see each other, to touch each other, after twenty years . . . Things that should be done, shouldn't they?"

"Why, of course, naturally," the man said quietly. "Listen," he then asked cautiously, "is it true, or is it one of the usual fabrications of the magazines, that in America they have television programs where they take a totally unsuspecting person and have him meet all sorts of friends and relatives whom he hasn't seen for years and years, gathered from all over the country and even the world—just like that, as a show?"

"It's true, it's true," Bernardo said quickly.

Piglioli-Spada sighed deeply. "Do you understand why I live here in isolation and I no longer read the . . . "

"Oh, yes, of course."

"You will find Corniano very different from the time when you were a little boy, I presume; for that matter, even in Venice there are a lot of neon lights. The magazines, at the time of the story we were mentioning, also carried some pictures of Corniano. But one reason why I hadn't forgotten the story was that the articles on the subject in *Roma Sabato* were written by someone named Massenti and were not bad at all."

"I know him. At Corniano, he saw my father too. I know Massenti and also Perineschi."

"Who is he?"

"The editor of *Roma Sabato*."

Piglioli-Spada pointed his butter knife at Bernardo: "I'll bet you he is illiterate. But not that man Massenti; there you could see the right kind of syntax." He put down the knife and got up. Bernardo rose too. Leading Bernardo back to the living room by the arm, Piglioli-Spada went on talking: "That's true, proper information doesn't exist any more, but after all, what can journalists do in some cases? What do we know about the dead, or the value that a soul has had? Did you bring anything with you? Of course, you Americans travel only with a toothbrush. I'll accompany you to your car."

They crossed the hall, with small Piglioli-Spada hanging on to Bernardo's arm; they went out into the cool morning and found Bernardo's car shiny with dew on the thin gravel in front of the entrance, with a few dry leaves on the hood.

But Piglioli-Spada did not yet allow him to get into the car: "Wait a moment," he said, and led Bernardo to the far end of the villa, toward the wall, where the chapel was.

They went in through a squeaky, water-logged door. The interior revealed the lines of a church in miniature. The little Gothic windows high up, the small steps to the altar, the narrow apse, the minuscule vault—all of it was completely bare; only spots of dampness interrupted the white and the void.

"And then what will you do?" Piglioli-Spada asked after a short silence, resuming their conversation as though he had simply moved to another room of the house, the difference here being the way his voice echoed in that emptiness. "Will you go back to America? Do you have a family in America?"

"I have a son by my first wife—a big American boy who lives in California with his mother."

"From whom you are separated?"

"From whom I am divorced."

"I see. And did you remarry?"

"And incidentally, my second wife is in Venice at the moment, I believe, with her mother."

"Why aren't you there too?"

"With Clare, my wife, there have been ups and downs. I came to Italy alone, before they did."

"Of course, you Americans marry many times. Long ago, when I believed one could entertain opinions of a general character without being precipitated into the ridiculous, I·thought that your habit of marrying many times was the right formula. The more so, since you keep in touch with your past wives in the most civilized manner."

"Yes, I am rather good friends with both my wives."

"There, you see," Piglioli-Spada said; and he fell into a long silence. Finally with a deep sigh he said, looking around the naked chapel: "That poor man Horst." He again took Bernardo by the arm to lead him outside. "Now," he said, while they were returning to the car, "There will be all those formalities. It is difficult to see any connection . . ."

Suddenly Bernardo said: "Once during the war in the Far East I saw a man die, and at the last moment he started reciting something unintelligible, it sounded like a formal prayer but I am sure that it was something he was making up as he went along." Piglioli-Spada listened to him intently. "If I remember correctly," Bernardo finished, "he was an Armenian."

"Think of that!"

Standing in front of the car, Piglioli-Spada took a notebook out of his pocket, wrote something rapidly, tore out the sheet and gave it to Bernardo: "If you want to send Genziana a line, I believe she would be pleased. I too would like to see you again, Partibon. Why don't you come to the funeral?"

"I'm afraid I won't go back to Rome," Bernardo said, getting into the car.

"Of course, you have your multiple family reunions."

They shook hands warmly through the car window; when Bernardo finally left, they went on waving until he had passed the gate.

CHAPTER FIVE

✵

Clement B. Blumenfeld:

Venice, hotel. Night 15–16 Oct. —I feel it is a good idea to take note of everything these days with even greater care than usual. An hour ago, the Countess appeared at the door of my room, and behind her was the shadow of my half sister, Mrs. Clare Partibon, née Flanagan, both of them with a superficial question on their lips: "What are you doing up so late?" A fake question. My mother knows my habits so well that at times she calls me from her room in the middle of the night if by chance we happen to be living together (i.e., in the same hotel; there have been no houses for some time).

Behind the fake question there was the real one, which remained unexpressed: "What about him? Bernardo? Did you bring him? Will he come?"

Then Clare yawns in the shadow (a spuriously relaxed and languid yawn; actually she is tense, and if she talked with sincerity she would say: "Let's postpone the whole thing. I haven't the strength to start talking about Bernardo tonight"). She tells our mother in English: "Well, I believe I'll go to sleep," so our mother comes into my room alone, shutting the door behind her. Here we are.

"Clement detests his mother"—that's perhaps the oldest among the erroneous slogans about me; psychological theories have been founded on just such a simple proposition; my mother herself has gone through periods of her life in which our whole relationship has been based upon that hypothesis. On the contrary, of course, I haven't the slightest animosity against the Countess. We have seen each other rarely, but every time we meet my attitude is one of affable interest. I am happy she comes in here to talk. (There isn't only my furious curiosity at this particular moment; there is also simple pleasure.) Between us, if I may say so, there is a man-to-man relationship.

I can predict within an inch every gesture she will make: the way she appears, dignified and at the same time businesslike; the way she looks at me, with interest and satisfaction, first of all evaluating me physically and guessing the level of my virility and of my social presentability; the way she takes a cigarette and waits for me to light it. I foresee the instant when she will spring the question on Bernardo, her smile, her style:

"Well, then, and what does *your brother-in-law* do these days?"

It is worth mentioning that we had dined together (or rather, she and Clare had already had dinner earlier, so they stayed on and kept me company, since I had arrived from Rome in the morning but had gone around Venice the whole day before coming to them at the Roman dinner time, the Countess being very much against delaying the hours of her meals), and that after dinner we had been sitting for half an hour in the hotel bar; but during this whole period there had been a conspiracy of silence, a heavy stone had been placed on the very name of Bernardo. Only the eyes of these two—similar in many ways, large, green-blue, unquestionably very beautiful—had continued to rest searchingly on my face as if to ferret out my secret thoughts. But nothing had been said. We had talked about things totally different from Bernardo, in Italian. Now, in my room, my mother's question had been put in English.

If one were to define my mother (or rather, if definitions of that sort had any meaning), perhaps one could describe her chiefly as an American lady. I don't mean only in the sense that by now she is more or less built with American materials (hair, diets, teeth, cosmetics, etc.)—I mean in the way she conducts her life, family and social relationships, etc. Will I clarify this idea later on? We shall see. At any rate, in spite of the fact that my mother's maiden name is so characteristically Venetian that it sounds made up—Nicoletta Benzon; however, she lets friends call her Nicole—only certain ridiculous social climbers, who occasionally surround her, have exclaimed ecstatically: "The typical Venetian lady." No. If anything, the Countess' original qualities have shown themselves in this: once she became an American lady, she set out to impersonate the character fully. Perhaps one could try to express the thing this way: my mother seemed to be saying, by her aspect, manner, attitude: "I could have become a competent doge's wife, but the Most Serene Venetian Republic was extinguished in 1798." (I put the date in; she wouldn't know it.)

It is true that, as is customary, I was given a middle name and this is her family name, so that one might suspect that she wanted to insert into her son's identification tag this fossilized relic of the doges' era. But that can be imagined only by people who know her superficially. Actually the idea came from my father, a Jew of Austrian origin, crazy about Venice. Later that fossil has been so much shuffled and reshuffled in the motions of our life that it lends itself very well to the wordplays with which I occasionally try to alleviate boredom: I turn it, e.g., into a Germanic or Scandinavian name—Bentzon or even Bengtson; and, in fact, in several respects (e.g., mountain climbing) I am a Nordic.

After having asked her rather roundabout question, "Well, then, and what does *your brother-in-law,* etc.," she did not wait for an answer, also because she could guess there would not be one, and she lowered her head somewhat like a catapult, throwing her look and her question at me: "You and Bernardo have seen each other, haven't you?" My mother, among other virtues, has a beautiful voice which is impressive even in the medium, sedate register.

Caught by surprise I reply immediately: "Seen? But we live together in Rome."

She frowns. In the act of concentration, she shuts and purses her American lips. Then she raises her cigarette to her mouth, inhales deeply, and slowly exhaling, looks at me through the smoke: "Well. Then let me ask you a question. Let us try to put the thing in its simplest terms. Has he become completely insane?"

To gain time I start murmuring: "I don't see, Mother . . ."

"You do remember an old idea of mine about good manners, an idea which you liked very much too, I heard you refer to it more than once: namely, that good manners are a convenience. They simplify relationships, they make life easier and more practical."

"Yes, Mother," I say with boredom.

She goes on: "The convenience of good manners. Now, I have never seen a more insane example of abandoning that convenience than the one presented by your brother-in-law in his recent actions."

"Well, if you put things on that level . . . "—this and other murmurs from me pass entirely unobserved.

For the thousandth time she wants to "recapitulate the

situation." She goes back to that day, crucial to her, end of November, almost a year ago now: "I was in town for Christmas shopping, I was staying in New York for three days, at our usual hotel. And the porter tells me that Bernardo is there too . . ."

"Mother," I say more firmly, "you've written this story to me, with all of the details, many times; and even if I didn't know it already, it wouldn't interest me. We are on a different plane."

She repeats only, looking at me but without seeing me, as in a dream: "On a different plane." Then she resumes, in full reality: "He was there in New York too, arrived I don't know whether from California or maybe even from Las Vegas; at any rate, when I met him he sort of looked that way—all golden with sunshine. It was the first time I met him after his separation from Clare, think of that. All right, you know these things, but I repeat them because I repeat them to myself and because you are a man and you must help me understand them. There was no reason why Bernardo and I shouldn't treat each other civilly, therefore it came quite spontaneously for me to say: 'You look wonderful.' He leans down to kiss me: 'I knew you were here,' he says. You know the way he does, he throws a half phrase like that, and even if he doesn't add: 'And that's why I came—to meet you,' you take it that way. I tell him, as a warning between the lines: 'Clare will join me here tomorrow.' He just looks at me, but the look means: 'I knew that too.' He immediately asks me to lunch; in moments like that Bernardo is irresistible." My mother says this in a dry tone, like a publicity agent recognizing the effectiveness of a competitor's methods.

One could continue like that for pages trying to reproduce my mother's speech, but it would be of no use. It amuses me to try and put on paper the way she talks, it becomes a sort of exercise; but her view of Bernardo's story does not furnish any useful contributions.

At any rate, let's continue for a while.

"As if that weren't enough, after lunch he also joins me for the Christmas shopping. And those were delightful hours, I want you to know that."

"All right, Mother, I know." I produce the trace of a yawn while I slip down into my leather armchair and cross my legs, so that now my knees are higher than my head.

"In other words, there were not, nor could there be, any doubts on this point: he had taken the initiative."

"What initiative?" I interrupt, this time with firmness, raising my hand like a journalist at a press conference. I feel sure that my mother cannot possibly think of using a term like "the initiative of a reconciliation."

She says immediately: "Well, let us say the initiative of a reconciliation. And I'll tell you more. From the way he talked and acted, and the way he made me talk and act, it seemed as though there wouldn't be any need for a reconciliation—as though there had never been a break. You know how Bernardo is? He is a *presence*."

At this point my mother was looking into empty space and it seemed that even she was at a loss for words, was guessing the complications of reality, was suspecting the existence of something not entirely reducible to her own terms: "It isn't that Bernardo at some point enters, or re-enters, your life . . . You only realize that he *was there all the time*."

I don't know whether these are my mother's exact words, but at any rate that's the idea, and it would have been an idea worthy of further development. Instead, she went on with her traditional tale: she and Bernardo, Christmas-shopping that afternoon; the perfectly natural tone of their question: "And what are we going to get for Clare?" and the answer: "Let's have fun choosing small things for the moment, we'll think of the important presents later on," and so forth.

So that when Clare arrives the next day in New York, she finds a husband already recaptured and reinstalled, a *presence,* an *a priori,* something one doesn't discuss, since it is already so evidently *there*: the huge bear with his large head, with his powerful, deep voice. Very pleasant evening, laughs, recollections.

And yet . . . Here is another phrase of my mother's that I find worthy of attention, this one also uttered with eyes staring into empty space: "And yet—how shall I say—he looked like *someone who is living in the third person."* She abandons the interesting observation and resumes: "But I assure you, quite soon they were very close to each other again. Later on, I heard them from my room." I don't understand why she says this as though she had made God knows what startling discovery. That Clare and Bernardo often found each other mutually desirable is the only obvious part of their relationship.

Sometimes I, too, observed them rather close, and this has always appeared to me as perhaps their main characteristic: at any moment they seemed ready to start making love. For example, that time they came to spend the day in New Haven, during my Yale period; when I had to leave them for a couple of hours in the afternoon they said: "Perhaps in the meantime we'll go up to your place and rest a while." Coming back I "heard them" from my landing, so I went out again and spent an hour at the library.

Or I remember that warm night in California, at Zuma Beach, when we stopped the car, and Ilse and I crossed the wide expanse of silver sand to go and swim in the Pacific, phosphorescent with moonlight (where can she be now, Ilse? Perhaps not far from that beach? Or has she left to come here to me? Is that why I describe the ocean and the sand with fabulously exaggerated adjectives? Is it because I see the stamp of her bare foot? It is afternoon there now, with the sun shining), the two of them, Clare and Bernardo, remaining in the car. There can be no doubt how they killed time while they waited. Et cetera, et cetera.

My mother is coming to the more recent developments of the situation: "Everything was arranged for our departure from America at the beginning of October; we had decided to take the boat for a change, also because it was his first trip to Italy after twenty years and he seemed happy at the thought of making it with both of us. During those years he had been in England and in France, but his return to Italy . . . well, it seemed that he had kept that in store, to do it with Clare, you understand. We were going to cross the ocean together, then I would leave them in Europe on their own. Instead, a month earlier, he leaves alone. In fact, as far as we are concerned, it isn't as though he *left,* he disappeared . . ."

"I know, Mother, I know."

For the first time I obtain a direct reply to one of my interruptions: "No, you can't really know. The difference between somebody *leaving* and somebody *disappearing.* It's worse than death," she says frivolously. "At least, in the case of death you know *something,* but when somebody *disappears* . . ."

While she talked like that, she seemed to ponder the mystery of things for a moment. Actually, however, what my mother feels is not anguish; it's simple panic, accompanied by irritation: panic, because she is left without that bear Bernardo, so big and protective, so vastly palpable, confirming by his very person her faith in the concrete reality, in the apprehensibility of life; and irritation, because after all, he had played a mean trick on her, hadn't he?

I ask myself whether my mother, in order somehow to explain Bernardo's premature and solitary departure, will mention certain facts, like the recent death of Bernardo's father, Odo Partibon, a rather extraordinary old man, whom I too have met (I have met practically everybody); or the story of Maria and her daughter Massimina, and certain newspaper reactions. It so happens that my mother and Maria "are good friends"—whatever that means in their language.

Instead she asks me: "And do you know whom he disappeared with? He didn't come to Europe alone, did you know that?"

"No, Mother, I don't know."

"You know Cecilia Ghezzi-Walther, don't you?"

"Certainly." I raise my eyebrows, casting preventive aspersions on what my mother is going to say.

She says it nevertheless: "He left America with her and came to Europe; or more exactly, he disappeared from America to re-emerge here."

"Accidental." I shrug. "Even if this were externally, chronologically true . . ."

She doesn't allow me to finish. "The first thing I did when I arrived in Milan was to call the Ghezzi-Walther house." Again I raise my eyebrows. She goes on: "I have known Firmino Ghezzi-Walther for ages, and he himself told me very simply that Bernardo not only had arrived with Cecilia but that he had been seen everywhere in Rome with her, and with a friend of hers, the little Fassola girl."

"Dora Fassola, Mother. Friend of mine. She is very fond of Bernardo."

"Another one. What does he have, a harem?"

I resume patiently: "In a way Dora is family to Bernardo, isn't she?"

She looks at me with suspicion. I want to remind her, at

least vaguely, that there are so many other worlds besides her own, so many other solar systems, galaxies, and that a story never is simple and lineal; in fact, that it is never finished and never fully understood. "Anyhow," I go on, "this picture, or rather, this vignette of Bernardo's leaving America and coming to Italy with Cecilia . . . I was trying to tell you that even if it were true, it would be irrelevant."

Strange—she is listening to me. It is the first time in the course of the conversation that she addresses me by name: "Well, Clem, what *is* relevant, then, in this world?" She seems to be sincerely looking for my help; in her green-blue eyes there is the shadow of a prayer and of childish confusion. Funny, but it is precisely moments of this kind that make me realize one thing (there is no less banal way to express it): that my mother has never loved me. This, however, has little to do with the present subject, which is Bernardo Partibon.

My mother, seeing that I don't answer, poses another question: "Do you believe that Bernardo wants to humiliate us?"

Here we are. There is a total rearrangement of the front line. She retreats to the kind of territory which is familiar to her: "Hasn't he had enough? How far does he want to go to prove that he has won? Why does he need this?" Et cetera. Questions of that sort. Even: "Didn't he feel he had been completely accepted by us and by our friends? What demonstrations does he need, of his success, of his power?"

In other words, the Countess goes back to what we may call her initial vision of my brother-in-law. When he was not yet my brother-in-law. When he was brought to her house in Connecticut the first time. Brought from California. Brought by me. So that there were various reasons for worry: (a) introduced by me; (b) coming from the Pacific coast; (c) Italian; (d) an Italian who "did not look like an

Italian." Et cetera. What could one do with a character like that in Westport? In that house? Then, essential discoveries: a Venetian, like herself; observation: Venetians are relatively rare in America; analogy of their destinies; Benzon, Partibon. Partibon, rather a well-known name. Secondary countryside branch of an illustrious Venetian family. Illustrious, but not without irregularities, ambiguous stories, complicated connections.

At that time her remarks about Bernardo were often of this tenor: "Quite an intriguing man, but very difficult to place. Art connoisseur. Art dealer. Designs houses for the rich, especially in the West, it seems. Looks like a farmer; there are long gloomy silences and sudden noisy laughter; but if he chooses, delightful conversation and manners. Without permanent address. Financial particulars altogether elusive."

I think of those days, rather far away by now, and I suddenly ask her: "Do you remember how many letters you wrote around, even to your social spies in Italy and to friendly bankers, to get information on Bernardo?"

"Why do you put things so crudely?" But while she says this, a very rapid sly smile passes over her face, which seems to imply: "I would do the same thing all over again tomorrow." Instead, she says ruefully: "I know, we treated him like a dog." That is to say, she exaggerates and dramatizes. Histrionic voluptuousness of self-recrimination. In fact, that mere dramatic effort seems to make her feel the fatigue of the late hour; she gets up to go to sleep. We go near the window together.

I raise the curtain. The embankment underneath is practically deserted, and at any rate people are made of shadow; the rectangles of the pavement are the color of lead and exhale humidity; beyond St. Mark's Basin, the island of St. George is cloaked in humidity and fog; yellow lamps on the water that mark the route to the Lido and to the port are out of focus, diluted into the dampness of the air. And so forth. The moaning of some foghorn, the flight of a rickety pigeon toward the monument of the nineteenth-century king with raised sword, looking like an orchestra conductor on horseback. Here, during our visits to Venice in my child-hood, I might have seen a miserable Bernardo Partibon wander, or Maria Partibon march in line, guided by nuns, and not known who they were. Here Nicoletta Benzon, my mother, took her walks, a Venetian child in the sun. And look at her now.

"Yes, like a dog, we didn't give him credit for anything," she goes on, "we were without pity. We were suspicious of him. And when he started showing interest in Clare, we were even less generous, including you."

"Me?" But I do not protest. I am tired of repeating cer-tain things. I repeat one of them nevertheless: "Mother, do you recall the first day that Clare and Bernardo met? Now, I'm not telling you that your daughter was in the habit of doing things of this sort, but the fact is that they went to bed together that same evening."

"Oh, that." It isn't clear whether "oh, that" means "that's old stuff, without importance" or "that's your old fantasy again." However, my words seem to have brought her to the breaking point of fatigue. She mechanically takes my head into her hands, and while she kisses my forehead she whispers: "Will he come to Venice? What will he do?" as if these questions were, shall we say, off the record, and did not count in the official game played between us: in other words, she would like answers for free.

"I don't know," I say sincerely. "Let's wait and see."

She is already at the door on her way out; she turns, she smiles and holds on for a moment to those comfortably use-less words: "Let's wait and see."

After I have shut the door behind her, I realize that we haven't talked about anything. Not even touched on any of the themes that form the texture of my life. Not a single word on my show, for example, even though later I am sure she will boast about the fact of having come to Italy in time for the opening.

And of course, not even the remotest allusion to Ilse. Better that way. I know very well that if I mention that name Ilse in her presence, she looks at me as if she were deaf, or like when I was a child and she taught me French, and if I didn't pronounce a word perfectly she pretended she did not understand. Come, come, Countess.

16 Oct. —The great encounter is perhaps on the horizon, the family summit meeting. Called Dora Fassola in Rome, told her that I had talked with her mother here, and that her brother Enrico was driving up from Rome in his car; she should take advantage of that. She hadn't known; they live together but they seldom meet; what would happen if I didn't organize things? Then, phone call from Bernardo in Bologna. He starts talking about how much he likes that city; then he says: "I spent an awful night here, I am sick again." I am rather used to Bernardo's "I am sick's." Then, curiously, he announces to me the death of Senator Horst—I had already read about it in the paper—and he adds confusedly that he was with Horst's daughter at the moment of the death. I ask which of the two daughters, trembling at the idea that it might be Genziana, whom I have loved for years at a distance. But he doesn't tell me. I haven't told either the Countess or Clare about this phone call; they just look at me with questioning eyes.

Night. —Awakened by Bernardo's call, this time right here in Venice. He went to a different hotel, more expensive than this one. I can already hear the Countess: "He wants to humiliate us," etc. She sincerely believes things of that kind. She will discuss it with Clare, offended and at the same time relishing it, reassured, after all, by such signs of Bernardo's prosperity.

Evening 17 Oct. —Long walk today with Bernardo around Venice. He tells me very little about his trip from Rome and the night he spent at the Piglioli-Spadas'.

We had already been walking for a while when one of us said the obvious thing—that it was the first time we were together in Venice. Other times perhaps we had seen each other but it was like being on different planets, etc.

"I am a countryside Partibon." This is one of his stock phrases. From the village, Corniano, they had sent him here to study, and he lived alone, in little boarding houses or rented rooms, although he had relatives here; in fact these relatives were the famous Venice Partibons, whom I don't know well, and among whom there were his cousin Elena, of legendary beauty, and her brother Giorgio, a kind of genius.

Bernardo tells me that he, a boy from the country, would occasionally go to the house of the Venice Partibons, which was at San Tomà; he pointed it out to me today, saying that to him some rooms of that house had been like inebriating dreams; there he had started becoming aware of differences in styles and periods of furniture, and of the human value that such differences could have. "They had a few astonishingly beautiful pieces, then they lost all of their money and sold everything; but at that time I had already left." Otherwise, he seems to imply, he would have bought the best pieces.

We went to the little square where Bernardo lived for a long time; it is a piece of interior Venice, all stone, not the

Venice where marble and Gothic windows and gardens face the water. Not the moans of boatmen, but chatting of women from window to window on the little square paved with irregular rectangles, and a stone well in the middle.

And we could see Bernardo, fourteen years old, already enormous, with countryside muscles, constrained within the little room with the iron bed, on which every now and then, even during the day, he would lie, destroyed by the heat; examination period; long hours of study; and he, so big, stooping over the little table two feet long, to study Greek and algebra; or, every now and then, going to the window:

"First I had a room facing an inside courtyard, then I obtained one with the window on the square, that window up there," he points out, and his breath seems to fail from the tumult of emotion, from the melancholy. "Examination time. The summer sun beating on these stones, which grow hot like sheets of steel. Cats yawning and stretching out, or eating fish heads, wrapped in newspapers and thrown to them from windows."

And then there were the winters. However incredible that may seem, observing the hands of the present Bernardo (strong and sunburned, the hands of a sailor or of a polo player), every winter in Venice he got chilblains. Even in the classroom he would wear *manopole,* gray woollen gloves that would leave his fingertips out, free to grab the penholder always dirty with coagulated ink—ink which, even when it was in its deep little well, before sticking to the fingers, was like black blood half curdled, or wine full of lees.

Some day when I write my *Contributions to the Biographical Study of Bernardo Partibon* (I'll write it in German: *Beiträge,* etc.) for which I am here taking disorderly notes, an important chapter will be dedicated to those Venetian years with their miseries, discomforts, ugly surroundings. This man who, not very many years later in America, was to handle paintings by the most splendid and high-priced painters in Europe, at that time in his rented room in Venice saw, as he told me, two little views hanging on the walls, as sole ornaments—one of the port of Trieste and the other of the castle of Miramare, printed *on celluloid,* as he himself underlined with a wild laugh.

"Did you have any friends?" I ask him at last, coming to the subject in a roundabout way, inviting him to furnish precise data on matters that I partly know, as befits a hypocritical biographer.

"Certainly not my schoolmates," he says.

"Umberto Boschinetti?" I try.

"Umberto," he says simply, "I could never take seriously."

"And outside of school?"

"Outside of school there were the Debaldès. Can you imagine? The De-bal-dès." It looked as though his eyes were going to pop out of his head. "Ugo Debaldè and his mother."

It may seem incredible, but the fact is that I have never met Ugo Debaldè (the mother has been dead for some time). I am planning to do it this time, if he is in Venice. I know something about the present-day Debaldès, and I always used to have wild fantasies about that name. From the first moment I heard it (it must have been during my childhood), out of pure imagination, and also on account of the echoes which that name, Debaldè, awoke in the caves of my linguistic maniac's mind, it was associated for me with ideas of corruption and images of punishment. *Debaldè*: I have visions of a man destroyed by vices; of a man from whom all hair has been plucked as a punitive measure; of a man blackballed from a respectable club for moral turpitude. *Debaldè*. My images are of course rather out of place, since the real Dr. Debaldè is very widely accepted by society; in fact, is thriving both here in Venice and in Rome.

In the distant years evoked by Bernardo, Ugo Debaldè and his mother (there is no trace of a father) were the proprietors of a boarding house here on the Zattere. Besides owning the boarding house, the mother also possessed, or perhaps had conferred upon herself, the title of baroness. The boarding house, whose interior resembled a middle-class Venetian house with terrazzo floors, little Murano chandeliers, eighteenth-century furniture, and a smell of risotto, used to have, unlike other, more normal Venetian houses, a crucifix in every room, or an image of the Virgin, or both. On the landings, holy images with oil lamps. In many corners, a prie-dieu.

I can smell an aroma of melting wax and incense spreading into the thick air of the boarding house (rooms small like eighteenth-century boudoirs, full of sacred and profane bric-à-brac), mixing with the aromas coming from the kitchen, where food of celebrated excellence was being prepared: risotto with green peas, creamed stockfish, fried fish of a delicately golden hue. So that this food, wonderful in itself, must have come out somewhat altered and ambiguous: around the rice, an aroma of wax; on the fried fish a soupçon of incense, if not altogether of extreme unction.

"There were autumn evenings when the Baroness, after I had had supper with them, would send me off with a little pot full of leftovers: 'It's all good stuff,' she declared, raising her forefinger with the smile of a sensual Mother Superior. I would carry the pot away wrapped in a large towel; with this fardel still hot under the linen of the towel" —Bernardo doesn't say: ". . . as though it were the body of a little child just killed," but it occurred to me—"I would walk part of the way in the fog of the Zattere, then turning into this street . . ."

(1 1 4)

We are walking through the same places. We turn into that very narrow street, our steps echo with a somewhat metallic sound between the houses: then the sound becomes fainter and more distant, like that of our voices, when we come out onto a narrow embankment at the foot of a bridge. On top of the bridge we stop, leaning over the parapet.

"Here I used to unwrap the bundle. I would raise the lid. I would look around to see that there weren't any shadows of people. And I would throw everything into the water. There was this gloomy sound, *ploff*"—here Bernardo looks into my eyes with feverish intensity—"of the food falling into the dark water. It was as though I had vomited. It was a way for me to try and liberate myself from the humiliation."

He has used that word several times, always in the same way, with the definite article: *the humiliation*. Not referring to any particular episode, but rather as though he said *the plague* or *the evil eye*.

"Never for a moment in my whole life, not even when I was practically starving, did I regret throwing that food into the canal."

He keeps silent for a long while. Then he resumes pensively: "And mind you, I *liked* to eat. It wasn't only the need for much food (imagine, in those years I was still growing, as if there weren't enough of me as it was), it was also that I really liked food. I have always liked to eat."

It was in that period that his mysterious diseases began. *Diseases* is too specific a word. "I wish they were that," he has told me himself several times. I have witnessed those attacks myself more than once, both in America and in Italy, and it is difficult for me to give them a name, or even attempt to describe them, but let's try: he is seized by a horrible and overwhelming feeling of sickness, something that I would call cosmic nausea. A kind of revelation of the world, in reverse: all reality turned upside down into nightmare.

"There were evenings when I could sit for hours in one of those little parlors of the boarding house, in the faint light of small Murano chandeliers and oil lamps in front of the holy images, and listen to the Baroness and her son talk interminably about their business transactions, their plans to buy a boarding house in Rome (they were not from Venice—in fact, no one knew where they were from; at any rate, Rome had always represented their supreme dream, with the Pope and the Vatican tourists), and then about their trips abroad to visit friends who had been their guests at the boarding house, about how little it had cost them, and about the profitable contacts they had made with past and potential customers. The Baroness used the same movements of her jaws to talk and to suck liqueur chocolates. It was during those evening conversations that I began to realize that besides running the boarding house they also engaged in another activity: traffic in small paintings, buying and selling little works of art. In fact, even with the religious objects that adorned the house one could notice a kind of rotation as some art objects were being placed with customers and others came in. And their trips abroad also had a commercial purpose: the Baroness was very clever, and she would boast about it with absolute naïveté: among the underwear in her suitcase she would hide little paintings and objects, which she would call her good-luck charms, eluding customs and avoiding complicated export permits. Smiling like a delighted child she would relate these small triumphs while her son devotedly approved, lowering his head like a purring cat. I repeat, I would spend hours looking and listening like that . . . ."

He stops and stares into empty space. "Nausea?" I suggest. "Horror?"

He laughs drily. "Perhaps I'll look for Ugo Debaldè. Perhaps he is the means for me to reach my sister."

"Of course," I urge him. "He is a very well-known person; besides, he often goes to lunch at Dora's mother's."

"You see how many things we have to do in Venice," he says evasively.

Now I must stop writing. The Countess and her daughter Clare are coming to my room, not without having announced their visit over the phone. For the time being, I carefully refrain from telling them that their son-in-law and husband, respectively, has arrived in Venice.

Night. —Why do most people dislike me? I fell asleep in the armchair, dreaming as usual about enmities and persecutions, and I woke up with that question on my lips, comparing myself to Bernardo Partibon, who is, contrarily, "a man one is naturally fond of," as for instance Dora Fassola says.

Bernardo was evoking his Venice life while church bells were resounding in the dark, humid air of the evening, and he told me a phrase which in various forms I've heard him utter before: "I have suffered and perhaps I still suffer for beatings which I myself have given to others."

There exists an external biography of every man (in the case of Bernardo, for example, his school in Venice, some passionate and solitary art studies at the Marciana and Querini Stampalia libraries, his emigration, the influence upon him of a very distant relative of ours, old Gutkind who was his mentor in New York, etc.), and there exists another one, formed of less-known but really crucial facts —the facts that alter and reform the vision that a man has of life, the way he treats his fellow men, and even the expression of his face, of his eyes (self-assured and opinionated in the foolish; doubtful and full of mutations in the thoughtful), the tension at the corners of the mouth, the tone of his voice, etc. There belongs to this deeper level in Bernardo's biography a certain relationship with his Venice schoolmates.

Perhaps because he looked like an older boy with a life of his own, Bernardo was left alone by his companions, surrounded by a certain silent respect. But between respect of that kind and persecution, the step is curiously short: all it takes is for one of the companions to open the smallest wedge, and all the others will throw themselves through it, euphorically, liberated.

That is what happened one day as they were coming out of school; there really was, it seems, one precise day. Bernardo had been called upon to translate a passage of Herodotus from the Greek, and apparently he had made a mess of it, so the teacher had sent him back to his seat, saying: "You waste too much time at the movies, Partibon," with the sour laugh of one who never goes there.

Obviously Bernardo had one of his small attacks of nausea: nothing disturbs and humiliates him more than a statement both false and inane. I can just see him: much bigger than the professor or any of the other students, back at his seat but still standing, disheveled and downcast, breathing hard in the silence of the classroom, which was now rippling with little waves of ironical laughter from the companions waiting in cowardly comfort for the development of the scene. And I can see him talk, turning to the professor, but actually as though he were talking to himself, or perhaps to the king of Italy hanging in a picture on the wall: "I wouldn't even have the money to go to the movies. Movies, my foot! Yesterday I walked around to look at churches."

"Which was true," he tells me now, a quarter of a century later. "Sometimes I would go to certain churches of Venice, alone, at the wrong time."

"Bravo," the teacher retorted, to aggravate his nausea, "recommend your soul to God, you certainly need that."

As they came out of school, his classmates surrounded him, at first with the usual respect and detachment, but without losing sight of him, as if waiting for a signal from somebody. Finally the signal came. One could have expected it to come from somebody older and more flippant than the others, but instead it came from Cerega (I know him by sight; he is now a well-known lawyer in Venice), a boy dressed even at that time with above-average elegance, precociously wearing a dark double-breasted suit, his hair precisely parted on the side and sparkling with brilliantine, a fat peaceful face, and wearing glasses, sparkling like his hair. It was this boy Cerega who placed himself in front of Bernardo, not aggressively but rather as if he were preparing to have a casual little chat, and yet blocking his way.

With a perfectly calm face and voice, and with just a tiny ironical curl on his thick lips, he produced at first a lame imitation of Bernardo's phrase in the classroom: "I wasn't at the movies, I went to church," in a falsetto, which didn't suit him at all. Then he brought his voice down to normal and concluded without the slightest amount of crescendo: "Priest. Big priest. Big dirty priest."

The others grasped those epithets immediately: "Big priest! Big dirty priest!" their only original contribution being the wildness and vigor of the cries.

At first Bernardo looked at them with surprise. They made more noise, and he started warning them in a low voice: "Drop it, don't get closer," because he was afraid, he felt a strength mounting within himself, which he could not yet analyze.

But the others were by now carried away: "Big dirty priest!" and at that point ("with a sense, as it were, of guilt") he thought of the Debaldès with their boarding house, with certain friendships they cultivated among prelates, with their rich meals, in which he had taken part, and with the sacred objects in that kitchen smell; then he said to his companions: "Don't humiliate me," but in a very low, inaudible voice.

"Perhaps I should have reacted at once," he tells me now, "but that first time I did nothing. So I allowed them to inaugurate a new style in their relationship to me, and I allowed this style to establish itself. I remember them one by one, my classmates: Cerega, Luigi; Vicini, Andrea; Scarpa, Achille; Bevilacqua, Leonardo; and so on. Boschinetti, Umberto . . ."

"Did he torment you too?"

"No, neither he nor Cerega, they were sort of apart, observing the proceedings but trying to act like young gentlemen; in fact, Boschinetti looked like an exaggerated Cerega, taller and more athletic, but he too looked very smooth, wearing a double-breasted blue suit, pomaded hair and even, I seem to recall, a starched collar. For a while he tried to act as liaison between them and myself, to give me advice: 'You have isolated yourself all these years, you are too much on your own, your schoolmates don't forgive things like that.' Even now, twenty-five years later, he gives me advice, but he has realized he has lost authority, so he limits his advice to where I have to go and have my shirts made, or my shoes, or things like that. He always acts as though he were my own particular friend, which I guess is understandable, because he has made a lot of money through me, and God knows how much more he is going to make." He laughs, but without malice; in fact, he seems to imply that by making so much money, Boschinetti has unwittingly put himself in a hell of a mess. Bernardo shakes his head.

"And what about the other classmates?" I ask.

"They would wait for me at the school door and then follow me, making faces at me and shouting insults. But by now everybody had lost sight of how it had all started; they just yelled anything that came into their heads, or they would make a sweeping bow, saying: 'Your Eminence,' followed by an obscene word. They would also come under my window when I was at home. I would dream of them at night, transformed into beasts hunting me. I would wake up in a sweat. Finally, one day, I reacted."

"How?"

"How? With the massacre I staged." He stops a moment, then proceeds, his head bent: "Smashing their faces. First one by one, then taking even two or three at a time. I had just discovered how strong I was."

He thinks it over a moment in silence, then resumes: "Not that I can express myself particularly well now, but I was fifteen then, and I talked even worse, so I certainly wouldn't have been able to put the thing into words, but if I had known how, I would have said: 'You used to leave me alone, and now, instead, there is this confrontation, which means that the only contact possible for us is through enmity, violence, the total abolition of pity.' I imagine that's why I beat them up. There were some spectacular exchanges of blows. Sweat, blood, black eyes, fingernails dug into faces, bites. Finally, one day when they had followed me after school to a quiet courtyard full of cats and garbage where they would start one of the usual attacks, I turned around and said: 'Don't get any closer. Go and leave me alone; let me stop, let me give this up. Don't you see what's happening to all of us?'

"This peculiar plea must have been accepted, because I remember that they all changed tactics and from then on simply looked at me in silence, darkly, with the welts and bruises caused by the blows to their faces, spitting every now and then on the ground in my direction. I realized that this was worse than anything. I gradually developed a frantic desire for them to start attacking me again. But it never happened.

"I shall never forget Cerega's face one day. I have already told you that he had kept away from the fighting. Well, one day I stood right in front of him, face to face, snout to snout, a few millimeters away. And I began by saying: 'Why don't you do something to me? Why don't you attack? It was you, Cerega, who started it by accosting me. Why don't you hit me?' And pointing to my cheek: 'Come on, try!' And he, his face all twiches, looked fixedly at me with vacuous, moist eyes like poached eggs, and said in that deep, unctuous voice he has always had, a voice he is now apparently employing with enormous success in court: 'But it was you, Partibon, who begged of us to stop. And anyway, it's not possible, because it wouldn't be a relationship between civilized men. It would be irrational on our part to go on fighting you. It would be like setting ourselves against a cannibal, a man from the jungle, or even . . . yes, a creature living in trees. In fact, that's exactly right—a huge monkey, an orang-utan.'

"You are probably thinking that the orang-utan should have smashed in his face then and there, but instead, not only did we not resume the fight, we didn't even look at each other any more. They left me alone, except Boschinetti and the gray mass of the neutrals, who must have been quite numerous, but I must admit I don't recall any of their faces or names. Only the enemies count, that magic circle which, if things had gone differently, I would have had to remember always as my schoolmates. So later on I left school altogether, I never went beyond the first year of the *liceo*."

And at this point, suddenly and in unison, Bernardo and I burst out laughing.

I was saying that every man has his own inner and deep biography made of episodes of that kind (which I shall have to take into particular consideration in my *Beiträge*). Now I am using a generic but useful expression when I say that there was formed in Bernardo Partibon the happy psychology of the bastard.

Alone as he was in Venice, he would have been particularly apt to find in the school a family substitute; but if that was the case, then he must have appeared as the son or brother with a stigma on his forehead, the one who keeps to himself, building his own defenses, becoming ever stronger and more solitary. He would spend as much as half a year without going to his family in the native village; and if he went to the house of the Venice Partibons at San Tomà, he would look at the faces of the works of art rather than at those of his relatives.

One should also remember what the Partibons in general were, as a family: some of them artists and intellectuals, all with touches of strangeness and rebellion, like his two young cousins—the very precocious Giorgio and the very beautiful Elena—or that uncle, Marco (more exactly, a cousin of his father's), whom Bernardo met years later in America, where they became good friends. Marco had had a peripatetic career and by his connection with a member of the Blumenfeld family, Stephanie, he had become the father of our distant cousin Manuela, thus creating even at that early date a contact, a point of fusion, between their clan and our own.

Therefore, in considering Bernardo against his family background (a good deal of which was only dimly known to himself), the present historian (myself, needless to say), aware as he may be of all that is perennially mysterious in the biographies of individuals and in the infinitely complicated textures of family histories and destinies, can nevertheless single out with almost absolute certainty these facts: that being a Partibon meant *per se* bearing a mark of singularity, of perhaps general alienation (i.e., from all other Venetians), at any rate certainly alienation from the various Cerega & Co. of the moment; and that, to conclude, the figure of young Bernardo, even compared to a classical black sheep like Marco Partibon, presents those family characters in such measure as to become the exception among exceptions, a bastard of bastards.

Then it happened that Maria, his sister, was sent to the convent in Venice (later to Treviso). It was typical of the Partibons that in sending the girl to the nuns in Venice, the thought that their son was already studying in the same city barely brushed, in the most casual manner, their minds. Different schools, different sections of the city, everything different. It was, so to speak, as though in sending her to the nuns in Venice they hadn't even had her mark down the address of her brother Bernardo in her notebook.

In those years she was a thin girl, with enormous green eyes, transparent skin, flushed cheeks. Photographs of that period have always shown her with a grave expression, not cross but rather abstracted. There is a group photograph with a couple of dozen Partibons from Venice and from the countryside, and various friends, shot at Corniano, I believe in the garden of the Fassola villa; in it, among all those pairs of eyes, the first pair one inevitably encounters is Maria's; she is the first person you notice, perhaps also because her marvelous cousin Elena, for example, is seen in profile, as one who obviously couldn't care less about the group picture, whereas she, Maria, trains her eyes firmly toward the photographer, standing still, in a self-conscious attitude and yet with an air of absent-mindedness, as if she could manage to be, at the same time, intrusive and uncooperative, aggressive and shy.

(1 2 4)

One must have lived here in Venice—which, as everyone knows, is not a city but a great complicated palace that has the skies of Carpaccio or Canaletto as its ceilings, the Piazza and the smaller squares as its main salon and its rooms, the narrow streets as its corridors—to be able fully to appreciate the expression *the girls of the nuns.*

Through the rooms and corridors of this palace at once sumptuous and familiar, exotic and domestic, they walk in what, originally and curiously, would be a military formation in two lines, but is reduced, in their case, to something so unco-ordinated and dragging that it suggests—to continue the military metaphor—the image of a disorganized remnant of a dispersed platoon of a peripheral regiment of a secondary army unit, which has not been reached by the news that the whole army was defeated months, perhaps years ago. So they continue to wander over serene fields untouched by the battle. They proceed like that, in practically troglodytical attire, with large straw hats the color of lead, with skirts absolutely out of any reasonable proportion to anything.

Not the historian (like myself) but the superficial chronicler might suppose that in the midst of such clumsy discipline and unbelievably bad taste, Maria, a Partibon, endowed since childhood with a beauty so aristocratic and ambiguous that against the background of her native village it had looked altogether alarming, would distinguish herself, let us suppose, by some external sign (brightly colored hair ribbon, sparkling pin or bracelet) symbolizing detachment and potential evasion, singling her out immediately as the rebel, the spinner of hidden plots, the one who secretly answers the *billet-doux* from the daring and dangerous page.

No, nothing of the kind. Her way of distinguishing herself (to me this has always been perfectly obvious even before the great and neglected journalist Tranquillo Massenti, for example, reconstructed it in his own way through testimonies gathered at Corniano itself) must always have been by her own brand of religious piety. Her own particular style. The manner, for example, of her attention to ritual— not exhibitionistic, not emotional, but intransigent, both in regard to the discipline imposed upon herself and to her eventual judgment of her companions. She knew more than the others. A kind of administrator of the cult, I am almost tempted to say. Or also, as the saying goes, more of a Papist than the Pope himself; the Pope, however, far away and a male, could hardly constitute a reference point for Maria Partibon in Venice at the nuns'. If anything, then, she must have felt like a kind of local monitor, a technician of rites, silent and absolute, superior to the very Mother Superior.

I am not surprised that Bernardo in those years was not even aware of those qualities in his sister. In Venice they saw each other—he, a boy; she, little more than a child. But precisely because they lived so separately, each in his own circle and with his own disciplines, those rare meetings with his sister, and the sight of her green eyes, her long eyelashes, her restrained and elegant gestures in spite of the absurd uniform, must have held for Bernardo the sweet and stealthy attraction of trysts.

A friend of the Venice Partibons once told me that in her opinion one of the most decisive characteristics of the family was a tendency toward incest. Naturally, one is tempted to apply this concept, as a working hypothesis, to the case of Maria and Bernardo.

"I would take her," he tells me now, "to St. Mark's Square to eat ice cream and I would look at her with pride. 'Why don't you let me dress you a little better?' I would tell her with absurd eagerness, considering that I don't know where I would have found the money to buy her clothes.

She would shrug and say: 'Oh, no,' and I am sure that she meant: 'What need is there of that, I am so beautiful anyway.' I resigned myself; feeling her close to me, dressed even like that, was enough. She was a child but she was the first woman in my life to make me experience a desire to transform her, to adorn her, as an act of homage." That's just about what Bernardo said. Actually he does not speak so pretentiously.

Toward morning. —It may be that people generally don't like me, but something else is also true: that I know everybody. In other words, I am obnoxious and intrusive.

I happened to be thinking that in our "international" milieu (my mother, Clare, etc.) the only person who really knew Massimina, who talked and played with her, is myself.

"Had you ever thought of that?" I ask Bernardo, who looks at me with fright. His attitude is useful, because it leaves me free to organize the family summit meeting. Which is good *for his protection*.

My mother and her daughter Clare still don't know that their son-in-law and husband, respectively, is in Venice. I had this confirmed when my mother called me over the telephone and then came here because she wanted company. She asks me about Bernardo only with her eyes. For the moment this is all right; meanwhile he is getting his bearings in Venice.

In a couple of days Maria undoubtedly will go to my mother's hotel to have tea with her. On that day, for example, after having let them talk by themselves for an hour or two, Bernardo and I will suddenly appear upon the scene.

He raises a weak protest against this plan: "I don't want to impose myself. I can keep in a corner without saying anything."

"We'll wait and see what you will do."

As with his classmates twenty-five years ago, he doesn't know his own strength.

"Don't forget how long you have been away from this scene," I tell him.

"Do you know what happened to me today? I saw two of my schoolmates on the street. One of them didn't even notice me, but the other one did; he recognized me, and do you know what happened? *We exchanged a casual greeting.* Why does this seem so crazy to me? When I think of the intensity during these years . . ."

He stops. Then I tell him: "Of course, all these years you have been like a great conscience functioning at a distance."

When I say things like that, Bernardo literally doesn't hear them.

So I shall simply clarify these ideas for myself. Given the premise that the most interesting people are not historical characters but rather what I would call the great ordinary characters, I try to gather some anecdotal material in order that one day, using also my *Beiträge,* a biographer with real talent may set out to do the complete job.

"When I think of the intensity . . ."

Bernardo does everything with intensity. "You are too intense," or something of the kind has always been said to him, even by doctors. I must write things down as they come, without much order; otherwise I forget.

I am thinking of a phrase that I heard years ago, shortly after the death of poor Dorothy Blaustein, uttered by her father, in Santa Monica. It was a brief period during which my Ilse was staying there with Manuela, and I with them. The Countess was in the East, and we were going through one of those phases in which she considered both Ilse and me total losses.

(128)

Manuela had been very friendly with poor Dorothy, and Blaustein was visiting her. Manuela had also been in a picture produced by him. At some point, without looking at me, his moist eyes turned toward the ocean dimly visible behind the palm trees, Blaustein addressed me in German, in a tone at once formal and dreamy: "You can't imagine, my dear Blumenfeld, what comfort the presence of Bernardo Partibon has been to my wife and me in our immense sorrow."

Now, the point is that Bernardo wasn't there, nor had he been around recently. He was, indeed, a couple of hours by car from where we were—in Pasadena—but we had not had any contact with him. One might say that between those two extremes of Los Angeles, his Pasadena and our Santa Monica, there was a distance comparable to the one between the two husbands of my mother, Stewart B. Flanagan and Herbert Blumenfeld.

I could embroider on this: on the biological difference, so to speak, between their world in that quiet and dry hinterland town with many rich old people in mausoleum homes, and our own on the ocean front, with the large white beach, seals in the foggy dawn, and among the inhabitants a nucleus of Mittel-europa immigrants, to which Manuela belonged, and, in a way, Ilse and I belonged also.

No, there was no contact. What Bernardo did at that time I don't know, but the fact is, he lived with his wife in her world; and he had never turned up at Santa Monica.

Now let us repeat old Blaustein's phrase to me: "You have no idea . . . what comfort the presence of Bernardo Partibon has been."

I: "Presence? Where? When? He has never been in touch."

He let a few moments pass before answering, then he said casually: "Well, he has called me on the phone." Then quickly, as one saying something too obvious: "No, no, what I mean is: the feeling that he is present. When something serious happens, you know that you are with him, and he is with you." Those were, more or less exactly, his words, and he didn't even bother to look at my face to see whether I had understood.

I told him with some resentment: "What do you mean? He isn't here, he is with a completely different group of people. What is this? Telepathy?"

I remember Blaustein, as though he were here in front of me now: all wrapped up within his idea, without answering or looking.

I insisted: "And what's the use of that kind of *presence,* may I ask?"

At this he turned to me for an instant, just enough to tell me in a low voice, and in a quick, matter-of-fact manner: "What's the use? To survive, of course."

I tried to put the thing on a level of reality, mumbling: "I didn't know that you and Bernardo were such good friends," but he didn't hear me.

Now I believe I understand old Blaustein much better than I did then. However, if I talked to him, I would tell him this also: "You, Herr Blaustein, are a rather rare, exceptional case. Normally, people with whom Bernardo is *present* are not even aware of it."

Let us hasten to add that I am not necessarily alluding to the fact that Bernardo "has helped so many people," to what he has "done for others" without their knowledge, or at any rate avoiding their gratitude like the plague. Even the Countess, to give an extreme example, practices anonymous charity, or rather, did so when she had enough money. One fundamental reason why Bernardo performs such actions in the greatest possible anonymity seems to me evident: it shouldn't even remotely occur to anyone, as it doesn't to him, that such actions may contribute to save or redeem or in any way help the principal, or that they may cure him (to use the particular Bernardo symptomatology) of his attacks of humiliation, cosmic nausea, and so forth.

The very fact that I have been compelled to use, a few lines above, the expression "anonymous charity," pretentious and revolting even at first sight, demonstrates that certain acts obviously should not and cannot ever be mentioned, etc. etc.

It goes without saying that one should avoid most particularly any kind of medals, badges.

For similar reasons it is also obvious (I continue to write badly and in a disorderly fashion) that our man Partibon will never fall into the habit of signing manifestoes or seeking memberships of any sort. I have heard him say once: "If anything, pretend that you voted for the party that lost." Question: Can one ever *embrace a cause?*

I am thinking of an afternoon last month, on Via Ludovisi.

I wish I could describe the face, the head, of the man whom Bernardo and I were observing: round, pale, and shiny, a sculpture in white soap, with straight hair combed back, glued to the skull with brilliantine. Eyes decidedly cheerful, sly, a general appearance that could be described with an expression I detest: happy-go-lucky. And this thick rubicund mouth, this soft rubber vent-hole moving without interruption, issuing a long monotonous stream of obscene Roman insults. The small woman, at whom the insults were aimed, with dyed, frizzly hair and a face stern and bizarre, let the fire of abusive obscenities hit her on the back; she would turn around only every now and then while she walked along that rich wall protecting aristocratic gardens, raise a finger and move it in the rhythmic gesture with which one threatens a child.

Bernardo's format is very convenient indeed. Any time he wants, he can induce a feeling of indisputable physical fear. He had no need to use special violence; almost delicately he took the man by the collar and told him: "Stop that, or I'll hit you." Or an equivalent phrase. I know Bernardo well, but I must say he caught me by surprise. The man, I believe, was ready to offer explanations, starting with: "Are you crazy? What do you have to do . . ." but Bernardo stopped him with a gesture of the hand, and walked away. That was all. The man stopped uttering obscenities; as for the woman, she was already far away.

Guessing my perplexity and questions, a little later Bernardo said quickly, in a low voice: "You have to embrace a cause before you get to know more about it." And he started to laugh.

After a while he added: "It was that way with the war." Apparently Bernardo did a stretch in the last war with the American Navy in the Far East, and he never talks about it. Here in Italy he often has various people tell him stories about that period, which he listens to avidly. He never talks about that either.

Since I heard that my Ilse apparently is leaving California to come here I haven't been able to write a single line.

CHAPTER SIX

The Italian consul at Los Angeles, Donato Plea, turned into Benedict Canyon Drive at his usual speed, which, muttering through clenched teeth, he described to himself as "purely insane"; finding a green light at Lexington Road encouraged him to accelerate; then he took a right turn, and driving up the winding road toward his house, on the first curves he made the car slide with an ear-splitting squeal; the package with the newly bought records lying at his side slipped down and planted itself in the space between the seat and the door.

Separated from his wife, who had remained in Europe, settled now in bachelor's habits, Plea rather often spoke aloud to himself: "How wonderful that records are made of plastic, in the old days they would have been broken." He smiled wistfully, recalling childhood gramophones in his grandfather's house at Lugo.

A car coming down decidedly toward him, speeding along the white curved wall, had its blinding lights already on. "Damn you," Plea murmured without anger, lighting his own. Halfway up the road toward his house he stopped abruptly. Against the white stucco, lunar in the sunset light, of a brand-new house with a high crystal door, behind which he could see a brass chandelier hanging from the ceiling, large flowers shone sharply with their violent colors, and bushes just planted but already tall, illuminated by blue spotlights. He had never noticed the house before and discovered it already complete, with lit verdure and all; the lot nearby was still a dusty jungle. He said aloud: "Altogether horrible," and he thought: "Sudden object in the midst of virgin nature. Marvelous. The magic hour." He seemed to remember something and tore himself away.

Farther up he abandoned himself to the pleasure of driving, telling himself: "The way Plea manipulates these curves is subtle embroidery," while, however, certain basic thoughts, the more ordinary murmurs of his mind, accompanied him. Dying; the imminence of unspecified but inevitable disasters; the folly of living in this expensive section of the city, all alone in a house sufficient for a numerous family; the ruinous inadequacy of a consul's salary; his whole career a failure.

First in his class at the entrance examination to the foreign service fifteen years earlier, praised and esteemed to an almost maniacal degree by all the heads-of-mission and the department heads who had had him as their collaborator, he liked now to remain at this rather inadequate post, far from useful Roman contacts, easily forgotten.

At a high turn, wide open like a balcony, there appeared on his left the usual view of the city spreading out to the distant line of the horizon, the ocean; a few spots of fog were suspended lightly above that valley covered with houses and lights. Every hour of the day and every season, he noticed, had overpowering attractions for him. High above him there was the rustling of trees in the sunset wind; here he was among cedars of Lebanon. At a new turn higher above he found himself among the eucalyptus.

He turned to the left and stopped at the opening of the

little passageway which led in sudden descent toward his house. At the corner of the little road there was the long line of mailboxes among the cactuses; he got his mail out and threw it into the car near the package with the records. He breathed deeply through his nostrils and noticed only the scent of eucalyptus wood, plants, flowers—no fog or ozone. The air up here was dry and gave an impression of full sudden heat, like a stove; the wind from the desert had started blowing and it entered the city this way, through the openings of the canyons.

In fact, Plea found all the windows open in his house and everything already intensely charged with electricity. The doorknob, the light switch, the thick soft towel, everything produced shocks and sparks at the slightest touch. From the window, the houses at the bottom of the canyon looked like lighted toys; the small automobiles ran with a swishing noise along the cleavage at the foot of the high, wooded hills. A dog barked with an already nocturnal sound.

He understood then that the idea of coming quietly home to write his long-projected letter to Enrico Fassola had been absurd. He knew that he would do many things at a time without completing any: try the new records; throw a few desperate phone calls around to make some not too desirable arrangements for dinner in order not to be left alone; read the newspapers with a desperate sense of emptiness; and above all, sit still, his eyes looking into empty space—and meanwhile he would start composing the letter to Enrico Fassola in his thoughts, with phrases that were already passing in waves across his mind and forming themselves into paragraphs, but with the vexing certainty that he wouldn't be able to remember them at the right moment, a feeling he had occasionally had in dreams tormented by his awareness of being a *manqué* writer.

Among his colleagues, Enrico Fassola was the one with

whom Plea let himself go most easily, writing to him every month or two; they had met in London in their early youth, later meeting again in various places, and also losing sight of each other for long periods of time. Rather recently they had met again in Washington on the occasion of the visit of important Italian personages on an official mission; he, Plea, had been summoned from Los Angeles while Enrico Fassola was in the group accompanying the eminent visitors from Rome; the result was one of the most pleasant times in their lives. They had agreed that the official mission was entirely useless; its success, consecrated by official communiqués which they had helped draft, had made them ecstatic with delight; the solemn words of esteem expressed by persons whom they considered irrelevant had had a practically inebriating effect on them.

I am sure you too have observed, Enrico, that certain families are fatally attracted to one another, they periodically come into contact, in various formations, like the little pieces of colored glass in a kaleidoscope. So it was between you Fassolas and the Partibons; the same also between certain members of the Partibon and the Blumenfeld families . . .

But this morning a new Blumenfeld had come upon the scene, *there are people that you have perhaps seen twenty times, but then the twenty-first turns out to be really the first,* Ilse, to whom, seated at his office desk, Plea had said: "All right, look, I'm just about to write to Enrico Fassola, also to congratulate him on his appointment to the London embassy, and I'll ask him to get some information on your case; you say you are a friend of his sister Dora's, so this seems to me the right thing to do."

"All right, write to Enrico Fassola," Ilse had said, "but what will be the point of that? And how long will it take to find out? I know Enrico a little bit, and I know his sister

Dora really quite well, she's rather a friend of Clement's."

"Who is Clement?"

"My twin brother, the one of the sculpture exhibition."

She always says "rather" as if to create a distance between herself and the things she is talking about. She appeared in my office at the consulate with the air of wanting to challenge me, which I found fascinating. She is small and intense, as if always ready to jump, or to shoot at you.

The gramophone was playing one of the new purchases, the air in the room was so dry that it made the pages of the newspapers curl; Plea went back to the window and saw through the screen a sky aglow with stars. A large night insect beat its head in vain against the screen, buzzing violently.

When a girl like that reveals herself for an instant, that is, when perhaps with a furtive look she makes you suspect that she is weak and needs help, she gives me a powerfully disturbing sense of tenderness. I am the first to deny that I bother with her out of a simple sense of official duty. And then I will tell you that you too are involved, Enrico. The name Blumenfeld reminds you of Berlin, when I was a half-baked vice-consul there, and you came accompanied by Giorgio Partibon. In Berlin, Giorgio was looking for traces of his uncle Marco, a rather curious and important character, but he found only his daughter, Manuela; it was I who discovered that Manuela was technically an Italian citizen, so that during the persecutions she could leave Germany with a passport issued by us. Many years later I found her again here, an American. She introduced me to a Partibon of whose existence I had not known, Bernardo, and it was through Bernardo and Manuela that I met Ilse Blumenfeld . . .

He said aloud: "But before this morning I hadn't *perceived* her." He realized that in the meantime he had poured himself a gin and tonic and had drunk three quarters of it. A new record was playing, ignored. The telephone rang and Plea jumped up to answer it. He was being invited for dinner on Saturday, the third of November; he lied, saying that he was already busy; invitations gave him a feeling of anguish. He saw himself confronted with long evenings of solitude; he sank in an armchair embittered by that thought and yet with a sense of relief, as though he had decided on a necessary surgical incision.

Ilse Blumenfeld was born in the United States of a Venetian mother; Ilse's father, Herbert Blumenfeld, who lives here but whom I have never met, was her mother's second husband. A half-hour apart from Ilse (a half-hour later, she told me, maintaining that she remembers the event) a twin, Clement, was born . . .

He said aloud: "Now I'll call her." But he had forgotten her number at the office; he did not find it in the telephone book. Meanwhile the telephone rang again. The same people of a moment ago had moved the date of that dinner—the evening of Saturday, the third, had turned out to be a difficult one for others too—and they were calling again in the hope of being able to have Plea on Tuesday, the sixth. Plea accepted immediately and threw himself again into his armchair with a sense of terror. He clearly did not tolerate either company or solitude any longer; he poured himself a new gin and tonic. He decided to call Manuela Bloom to ask her Ilse's number. He would say: "I remember her personal statistics very distinctly, but I do not remember her phone number."

Father: Herbert Blumenfeld; mother: Nicoletta, née Benzon; divorced since 1929; both parents and daughter U.S. citizens. The episodes which created difficulties for her in Italy took place in September—between the sixth and the tenth approximately—of last year, at the Venice Lido.

(1 3 8)

They apparently resulted in a police order to leave the territory of the Italian Republic within a week.

It turned out that Manuela was not in, her answering service did not know where she was, she probably had left for New York. Nobody was at home; for many people now, Plea noticed, leaving constituted the main occupation. In the sky of the city, in the dry electric air hanging over those prairies covered with lights, he thought he could see the vast net of telephone calls among people who had left. No one *was there. We never are in the place where we happen to be, we never do what we happen to be doing.* Who had told him these phrases? Writing to Enrico he would make them his own, and he could already see him smile with pleasure. Whom could one ask about Ilse, ask who Ilse really was? He tried to think of connections, contacts, he searched his memory for names of friends that Bernardo Partibon had here; Bernardo himself must now be in New York or perhaps even in Europe. He evoked some names: the Blausteins, all departed, or dead; Berger, in Europe for film co-productions; Rust, that would be absurd—it was at his house that Bernardo Partibon had denounced the fake Modigliani paintings; Flanagan, perhaps even more absurd —one didn't quite know whether at the moment Bernardo was on good terms with his second wife, a Flanagan girl, or was separated from her.

Actually Ilse is only distantly related to Manuela, and her relationship to Bernardo Partibon, strictly speaking, doesn't exist: she could be defined, with unusual and, at best, inexact terminology, his half sister-in-law. And yet, Enrico, these clans possess a violent centripetal force; the members of families caught in the fatality of attractions discover the existence of relationships and conjunctions between them, of which they were not aware—this is one of Plea's Laws. As a boy, for a while I thought I was a writer;

(139)

if I had had any talent I would have become the chronicler or the poet of such situations; now I am the bureaucrat, and I write them down in terms of civil register, passport, and other unrealities.

"This used to be enough, I almost liked it. Doing one's job well. Now I am losing my mind." He poured another gin and tonic. He knew he had a great capacity; he had never been drunk in his life.

He went to the kitchen. Here too, through the screens, he could see the city, the valleys, and the vast expanses of lights, and nearby the eucalyptus trees moved by the hot wind, white in the night. The spaces between houses were a tangle of dried twigs; one look could embrace the electric gadgets in the kitchen and those fragments of night jungle, impossible to cross but close at hand. Plea would have liked to have somebody to talk with about these visions. *And instead, I'll never get to say anything: my whole life is a mistake, Enrico.* The crickets were deafening.

Out of the icebox he took a plate of cheese, which the Negro maid had left for him. He usually was at the office when the woman came to clean the place. Only once, in bed with a fever, had he allowed her to serve him, make soup, go and buy medicine and food. The woman had discovered his avid taste for cheese. At the end of that day of unusual attention, she had told him very gently: "I have enjoyed your company very much," and from then on he had always found a plate of cheese ready in the icebox. Plea took a huge piece of Gorgonzola and put his teeth to it with greed. He felt a timid but distinct affection toward the absent woman. He was relishing the strong cheese with its metallic tang when the telephone rang again.

Only listening to her now over the telephone, Plea found the right definition for the voice of Ilse Blumenfeld, with that guttural *r:* "She talks like a German child raised in Italy."

"Listen . . . look, forget about it. I'm leaving for Italy anyway."

"Where are you? What are you doing? What are your plans for tonight?"

"Why? You want to take me out to dinner? Does it bother you that I called you at home? Do you have company? I hear music. I just wanted to tell you not to bother about me."

His reply came quickly, as if incidentally: "No, no, you just come over here."

"Why?"

"Well, to begin with, your problem is not completely clear to me, and if I have to write to Fassola I believe I'll need some other data."

"But I'm telling you that I have decided to leave anyway . . ."

Plea interrupted her, speaking in a magician's tone: "Do you still want to be in Italy by Friday next week? I'll send a cable in code if you want."

The girl laughed. Then the laughter died out and there was a long silence.

"Hello?" Plea said.

Ilse spoke slowly, with gravity: "You are very amusing. Very messy. But look, this evening I can't, you know."

"What do you have to do?" Plea asked challengingly. By now he was sure he would spend the evening with Ilse; in fact, the thing was beginning to worry him.

"I have to go by two places. Well, of course you could come too."

"Where?"

"Houses of people. I'll give you the addresses if you

want." Plea was caught by dismay and she seemed to realize this: "It's nothing very formal, you know. I go because I have to talk to certain people."

"And where would it be?"

Ilse started explaining an address to him; at the third street name she realized he was lost.

"Listen . . . look, already this morning I realized that you are a disorganized person; so—look, I'll come up to your place, then we'll go together, it's simpler."

Other words that she always says are "listen . . . look."

"Do you know where I live?"

"I know that section very well."

As soon as he had put down the receiver, Plea automatically ran to check whether there were champagne bottles in the icebox. There were two of them at the right temperature; as soon as Ilse Blumenfeld arrived he would pour their contents into a carafe. "She will come wearing pants like this morning at the office," he said, "pants, and her hair like pieces of string, to take me to the beats." He felt a sense of relief, because Miss Blumenfeld fixed up in that offensively conventional manner would cease to exist as far as he was concerned.

Much sooner than he had predicted, he heard the sound of the motor and saw the reflections of the headlights on the white walls of the room and on the book shelves; Ilse was putting her car in the garage next to his own. Almost immediately the doorbell rang.

She was swathed in a tight, very plain semiformal dress. Small, with a calm and pretty face and exactly the right amount of make-up, she seemed much younger than in the morning; always to him a bit mischievous, looking rather like a little girl trying to behave herself; the formal dress seemed like a superimposition, a costume. He made her sit down, but she got up again immediately to follow him into the kitchen. She was quiet, watchful, ready to help. In silence she looked at him while he uncorked the bottles; while he poured their contents into the carafe, she followed his act with a smile that did not even express much curiosity. "And then who is supposed to drink that?" she asked.

"We will. Come on, we'll sit down and listen to the new records I bought."

"What records?" she asked, favorably disposed, compliant. In fact, she took a tray herself, placed the carafe and the two glasses on it which Plea gave her with a smile, yielding the management of operations to her. They were ordinary glasses, Ilse noticed, thick and cheap. "I like to drink it from the tall narrow ones," she murmured, but meekly, "don't you have any of those?"

Plea mumbled: "I don't know where the champagne glasses are," cutting her short, and preceded her into the living room. She followed with the tray. She placed everything on the very low coffee table with an enormous, leaf-shaped marble top. "Shall I pour?" she said, taking the carafe and already serving. She offered a full glass to Plea, who followed her very attentively. "Drink, it looks good," she said and poured a glass for herself. She made a perfunctory toasting gesture, then with gusto she drank half of it in one breath and put the glass back on the marble table. But she kept herself seated on the edge of the sofa as if at a formal visit.

Plea asked with studied, official somnolence: "Well, then, tell me something more about your problems."

Ilse smiled with restraint: "You mean that story in Venice, don't you? Well, there were these boys, and they started to make a little noise, first in the house of a friend of Clement's, Cristina Benzon—she's the daughter of relatives of our mother's and she has a motorboat—and then they went on to Beddoes' place, you know, the painter? Beddoes then lived in a rather beautiful palace. Look . . . listen, do you really want me to tell you everything? Actually, they sang folk songs rather than anything else, but then there was this business with the strip tease. There were some very young Oriental girls, really extraordinarily beautiful. We all went to a place on the Lido, and there they started a kind of show. But I believe the authorities had been watching Beddoes for a while already, to kick him out of Italy eventually. He's very rich, you know, but he is not an unpleasant person. In Italy it's really incredible—you can live wonderfully well there, but then it can happen that they pick for instance Beddoes, who by the way is rather interesting as a painter, and they kick him out, with his group of friends. It's difficult to understand why things happen, the criteria; it's even more difficult than here in America. Except that in Italy there is no death penalty. I think about things like that a lot, you know. I knew Markham rather well, the one who was executed on April fifth of this year. We were rather good friends." She finished drinking her glass of champagne and poured another one for Plea and for herself. "Do you like being a consul?"

"No, not particularly."

"It must be a rather atrocious thing, because criteria obviously can't exist for you either. Isn't that so? Sometimes I think of the administration of justice as one thinks of a force of nature, mysterious," she said, seeking his approval by staring at him with her large eyes of an unexpectedly light color in contrast to her very dark hair, "or else the way one thinks of very small children, as if they were all crazy, unpredictable."

"A consul does not administer justice, you know. At any rate, what did you do to get yourself expelled from Italy along with the others?" Plea asked. That girl, talking like a grave and monotonous German child, with that tight dress revealing her shapely form, with that proper hairdo some- what in the style of the twenties, and with that classical pro- file, gave him stings of irritation. *It would have helped me to develop that irritation into a complete and decisive feel- ing.* "You must have done *something.*"

She looked at him, for a quick moment, in humiliation and terror; it was as if Plea had made a gesture to hit her. She got hold of herself immediately and spoke now with vehemence: "I started yelling anything that came into my mind. It was the least I could do, wasn't it?"

"At any rate, as far as I can figure out, there has been a police order. I'll cable Fassola asking him to get some in- formation at the Ministry of the Interior, or to do some- thing anyway."

"Forget it." Ilse just sat and watched him in silence for a while. Then, she concluded in a sweet voice: "You are very nice. Very intelligent. Very brilliant." She seemed to be reading him: "With that upper lip just jutting out a bit, like a lid over the lower lip; and then, the way you frown—a stubborn, annoyed child." She mimicked him: " 'As far as I can figure out there has been an order . . . I'll ask for in- formation . . .' At any rate, I'll leave tomorrow or the day after at the latest."

"But why? If you don't have to be in Rome until next Friday?"

"That's why I'm leaving now. My trip is a rather special one; my father arranges it for me, he is associated with a travel agency, and if I do it this way it will cost me much less. I haven't got much money."

"Do you live with your father? What do you do for a living?"

"No, I live alone. I have always managed rather well. I only know how to do two or three things, but I do these two or three things rather well."

(145)

"For example?"

The hot wind was agitating the curtains, the window frames were squeaking, making noises as in a sailboat; finally a floor lamp with a long stem and white parchment shade fell on the floor with a crash. Ilse got up, put it on its feet again: "Nothing broken," she said. "But listen . . . look, if I shut the window it's less hot." She readjusted the shade on the lamp, she shut the window. All objects that she touched produced very visible shocks; the champagne was absorbed and went to one's brain immediately; she felt she was flying over the furniture, over those prairies covered with city lights; she came back and sat down again on the edge of the sofa near Plea, answering him: "For example, you know Chet Marshall, the one who is now in Rome to do Caligula in *Caligula?* Well, that book he wrote—I wrote it with a friend of mine, as ghost writer, you know?"

"What's the matter with him? Is he a moron?"

"As a matter of fact he is rather clever, but he can't express himself. Harry Berger's idea would be to do a neurotic Caligula, you know? Then, I play the piano rather well, I played in a restaurant in Santa Monica. Lately, however, I worked as an accountant—the working hours suited me— in Hollywood, in a large furniture store."

"But what would you actually like to do?

"I don't know. I always seem to be so busy."

"Busy doing what?"

"I don't know. *People* . . ." She spoke with warmth, shaking her small, well-built body, making gestures with her little hands: "For instance, this morning a boy woke me up, he is seventeen, he is very serious and wants to become a painter, but he has nobody to talk to. He spent three hours talking to me. And I won't even begin to tell you how women friends are, they come to me because they consider me older than they, even if sometimes I am younger.

In Europe you consider American women as hare-brained; you try to make them and that's all; there is nothing I detest more. On the contrary, they are very complicated. Full of strength and with a certain quiet way of bearing pain. I like them enormously; now you'll think I'm a bit lesbian. All things considered, you know, I have no country of my own, and I have lived alone a lot. However, I see a tremendous number of people, and we talk, we talk. But look . . . listen, we've got to move and go to the Rusts', otherwise I won't find . . ."

"To the Rusts'? You hadn't told me. You mean the ones who had that story with the fake Modigliani paintings?"

"Yes, of course you know the story from Bernardo Partibon. You weren't here at the time; the counsul was Menichini."

"Yes, Walter Menichini."

"You know Bernardo well, don't you? He is the husband of my half sister, Clare Flanagan. Look, let's finish the champagne, because it's a pity to leave it here; then we'll take my car so I'll drive and we'll get there more quickly; then I'll drive you back home."

Menichinio consule. *The interesting thing is that W.M., when invited to important homes in Beverly or Bel Air, would shiver with delight. His superficial involvement with questions concerning art, fatally coupled with his desire to affect an authoritative approach to art itself in a time of cultural vogue like our own, induced him to pronounce a verdict, at the social rather than the official level, on the Modiglianis in question. "Beautiful, some of the most beautiful I have ever seen," he ventured, and Mariachiara, his wife, excitedly joined him in praise. There were on W.M.'s past record utterances like "I can't take those oblong Modigliani faces," although being a patriot he would always de-*

fend the Italianism of the painter if anyone considered him Parisian. Besides, in this particular case the proprietors of the canvases, socially speaking, made his mouth water. He talked to Bernardo Partibon. W.M. saw this as a quid pro quo *arrangement: Bernardo, he guessed, must have contacts that could turn out to be interesting, and on his part he was offering the Rusts as in an exchange of stamps. At the first descriptive hints that W.M. dropped: "Splendid house, important paintings," B.P. replied: "Not to my knowledge." But to Menichini this was not enough of a warning. A curious opacity, since B.P.'s face in such cases literally changes, and even the least practiced eye sees the usual, generous, slightly confused Bernardo, whom I too know rather well, turn into the austere arbiter, the businessman-censor, known in the world of galleries and art auctions. So that, brought by the Menichinis to the Rust house, the arbiter, right from the threshold, as if rather than seeing the paintings he could smell them in the air of the living room, says: "They are fakes." A smile from the consul, meaning: "Partibon, here we are among well-bred people, I am sure you'll correct yourself immediately." Mariachiara, absorbing the paintings with her vitreous eyes: "I find them so beautiful." There is a heavy silence; evidently here we are no longer within the boundaries of social manners; terror has set in; this is the wrath of God; but Bernardo Partibon hath spoken, in fact he gives a quick little shrug, the thing no longer bothers him. Mariachiara emits a cry: "How horrible!" Not so much on account of the fake paintings as on account of Bernardo's* faux pas. *They all wait for his words a long while in vain. The silence is broken by the host, who takes Bernardo to one side like the patient's relative wanting to know the whole truth: "What should I do?" Bernardo appreciates that; the man knows how to lose like a sportsman. "Keep them if you like them." But a moment later he will whisper: "Throw them away. I'll throw them in the fire for you if you haven't the courage," as if he offered the confused man a beneficial injection.*

Already at the very first glance, Plea saw several known faces in the crowd at the Rust party. He prepared to cross the living room, looking for the den, which in houses of that kind always exists. He and Ilse lost sight of each other immediately. It must have been a rather important party: moments later he felt as if it had already lasted two hours. He saw everyone from the back or from side angles, except for physically remarkable ladies: these knew that they were conspicuous and seemed intent on contemplating themselves from the inside; they carried their faces around; showing them was sufficient, there was no need for them to express anything. One of these ladies stopped in front of him a moment, looked beyond him as if he were a fortunately transparent obstacle; she cried ecstatically: "Plea! Donato Plea!" They kissed each other and did not see each other again.

From the leather sofa in the den, which he had finally reached at the cost of innumerable repeated gestures and greeting formulas without possible identifications, he saw through the door a neat segment of the party; curiously, this included Ilse, whom he had considered lost. With a jolt of affection, which he diagnosed as paternal pride, he saw Ilse cope with this milieu and group of people with an air of masterful casualness. From the view of that rectangular fragment of crowd seen through the door he derived the impression that that irritating German girl knew everybody. She moved well. She treated people with the right tone. He saw her stop and talk to a sixty-year-old gentleman with very clear eyes, extremely tall and childish-looking, bald, the top of his head being a cap of sun-tanned skin. Plea would have liked to linger with his eyes on Ilse, but the den, where he had looked for a restful pause, was not empty; and from among the other persons occupying it, one man suddenly identified himself as a compatriot. A voice hit Plea sideways—the voice of a man already seated near him on the leather, a voice nonchalant and self-confident, revealing that the compatriot had had his look turned in the same direction as Plea's. "That Blumenfeld girl, she's real cute," Plea heard; he turned around and saw, already offered to him, a smile with a wide display of teeth, and a large soft hand: "The name is De Dominicis."

"I remember you. How are you?" He had seen the man once; as in a compulsive tic, he had retained the useless biographical data: Arrived here via Argentina; previously had lived in the South of France; settled in California a few months ago with some money and the idea of making a splash. Plea listened to himself ask: "How are things going? Are you happy here?"

"I like California, you know, I adore it, otherwise my place would be the French Riviera. The French Riviera is really tops, you know." He displayed again his whole healthy line of teeth: "That Blumenfeld girl is real cute."

That insistently nominal comment induced Plea to ask without curiosity: "Do you know her?"

De Dominicis spoke in a benevolent tone: "She's a whore. They've thrown her out of half the countries in Europe. Real cute, though. You know, these American girls?" He smiled the virile Latin smile, his eye squinting knowingly in the direction of Ilse, who was now talking intensely to a very young athletic-looking boy with a crew cut and glasses, and wearing a dark-gray flannel suit. He returned to Plea: "Dear Consul, some day you and I will have to have a nice long chat."

Plea got up: "Come to my office some morning," he said,

consciously self-destructive. "Why don't you call my secretary and have her give you an appointment?"

He got away, formulating a little wordplay to himself—*olio,* oil: *odio,* hate—how far would the hate-stain expand? In the past, some stains had expanded considerably, marginal points had reached Rome. But in Rome, Plea thought with sadness, he had friends, prestige, in such measure that all rumors were shelved and things were left forever unexplained.

He went back into the living room, finding it more and more fluid and wavy with tobacco smoke and the deafening din of voices; the crowd was thicker than ever; he asked himself which could be the host and hostess; however, on second thought he was sure he had already recognized and greeted them on his initial trip across the room. Mr. Rust must have been that robust and friendly man with thick eyebrows; his wife, silver-haired and wearing glasses with a very sober frame, oozing friendliness and hospitality, had told him: "Happy you could come, Donato," with disarming sincerity. Had it perhaps been cruel of B.P. to upset their artistic ideals? No. All was well. Menichini punished. And these two had taken the thing with sportsmanship and in the end got the proper orientation; sooner or later, in fact, they became the specialists, the experts. The fake Modiglianis had disappeared, perhaps Mrs. Rust was hunting for authentic ones, and at any rate she favored the local abstractionists. Plea thought with nostalgia of Bernardo the arbiter, he asked himself where the man could be; he would have liked him to be present here. He looked for Ilse and unexpectedly found her near him, putting her arm around his waist and whispering: "Shall we leave?" taking the words out of his mouth. "I've done all that I had to do, more or less," she added.

"You are the only person I know; let's leave, the two of

us, I'll take you somewhere to eat; then we'll stay together and talk all evening; you are my only friend."

Ilse took him tenderly by the arm, as if they belonged to each other; he was thinking that perhaps he would take her to Italy himself, making a break, forcing their way across the border.

But there was the second visit to be made. In the car, riding toward the hills in a northeasterly direction, they reviewed the Rust party, the guests.

"Didn't you realize?" Ilse was asking. "Very tall and very thin; he gets a lot of sunshine playing golf; dear Stew, my stepfather, of course. My mother has no rapport with me, but Stew follows a rather conciliatory policy."

"I don't know anything, I don't know what relationships there are among all of you."

"Well, he and my mother see very little of each other; they've been married an enormous number of years, adding together the first and the second time. He doesn't understand Clement very well, but he wanted more or less to adopt me; I interested him more than Clare, who is his real daughter. However, he doesn't tell my mother that he and I meet, and he has not given me any money for my trip to Europe; not that I have asked him for any, and for that matter he hasn't got much, you know. In fact my mother and Clare are running after Bernardo, who is the richest of all anyway. I believe Bernardo is quite rich. My stepfather is a Catholic and when I was very young I believe he would have liked to convert me."

"From what?"

"I don't know. On the other hand, he also liked me very much. I'm sure he would have been ready to establish any kind of relationship between the two of us. He knows what kind of relationship I have had with men since the age of sixteen, and this horrifies my mother but excites him. Technically speaking, with him it wouldn't even have been incest. But I treat him with kindness, he had called me to say that he would go to the Rusts' and I went there also in order to see him. Many other things too—I had to try and calm that boy a little, you know? He is the son of the Rusts, and he's afraid he has made one of my friends pregnant."

"All of this doesn't interest me and at any rate, Ilse, I believe you're wasting a lot of time."

"I like it when you call me by my first name. And I'm happy my stepfather saw me arrive with the Italian consul. He notices things like that."

"He doesn't even know me."

"Everybody knew who you were, you are very popular."

"You are all unbalanced; I don't want to have anything to do with you."

Ilse raised her right hand from the wheel and patted Plea on the head; then with the back of her fingers she caressed his ear; she brought the hand back to the wheel and drove for a long while in silence.

Plea asked: "Must we really go to this other party of yours? And where is it? Much farther up?" They had been riding along Sunset for a while, then they had gone up Laurel Canyon, leaving it to take one of the steep little roads on the left; now they were riding close to the houses, some of them Spanish, others mountain châlets.

Ilse brought the car to the side and stopped it there, heavily slanted to the left. "Listen . . . look, let's go back if you want, let's drop the whole thing, I'll take you back to your house."

"Why did you want to drive? Carry me around like a piece of baggage?"

"I liked the idea. Forgive me. The car is so old and miserable."

In the reflections of the car lights and of the street lamps they looked at each other a long while in silence, then Plea said: "Come, come, let's go, let's do what you want." He added: "You talk so much . . . Your families have been haunting me for years."

Ilse gave him a quick smile and said only: "The house where I have to go is a little farther up; it isn't a real party; I'll just go in a moment alone, you wait for me outside and then you can take me to dinner." Plea nodded and she kissed him fleetingly on the lips, then immediately started the car again. After two turns she stopped in front of a little wooden gate, its white paint peeling off. She got out of the car, slammed the door, and without another word went up into the house leaving him alone in the car, a few inches away from the peeling gate and a bush with flaming red flowers. The gloomy ironical cry of an owl marked the time. Soon Ilse came back, sat behind the wheel, and before starting the motor she threw an envelope with the letterhead of a travel agency into the glove compartment. "Tomorrow I'll go to New York," she said, "I'll go that far at least, for the time being."

He took her to a very expensive restaurant, with wood paneling and soft lights, operated by Italians. The Italian maître and three Alsatian waiters rushed to him. Plea sat down and started to order; Ilse sat delicately on the edge of her chair, holding on to the shiny white tablecloth covered with glasses and china of various sizes, sparkling in the shadows; she looked at him, composed and rather tense.

The maître prepared himself to take the order. At the mention of a certain vegetable, he stooped close to Plea's ear and whispered in it, conspiratorially: "Oil and garlic, Mr. Consul General?"

(1 5 4)

"Consul is already more than enough, cut out the General—but excuse me, Sanzio, forget it . . . " Plea said, getting up suddenly. Immediately Ilse rose from the edge of her chair. "It occurs to me that perhaps it's still a little too early . . ." Plea mumbled, "perhaps a little later . . ." He took Ilse by the arm and was already going toward the exit, he put his hand on the maître's forearm, shaking it with friendliness as he was taking leave. With a wave of the hand and a vibrant smile he greeted De Dominicis, whom he had discovered, with voracious wife, at a table. Respectful whispers from the maître and from one of the Alsatians followed him to the door, thick and polished like that of a safe. Outside, with acrobatic speed, one of the parking boys recognized and brought back Ilse's threadbare little car.

In the car, headed west, Plea said: "You are happy that we left, aren't you? Now we'll go and eat wherever you want."

She brought him to that place near the Pacific Coast where some time before she had played the piano. Inside, the humid pungent air from the ocean mixed with an air thick with alcohol, and smoke from charcoal-broiled meat. The floor was slippery, with sawdust on it. The light came from candles in opaque glass tubes; there were red-checked tablecloths; the menu was printed on glossy cardboard, large as a newspaper. The proprietor, Dave, wore sports clothes; he and Ilse kissed each other on the cheek, and it became evident from their conversation that they had some little deal on concerning the purchase and sale of a gramophone. They ordered steak. Waiting for the steak, they ordered some oysters. After tearing the oysters from their shells and devouring them, they would raise the shell to their lips and drink the remaining salty water impregnated with lemon. At first Dave would come to their table and exchange a few words, but then he left them alone and Ilse could talk to Plea uninterruptedly.

Already in the car she had started to talk about Herbert Blumenfeld, her father; she had met him in the house of her second stop, to get her ticket for the trip to Europe from him. "I would have liked to meet him," Plea had said, "I would have come in too if I had known he was there," and Ilse was resuming now: "No, you see, my father is sort of eclipsed. It isn't that he is sick or anything like that—he is eclipsed. In fact, he is very well, takes wonderful care of himself, has enough to get by. He is happy. Do you realize that? *He is happy*. It's hard to imagine how he must have been when my mother first knew him. She was still married to Stew, and people have said that from the moment their eyes met, Stew just dissolved from her mind as though he had never existed. When they talked to her about divorce proceedings it seems that she just said: 'Divorce from whom?' She couldn't remember him. She remembered him twenty years later and in fact married him again. Her union with my father must have been a moment of furor, the only one in which my mother has known sexual fulfillment. She and my father met in Venice, he was insanely in love with Venice, so much in love that he could have knelt down to kiss the ground, lick it, and finally he found the embodiment of Venice in my mother's body—so you can imagine. In Venice he had lived like a native, he would row in a *sandolo* in the Burano fashion, with oars crossed, he was strong and apparently very handsome, he rode on horseback at the beach on the Lido, and he would swim for hours at a time. We, Clement and I, were conceived in Venice during that fantastic period. And then, since she had become an American through her marriage to Stew, and was also very much attached to American wealth, they came

(156)

here, he had friends and relatives in Santa Monica. Seen from here, their Venetian furor must have looked to them like something of a tourist souvenir. And meanwhile, we were born; they saw this pair turn up, two problems instead of one, when the thing between them had already more or less petered out, you know how it is, some meetings are like that; there is a flare and then everything ends, and when the moment comes to put the cards on the table, the two don't know what to tell each other any more. So they just looked at each other, and they realized that they had never explained themselves, they had only made furious love—enviable, as far as that is concerned; and then they didn't even understand how it had all happened.

"And there we were, Clement and I, reminding them of the thing by our mere presence. All children are irritating but we must have had, already at the start, a charge of irritation much above normal. Actually, Donato, the best thing that could have happened to them was to die in Venice, in the flare." She realized that Plea had been pouring red wine in her glass and took a large swallow.

Plea shrugged. "A romantic idea. And then, you know, you would also have finished in that flare." But he spoke defensively, without conviction. Ilse had bitten into a piece of steak, bloody inside and charred on the outside; while she chewed she kept fixing Plea with incredulous eyes. "In that case," he repeated, "you would have finished too; in fact, you would never have started."

Ilse swallowed and interrupted him with conviction: "I have thought about that many times. And as a solution, especially for Clement, perhaps it would have been . . ." But she stopped abruptly, then spoke slowly, with detachment: "I wouldn't want you to misunderstand me. Clement is the human being I love most in this world. I'll admit that these words are rather vague."

(1 5 7)

"They are not vague at all."

"We were born together. I imagine we felt we were together against the rest of the world, so to speak; and instead, they kept us apart quite a lot. In other families with children there would be little colds, an occasional tonsillitis; between Clement and me, however, there was also 'the morbid attachment,' but it was referred to in the same tone as the little colds or the tonsillitis.—Perhaps it isn't even our parents' fault that they haven't followed us much in life. For that matter, family relationships have a rather vague meaning. Dora Fassola once, talking to me about the Venice Partibons, whom she admired madly as a child, told me about a theory they were always propounding about family relationships: they claimed that the formal ones, like between father and child, do not count, whereas those that count are the ones they used to call gratuitous, invented. In order to function, they said, even the conventional relationships should be treated as though they had been created. I know nearly nothing about those Partibons, but I never forgot that theory."

Plea nodded, caught in the talk, but gloomy; he felt almost physically enveloped in the net of those families who always found a way to recapture him, through the years and the different countries. Still defensive, he said: "Perhaps that's nothing but a justification for incest."

Ilse shrugged: "Yes, perhaps. At any rate, what I was getting at is that just as a relationship between father and child can be invented, so you can be a bastard even having legitimate parents alive and kicking like my own."

Plea again tried to disentangle himself from the net: "You say all this because you don't get along with your mother. And why don't you? Perhaps she disapproves of the way you live. I'm not telling you that she is right."

"You know what started my mother's intolerance toward

me? Do you think it was because I ran around with men and things like that? Maybe later, but the basic reason is that I was a sickly child."

"What do you mean?"

"I was ill, I was never really well." After a pause she resumed in a reasonable tone: "Listen . . . look, perhaps she didn't understand it herself, but that is the origin of it; she is a woman of great strength, and seeing this little girl around, who was never well . . ."

"You're crazy. A mother, on the contrary . . ."

Ilse looked at him with surprise: "I admired her for that, you know." She sighed. "I spent some time in a sanitarium," she said. She paused again. "You knew poor Dorothy Blaustein, the one who died?" Plea shook his head without interrupting, listening intently. "She too was in the sanitarium at that time. The horrible thing with a sick person is when she loses her dignity. Certain animals who suffer a lot, still don't lose their dignity." Now she was silent for a long while.

Over the red-checked tablecloth, Plea took Ilse's hand and held it tight under his own.

Ilse looked at him with gratitude and resumed: "Dorothy was a person whom I loved very much. She was a virgin. She died a virgin. She never had a man. One day we were both lying in deck chairs on the terrace, and I happened to notice black rings under her eyes; and she told me: 'I've been ill so long now; I am alone,' explaining how she had excited herself with her own hand, and she said this with a smile which was much worse than if she had been crying. I tried to laugh the thing off, but it was a total failure, I assure you I didn't succeed. Then when I got better I told myself many times: never, never, never be like Dorothy, never." She freed her hand from Plea's to blow her nose; she returned her hand, with a smile.

Plea said: "Let's go, let's go back to my house."

"Listen . . . look, I like you, but I'm leaving tomorrow and we can't start a thing now. Please." And she resumed: "Above all, don't believe that I worry about my mother. My mother is intelligent, true, but she hasn't got many interests outside of money. It's hard to understand what makes people like that go on living. Clare is stupider, and then, she's younger. Now she has a lover."

So they came to talk again about the sometime husband of Clare, Bernardo; and they went on talking into the night, losing themselves in the branches of that multi-family structure, and always coming back to Bernardo Partibon, as if his very bulk made him omnipresent, a reference point, a center; or as if that complicated genealogical tree had been growing backward, starting from its infinite ramifications and finally finding a trunk, a gathering nucleus somehow more solid and well rooted, better suited to give sustenance and nourishment. To give nourishment, but also to absorb:

"He is a perfect combination of altruism and egotism. Take for example Gutkind—Bernardo's relationship to Gutkind. Gutkind too was related to us, you know."

"Wherever you touch, there is a connection," Plea said. "Bernardo himself told me once that what little he knows about art he has stolen from Gutkind. He laughed in a curious way."

"That was especially during the period when he was divorcing the Peach. That's what we call his first wife. She now lives here with Larry, their son Lorenzo. By Clare, Bernardo has no children, although it seems that in the early days they practically lived in bed. Gutkind was a rather decisive influence. Bernardo knew Gutkind at the end of his golden age. I've seen Gutkind's house in New York once myself. Bernardo lived there for some time."

As a boy, perhaps he had brushed elbows with people like that, in Venice; here he must have entered their world at first somewhat like an apprentice. All in all, he was a more conventional type of emigrant, whereas these people had settled into exile irradiating their milieu without ever ceasing that irradiation, exuding Mittel-europa, recomposing their houses so that they almost seemed like snails that had brought it along with them—servants, library, and all. So, I suppose, was Gutkind. And Bernardo Partibon must have digested him like a huge philosophical treatise or a book of wisdom or etiquette—or even like a whole course of study, learning his secrets, discarding his pomposities and weaknesses, finally emerging beyond him and discarding him altogether.

"And then there was the marriage to Clare, rather a failure, but important too, in its way; now it even looks like my mother is trying to arrange a reconciliation. My mother resembles him in some ways. The Venetian element. We all resemble each other in some ways. But Venetians are very resistant. Venice, you see, is a little bit putrescent, so a kind of immunity is created—they are somehow inoculated against total corruption. And then, they talk so much. That saves them. Bernardo! I wonder how he will end up."

CHAPTER SEVEN

✣

Suddenly in Bernardo's dream there appeared a woman dentist who inserted a drill in his mouth; but Bernardo did not feel anything, the drill was weightless and gave the sound of plastic. "Signorina, stop that," Bernardo was saying, "what you are doing is all wrong." The dentist stopped drilling; she shrugged, put the instrument back into her small case, and left. "We are in a hotel room," Bernardo said to himself, "and that was not a dentist, she was a barber with an electric razor." At that point the sound of the plastic drill started again and kept buzzing interminably. It was the telephone on the night table. Awake and conscious, Bernardo raised himself slowly against the pillows: the telephone went on with its hollow vibration and he continued to stare at it with a kind of quiet suspicion while he blew his nose slowly. He threw away the tissue, raised the receiver to his ear, recognized the voice immediately: "Dora?"

"I'm here in Venice, you know," Dora Fassola said, disappointed at not having managed to surprise him.

"So you are here in Venice. Well, it did seem to me that I wouldn't have heard you so well if you had been in Rome for example."

"Do you know what I just got?"

"No, I don't know."

"I just got a wire from Ilse." Dora paused, "Aren't you going to ask me anything?"

"I'm waiting for you to tell me."

Dora's voice gave him a feeling of tenderness. It was obvious that Dora was at home, at her mother's; she spoke in a clipped modern tempo but with occasional traces of dialect. She resumed: "A cable, that is. She says she is coming here; in fact, she is confirming it. Even the consul there did something about it, you know? So Enrico was saying. I came up here with Enrico."

"Where is Ilse now?"

"In Santa Monica, I guess."

"So the consul is Plea," Bernardo said, "pleasant and clever, just the opposite of his predecessor, Menichini."

"Some of the people who were in Italy with Ilse last year had their residence permit taken away, or something like that, but she had nothing to do with it, actually." Dora would have liked to see Bernardo interested, excited.

"Is that so? She had nothing to do with what?"

"With that big mess." No reaction on Bernardo's part. "I have just heard," Dora went on, "that you and Clement went around Venice for hours talking all the time. What a pity—I should like to have been with you. Wouldn't you have liked that—all of us together?"

"Oh, I don't know . . ."

"You woke up in the wrong mood."

"I was dreaming of a lady dentist with a plastic drill."

Dora burst out laughing; Bernardo was caught and laughed along with her. "You are at your mother's, aren't you? I can tell from the way you talk."

"Yes . . . you are glad I'm here, aren't you? I was afraid you didn't like me any more. There is a young man in Rome who likes me, but really, seriously. He is a professor but he's terrific; he was at the Solmis' the other night. You do remember him, don't you? Ovidio."

"Of course I remember him. What did you do to him?"

"Nothing. I was supposed to have dinner with him tonight, imagine that."

"And why aren't you?" There was another pause.

"Listen, I'm coming over now; meanwhile, you try and wake up. You are not awake yet. You have a bedroom and living room, haven't you?"

"Yes, why?"

"Otherwise they won't let me come up, you know hotel rules, and I want to come up and talk. That is, I want to talk with you."

"About what? Why?" It seemed to him that his days always started like that: invasions on the part of people he hadn't invited. It was like discovering a black-and-blue mark somewhere on his huge body without knowing what he could have bumped against.

"Now I'll call the gondolier and I'll be there in a few minutes," Dora said, hanging up.

So Dora was staying at her mother's, and Bernardo knew what that meant. It meant the house where she had lived as a child when the family was very influential. At the beginning of their ascent, thirty years earlier, the Fassolas had bought that palace which, although ancient and Gothic and therefore corresponding to their notions of a Venetian palace, had, through improvements and cleanings, acquired a glossier and more expensive look than that of other buildings of the same type. This morning in the leaden gray light, it appeared discolored and stained not only from time and brine but from autumn rain and fog.

Of their palace, the Fassolas had kept only the mezzanine floor with its cozy rooms and low stuccoed ceilings, where Fausta, Dora's mother, lived alone during most of the year; her husband, Augusto Fassola, who for almost fifteen years now had considered himself a dying man, remained in the country all the time, at Corniano, near the grave of his younger son, Massimo; Dora lived as much as possible in Rome with Enrico, who had an apartment on Via Denza; she occupied it also when Enrico was stationed abroad.

That Venetian palace, not far from the widening of the Grand Canal into St. Mark's Basin, was on the opposite side of the canal from Bernardo's hotel. Twenty years earlier, when he lived on a small square in the inner city with chattering of women from window to window amid hanging laundry, the region of Venice inhabited by the Fassolas had been, to him, a world high and remote, filled with dogal history and open to winds from the sea; at that time, "calling the gondolier" would have meant to little Dora or to her mother having one of the servants tell the house gondolier to keep the boat ready at the canal door. Now, instead, it meant that Dora would call the nearby ferry service, the *traghetto,* or would perhaps simply go to one of the windows of the mezzanine, low above the water, and make a sign to the gondoliers of that public service; one of them, rather out of old familiarity than because of any particular prestige surrounding the Fassola name, would make an exception and pick her up at the house to ferry her across to the hotel on the opposite side.

In fact, less than fifteen minutes had passed when Bernardo, in the bathroom, heard Dora knock at the door of the living room. Walking into the bedroom, he saw her standing straight at the opposite door, which was open. Dora knocked on the door frame, saying: "May I?" and she entered the bedroom, adding: "You look wonderful in your dressing gown, you look even bigger; you are majestic."

Bernardo sighed and settled himself on the bed again,

propped high against the pillows; the girl sat on the edge so that they were face to face; they smiled at each other.

"When did you arrive? And how did you find things in Venice?"

Dora answered as if she gave an announcement: "Here in Venice it's really nightmarish."

"Why?" Dora and her friends often used words of that kind, without emphasis or conviction, as if they mentioned what temperature it was.

"All of a sudden Clement calls me in Rome and says: 'Look, we're all here in Venice, your brother Enrico is coming up too . . .'"

Bernardo felt he was being fenced in; he smiled, looking at her talking, while he warned himself: "Here we are; now she will go on like that, she will say things that I already know, as if it were agreed that here you go on and on repeating things that you already know, telling each other stories, giving long quotations from other people's talks, with imitations of their voices, reviewing events and translating them into comedy; then I'll go on listening as I listen to the swishing noise of the water beating on the marble steps, just like that, with a light ear, and then I'll yield and she'll have me talk, and I'll throw myself into it, and I'll talk . . ."

Dora asked: "What are you thinking of? What are you looking at?"

"I'm looking at you, and I'm thinking that we are in Venice."

"Of course we are in Venice. Aren't you happy? Think how much we owe to Clement, bless him. I didn't know that Enrico was going to come up. In Rome he stays in his office at the Ministry until very late, and we hardly ever meet. Enrico has now been appointed to the London embassy so that Father apparently has been sending desperate messages from Corniano: 'Enrico, my dear, before going away from Italy again, come here, stay a while near us.' *Us* means of course Father and Massimo. Massimo is buried at Corniano, you know, because he liked Corniano better than any other place in the world." Dora moved her hand forward to insert it under Bernardo's pajama jacket and place it on his chest as if she were feeling his heart. It was a small warm hand. "You are really the postcard image of the strong man, I didn't know how thick and curly the hair on your chest is too."

The sensation on his chest was very light, yet it spread all over him, simple and very complicated at the same time. Dora had very dark eyes, a round face, very regular and pleasant, a mouth well shaped and still extremely youthful, without bitter lines—a calm mouth, at worst set in a vague, sly smile; only those dark eyes, without luster, had a kind of congenital sadness, left there by the years, forgotten.

"I came over because you were here and you are threatening to leave for America any moment . . . " She took a sip from the glass of mineral water on the night table. "You're threatening, but you won't do it, I'm sure. Or perhaps you don't want to abandon your important business in America for too long; is that it?"

"My important business in America is nothing."

"You won't deny that you have a lot of money. Once upon a time, when I was a little child here in Venice, we were very rich, imagine, then we went down the drain; obviously, however, I wouldn't marry a rich man, money in itself is not worth-while. You know, I would marry somebody like Ovidio. I had promised I would have dinner with him tonight; instead, I saw him a moment yesterday at a café, to tell him that I couldn't, that I was leaving. It's curious, but the thing becomes more important that way. I saw him a quarter of an hour at the café in a hurry, a café where

I usually never go, and we were holding hands all the time. Think of that. But it was a rather important thing. And why do you say that your business in America is nothing? You are an enormous success, aren't you? And if that sort of thing has no value, then what does? Eleonora Conti, who has been to college in America, introduced me to some American girls some time ago—one was the daughter of a senator, or of a governor of a state, something like that, one who has a chance to become President of the United States, it seems, perhaps you know him, and she was mentioning this father of hers, who is still a young man and then also terribly handsome, and he says that the only occupation worth bothering with is politics. Do you think that's right?"

Bernardo sighed, then shrugged his shoulders. Now Dora had taken one of his hands and she looked at it, holding the large fingers tightly in her own hand, caressing the finger tips with her thumb. "I, on the contrary," she went on, "do not consider politics so important. Perhaps I'm influenced by Enrico. You know the way he feels."

"I always remember the letters that we wrote each other during the war."

"Yes, I know; you told me bits of them from memory." Dora's face darkened a little; she watched Bernardo attentively, as one who sees a recognizable but incomprehensible symptom reappear in a sick person. She remembered Bernardo's deep slow tone in quoting words from one of the letters that Enrico had written to Bernardo from the neutral country where he had been as a young diplomat during part of the war, after the two of them, strangers to each other, had made contact through information gathered from relatives spread around the world—the precious and absurd contact between two men who, from reversed points of view, had sought each other with a kind of blind hope. There was, of course, also the abnormal family relationship

(1 6 8)

connecting them—Massimo dead, Maria left with Massimo's child—but such episodes by then were submerged under the events of history, of a history neither willed nor understood by the two, who, with a kind of passionate detachment, conducted that dialogue so arduous even from the simply physical, postal point of view, while their last thought in the world, even granting that someone might propose it to them, would have been that technically they could be defined enemies, in a state of war.

They had addressed each other quite formally. From this unknown and contemporary relative, Bernardo had received disconnected information, a few hints at Massimo and Maria, and even vaguer ones at the Venice relatives (Elena, Giorgio, toward whom Enrico seemed to have felt an attachment both deep and desperate), immediately accompanied by more general comments on the war, on Italy; it was on these that Bernardo had lingered avidly, in fact they had dug themselves in his mind from the very first instant, as if they had been there always. It wasn't as though he had carried the letter in his pocket, more and more rumpled and worn out, in order to read it until he knew it by heart; rather, it was as if its words had printed themselves on his mind the minute he had torn the envelope open and set his eyes on that sheet, coming down the steps of a Spanish post office in a California town, with a sense of revelation, and, at the same time, of recognition. *Because you see, Bernardo, there exists such a thing as noble defeats. There are moments—I do not need to tell you—when embracing an absolutely desperate cause and marching toward certain disaster is a glorious act, or at least one possessing its own pathetic grandeur. But there will be nothing of the sort in this case. Here there isn't only an army ill-equipped, ill-organized, obviously directed to its ruin. The tasks that this army will be ordered to fullfill are not only*

(169)

predestined to the most miserable failure, they are not only sad errors; they are also universally considered dishonorable. Tell me, Bernardo, what more do you want?

"But then," Dora said, "when you came to Italy after such a long time, you and Enrico hardly saw each other."

"We still have time, especially if he's in Venice now. He's a very kind man."

"Later we'll call him . . . What do you mean? How did you expect him to be?"

Bernardo sagged down: "I don't know. I don't know anything about anybody."

"Enrico is doing very well, you know, as a diplomat—he's very conscientious, intelligent, a terrific worker: that's because he doesn't care for it at all, you see. Pity that Marco Partibon is not in Italy, you could have talked with him, don't you think?"

"I knew him many years ago in America; it was he who put me in touch . . ."

"I know . . . of course. Years and years ago Marco Partibon had quite a thing with my mother, did you know that? Now he must be in Germany, or perhaps in America. Perhaps you could have talked with him." She looked Bernardo in the eyes, as if to read something there, and she sighed like a worried nurse. Actually she did not quite know what Bernardo could have wanted to talk about with Marco Partibon, or with anybody else for that matter, including Maria. She tried to help him blindly, like a student offering the few data he knows in the hope that they will fit the examiner's questions: "At some point during the war Marco, if I remember correctly, was also in jail, then he escaped to Switzerland with your cousin Giorgio, I believe. That sort of thing, you know? Giorgio adored his uncle Marco. Giorgio was a great love of mine when I was twelve or thirteen; now he is terrifically successful, he has been invited to give lectures at the Sorbonne, and at Oxford too, I believe. I haven't followed them very closely, Marco, Elena, Giorgio, but in some ways you make me feel that I am in their presence again. You look like them. You are even bigger than Marco Partibon, who was a terrifically huge beast himself, and you have the same eyes as Giorgio, set the same way. How sad it is . . . you know, I remember one time when a friend of mine and I were little girls, and we accompanied your cousin Giorgio to the station here in Venice in our gondola. Memories, evocations . . ." Dora uttered the words as though she made fun of them a little, with a kind of sob of laughter: "How sad, and now, my uncle Ermete in South America, my father retired at Corniano, you don't know how sad it is to compare the present with those days long ago, like when Massimo died, which were sad times to begin with. In fact, tragic, weren't they?" She sighed deeply, revealing the contour of her small but well-formed and solid breasts, giving an impression of extraordinary physical well-being. "You don't know how it is," she resumed with vivacity, "with Venetian families. However, Mother and I love each other. Venetian families . . . Italian families, we might as well say. Even now, you know; you have no idea. I don't know a single marriage that turned out well."

"Maybe you think American marriages are terrific successes . . . I'll tell you, they are nothing to brag about either."

Now Dora laughed more overtly and she knocked on Bernardo's chest with her small fist: "You mean your own little private messes, for instance? You've always been marvelous at making a mess of your love life, haven't you? How was your first wife? Was she good-looking?"

Often, when confronted with questions of that kind, Bernardo showed the expression of a man with his back to the wall, or even of the captured animal. "That was long ago, you know," he attempted.

But Dora insisted: "What did she look like?"

"As for her appearance, how shall I put it, she was a little bit like a peach, and that's actually what they call her, the Peach."

"You mean round and velvety?"

"Well, I don't know—a peach."

"So you liked her?"

Bernardo seemed to discover an easy and unexpected way out: "Of course . . . yes, I liked her."

"Why did you get a divorce, then?"

"Yes, of course—we were divorced." There was a long silence.

"She drank a lot, Ilse always said."

"What is Ilse supposed to know? Well, yes—she did drink. There was a period when she drank enormously."

"A peach in heavy syrup."

"What?" Bernardo seemed frightened. "Well, yes—something like that," he murmured abstractedly. He looked into empty space, there was an apparition visible only to himself. He said: "Remembering it is even worse than living through it."

"Now, really." Dora was going to add: "There we go again." Already on previous occasions Bernardo had come out with statements of that sort; it was entirely incomprehensible to Dora how one could feel so intensely about something that didn't exist any more; on the other hand, she remembered that according to widespread opinion among her girl friends, it was fixations of that kind that "made Bernardo fascinating." She knocked on his chest: "Talk to me about your peach-wife. Her name was Beverly, wasn't it? As in Beverly Hills?"

Bernardo took her little hand: "I've talked to you about

(1 7 2)

her already, haven't I? She was a college student when we met. She was from Ohio, and she had come to college in the East. At that time I was more or less settled in New York, things were beginning to go rather well. I never even finished secondary school, so at first in her circle of friends I felt uncomfortable—girls who read, painted, did all sorts of things. She belonged to the most fashionable group in a college which was rather fashionable to begin with. Later I realized that these girls treated me like a god because I knew about art."

"And because you are fascinating, Bernardo."

"So?" Bernardo said gloomily.

"You and the Peach had a marvelous physical rapport, didn't you? Ilse used to say . . ."

"There you go with Ilse again."

"Ilse is one and the same thing with Clement, and Clement is one of the main experts on you. At any rate, it is a well-known fact that that marriage, sexually speaking, was a terrific success."

"Why not? For some time now, she has had a liaison which from that point of view seems to be a phenomenal success."

"So the Peach is all right now?"

"Yes, yes, she is perfectly normal."

"Since you are divorced, why doesn't she marry this new lover?"

Bernardo shrugged. "It's one of those halfway things, you know," he mumbled. Through his business manager he paid his wife a sum of money every month, which would be reduced in case she married again.

Dora studied him intently; she said: "Ovidio maintains that in the Italian way of life, women are the victims." Bernardo did not react. "Is Beverly happy now?"

"Now she is perfectly normal," Bernardo repeated. "Our

son lives with her and is growing up beautifully."

"Do you think a lot about them?"

"I think about them."

"But then you always think about everything and everybody, don't you?"

"Well, maybe."

"Is it true, though, that the Peach used to get drunk?"

"As a student in college she would sometimes shut herself up in her room all alone, and drink until she passed out."

"I have never passed out drinking."

"Bravo."

"Should one try, do you think?"

"That's not the sort of thing you either try or don't try; it's something that either happens or does not happen. And at any rate, when she shut herself up in her room like that, she was probably six or seven years younger than you are now, so in your case it's perhaps a little late to start."

"And if she did that even before you got married, how come you married her? Did you want to cure her? Did you feel pity?" Dora was trying Bernardo from all sides, she probed the terrain at various points to try and find the right vein, and then she would let it gush out and watch it run, with delight.

"Cure her . . . pity . . . pity," Bernardo repeated. He shook his head: "First of all, I was trying to understand. From the time I met her, long before we got married, I would just sit there and try to understand. When I went to visit her in the early days, if she was alone in her room, in that state, she would first say that she wasn't in, then I would insist and she would suddenly yield and let me see her. In fact, in the end, it was she who looked for me when she was like that. She seemed to be saying: 'Apparently you are interested in seeing me like this—well, here I am,' and she would stand in front of me looking like a beaten animal, but at the same time with that expression drunk people have, arrogant and insensible, and that air of cunning that they have, but contrived, without backing. I don't know whether you have ever seen that. As far as I'm concerned, it was the first time I saw it in a girl."

"What impression did it make?"

Bernardo answered slowly: "I'll tell you, I believe I wanted to see her in order to suffer; it was as though I felt that my suffering would do her good. I'm trying to tell you how I felt then. And I don't think I can make myself any clearer."

Dora took his hand and held it tight in both of her own; she bit her lower lip, concentrating on studying his face. She felt happy. Her trip to Venice had evidently been the right idea. "I adore Bernardo," she was telling herself; and his confidence made her feel proud. She thought of Ovidio, with whom she had talked about Bernardo; and she guessed that somehow this growing intimacy with Bernardo would increase the already considerable attraction that Ovidio felt toward her. Things, she thought, were going rather well.

"Go on, Bernardo," she whispered. "When you married the Peach, was she still in college?"

"No." Had she lost the vein again?

"But you had already gone to bed together?" Bernardo didn't move. "Well, at any rate, to bed or somewhere else. Once you did it under a grand piano." She squeezed his hand to stop him from protesting. "I know it from Ilse." Bernardo remained silent. She asked in a low voice: "And when did you finally get married?" There—the vein was struck again.

Bernardo resumed with gusto: "First, this is what happened: she left school. One day I went as usual to look for her, and she had left. None of her friends could give me any address, except that of her parents, whom I didn't know and who lived in Ohio. I put a call through to Ohio, but of course she wasn't there; her parents at that point still believed that she was at the college. Her father was very kind, he was in the carpet business; he asked me to leave my name and address, and a couple of weeks later it was he who called to tell me that his daughter had settled in New York to devote herself completely to painting; he sounded rather proud of that. He gave me his daughter's address in New York; I went there but I didn't find her. At some point I realized that I didn't understand why I continued to look for her. Finally, I forgot about her. Do you understand? Sometimes I forget, just like that." He looked at Dora with anxiety.

"Why not? What's so strange about that, Bernardo?" He seemed to her a little bit like a child with nightmares.

"I don't know."

"You are quite extraordinary, Bernardo." Dora's happiness increased. From the foggy canal she heard the whistle of a little steamer; through the light curtains and on the high stuccoed ceiling she perceived the gray restless reflections of water. She was happy to feel herself in the autumnal Venice of her childhood, so many years later, receiving the confessions of this new Partibon, recently discovered and already so close to her, closer, in fact, to her than to any other relatives. "Go on, Bernardo," she whispered.

"Well, one day, one afternoon, in an art gallery on Fifty-seventh Street, I accidentally found her. She had very long hair. A few months had passed, yet she seemed five years older, but I don't mean that in the sense that she had withered; in fact she was stronger, more mature, especially in the motion of her hips." He shrugged and concluded: "We got married the following week."

"Simply like that?"

(1 7 6)

"When things happen like that, it is as though they had already happened, and the act itself is just a formality."

"At that time you had a little bachelor apartment in New York, didn't you?" she asked, as if jealous.

"No, I had lived in a hotel, run by people I knew, a hotel where long before I had also worked as a waiter for a while. The little money I made I invested in paintings. Beverly and I settled in the country, in a rather dilapidated frame house, but among stunningly beautiful trees, in Connecticut, but in one of the less chic sections. We had been in our house for about a week when I had a chance to buy, imagine, a little Modigliani, a very beautiful one. Those were different times; if I told you the price—paid in installments, too— you would be surprised. And instead of selling it, I put it in our own house. I already had two or three paintings which I considered my own, but none of that importance; I had bought that one with difficulty and with the idea of selling it to rich people in California. The decision to keep it for us was therefore a little symbolic—it meant that I planned to make money fixing up other people's houses, but the one that interested me most was our own; and don't forget that at that time I was just beginning, and although in appearance I was more or less the same as now, I was only twenty-four. Some mornings she would get up earlier than I, and then I would find her in the living room downstairs, wearing her gown, sunk deep in the sofa, her naked legs comfortably stretched on the coffee table, her eyes glued to the picture. I was ecstatic, I was mad with pride. Then we would prepare our café au lait together, we would drink it in the kitchen, looking through the window at the trees that grew in that wonderful country. I also bought her a dog, an enormous Weimaraner."

There was a long silence. "Why don't you go on?" Dora asked.

Bernardo said: "She loved those enormous dogs." And he could just see that one, with its long, simplified lines, a heraldic animal. "He was almost bigger than she."

"Bigger than the Peach?"

"Yes, bigger than the Peach. And although I liked it in the East, I would tell her: 'Let's go west, and there I'll buy you a horse as well.' Meanwhile, I took a trip to California by myself."

"That's when you met Manuela. And Ilse and Clement," Dora said possessively, and she went on, reciting: "And so you planted the seeds of your second marriage . . ."

"No. I had already met Manuela just after she came to New York from Europe. She arrived fom Germany around that time, after the first big persecutions. Marco, her father, had written to me."

As though she had lost one point and wanted to make it up immediately, Dora said: "During that time there was a *thing* between you and Manuela, wasn't there?"

"No."

Another point lost. "Go on with your story, Bernardo."

"Well, Manuela herself was just beginning to settle down in California, they had given her a small part in a picture—people she had known in Berlin in the past, emigrants like herself, who helped her. And she gave me some leads too. In the East I had Gutkind. But in the West she was the first to help me. Why does all this interest you? Things that are already very far away. Ilse and Clement were fourteen, and only Clement was living in California at that time. Perhaps Ilse was in Europe; they kept them apart, I don't know whether this was a curious decision taken by the parents at the time of their divorce—keeping one twin apiece, so to speak—or whether even more curiously they had been advised to do so by one of those psychoanalysts, you know? Clement would take me to the beach in Santa Monica; he was a slightly irritating little boy, with that classical profile and that incessant talk: he wanted me to explain the political systems of Europe, which seemed to fascinate him—not the totalitarian states as they existed then, but the absolute monarchies of past centuries, France, Czarist Russia. He had spent long periods of time in Venice, he knew all about the Venetian Republic, and he wanted to check his information with me, who knew much less than he did. You know how meticulous Clement can be sometimes even now? Manuela was an extraordinary person. On the whole she has done much less than she might have as an actress. I'm still in touch with various people I met that first time. But what I remember most distinctly about that trip was the pleasure I felt going back home to Connecticut, to my house, to my wife."

"You used to take your bath together in the tub, didn't you?"

Bernardo shrugged, with a spurt of laughter. "Poor Dorothy Blaustein was a little bit like you, with that kind of curiosity; Ilse, too, is a little bit like that."

"Knowing certain things about you makes me feel I am a closer friend."

Bernardo looked at her with an air of intense interrogation. When he acted like that, she found him quite lovable. She ordered: "Do finish your story about the Peach. It's a marvelous story."

Bernardo sighed: "Well, I came back from California, as I was saying, with much desire to be in our house again." He frowned. "And at the door, I didn't find *her* to receive me."

"Who was there?"

"A man wearing dark glasses, small, with a little white mustache. Finally I recognized him by his voice, sweet and thin; until then, you see, I had only talked to him over the telephone. He was my father-in-law. His name is Mervyn.

I don't know whether this is an impression that I formed only in memory, colored by what happened later: at any rate, as I see the scene now, it seems to me that he looked like the relative of the patient, the one who waits for the visitor at the entrance to forewarn him about the gravity of the situation. And there's another thing that I remember about that scene, and about all subsequent days, a vision which is stuck in my mind with the same clarity as that of Beverly and her father—the vision of the ants."

"What ants?"

"What do you mean, what ants? Ants. Have you ever seen ants in really extraordinary numbers?"

"I don't know what you mean by extraordinary."

"Something like this"—and Bernardo put his hands forward to indicate about sixteen inches—"imagine something like a ribbon, this wide. A black ribbon, lying on the floor. Well—it was made of ants. From the door between the kitchen and the garden, through all of the kitchen (with various ramifications, minor ribbons climbing up the cupboards, the drawers), farther on into the living room (here too, ramifications up the tables, the book shelves) . . . well, all of these ribbons were formed by ants; bending forward to look closely you could distinguish them, you saw all of that motion, of that frenetic coming and going."

Dora murmured: "You describe it beautifully."

Bernardo did not see her any longer, captured by his memory: "To give you an idea," he resumed, "when Mervyn, her father, realized that I was looking with astonishment at those black ribbons, and all he did was say in a thin voice: 'Yes, ants,' I didn't even react. I didn't say something like: 'You moron, why don't you move and do something?' I just stood there too, without saying anything."

"Without saying anything."

"Do you understand?" Bernardo asked, brightening up.

"Fantastic."

"Only the following day did we make the decision to go down and buy poison. It isn't a poison that kills on the spot. You place these little bottles of poison in strategic positions, on the side. They have a little metal cap, which you can leave there, screwed on, because it has a triangular opening in the middle. The ants go into that opening and I don't know whether they also have a little drink of poison syrup on the spot; at any rate, they pick up a little bit of poison and bring it back to their nests. So you poison the whole species—at the source, so to speak—in its secret caves. So that, when everything is over, you don't find the little corpses in the house as you do with sprays—you find the void."

They looked at each other a long while in silence, then Bernardo resumed: "In other words, I had realized immediately that the two of them, father and daughter, had not been able to act, they had had to wait for my return. Father and daughter (the mother had stayed back in Ohio) resembled each other. Same round head, same clear eyes—luminous but weak. He had come to New York for a convention, representatives of his carpet business, I suppose. It was the first time I saw him. And for that matter, the last. And I don't know why my return home, the apparition of the father at the door, the ants, all of this is connected with me in memory with the fact that she started to drink again. Mervyn at the door had been like the bird announcing a storm. But why do you want me to tell you all this?"

"Talking with you like this is one of the things I like best in the world." At those words, Bernardo was paralyzed for a while, staring at her. "So, then," she encouraged, "it was at that time that the Peach started drinking again?"

"I can't tell exactly. When a memory is so intense, you always have everything with you; it's as if facts were not lined up in time, but all present somewhere in space. Well!" Bernardo gave a brief spurt of laughter which Dora did not understand. "Well! Time becomes a spatial dimension. And can you tell me," he asked with urgency, while Dora understood him even less but was watching him ecstatically, "can you tell me why so many people, doctors too, have always told me that I can't go on thinking, living, this way? What other way is there to live?"

"But it makes you suffer"—and Dora squeezed his hand and raised it to her chest—"doesn't it? Well, then, why look for things that give you pain?"

"The pain is nothing." Bernardo looked at her with still, darkened eyes, heavy with melancholy. "I would find her in the kitchen. I would discover her drinking alone." After a pause he resumed in a quiet, precise tone: "I waited a little. I studied the situation for a while. Then I started telling her: 'Listen, do this: go ahead and drink, but before you start drinking, come and tell me. I won't open my mouth, I'll only come to the kitchen (since that's the place you have chosen, for your drinking) and I'll just sit and look at you.' Now, this may seem strange to you, Dora, but I tell you, talking to her like that, my lips trembled, I felt a lump in my throat. *Since the kitchen is the place you have chosen for your drinking.*"

Dora looked at him with admiration: "Did she take drugs too?" she asked in a low voice.

"No. She only drank. Gin. 'You always drink gin, like an eighteenth-century English prostitute,' I would tell her. I can just see her—her blond soft hair on her beautiful round head, and that red face—a fruit full of juice. She would tell me: 'Take me now, because if I lose consciousness it's no fun.'"

"A very reasonable idea, after all."

"Well—I guess so." He resumed after a pause: "The ants

disappeared and her father left too, a few days later. I haven't seen him since. But I'm sure he is still doing very well with his carpets. He never explained to me why he was at our house precisely during those days of the ants, but I have the impression that he wanted to tell me something and didn't know how to express himself. Perhaps he simply wanted to tell me: 'Watch out, Beverly will start drinking again,' and then perhaps confess to me: 'I used to drink a lot too, before my ulcer.' At any rate, on a perfectly ordinary morning after her father had left, she had gone downstairs before me the way she did when she used to sit and admire the Modigliani; and when I went down I found her alone in the kitchen with an empty gin bottle. In appearance she was her usual self, with her round, juicy face . . . I can just see her."

"I can see her, too. I have a feeling, Bernardo, that just *being you* must be incredibly interesting. I feel you must always be telling stories to yourself."

"Call that interesting."

"Go on, please."

He was looking into empty space, whispering softly: "We had made up a way of talking Italian occasionally, a mixture of baby talk, of dialect, also of invented words. Now I started to tell her: 'Do you like the sbronza? Do you like the sboba?' with this tone of voice, as though I were addressing an idiot child who had gone to a corner of the room with her face to the wall, thinking that no one could see her. 'Are you happy? Eh? Beverly in a corner, Beverly in the dark, Beverly disappeared, fire, little fire, little water, water, Beverly is drowning . . .' and she would echo, looking at me with her round eyes: 'Beverly is drowning,' and I would start scolding the little girl: 'You didn't keep your word, you had promised that before going to the kitchen to drink you would come and tell me; I had promised in return

(1 8 3)

that I would look at you without saying anything,' and as a matter of fact, she had confessed to me that a couple of times the idea of inviting me to the show had made her laugh, so that she had just sat in the kitchen, with the bottle on her lap, unable to open it because that made her laugh.

"Finally, one day, not in the morning but toward evening, I found her in the kitchen with an empty bottle, and this time she looked as if she were dead. I took her up to bed, in my arms. Her eyeballs were rolled back, so that you could see only the whites. She fell asleep, as she always did, for that matter—she snored a little; and she could go on sleeping for fifteen, twenty hours.

"But that time, while she slept like that, I started walking through the country outside, it was winter. A winter sunset; the long, still shadows of trees; and the trees themselves dry, clean, there is nothing cleaner than the wood of trees in winter. I realized that nothing mattered to me any more. I was like one who has been beaten too long. Well, no, I can't even say that nothing mattered to me—I had gone beyond the limit, I didn't perceive even the absence of feeling, I had lost the sense of the difference between something that matters and something that doesn't. I wanted to go away; divorce to me was like the thought of the knife to one almost anesthetized.

"When she woke up the next morning, she told me herself: 'Drive me to the sanitarium and leave me there.' But at that point I insisted that she not leave me. She didn't even listen, she was already on her way to the automobile. I took her to the sanitarium, a place where they did things very nicely, but one of the conditions was that she not see me any more. I went back to our country house alone, and except for a few trips to New York on business or to visit the Gutkinds, I stayed a long time in the country, absolutely alone."

"Who are the Gutkinds?"

"Relatives of the Blumenfelds, art dealers, et cetera. For a while they sort of adopted me, they helped me a lot." Bernardo stopped as if he had hit on something, and didn't want to move any more.

"Go on with the story of the Peach. You were left alone—then what?"

"I would prepare my own food and eat it by myself, or with the dog. And I ate a lot, I was disgusting to myself. The house was a pigsty. One evening, I don't know how long after she had left, she arrived at this pigsty. I watched her with suspicion, trying to make out whether she looked like the girl who had escaped from college. She was all right, even though there was something contrived in her appearance and gestures, as if she was made of pieces held together artificially. The house around us was just continuing to function on its own. She tried to tidy things up a bit—there were also a few dying ants scattered around remains of food—but nothing seemed completely real; she didn't even look at the Modigliani; the dog was sick but she didn't bother about him either. We talked very little."

"Did you make love?"

"Imagine, it was during that period that we conceived our son."

"You were telling me he is very handsome now."

"That's right, and very strong."

"So you could also be happy?"

"Words like that, you know, Dora, don't mean much."

"How did she happen to go away again?"

Bernardo took a deep breath, then spoke as soberly and clearly as he could:

"One morning she just sat in front of me, she hadn't been drinking or anything, her appearance was completely normal; she looked as though she were going to discuss house

(1 8 5)

problems, projects, bills, and she told me in that tone: 'Let's quit, Bernardo, let's kill ourselves.' Well, Dora, this is what happened: we understood, both of us, immediately, that that suggestion, even if we didn't follow it, made its own sense; and that's why I remember that moment as a *right* moment or, if you wish, a happy one. We understood each other as never before, and it is because we lived that moment together that we shall always be friends, that we shall never harm each other."

"Oh, Bernardo," Dora said with a brief sob, and raising her arms she hung around his neck, pressed her cheek on his chest. "Go on, finish your story," she said with that tearful, suffocated voice. "Did she leave then?"

"She went back to the sanitarium. They really did an excellent job with her. Now she is in California with our son, she is full of concern for him, and very strict. To tell you the truth, she has become a rather boring woman."

From her position curled up in Bernardo's arms, Dora raised herself, her face free again, her eyes still moist; she laughed. "Do you know what I'm going to do now? I'll call Enrico, he is at Mother's; in fact, we'll all go and have lunch at Mother's, the food is heavenly." Happy with this program she embraced Bernardo, curling up in his arms again; then suddenly she asked: "What about your sister? When you heard the story of her being seduced by my brother and left pregnant, what was your impression?" Bernardo did not answer; Dora resumed: "As a boy you knew Debaldè, didn't you? But it isn't true, you know, that he had an affair with Maria."

"That's all news to me."

"You know what? I believe Debaldè is a virgin." Bernardo felt Dora's body within his arms, shaking with laughter. "Clement is very curious about Debaldè, I told him I'll

(1 8 6)

have the two of them meet; Debaldè often has lunch at Mother's, and Clement wants to hear the way he talks."

"In Venice everything becomes a stage, somehow."

"Not everything, Bernardo," she said, raising his hand to her lips.

"You're right, not everything," Bernardo said clumsily; the sound of his words was suffocated also because the girl was pressed tightly against him; he felt that small body, with limber joints and yet solid, the body of a golf player. Still contained in his arms, and turning around like a child in sleep with a kind of unconscious and voluptuous languor, Dora exposed her breast toward Bernardo, who casually put his hand on it. Once before, in Rome, in the same accidental way, he had found himself caressing her and returning her kisses without any words between them. Almost at once now the girl freed herself slowly, raised herself, and smiled.

"No," she said. "I'll admit that it would be . . . It would be curious perhaps; who knows?" She looked at him with unusually bright eyes: "Bernardo. Bernardo," she repeated to herself, as though savoring the name. "In Rome I had a reputation of being easy to get, and I would have had it here too, except that here in Venice people had rather lost track of me. And do you know why I had that reputation? Because I *was* easy, in a way, perhaps. Now I have been chaste for two years. That's something you didn't know, you who know everything."

Bernardo stretched out his arm and lifted the receiver from the cradle. "Didn't you want to call Enrico?" he asked without raising the receiver to his ear while the operator's voice could be heard from it, and then immediately that of the concierge who was audibly saying: 'Mr. Partibon, Mr. Partibon,' but Bernardo held the receiver away from himself, hanging between two fingers, black and buzzing like an insect, handing it over to Dora: "Take it, tell them to leave me alone."

Dora pressed the receiver to her ear, listening for a moment, then she said: "No, Mr. Partibon will not take any phone calls." She listened for a while longer, and then, covering the receiver with her hand she told Bernardo: "He says that they've been trying again twice to reach you from London, and if you are here, why don't you want to answer, he says." Bernardo took the receiver from her hand, sighed deeply, and said into the telephone: "Thank you, Predazzi, but please, forget it. Tell them that I'm not here. Right? And listen, Predazzi—that call to New York, please cancel that too. Thank you, thank youuuuu," he said, blocking the man's reply and handing the receiver back to Dora: "Go on, call Enrico, I really want to see him."

Enrico Fassola went into Bernardo's living room and found him sitting there, all dressed up, in deep conversation with Dora; he stopped behind her and caressed her hair, then shook hands with Bernardo with an amiable smile; one of his bicuspids was missing and he had a timid, slightly sibilant voice: "You'll stay here awhile, won't you? I hope we'll finally have time for a chat." He wore a very tight, dark-blue overcoat; in his left hand he held gray gloves and a black hat. He put them down, took off his overcoat and without taking his eyes away from Bernardo, asked: "How are you, Bernardo? I can call you by your first name, can't I?" as he sat down in an armchair between him and his sister.

With suppleness he raised his long narrow foot from the floor, to hold his knee in his interlaced hands; he frowned as if trying to recall something. "A lot of people," he said, "have talked to me about you with great admiration. With

(1 8 8)

great affection. Umberto Boschinetti. Firmino Ghezzi-Walther." He spoke in a precise and colorless manner, as if fulfilling an official duty.

"Bernardo's specialty," Dora inserted, "is to make friends with the husbands of his lady friends."

Enrico interrupted her with a look; he went on as if completing a list, for Bernardo, but there was a questioning shadow in his voice when he pronounced the new name: "And . . . Debaldè. Ugo Debaldè." He shrugged almost imperceptibly and had a vaguely apologetic smile; he threw himself back in the chair, stretching out both legs: "Mother used to know the poor Baroness. Debaldè is dying to see you. Tell me about America." But he did not wait for a reply, in fact his tone became lively and amused: "You'll find a different Debaldè from the one you used to know—all cleaned up—and he won't leave you in peace, because he is planning, among many other things, a trip to America; nowadays, for all kinds of people, a trip to America is the thing; are you aware of that, you who live there? Getting an assignment in America would horrify me because of the great number of people that would pour in on me from Italy."

He turned his head abruptly toward the door; somebody was tapping rhythmically on it with his finger tips, like a message in Morse code.

"That must be Clement. He brought me here in a motorboat, I don't know whose motorboat it was; he stopped to talk with some Americans he met in the elevator."

Meanwhile a young man had come in—not too tall, wearing a tweed jacket, corduroy pants, and dirty, thick white leather shoes; around his neck he wore a huge scarf in bright colors, which he unwrapped and threw near Enrico's overcoat. He asked: "What were you talking about?" He had intense, quick eyes; when they happened to linger on

(1 8 9)

something—an object, a person, as they did now on Dora —they seemed to soften and became questioning, worried.

"Clement, my love," the girl whispered. "Imagine, we were talking about Debaldè and his projects."

"I know everything." Having obtained Dora's answer, Clement started moving his eyes around again, on Bernardo, on Enrico. It was as if he had a particular understanding with each of them. But then his eyes returned to Dora; he sat on the arm of her chair, putting a hand on her shoulder. "I've received a cable, too," he said. Without interruption he turned to Bernardo: "I was with relatives of my mother's; Cristina let me have her motorboat; shall we go to San Piero in Volta to eat fish risotto? No—one does that sort of thing in the summer, and then, anyway," he turned to Enrico, "we are going to Mother's for lunch." And to Dora: "I mean of course your mother. She has guaranteed the presence of Debaldè."

"Did you talk to your mother about Ilse coming to Italy?" Dora asked.

Clement gave a restrained laugh, which Dora somehow found painful: "There is nothing to do. You can't talk about the dead."

"That's not true, Clement."

Clement smiled: "What do you know?" Dora kissed him on the cheek. "I was at the beach on the Lido," he went on, "the lighthouse pier. The military zones, the hospital. That waterfront line of hotels, far away, all closed. Look at this"—he offered Dora a pebble smoothed by the water, taking it away from her almost immediately—"it isn't much," and he put it in his pocket, laughing happily. When he was silent the others were silent too, acting either worried or as if he had promised them a show. "As a matter of fact," he said, raising his forefinger, "my mother and I are getting to be rather friendly; at any rate, we are mutually feeling the ground, getting to know each other; it's a little bit as though we were engaged." There was a new long silence, which he interrupted with a whisper: "Listen, listen," and they all could hear the siren of a boat from St. Mark's Basin, and then, at the striking of the hour, the church bells from Santa Maria del Giglio or perhaps from Santo Stefano, finally also the deep, precious ones from St. Mark; and here in the room, Clement's whisper: "Listen, listen." They were consciously savoring Venice, they let the sounds flow into them, also gondoliers' voices from the *traghetto,* the bumping and squeaking of boats against the wooden piles planted in the canal bottom, the deep dull honking of a public motorboat in the fog.

Bernardo had visions of childhood visits to Venice, he recalled the mixed smell of fog, of burning coal, and of food in the kitchen of the Partibon house at San Tomà, the smell of oil paint, varnish, and turpentine in the studio of his painter-uncle; and in the living room the mysterious and sweet smell of antique furniture.

"Why aren't we always together, all of us?" Clement asked. "You see, my idea of a Venice gathering was a good one; in Rome we hardly ever see each other."

He rose abruptly and went to the window; he raised the curtain and caught a glimpse of the Church of the Salute in the gray air, and said to himself, smiling: "That solid bulk with the curls," then he turned again to the others, and his eyes, full of doubt and pain, stopped on Bernardo: "Ilse and I," he asked, "why weren't we children like you?" His eyes moved on to Dora and Enrico: "I talked with your mother for hours," he said, "she has an incredible knowledge of three generations of Partibons, she told me stories about Bernardo here . . . Do you remember, Bernardo, the day of your cousin Giuliano's confirmation, here, in the Church of the Salute?" With his thumb he pointed to the window.

"Now, really," Bernardo said.

"She saw you that morning—she remembers you." And turning again to Dora and Enrico: "He had been brought from the country, a four-year-old child, and after his cousin's confirmation, everybody moved to the house for refreshments. And there he drank, all by himself, three quarters of a bottle of liqueur. I can see it myself . . ." Now he walked up and down the room, his eyes raised to the glass chandelier hanging from the ceiling: "I can see him, I can touch him, this child, himself not much bigger than a bottle, filling himself up with liqueur, his round face getting red and shiny, his blue eyes afloat . . ." Clement lowered his voice as if passing to an extremely confidential and delicate theme: "In his clenched fist, chubby and already robust, he was holding a biscuit, a *savoiardo*. 'Come now,' they said, stooping over him and trying to make him open his hand, 'we'll make a nice little package of *savoiardi* for you, so you can take it with you to Corniano,' but he didn't budge, his hands squeezing that particular *savoiardo* . . .

"He is a Partibon from the countryside, the rustic little cousin, already big at four years of age, and he was storing liqueur like a tank, since he couldn't take the bottle with him; and accustomed as he was to coarse country bread, he hung on to that fine biscuit, ready to defend it, like a mastiff puppy, meanwhile rendering it, by the way, inedible . . .

"Why," Clement repeated, "why weren't Ilse and I children like you? Why is it that in front of Ilse my mother can never, absolutely never have felt what anybody would feel in front of you, a four-year-old child, drunk with liqueur, and with that biscuit pasted in your little hand? Why?"

His voice was trembling, he had a lump in his throat,

(192)

perhaps tears in his eyes. "Clement, come here," Dora whispered. Meekly the young man went to sit near her again. Then he shook his head, passed his hand through his hair, smiled: "Don't be afraid," he said, "even if Ilse comes. This time I'll be much better. We are all getting older. We are getting at the *modus vivendi.*" Bernardo got up, grabbed Clement by the shoulders, shook him: "That liqueur introduced me to drinking," he said, as if comforting him, "it inoculated me. We at Corniano got our inoculation rather early, as far as that's concerned. If necessary, I can outdrink anybody, Americans, Bulgarians . . . In the country, from childhood on, who has ever drunk anything but wine and grappa?"

They all laughed with exaggeration; it was as though they wanted to show that they were happy together, that there was hope.

"And by the way," Bernardo said, "having lunch at your mother's is fine, but first I'll take you to St. Mark's for a drink." The idea of the Square in the autumn, the silver-lead color of the air, which covered even the gold of the church, attracted him enormously.

"What a divine day," Dora said while they got ready to leave.

CHAPTER EIGHT

Ugo Debaldè had started, immediately after the death of his mother, to dress much better; he had ordered even his deep-mourning suits in Rome, abandoning his old Venetian tailor, Gelusian, a man of distant Armenian origin. A veil of fat had grown on his healthy rosy flesh. He lived between Rome and Venice; when he was in Venice he spoke the dialect with ostentation and favored the company of ladies older than he, who could provide him with affable hospitality and a certain social luster excluding erotic pressures; Dora and Enrico's mother was one of them. Talking about her, Debaldè would say: "Fausta Fassola is one of my great passions," and in return would sometimes help her handle her affairs, thus substituting for her husband.

He liked to eat well; and the Fassolas' cook, Ortensia, was a pillar of the house left over from the family's grand epoch; she was seventy-five years old, very vigorous, and she cried easily; if untouched food was returned to the kitchen, Ortensia would break into sobs full of anger and melancholy.

Debaldè was now in Venice to stay at least one month, devoting himself to his favorite activity—organizing, as secretary general, large international cultural conventions.

The present one would have as its theme St. Mark the Evangelist, and scholars from all over the world would attend it, even American and Japanese. Pamphlets and leaflets were already being circulated, bearing as a coat of arms the noble, austere face of the winged Lion, emblem of St. Mark and of Venice. The seat of the convention would be the Orsenigo degli Specchi palace. Debaldè considered Venice supremely suitable for conventions of that sort; he saw them destined to bring new life to the city and to its old palaces, which, as private homes, were often too costly and uncomfortable.

Not so much because Debaldè was expected for lunch as because Dora and Enrico were in Venice and would bring Bernardo Partibon and Clement Blumenfeld, Mrs. Fassola had gone to the kitchen to help Ortensia. Dora, arriving with a shiny red face, found her there; with an arm around her daughter's waist, Fausta drew her close and they exchanged a long kiss. "They are all in the living room," the girl said somewhat redundantly because they could hear Bernardo's and Enrico's loud voices.

"Is the boy there too?" the mother asked, meaning Clement.

"Yes, he's there. Debaldè hasn't come yet. I am desperately fond of Bernardo." There was a damp wind outside, and walking toward the Piazza, to warm her hand, Dora had put it in Bernardo's overcoat pocket, entangling it with his own, and whispered to him: "Our hands are in bed together." Her bosom swelled visibly as she looked around and inhaled the air of the kitchen. She very much liked to eat; in Rome, she would know restaurants not according to the criteria of fashionableness but according to the quality of their cuisine, and she kept up to date on their specialties, and their ups and downs. Curiously now she realized that the most exciting smell in the Venice kitchen was that of celery mixed with the basic, steamy air of rice cooked in broth. "I have also prepared two or three very simple things, among others. I know Enrico likes them," the mother said, and Dora at once announced possessively: "Bernardo too."

Clement came in, looking around. He smiled and embraced Fausta from the back, kissing her hair. He left her abruptly and went to a window while her tender gaze followed him. From the window Clement looked below: there was an inside courtyard, very narrow, full of cats drenched with humidity. Then he turned his intense, restless eyes toward mother and daughter; he asked: "Where is Debaldè? Hadn't you promised us Debaldè? He and Bernardo haven't seen each other in twenty years."

"Think, how many things are happening," Dora said. "I've talked to Bernardo for hours and he has told me everything."

"What do you mean, 'everything'?"

Dora shrugged; with a toothpick she stabbed a roast potato and raised it to her lips: "Everything," she repeated. After tasting it, she said in a low voice: "If I could I would eat only potatoes."

"I made *Bratkartoffeln* the way Enrico likes them," the mother said.

"Bernardo and Debaldè," Clement was saying, "used to see each other when Bernardo was at school in Venice and that crook, the Baroness Debaldè, ran a boarding house on the Zattere."

"The passion for Central European food is something Enrico developed when he was consul in Austria," Dora said, stabbing another potato.

"Mrs. Debaldè was a friend of mine," Fausta was saying to Clement, laughing softly. Fausta was a small, compact woman, much more active now than before the war: her sky-blue eyes, for which she had always been famous, stood out with greater intensity and beauty than ever, now that her hair was a dark silver. "Debaldè is still the owner of that boarding house," she added.

"Among many other things," Dora said.

"Among many other things," said the mother.

"I have decided that perhaps I'll marry a professor without a penny," Dora said.

Fausta bent over the gas stove to put out the fire under a little pot containing an important sauce; she took her apron off. Ortensia, after her major labors, had placed herself on a straw chair in a corner, supervising the final cooking operations with a fixed smile. "Relax," Fausta told her, caressing her cheek, "everything will be all right." And to her daughter: "Did you give those people something to drink?"

"Enrico made a martini."

"No, I made it," Clement said.

Dora looked at him with anxiety. Clement was like that: he would say perhaps the most insignificant thing, and yet everybody would stop talking and look at him with worry. He was the only man who sometimes made her feel certain that he was suffering. On the contrary, Dora mused, compared to Clement a man like her father made you laugh, who for at least twelve years, retired at Corniano, found in suffering his main occupation. She went over to Clement, and before taking him by the arm to follow her mother into the living room, she embraced him, pressing her forehead on his chest. "You always smell divine," she said. The doorbell rang three times, one long and two short. "This is Debaldè," Fausta said.

They went into the living room to wait for the new guest. The room had a low stuccoed ceiling, the furniture was eighteenth century, fluid silver reflections from the canal filtered through the light yellow curtains. Enrico was talking to Bernardo with unusual liveliness.

" . . . oriented toward the extreme right . . . stronger in the West than elsewhere . . . tell me if I'm wrong . . . where do you usually live?"

Bernardo was taken aback, speechless, as if he himself were wondering where he usually lived. He seemed relieved when Fausta and Dora appeared; Fausta went to him with arms outstretched, rose on tiptoe to put her hands on his shoulders and kiss him.

There were squeakings of steps in the entrance, and soon Ugo Debaldè came in. He was wearing a light-colored flannel suit, thick and soft. Blond, he had blue eyes and a rich velvety mustache. He kissed Fausta's hand, looked around, and his eyes stopped on Bernardo: "Am I dreaming?" he cried happily. "Partibon! Bernardo Partibon!" He turned to the others and asked in a suddenly shrill voice: "Do you realize what an extraordinary moment this is?" But he stopped abruptly and threw himself into an armchair, seating himself comfortably and looking all around with bright eyes.

From near the window Clement moved toward him; when he stood in front of him, he pointed his finger: "So you are Debaldè," he said. "Very good. You were missing in my collection."

"But we know each other," Debaldè said encouragingly. Seeing that Clement had decided to regard this as their first encounter in life, he said: "I am delighted," and although the move cost him some effort, he got up, extending his soft hand.

Clement shook it and looked at him with a quick smile instantaneously turned off again. "How are you?" he asked. "And how is Christian civilization? Are you saving it?"

Once more he produced his unyielding smile, then his face darkened: "I saw some of your recent announcements, and I must admit that your idea of an international convention of St. Mark scholars is your best yet. You didn't know you were being followed so closely in your cultural activities? Look at this." He pulled a leaflet out of his pocket and gave it to Debaldè. With a kind of stubborn sadness he went on: "I'm a stranger in Italy, I'm observing Italy as a stranger," while Debaldè sat down again, drew out of his breast pocket a beautiful pair of glasses of a somewhat antiquated style, put them on, and threw a glance at the leaflet, immediately returning it to Clement; his quiet, watchful look lingered on the young man; he clearly postponed the idea of answering him.

Enrico was following them with increasing interest; he told Debaldè: "I read somewhere that the Cardinal Patriarch has given your project his patronage. What would you like to drink? Shall I give you some vermouth? I find you looking very well, Debaldè, you've put on some weight."

"Yes, Enrico, thank you, some Punt e Mes vermouth."

Bernardo was seated in a deep chair and moved his large oval eyes around: "I see some beautiful things here," he said. "Those two little chairs especially, they are worth the rest of the furniture put together." Debaldè looked at him in astonishment.

Fausta, who was standing, small and straight, near Bernardo's chair, exclaimed: "What an expert you are, Bernardo; they are the best things we have, and no wonder: they come from the former house of your cousins at San Tomà." With her hand she smoothed his curly hair: "I'll call you simply Bernardo, is that all right?"

"Thank you," Bernardo said.

"At some point your cousins lost everything and their home fell apart," Dora said. "Later, for that matter, we lost everything and fell apart too, except that perhaps at our stage of the game things like that did not mean much any more."

"Did not mean much?" Debaldè asked with curiosity.

"It's people like you, Debaldè, who still have a fixation about money," Dora said affably.

Ortensia came in, wearing a very complicated apron covered with lacework; she carried a large tray with cocktail hors d'oeuvres.

"How marvelous," Fausta exclaimed, "put it here."

There were very thin slices of prosciutto wrapped around delicate breadsticks; little disks of toast were supporting a thin slice of lemon and an anchovy; there were even candied chestnuts wrapped in an Italian equivalent of bacon. All looked at the tray with interest, pondering their choice. While Clement was making another pitcher of martinis, the conversation continued in part between full mouths.

"I'm crazy about all of these American-style things," Debaldè said, swallowing a bacon-chestnut. "I don't care for cocktails, but little hors d'oeuvres are one of my passions." He turned to Bernardo: "As an American, you are probably already bored with this sort of thing, but as for us . . . Fausta and, I must add, my poor mother, were pioneers in the field. The salads, too." Bernardo did not react. "I'll come to America, perhaps rather often in the next few years. They do great things, in my area of activity. You and I must have a nice long chat. They have great means. When are you going back?"

"Back where?" Bernardo asked with such a dumfounded air that Debaldè was paralyzed in his turn and lost the thread of his talk.

Clement was pouring fresh martinis. Enrico told him: "You are a real master," and let Clement fill his glass as if it had been plain water. Enrico seemed to be quietly sparkling, he was studying Debaldè with a sly, intent look. "He is marvelous," he murmured to himself, "he is sublime." To find something comparable, he had to look back in memory to some Washington days with Donato Plea: then they had been especially fascinated by a government man on his first American visit; but Debaldè seemed even more promising. He had known him for at least thirty years but he had never had a chance to examine the present Debaldè in detail. Still quite young and even rather *handsome*. When they moved to the dining room and sat around the table, Enrico observed that Debaldè wore a waistcoat and that an ancient watch chain, of very fine gold, was festooning it. Besides, he pushed a corner of his napkin under his collar, and he had that nineteenth-century mustache. He was speaking about some of his recent reading.

"There is a flourishing of the novel in Italy too, but one has so little time to read. My favorite would be Perucchini; have you read his novel, Bernardo, *The Idiosyncrasies?* It's an extremely perceptive book, with some extraordinary grafts from the vernacular of the Mantua region."

"It's amazing, Debaldè, how you can talk about any subject in the appropriate language," Enrico said.

"But why don't you tell us about America," Debaldè said to Bernardo. "What's being written in America? I must confess that I'm still back with Hemingway, I've read everything he's written, but God knows what exciting things are being written now by the young. Isn't it true that there is a new eagerness, a new wave of spirituality?"

The agape was conducted on two food levels. A main basic line was represented by rice cooked in broth and boiled meat, as ordinary as bread; minor lines were superimposed upon it, crossing each other, comprising dishes which went all the way from very minute and immensely appetizing shrimp to vegetable soufflé with béchamel sauce, of sublime simplicity. The most classic pieces, along these minor lines, were broiled fish and liver alla Veneziana; each new dish tickled the taste by never being offered in excessive quantities. To dishes of her Venetian nation—where the Mediterranean, the Near East, and Mittel-europa crossed— Mrs. Fassola's genius had adapted principles of variety and distribution borrowed from the Nordic smörgåsbord. The discovery was part of a way of life adopted by herself and her daughter when the father had settled at Corniano and the two of them had become like sisters, united in their survival to many domestic and national misfortunes, maintaining their feminine symbiosis even after the girl had gone to Rome to live with her brother Enrico. By letter or *viva voce,* Dora always told her mother everything, important events and trifling ones, jokes, worries, and loves. This confidence was their secret, and it would last forever. Dora sensed that she would soon get married, which meant that that capacity for survival, so acute in their small and malleable Venetian bodies, those tastes and pleasures, that cuisine, would be perpetuated and grafted by Dora, through marriage and a home of her own, into the wider pattern of the Italian nation. This, she felt, was the sense of her migration to Rome. She looked around herself with pride. Even the wines were very familiar; the basic one of the house came from Corniano, the others were from the province of Verona. She drank much wine, she and Bernardo exchanged looks that were frankly brightened by the remembrance of the long deep kiss they had exchanged that morning. Exalted, she listened to the calls of the gondoliers, the honking of motorboats in the fog, she saw familiar furniture and house objects: the multicolored porcelain birds, the silver snuffboxes lying on damask tablecloths, and stirring softly above her the ghostly reflections of water on the ceiling, which were to her like the very rhythm of blood. This rhythm Dora would reveal to a man, giving herself to him; but it must be a man wanting to be absorbed and dominated by it, so that she considered she had been right in keeping within certain limits with Bernardo. She had used him, because their brief embraces had contributed to making her feel that her period of chastity was coming close to an end; next week, almost certainly, she would give herself to Ovidio.

Debaldè was talking about scandals on the Lido during the previous summer.

Clement was saying: "Don't tell me, Debaldè, that you too are a police worshiper."

At first Debaldè's voice was like a shrill sob: "Police worshiper?" Then in a practical, debonair tone, affecting a local accent: "Enrico here, who for God's sake is a man of order, knows very well what I mean. Hmm."

"Explain to us what you mean," Fausta's harmonious voice intervened.

"Explain to me what you mean by 'man of order,' " Enrico inserted.

"Oh, come, come," Debaldè said, sounding now like an old Venetian, a sweet-sour Pantaloon, "why should we allow our Venice to be the stage for stupidly dirty shows? Let them stay back in their own countries. Desecrators. Dirty little pigs," he added domestically, as though he were scolding children, "with their little orgies, their strip teases"—he raised his voice conclusively—"and their perversions."

"Be precise," Dora said.

"The things that happened in the house of that . . . what was the name of the painter?"

"What painter?" Bernardo asked as if waking up.

"Beddoes," Fausta said.

"That's it."

"Beddoes is not a pansy, you know," Fausta volunteered evenly.

"Craig Beddoes? An American painter?" Bernardo asked.

Debaldè said, encouraged: "An abstract painter. And mind you, I am very much in favor of abstract painters; in my house in Rome I have nothing but abstractionists."

"Why?"

"You haven't told us yet what they were doing," Clement said, and everybody turned to him.

Debaldè seemed to remember something; he asked Clement: "Did you know that man Beddoes?"

"I know him, and my sister Ilse was present that evening on the Lido."

"Now I see the connection. Ilse Blumenfeld." Affably: "Well, then, my dear, you know things much better than I, don't you?" Then, reflectively: "Besides some American girls, they also had some strange little dancers whom I think Beddoes kept in his house—adolescents, I don't know whether from Java or Tahiti—and he wasn't content with having them dance naked in his own house, he had to have them do it also on the tables at this place on the Lido where they went in a state of already advanced inebriety. When the police came, they were all ready to come out into the street, and they were planning to repeat the show on board, on the boat going back to Venice, so they just had to be stopped. Among the misfortunes of that painter Beddoes there is also the fact that he is very rich; he comes here with the idea of making a harem for himself and a Lord Byron kind of life; he buys one of our magnificent palaces—lucky thing they stopped him in time. I've been told, I don't know whether it's true, that he was associated with the ill-famed Rioseco."

(204)

"Who is Rioseco?" Bernardo asked.

"A very high-ranking pimp."

"Have you already tried the broiled fish, Debaldè?" Fausta asked.

But Debaldè was elaborating: "He wanted to buy one of our magnificent palaces on the Grand Canal, the whole building, to transform it from top to bottom into a bordello."

"He had got it into his mind," Fausta explained to Bernardo, "to resuscitate the type of well-bred Renaissance courtesan like Veronica Franco, for example. Sumptuous background, very high prices."

"Good music, good books," Enrico said.

"Now, I hope you won't call a man a police worshiper," Debaldè said, still in his vernacular debonair tone, "if he warmly approves of certain measures."

"What measures?" Fausta asked in a conversational tone; she put her hand on the back of Clement's and looked at him with tenderness.

Clement in turn caressed Fausta's protecting hand, murmuring to himself: "Loaded with wine. When they are like that, they look like girls from the Venetian countryside. Besides Ilse, another one was Corinne Pauling, a great friend of mine, with glasses and a round head, a graduate of Bryn Mawr. She too, when she drinks, looks as though she were born in the Venetian countryside; wine drunkenness gives that kind of coloring."

Debaldè observed him, shaking his head as though he were watching a delirious man; Bernardo listened to him, understanding everything, but keeping his eyes half closed, lowered on his plate.

Then Debaldè reacted to Fausta: "You ask me what measures?" His voice was guttural but still friendly: "Heavens, police measures, of course. Throwing them out of the country, politely but firmly—that's the only way to handle individuals like that; they gave them a week's time to go and camp somewhere outside of Italy."

"The interesting thing about Ilse . . ." Dora was starting.

"Cut it out," Clement whispered, "change the subject."

In the distraction created by Ortensia, who came in too early with a pastry tray, Enrico whispered to Clement: "My colleague over there is doing something about it too; I got a cable from him. You told me yourself that Corinne Pauling has been readmitted into the country, so you'll see, Ilse too will be in Rome for your exhibition."

"Change the subject," Clement cut him off too.

"My dear friends," Debaldè announced," I ask for nothing better than to change the subject. I just don't like dirt, that's all."

Enrico was absorbed by a vision of Debaldè as a boy. On account of the boarding house, Ugo had had English friends, a bit clumsy, well scrubbed with hard brushes. For a time, he had imitated them. Athletics. Soap and showers. His phrase: "I grant you that the cleanliness of the soul is more important, but I assure you, I can't bear bad odors." Some writings in chalk had appeared suddenly one morning on the walls of the boarding house: UGO FAG, and then, in a more cultivated style: DEBALDE SODOMITE.

Debaldè turned to his old companion Bernardo: "You are not saying a single word, Bernardo, my friend. And I'm sure you have so much to tell me."

"I am listening to you. I am even more of a stranger than Clement. In fact, much more; he has been in Italy a long time—Rome, Venice, Corniano too."

"I'm trying to persuade Bernardo to come to Corniano with me today," Enrico said.

"You are a sculptor, aren't you?" Debaldè said to Clement. "You see that I am well informed about *your* activities too. When I'm in Rome I don't miss a single show; unfortunately I'll miss yours because I have the convention here. Is this pastry," he said suddenly, turning to Fausta, overwhelmed with admiration, "really made at home?" In his look he included Ortensia, who blushed. "I don't know," he went on, "perhaps it's because I am older than you all and have mellowed with age like a good wine. Do you know how I see myself, the older I get? Like a Dutchman. One of those large, placid Dutchmen with very comfortable shoes? I remember one of those at the boarding house, he was so very devoted to Mother."

Enrico commented cautiously: "But you, Debaldè, are a very active man . . ."

"For instance, I have never been in the least interested in getting into Parliament. Believe me, I am a lazy man." After a moment of reflection, Debaldè turned to Clement and added: "You artists have the right idea."

"Why didn't you ever get married," Bernardo asked, "perhaps to a nice Venetian girl like our Dora here?"

"He would never take somebody like me," Dora said sweetly. The two exchanged a curiously sad look.

Then Debaldè, as if announcing that for the moment he had stopped eating, threw himself back in his chair and put the napkin on the table. Looking at Bernardo, he sighed deeply. He asked: "Have you seen Maria?" A long silence followed.

"No, he hasn't seen her," Clement answered rapidly. "You would know it if he had, wouldn't you, Debaldè? You control Maria, don't you?"

"What a curious idea." Debaldè looked around, appealing to the others.

"It isn't that you are lovers," Dora said, "it is that you help her as you help other people. Everybody has been telling Bernardo that you were the person to go to if he wanted to get in touch with Maria, especially since she and her husband separated."

"That was a very, very sad decision," Debaldè said.

"Not at all," Fausta cut in, explaining to Bernardo, "on the contrary, I think that your sister's marriage to Gervasutti was a mistake from the beginning; by separating from her husband she has slightly corrected the error she made fifteen years ago, or whenever it was; anyway, shortly after my Massimo died. I remember Vittoria Partibon, the most balanced person in the family, saying even at the time: 'What this boy Gervasutti is doing, marrying Maria, who is already pregnant, is not a *beau geste;* in fact I find it rather repulsive.' And I would have liked to stop him, precisely because Maria was bearing the child of my child, if you really want to know."

"But of course," Dora said, "in fact the *beau geste* element was the creepiest thing in the whole picture: *beaux gestes* are always very creepy things."

"I know all about it," Bernardo said, "I have always known everything from afar."

"From afar," Debaldè said with relief, "so you can't have the right perspective. Who could ever have told you that I control Maria, and foolish things like that?"

"I'll mention one case," Bernardo said, "that English Monsignor, when I was in Rome and I asked for the hundredth time about Maria at the San Luigi Hotel—he told me you would know everything."

"Which Monsignor?"

"He lives in Rome," Clement said, "at the San Luigi, which, if I remember correctly, belongs to your hotel chain, Debaldè. Monsignor Ashton. A terrific connoisseur of wines. I studied him one evening at the restaurant. He doesn't know me."

Debaldè shook his head: "The hotel belongs only partly to us," he said, "and I bet you," he added affably, "that in a moment you, Clement, will be describing Monsignor Ashton to me as the priest who eats capon and fills his belly with wine—a propaganda vignette of fifty years ago."

"Not at all, he is a very elegant Englishman and a real expert, he knows French wines magnificently. I've only talked to him over the telephone. He believes I'm German or Russian."

Debaldè shook his head again, without wanting to understand more and without appearing at all disconcerted. "All right then," he said to Bernardo, "why didn't you look for me? It would have given me great joy."

Bernardo, his huge head bent, mumbled confusedly: "Well, I have understood that one had better let things happen, just like that."

Clement raised his voice: "Bernardo Partibon has come back to Italy after twenty years to try and establish authentic relationships, with people, and with his own memories. The authentic relationships he has found are mostly accidental. With new people, or at any rate, not with the people he was looking for."

"Did you go to Corniano to your mother?" Debaldè asked, sticking to the obvious.

"Come to Corniano with me," Enrico said. "You can stay there a couple of days. I'll call my father's house and tell them to inform your mother and Caterina. Nothing could be simpler."

"Nothing could be simpler," Bernardo said. "I haven't seen Mother in twenty years."

"Shall we have coffee in the living room?" Fausta suggested.

In the living room, besides coffee, of perfectly correct strength and temperature, Ortensia had also prepared a great variety of liqueurs and of bitter chocolates. Debaldè took a crème de menthe and sank down in a large sofa next to Clement, a young man whom he would remember and describe, by and large, as attractive and redeemable.

"I know a lot about you, Debaldè," the young man was telling him now with some sadness while the women were pouring coffee, cognac, kümmel, and offering bitter chocolates on little trays in the San Marco style of silverware, "also because, gathering data on Bernardo for a possible biography, the name Debaldè occurs . . ."

Debaldè was now smiling like a huge, peaceful cat; he relaxed, convinced that only half of what Clement said was understandable. "Well, of course," he said vaguely, "our friend Bernardo, all these years . . . But it is true, isn't it," he asked Bernardo, "that it was my mother who started you on your career?"

"No," Bernardo said, "that's not true. The one who did, if anybody, was a man called Gutkind."

"You oversimplify things, Debaldè," Clement said. "Ask me. I know everything."

"Of course, Bernardo, you've been away a dreadfully long time," Debaldè resumed. "And now you find yourself in a completely different Italy—let alone what happened in your own family. You must really feel lost," he said, scrutinizing Bernardo while he stroked his mustache with his forefinger, "I can't even imagine how lost somebody like you must feel: you have chosen a life of uprooted internationalism, you have dissipated yourself in places like Texas, like California, haven't you?"

Bernardo did not understand him and did not know what to say. He offered some words to fill the silence: "I have friends in California. Among others, my son lives there with his mother."

"You see?" Debaldè shook his head.

(2 1 0)

"I tried to talk with my son yesterday, but when I called he was out."

"On Bernardo's biography the sun never sets," Clement said.

"What?" Debaldè asked.

"In California it's nine hours earlier than here," Dora said, "for example."

"Time-space," Debaldè observed, becoming eloquent again. "Multiply the thing by a thousand, by a million, and it will be like communicating with a different epoch, won't it? These are the immense perspectives opened by space exploration—or by science fiction, if you wish."

"As long as it's only a difference of nine hours, I find that much more amusing," Dora said.

Debaldè shrugged. Then he started thinking aloud: "Well, Bernardo . . . really, you know, you've lost the rhythm. Let's hope you stay a long while among us, so you'll really be able to try and understand what has happened here. And, yes, I am talking also about your immediate family circle—Maria; her daughter."

"Look, Debaldè," Clement cut in, "don't forget that I knew that girl better than you did." Dora looked at him anxiously.

"That may very well be, my friend," Debaldè agreed.

"Change the subject," Dora said. She exchanged an understanding look with her mother.

But Clement went on: "I even accompanied her a couple of times to the mental hospital where she visited her old schoolteacher. It's because of those visits that you gave her a medal, isn't it?"

Debaldè said soberly: "They awarded her a Caritas award. These awards are given for signal acts of charity. A very beautiful institution, which deserves to be expanded." He smiled at Bernardo, at Enrico.

Then Clement also turned to Enrico, almost crying. "I don't know what you ever thought of her, of that little girl of your dead brother, but I'm telling you, when she died too, and they started wanting to make a little saint of her, in the same way as they had once made him a hero of the fatherland, it was I who went to implore Massenti: 'Tear the whole thing apart, try to stop . . .'"

Enrico was silent; there was a contraction of his lips, a grimace rather than a smile.

Meanwhile Debaldè was saying: "Massenti, that's a good one." He sniffed.

"I have talked to that fellow Massenti," Bernardo said.

"Pernicious," Debaldè went on. "First in that infernal magazine he handles the Caritas awards—which are a fine, dignified institution—as if they were a beauty contest. Then, for example, he goes to your dying father and pulls out of him statements which we may well call iniquitous . . ."

"What statements are you talking about?" Fausta asked.

Dora answered her: "You know it too. Maria's father said that she would have been perfectly capable of making her daughter a martyr in order to have her die in the odor of sanctity. Rather witty, I find. I adored Odo Partibon."

"Unforgettable old man," Fausta confirmed.

Debaldè went on: "Massenti finally produced just a couple of local-color sketches rather than anything else; I'm sure Perineschi must have put the brake on him; but suppose that some day, drunk with grappa as he is practically all the time, he should go around repeating iniquitous statements like that . . ."

Blandly, courteously, Clement asked: "Would that endanger your chances to make the right moves in order eventually to initiate a beatification trial?"

While Clement was formulating his question, Debaldè

followed him, soundlessly moving his lips as though he were mentally repeating Clement's words to himself in order to believe his own ears. Then he burst out, dazzled: "Fantastic—this picture you've made up of the whole thing. Fantastic. So that's the way you visualize Debaldè: the man in Rome, the influential friend, the one who can obtain favors from government offices. Except that here, instead of a government office, there is a Church authority, and the favor would consist in pulling the right strings to obtain the beatification of a relative. That's it, isn't it? I've hit the bull's eye, haven't I? And a perfectly smooth story it is, too. It has only one drawback: even as simple hypothesis, it is the wildest and most grotesque fantasy, coming from people who"—and his voice became suddenly low and warm— "like you, Clement, are looking desperately for something in which to believe."

There was a considerable period of silence.

"I know what I'm talking about, my boy," Debaldè added by way of softening his formal speech with a kindly domestic appendix.

Clement observed him pensively; then again in that courteous manner he said: "Perhaps neither of us knows what the other one is talking about. As usual, words have no value. If, for example, I should say: 'I was very fond of that little girl, I loved that little girl,' these phrases would be devoid of meaning. I know that."

Debaldè brightened up again: "That's what I'm telling you. You are feeling your way in the dark. You are afraid to admit your very . . . " He stopped; by now Clement was very obviously redeemable; Debaldè could listen to him with a compassionate victor's smile when Clement resumed:

"In fact, Debaldè, I could give you some ideas. Let's start from the concept that that extraordinary little girl may have created a halo of charity for herself, in perhaps heroic measure, going to visit the sick, et cetera. Isn't that it? Now, these sick people, as in the case of her old teacher, often happened to be the mentally ill. Well, you know better than I do that for a beatification you have to have miraculous recoveries that occur through the intercession . . . "

"You know more than I do, my boy," Debaldè said, now almost amused, the cheerful Venetian.

"Well, briefly—have you ever thought about miraculous *mental* recoveries? Think about it. You have at least thirty years' time and you need to prove two miracles, if I'm not mistaken."

"You are more of an expert than I am. But if you loved that little girl, stick to that. It's a beautiful memory. An incarnation of goodness. Don't smile like that. Petty cynicism."

Now it was Clement's turn to look around and appeal to the others; then he came back to Debaldè: "I like you, you know. You sit there, so cozy and happy . . . You decide about good and evil . . . Now, take a man like me. You see, Debaldè . . . for example, let us say I think of the last twenty or thirty years of history, and then I tell myself, if you belong to a human race that has allowed certain things to happen without at least committing universal suicide as a gesture of collective logic—I am not saying 'expiation'; I say 'simple logic'—then you have no right to decide . . . I keep quiet . . . "

"Oh, no, no, my son . . . " Debaldè broke out. He sounded a little theatrical, but he was deeply moved: "How can you claim so much despair, all for yourself?"

"Try to understand me. I live very well, you know. Don't worry about me. I have friends, I even have some family, imagine that. My sister and I are like one—even if we were often kept apart—also because she gets expelled from coun-

tries, as we were mentioning earlier. I am very interested in
my sculpture. I am curiously lucky with women. But I tell
myself: the whole thing is a gift, an absurd gift. I mean that
if we are going to get one of the bombs, with global destruc-
tion and everything, I will think: Well, what else could we
expect?"

Debaldè let his eyes wander over Clement's face. Then,
lowering his eyelids, he concluded: "A struggling soul. I am
happy to have met you. I should like to have a long talk
with you." Then, cheerfully, fraternally: "Why don't you
come to one of our conventions? I would be infinitely interested in a contribution from you—a young man's testimony."

Ilse was awakened by the glare of fog from the canyon,
even more piercing than that of the sun. She didn't immediately recognize that small wood-paneled room with the red
carpeting. It wasn't the very first time that she slept in a
man's house without going to bed with him, but at any rate
the situation was rather unusual. Also because she did not
remember exactly when she had got there and gone to
sleep.

Plea came in bringing a tray with orange juice, tea and
toast: "I heard you move," he said, "in a moment I would
have called you myself. It's very early; you probably slept
about three hours. You told me that you want . . ."

"I did? Yes," Ilse said in a raucous whisper, "the airplane
at noon, and I still have things to do. Everything, in fact."
She rubbed her eyes with her fists; she still felt the anguish
of sleep. Plea placed the glass in her hand; she drank her
orange juice blindly. She began a series of sighs and cough-
ings in various tones; she blew her nose; finding her voice
again she spoke, forming each word with care, as if answering a difficult question: "If I had come to bed with you,

I wouldn't have been much good." She seemed pleased at having been able to organize coherent words. "But I swear . . ." She took his hand and smiled; her face looked childish but destroyed, desperate with sleep. Her widened eyes could not yet see. "Listen . . . look, I swear, I'll come back from Europe quite soon, and I'll come and live with you. For a while."

"Do you really want to leave now?"

"Oh, yes . . . yes. Yes." She smiled. She was almost awake.

"Our cables are in Italy now, they must have got there several hours ago; while you slept I sent some others to various people." Ilse looked at him with gratitude but without really listening to what he was saying. Plea made much use of the telegraph and the telephone, prompted by a kind of generic nervousness rather than by real belief in those phantom contacts.

After they finished their tea, Plea put the tray on a chair and left the room. Coming back a few minutes later, he found Ilse all dressed; she took him by the hand. "First thing, I have to go home and change; dressed like this in the morning, I look a little bit like a whore; at any rate, I have to change, I'll put on my traveling clothes; I'll take only one bag with me. Then I have to leave the car . . ."

There were always problems with cars. "Where? Who is going to keep it for you?" Plea interrupted her also because he had decided not to let her do all the talking, these few hours they were going to spend together.

As if guessing that, Ilse said only: "Larry," but now that the way was free, Plea kept silent; so she resumed: "Are you going to take me to the airport? Last night you more or less promised you would." She looked at him, still holding his hand, then she rose on tiptoe to kiss his forehead.

"Who is Larry?"

(2 1 6)

"The son of Bernardo and the Peach. Come with me, and you'll meet the Peach."

In little more than an hour she changed clothes, packed, locked up the house, and put her one bag, not too large, into the trunk of the car.

It turned out that the divorced wife of Bernardo Partibon lived with their son on the old Topanga Canyon Road. The house was old too, large, white frame, with a lot of staircases, and an intricate garden, which originally had perhaps been devised as a Japanese garden and was now cluttered with laundry hung out to dry, a barbecue pit, faded canvas chairs, and unusually meek cats. Ilse came in through the kitchen door, which they found open, and signaled their presence by a whistle. She made Plea sit in the little living room filled with old American furniture, an upright piano, a telescope, a reading desk with the huge Webster dictionary open; and she went up the wooden staircase to call Beverly and her son.

They all came down and greeted Plea as though they knew him already. The Peach had blond hair turning gray; actually rosy, velvety skin; and affectionate, questioning eyes. Larry was already almost the size of his father, and he had his mother's eyes; Partibon family traits were evident in the shape of his face, especially in the distance between the eyes. From deep stratifications of memory, there came back to Plea visions of the now remote Giorgio Partibon, except that in the case of Lorenzo, or Larry, those traits reappeared in gigantically magnified forms, as was the case with the local forms of nature, such as trees or waves. Plea felt he was being caught in the net of those families again. Almost defensively he accepted Beverly's offer of a Bloody Mary.

While Beverly was pouring the tomato juice into tall

glasses, adding vodka, pepper, and lime, Larry was talking to Ilse in what sounded to Plea like college-student English; he was promising her that on her return from Europe her car would be like new; he announced with knowing pride that he would perhaps, for his own amusement, put a new engine in the car. He shifted to Italian, which in his case was a Venetian-American mixture, as he said reassuringly: "I'll take care of everything." Then he gave Ilse a large bulky envelope: "Will you give this to my father? There are also newspaper clippings here that will make him laugh." He seemed to imply that his father wouldn't want to miss the sequence in some of the comic strips.

Larry had sat down near Ilse on a small Victorian sofa; they were holding hands; he was twice as big as she but she treated him like a son or, say, like a kid brother. Over the mantelpiece hung a portrait of him at the age of eight, not very different from now, painted by his mother. Plea was turning his eyes from the original to the portrait when Beverly interrupted him, laughing, asking him in English not to look; she put the tall Bloody Mary in his hand.

It was so strong and peppered that it brought tears to his eyes. Beverly took a sip from the other glass she had prepared and passed it on to Ilse after an approving nod; she lit a cigarette and sat down with the others. She asked her son whether he wanted to prepare a drink for himself but the boy said he was in training; both mother and son laughed.

Plea turned to Ilse with worried, questioning looks; in about two hours her airplane would leave; the airport was in a different part of the city; the girl looked serenely comfortable, as if she were planning to spend the day in this house.

"Where will you go?" Larry asked idly. "Only to Rome, or to Israel too?"

Ilse explained to Plea: "Through my father I'm getting a

ticket that will take me as far as Israel, if I want to. Of course I pay for it, but rather less than the regular price." She replied to Larry: "I have two weeks' vacation in all, you know." She took a sip; she lit a cigarette.

"How do you like your job?" Larry asked. "How do you like putting numbers into squares?"

"I'm very good at it. And then, the hours suit me. But if I find a job in Rome, perhaps I'll stay there a while."

"With Chet?"

"No, not with Chet."

Then for about a half-hour they went on talking about people Plea didn't know. He was overwhelmed by a feeling of serenity. He felt neglected but absolutely happy. He decided that if Ilse was going to miss the plane, so much the better; he realized that he felt comfortable in this house, nobody was bothering him, he wouldn't go to the office in the afternoon either. He sincerely praised the portrait over the mantelpiece and persuaded the Peach to let him see her other paintings.

They crossed a corner of the garden, unkempt but well utilized; they had to stoop as they passed through the wash hung out to dry; they got to the little wooden structure among trees where Beverly did her painting. On the walls and on the easel were several portraits of the same man. Plea even recognized him—a man called Tynant, art critic on a local newspaper; Beverly, laughing, described him as her fiancé. The rest were portraits of children with a pensive expression, which in some cases degenerated into open sadness. Beverly said that she did a number of them on commission, and that by adding this income to what she received through Bernardo's business manager, she and her son lived awfully well. In a corner of the room there was a little bed; Beverly went over and lay down across it with the back of her head against the wall and her chin pressed on her chest; from that position she studied the latest portrait of Tynant on the easel for a long while. She seemed to forget Plea's presence.

Ilse's and Larry's voices were heard from the garden; then the two of them came into the studio talking incessantly, exchanging little wordplays and jokes. There was very little time before the plane left, and there was the problem of transportation, which until then they had not given much thought. After a prolonged discussion they concluded that they would leave without the Peach in Ilse's car, which Larry would later bring back and keep there after taking Plea home—unless Plea wanted to come back for lunch, a decision which they finally agreed to postpone until later. Larry was driving, so that Ilse sat between him and Plea.

As soon as the car moved, Ilse started talking and never stopped. She talked all the way down the canyon, and then along the ocean with its fog, its powerful sea gulls and mammoth, gray breakers; Plea not only listened to her, he felt her talk like a vibration as she lay in his arms against his chest. "You are like a waterfall," he cried in the wind, and he was really hoping that she would soon return and come and live with him for a while.

"Look . . . listen, that's what keeps you alive, you know—words. That's why it doesn't really feel as though I were leaving, going rather far, in fact. Wherever I am, the circle is formed again, and one talks. Italy is extraordinary from that point of view, and Venice beats anything. I'm a Venetian on my mother's side, as you know; between her and me there is no rapport."

Larry was driving at top speed but with such steadiness and self-assurance that he gave the impression of going slowly. After some reckoning Plea concluded that the boy couldn't be old enough even for the most precocious of driving licenses; on the other hand, he was sure that Larry at forty would look more or less the same as he did now. He was hoping that Bernardo too would come there soon. Ilse kept reviewing themes of the night before, her mother and Clement, Santa Monica and Venice, the Partibons, the Blumenfelds, places and events, which her words seemed to liberate from space and time—with Plea listening, caught again in the net, squeezing her as if to hold her back. She did not stop talking until they were separated by the gate and by officers in light-colored uniforms. At the last moment Ilse did not bother about Larry's presence and kissed Plea repeatedly.

It had been decided that Bernardo would go to Corniano with Enrico. By now, each person in Fausta's living room had his own conversation refrain. "You've lost the rhythm, Bernardo, but I really hope we may recapture you. Big things. That little girl . . ."

"No one in the world has known her as well as . . ."

"Tell us how she really was, Clement, since you . . ."

"She was a child but she was already wonderful company. In appearance she was something of a tomboy. I would have her ride on horseback with me. A serious little Venetian country girl, with a straight nose like Signora Margherita, Bernardo's mother; do you recall, Bernardo, although it's twenty years ago, how straight your mother's nose is? At school with the nuns, the child must have looked a bit aloof, keeping to herself, like her mother when she was with the nuns here in Venice and had secret meetings with Bernardo. Even this solitude could be used to build your stories on, couldn't it? An isolated girl, one who was listening to inner voices, wasn't she? I am talking to you, Debaldè. She would read about the lives of saints. I remember her telling me about a saint—Elisabeth of Hungary, if I remember correctly—who one day drank the water with which she had been washing the sores of a leper. I managed to love her even when she was saying these dreadful things. She was of extraordinary beauty. How lucky, being a sculptor and not a writer; if one had to put everything into words, what pain! Whereas sculpture is mute. One day we were at your house, Bernardo, at your mother's house, rather, at Corniano; your mother and Caterina Visnadello were cooking a wonderful polenta. Massimina pulled me by the sleeve (your mother and Caterina, after all, always looked at her with a kind of suspicion or worry) and talked to me the way little girls sometimes do, especially little Venetian girls from the countryside, in a kind of deep thick whisper, which can suddenly turn into falsetto: 'Please,' she said, 'come away with me a moment.'

"She took me upstairs to her little bedroom and there she said: 'I'd like to cry for a while,' as if she were saying: I'd like to take a nap.' But she didn't break into sobs or anything, she just stood there, looking at me. Finally, with the manner of a mature, practical person, she said: 'Well, the fact is that I don't feel well at all.' She had wanted to be alone with me to say this. Her eyes were darker, shiny but without transparency. It is possible that she may have caught typhoid fever visiting the sick; at any rate, they did not handle her properly; that's what Moscato said, the old doctor of the Venice Partibons. For that matter, the sick that she had visited were mainly those in the mental hospital, where her old teacher was, a quiet, very sweet old woman."

He turned to Debaldè: "Our meeting has been useful. I've got the picture now." Then, turning to Enrico and Bernardo: "You go to Corniano; Dora and I will take Bernardo's car and drive back to Rome; there I'll take care of everything. I'll pay a visit to Genziana Horst, as you told me. Perhaps I'll arrange a family summit meeting in Rome

(2 2 2)

rather than here. It appears that Maria is there." He looked at Debaldè for a sign of confirmation. "At Corniano, Bernardo, let them talk to you about the little girl and everything. No point in your going with Enrico to see his father; he would take you to Massimo's grave the way lady tourists go to the English cemetery in Rome to see where Keats is buried. Rather, you should get your mother, Signora Margherita, to talk."

There had also been a problem with transportation. Enrico and Bernardo would go to Corniano by railroad because there was a very convenient train; Enrico was leaving the car in Venice for his mother to use; he would later go back to Rome by train and leave a few days later by air for London.

Rather out of habit than out of real conviction, Fausta observed: "You are a little ponderous in your moves. You organize something and then you do something else. Your continuous displacements are, after all, a little absurd, and I don't see how you can help feeling a bit dizzy."

"In Italy now, one lives in Italy," Debaldè explained. "It's like one city; and the cities—Rome, Venice, Milan— are what city wards used to be; there are times when I don't know very well myself where I am."

Bernardo adapted himself to Corniano immediately, as he had to Venice, in spite of differences between the two homecomings: in Venice he had found the old familiar places mostly untouched and had breathed recognizable air; at Corniano, as if this were also a form of recognition, he realized from the first moment that things had completely changed; it was no longer a white dusty village, it was a little town full of motors, even with a couple of traffic lights. He liked the air, the wine, the tower clock with its blue dial and golden Roman numerals; the high, grass-covered hills rising steeply behind the houses; he liked the local speech, much harder than he remembered it; finally and above all he liked the so-called Mexican, Margherita Partibon, his mother.

In spite of Enrico's telephone message, she was not at the station to meet him. When they came out of the station into the street, Enrico left Bernardo immediately to go to his father's villa. A woman about thirty, dark-haired and dark-skinned, was waiting for them; before taking a taxi by himself, Enrico kissed her on both cheeks and delivered Bernardo to her; she and Bernardo got into another taxi. The taxi was shiny, rode softly, and smelled like new; the only difference from the most beautiful taxis in Milan or Rome was that the woman, Caterina Visnadello, called the driver by name, Menegato.

When they were on their way, Caterina said to Bernardo: "Your mother wasn't really convinced that you would arrive; that's why she didn't want to waste time waiting for you at the station."

"Is she sick?"

"No. And how are *you?*" Caterina studied him with admiration, her full lips parted: "How big you are," she said, laughing, "quite a bit bigger than your father. If you had come last year, you could still have talked to him."

"To whom?"

"Your father, of course. And how are you?" She took his hand; she herself had a large beautiful hand, very expressive, carefully manicured.

"On the whole I am quite well."

They stopped in a steep narrow street in the high old section of town, and Bernardo hardly recognized the "little palace" where his mother had her apartment; it was the apartment which his father, during the years of his disastrous investments, had unreasonably referred to as his "business office." Their house in the open country had been occupied by his father's cousins, Paolo and Vittoria Partibon, the parents of Giorgio and Elena, the so-called Venice Partibons, who had settled there after their own economic ruin. The courtyard of the "little palace" looked all cleaned up now; it had once reminded you of a stable, with strong smells, open to the wind; the war had destroyed part of it, and now it looked like a small and sober sixteenth-century stage, all nicely brushed up. They went up the wide staircase; on the first floor, the doors that led from the main salon had been room doors in the old days, but now for at least half a century they had been doors of apartments; the bellpulls of Bernardo's own time had been replaced by electric buttons. At the door of her own apartment, his mother was waiting.

She was sunburned; she had wrinkles like a sailor's rather than like an old woman's; she was thinner and stronger than she had been; the shape of her face appeared simplified, straight nose, straight mouth, suggesting irony rather than harshness; her lively, alert eyes shone against that leathery skin. From the very first moment, she held Bernardo uninterruptedly under her inquisitive look. She was a perfect stranger; photographs sent to him by Caterina in the course of years had not managed to evoke her at all. He had an old vision of her as rather gloomy and taciturn; on the contrary, she dressed in light colors, she talked a lot, and very well. "What a smart lady," was her son's first impression as his mother, leading him inside and showing him the apartment, kept saying, studying him: "What a character."

At first there were moments when he thought that his mother might be a bit confused, ever so slightly out of her mind; but then he realized that even in her vaguest and most wayward talk, his mother in the end managed to reach a solid bottom of clear consciousness and decision; then he began to admire her boundlessly.

As soon as she had preceded him into the room with book-covered walls where she normally lived, she said almost by way of introduction: "Look, Dino, I won't go to Venice, you know. Some of your relatives have written to me on the subject, and I told Caterina she shouldn't even answer them; I know about them; I know that they have arrived from America by themselves, not with you; and then, for that matter, I knew your mother-in-law when she was a child; they used to come here during the summer, forty or fifty years ago. But I have no intention of pretending that we are friends, and even less that we are enemies; we are nothing to one another. As I see it, your relatives have only one fear: money. Meanwhile, your mother-in-law lives in a luxury hotel, and your wife . . ." She was not accusing anybody; she spoke like an alert, well-informed child.

Bernardo interrupted her, embraced and squeezed her, kissed her face: "You are wonderful," he exclaimed; then he turned to look around the room: "You are very nicely fixed up here." A little piece of furniture in a corner made his mouth water.

"I don't know whether you have realized," Caterina said, "that all these years you've been sending a good deal of money."

"I'll send you more," Bernardo said to his mother, "you can buy yourself a car, and then Caterina here will drive it. Besides"—he went to a window—"you'll get some new curtains." He pulled at a curtain as if to tear it off.

"If you go on like that, big as you are, you'll smash up the whole place," his mother observed.

"I'll fix up this room for you, and the rest of the house too. What kind of a bed do you have? Do you have a beautiful bed? An old one that was in the house?"

"What a character you are!"

"Well, it's his job," Caterina said in her deep voice, unchanged since childhood, "furniture, fixing up houses."

"Do they have beautiful fabrics anywhere here?"

"Mrs. Bettanini's shop," Caterina said. "Well, anyway, what used to be Mrs. Bettanini's shop in your days."

His days? Bernardo looked at her with blank eyes; he remembered absolutely nothing. "I met some people called Bettanini once in Texas."

"Maybe they are cousins," his mother said just to say something, laughing lightly.

Bernardo was thinking that Rodolfo Pigliolo-Spada had been the only person who had shown any true curiosity about America; Debaldè did not count; Enrico already knew all that he wanted to know; Dora was interested in sex matters rather than anything else. Here at his mother's, it seemed to him as though his American years did not exist at all. He was also surprised to see how much his mother and Caterina had managed to do with the money he had sent them; there was even wall-to-wall carpeting. And a couple of admirable table lamps with bright-colored lamp shades; no rickety chandeliers hanging from the ceiling.

"Caterina here, does she live with you?" he asked.

"Yes, but now she's engaged again."

"Not at all. Would you like some tea, Dino? Some coffee?" Mother and son were now seated; Caterina was still standing, waiting to serve them.

"Well, yes, a nice cup of coffee."

When mother and son were alone, she resumed: "I very much hope so."

"You hope what?"

"That she finds herself the right fiancé," the mother said.

"I very much hope so too."

"Her first husband—he died tragically." Bernardo nodded. "They used wire to hang him. One of the streets

(2 2 7)

has been named after him, down toward where we used to live."

"Mother, I know everything, you know."

"Unlucky you, if you know everything." Bernardo's shoulders shrank, as if apologetically. "Among your American relatives," she went on, "the only one that really exists is Clem."

"He has a fixation about being disliked by everybody."

"That's not so." She added immediately: "Oh, I know that. You were pretty difficult too, as a boy. As for myself," she went on without interruption but raising her head abruptly, "I feel no pity for anybody, and least of all for those who consider themselves good."

His mother's words seemed to settle in the air, in the long silence. Then Bernardo realized that he would have liked to get up and embrace her; he had no idea where the old lady, with that straight nose and that sententious air, had gathered such thoughts; he knew only that he would like to hold her in his arms. "You get better as you grow old, Mother. But then you are not old."

"Of course not."

"A journalist, a man by the name of Massenti, has described Father's death to me, and his funeral."

"Did he tell you what a display it was? And imagine, he hadn't wanted any flowers."

Caterina came back with the coffee tray, on which she had also placed two telegrams. "You've just arrived and there is already mail catching up with you," Caterina said, looking at him with questioning eyes. "I find this a little crazy." Bernardo took the telegrams, glanced at them without opening them, and put them in his pocket.

"What a character," his mother said. Without asking for his approval, she also poured into her son's coffee a generous amount of anise spirit, *mistrà,* from its chubby little

(228)

bottle with a cuspidal metal tap; with interest she studied her son's reaction to his first sip of that hot beverage: "How is it?"

"Magnificent," Bernardo exploded. His warm look embraced Caterina too.

"And listen," his mother asked, "did you see Maria?"

Bernardo put the cup back on the saucer, and said nothing.

"Since she is always between Rome and Venice," his mother explained, "you have more opportunity to see her than we have. You probably know about that poor little girl. But of course, you told me you know everything."

"About Massimina? What's that hullabaloo the newspapers have been making?" Bernardo asked, trying to find out his mother's attitude.

But she shrugged, as if she ignored the whole thing.

"What kind of a child was she really?" Bernardo asked.

"She was never really an obedient child."

A grandfather clock was chiming three quarters of an hour. Beyond the thin, half-open curtains and the uneven windowpane, Bernardo could see the green damp hill with a few scattered houses and a small closed chapel, exposed to the wind, with a cypress tree near it. He was slightly nearsighted but he thought he could also distinguish cows at pasture. It was rapidly getting dark; the first lights had appeared.

"She would go her own way," his mother elaborated, "without even turning to look at anyone."

"One Sunday morning," Caterina said, "one of the very last times that Maria came to see her father, I was with them, and Odo was very ill; well . . . she, the little girl, could think of only one thing: leaving in a hurry, as soon as possible. 'Mother, you stay here if you want, but I have things to do.' Which meant going to church and perhaps to

(2 2 9)

her crazy old teacher to bring her mints. I looked at her from the window, and I can still see her with her polished, solid little boots, sounding away along the pavement. She liked to dress with class. She was so strong, and very, very pretty too."

"A little bit of a tomboy," Bernardo said to himself.

His mother spoke in her sententious tone: "She certainly wasn't the type to go barefoot. Or to subject her body to any sacrifice. However, she was not greedy or anything. She was a little woman who knew what she wanted. She was very intelligent. She would have done great things if she hadn't died. But what's the matter with you?"

"Sometimes in the evenings, Mother, I don't feel well at all."

Caterina felt his forehead. She was silent. Then she said to the mother: "You try too."

The two women were standing close to Bernardo.

"Sometimes it's just fatigue," his mother said.

When they were seated at the table, he felt worse. They had prepared many excellent things for him, but he wanted only some light soup, which he left unfinished. He went to bed. Rather logically, they had prepared the room for him in which his father had died. His mother and Caterina stood on either side of the bed while Bernardo kept gasping, tossing and turning, throwing aside the blanket, which the two women would immediately tuck in again. They were not used to his ways of thinking, and therefore, even though they asked each other, they could not decide when he was speaking in full consciousness and when he was delirious. Without any explicit agreement between the two of them, they followed the policy of seconding him in anything he said, pretending that they understood; there was, for example, Bernardo's insistence in asking them to "get in touch with Clement immediately" and remind him "to go to the Senator, that is, to his daughter, if possible to the funeral, or if he does not get there in time, he should talk to her somehow in my behalf too—he'll understand, he knows," and the two women would reassure him, reminding him, in fact, that a telephone had been installed in this house too—with Bernardo's money, incidentally—and that they had not understood why today's message from Venice had been sent through the Fassola villa.

"You women tell him that, he'll understand, he is a boy who understands women; I behaved horribly," he would say and that simple cue which he volunteered seemed to develop into a total and overwhelming sense of inadequacy, of failed duties, which obsessed him: "I know I have always forgotten everything, but I'll give you the money," he would say, for instance, trembling, "don't even mention it, I'll give it to you . . . " and he would provide questions and answers: "Would a hundred thousand do? Two hundred thousand? Dollars? No, that's not it, we can find money like that ourselves. Then what is it? Is it the end, then, the total void? Or is the figure too small? Is that what it is? If it isn't enough, I'll try Gutkind. Gutkind? Don't make us laugh."

He continued nevertheless to be aware of the fact that he was Bernardo Partibon in bed, and that he felt sick, considerably more so than usual. He tried the old definitions, nausea, horror, humiliation, but this time he felt he was losing consciousness; to begin with, there was no doubt that his sense of time was gone, and the faces which began to emerge around him, not those of his mother and of Caterina (from them he perceived only voices wrapped in cotton pads of fog: "We must call Moscato. Like a bull's fever") but those of unknown stiff-necked hypocrites, holding mysterious rights, mortgages, transit privileges over his person— these faces did not find any recognition, did not ring any bell in his memory. "If at least they would send me the right people," he said, "but where is everybody? Where are they? And why?"

He had no doubt that there were many people in the room, wrapping him in moist clothes, probably to carry him away.

He said: "One night in Michigan, we were wading across a lake. Autumn leaves. There were hundreds of lakes. Peace. Never laughed so much. But then? Then? I have exploited everybody. I have betrayed everybody."

The two women bent over him, smiling at these rather undecipherable messages. The mother, in a quite skeptical tone, mentioned past illnesses overcome by the boy, native strength, inexhaustible capacity for physical suffering, and recuperation in the cisalpine Venetians. Caterina massaged his forehead with ice, murmuring: "This boy is going to burst into flames," and the mother would reassure her: "No, no, it takes more than that."

It was always evening, but for some reason it was early dawn; and even though he knew he was in bed, he saw himself sitting at the table, and he realized that one of the stiff-necked dinner guests was a doctor. "No! I don't want him," he warned, jumping out of the bed and dragging the sheet with him which, being also a tablecloth, left behind a trail of falling dishes and silver. Since the tablecloth-sheet was also a carpet, the doctor stumbled and managed to throw himself out of the door before falling. "Bar that door," Bernardo ordered; and at that point he was sure that he had lost consciousness and at the same time that he had regained it—he was, in fact, catapulted into sleep, or rather, he found himself surrounded by an enormous, grassy expanse of sleep, and he threw himself into it. He slept consciously, furiously; he set his teeth into sleep and chewed it, getting

(2 3 2)

nourishment from it, feeling it as it spread all through his body. Thus sleep took the place of everything else, actions, thoughts, words, it was his only way of existing and of expressing himself. He felt he was the child Bernardo, Dino, at Corniano, and that this was a reality without action, a speech without words, something that in order to exist did not need either space or time, house or hours. It was rather the sea, an endless wide sea, smoother than he had ever seen it.

With eyes half closed, he noticed the sun entering from the tree-lined street, creating aquarium transparencies; and he heard his mother's voice:

"The fever has come down completely."

He pretended he hadn't heard her; cunningly he knew that his recovery had begun. In fact, that it had already made considerable progress. Every object confirmed this, revealing new aspects, fresh, clean, with special understandings for him. He himself was carrying on this recovery. He realized that health was not granted to him directly; a new strength was flowing into him, and with full consciousness he used it to recover his health. Now he made it official that he was awake.

"You've had one of those big flashes of fever like a three-year-old child," his mother said. She must have said that a half-hour earlier, but the phrase had remained frozen within the image of his mother; now that that image was becoming alive and warm, the phrase was defrosted too. "What did the doctor say?" she asked.

"I threw him out," Bernardo said, happy to be able to assume that at least one of the stiff-necked visitors had not been a nightmare, "before he could touch me. And please, Mother, tell that fish not to come here any more."

"We tried to get Moscato but he's in Venice; and how could you have seen this doctor if you were delirious when he came?"

"What do you mean, delirious? I was my own doctor. Or rather, you cured me." He threw out his arms; she bent over him and let him peck her on the cheek. She emanated a strong fragrance of lavender. "Do you always get up so bright and early in the morning?"

"Apart from the fact that it is now two in the afternoon, in the morning I get up around nine, Dino."

Caught in an error, Bernardo jumped out of bed: "Then I'll have to take a bath."

"Yes, you may do that, you are better now," his mother said offhandedly.

"I have brought attacks of that kind down to three hours and even two," Bernardo said with a kind of athletic pride, or as if he were talking of an industrial production cycle. "How long was I sick?"

"Longer than that. And look, apparently there was a phone call from London, and even one from America, Mrs. Bergalli said."

"Who is she?"

"One of the telephone operators."

Now Caterina too appeared at the door: "They were calling you from New York. Yesterday the mail, and now the telephone." She giggled good-naturedly.

"I am sure it's some perfectly stupid thing! It's not my fault! There is a diabolical concierge at the hotel, who tracks me down; he seems to believe that's very American."

"Do you want us to tell Mrs. Bergalli something?"

"Nothing."

The mother said with resentment: "Caterina's little girl will be sorry. She was so thrilled at the idea of talking with America."

(2 3 4)

"I didn't know Caterina had a little girl."

"She looks just like a flower. Nice and straight. Perhaps you should call her from America when you go back there."

Getting out of the bathtub, he realized that the bright yellow bath towel, prepared for him on the white metal chair, was actually in the form of a robe, and had obviously belonged to his father. He draped himself with it, and returned to the bedroom. Here Caterina was waiting for him, standing near the bed. "How do you feel?"

"On the whole, quite well."

"You always say that, and then you are so sick you are ready to die."

Bernardo placed himself on the bed, bathrobe and all; Caterina covered him with a woolen blanket, then she tucked it in under his supine body, his legs. "What a mountain!" She had to walk all around the bed to fix him up at the various points.

"Keep quiet now," Bernardo said to her, "sit down here." He made room for her on the bed. He was the master of the house; his sickness, even if dazzlingly brief, had installed him, had given him seniority, as if he had spent months there. "What did Father actually die of?" he asked.

"Kidney and cardiovascular complications." Caterina saw the *Gazzettino* of that day, still folded, on the night table: "Would you like me to read the paper to you?"

"No, for God's sake."

Caterina opened the paper and read it for a while by herself; she moved her lips while she read, as if in prayer.

"But I wanted to make conversation," Bernardo protested.

Obediently, Caterina folded the paper again. They looked at each other for a while in silence. Bernardo observed her, from the wide round forehead to the structure of the shoulders and the breasts, down to the hips; he liked to see her sit so solidly in front of him. "You have always been quite big too," he said, "but one doesn't notice it because you have the right proportions." He took her hand and made her move closer to him. "Right temperature too," he went on. With his large hand he caressed her face, her shoulder, pressing, modeling. "You are made of the right kind of dough," he said.

"What a way to talk!"

"Nice, wide face." There were long intervals of silence, filled with their anxious breathing. "People with nice palates," Bernardo went on—and that must have been a very old phrase of his uncle Paolo's, the painter, who saw in the palate the secret supporting arch of the face and therefore of the person. Caterina laughed and Bernardo took that laugh as a challenge; he pulled her to him, and as soon as he made a move to kiss her, Caterina shut her eyes with a kind of solemn gravity, and let him do it. Then she herself grasped Bernardo's shoulders, feeling them under the robe with expert fingers; finally she took the lead in a long, involved kiss, in which they lost themselves. When they parted, they looked at each other, laughing. Then, serious again, studying each other with agitated eyes, they began to whisper.

"Where is Mother at this hour?" Bernardo asked.

"She sleeps until exactly five-thirty."

"Really?"

"Then, many times in the evening she stays up till late to play cards, and she is very good."

"You have no idea how I would like to see you without clothes on."

"Oh, dear," Caterina said with a shadow of fear and awe—as one facing an event which seems surprising and yet has been predestined since time immemorial.

She went to the door and locked it. All of this she did very slowly, with deliberately long periods of silence; they heard the ticking of the clock and, from the village, a car horn honking far away, the muffled sound of a bell, a train whistling in the humid wind. Bernardo waited for her, stretching his arms out to urge her to return to the bed, but the woman kept moving around the room, not uncertain but rather as if studying the place, tidying things up. Finally, keeping her eyes fixed on him, she started undressing with a kind of abstracted slowness, folding each garment diligently on a chair.

She went back to him and made him step out of bed; she took the large yellow bathrobe off him; made him get back to bed; and followed him. Sheets and blankets were stirred, agitated, finally completely overturned by their increasingly vast and deep motions; kissing Caterina's breasts, Bernardo held them with both hands as if to quench a thirst; from there he descended slowly in the darkness toward her womb until she warned him: "You're going to drive me insane." Saying this she freed herself, and performed the most decisive of their motions by rising from the ruins of the sheets and blankets; she clutched him and finally climbed on him, placing herself there, victoriously in the open. Thus she made him initiate love in her, and when she felt sure of it she turned him and herself slowly, performing each motion with masterful cautiousness, looking fixedly in his eyes as if to guide him.

That evening Bernardo got out of bed and insisted that he wanted to hire a car and take his mother and Caterina to a nearby village to have dinner at the celebrated Oselladore Inn, but his idea was considered insane. So they had dinner at home, with Caterina bringing the dishes from the kitchen.

(237)

"Coming here has been very good for me," Bernardo said to his mother, who looked at him incredulously.

"It's been as good for you as it has for us," Caterina said. She had found a way of communicating with Bernardo which could be used in the presence of his mother. After serving the soup, sitting down, and taking a first spoonful herself (they had old silver, large in size, and very beautiful), she said: "Since the time when I was a girl and I used to go with your cousin Giorgio, I've always known that one of the things that keep us going is men like you, who are kind."

The mother coughed. "Oscar was the best," she said in the tone of an often-repeated phrase.

Caterina said to Bernardo: "No, you didn't know him. He was from Friuli." All three were silent. Then Caterina seemed to speak mainly in order to fill that silence: "I wanted to die too, but then I went on living."

"So many deaths," Bernardo said. The hot bouillon was doing him good, but he perceived, however distant, the possibility that he might suddenly faint, though as long as he felt himself holding the attention of these women he felt sustained, in fact nothing could make him really afraid. "Now I know why I'm sick sometimes: it's because I have abandoned everybody." They looked at him with curiosity. "Everybody. Starting from here, Corniano, yourselves . . ."

"Nobody ever abandons anybody," the mother said. She had a curious way of immediately giving a phrase her own meaning and of replying before it was even finished. "And then," she said as if wanting to avoid a lot of useless further talk, "Corniano is a little town full of life."

"I wouldn't mind staying here," Bernardo said, and immediately caught a quick, unconscious exchange of looks between the two women; he clearly understood, once and for all, that if he stayed he would be a nuisance.

"You will probably say, and with reason," the mother went on, "that quite often the people who bring life to the town are hardly the right ones." Bernardo cocked his ear. "Am I right?"

"Who, for example?"

The mother shrugged. Caterina laughed, and said: "Once upon a time it used to be the Fassolas, they had everything. Massimo, before getting Maria pregnant, was wild about me, but I never . . ."

"Who has everything now?" Bernardo cut in.

"Now it's a little more complicated," the mother said, "also because there are many more people."

"Do you know a man called Debaldè?" Bernardo asked casually.

"The mother said: "Hmm, Dr. Debaldè," and she turned to Caterina: "You tell him."

"There is nothing to tell," Caterina said. "He used to help the Fassolas a little with their business problems, since Augusto Fassola has been so ill for so many years."

"Debaldè knows Maria well, doesn't he?"

"Hmm," his mother said again.

"Well, what I mean is, didn't he have something to do with . . ."

The mother interrupted with an insinuating laugh: "He would have liked it a lot if something big had developed with Massimina's story. Hmm."

"As for instance what?"

The mother turned to him very excitedly, waving her hands in the air: "Well, perhaps . . . you know, pilgrimages, a sanctuary, things like that." Then she became her usual calm and sententious self: "Everything has to do with the increased wealth of the country."

"Perhaps Debaldè still has hopes." Bernardo was tempting his mother, trying to arouse a lively reaction. "You should have heard what Clement suggested to him—the idea of mental recoveries."

"Oh, that," the mother said. She turned to Caterina: "You tell him."

Caterina seemed happy to be consulted—to guide Bernardo, a stranger in his own village: "They would refuse. They would block the thing." At every phrase the mother nodded, as if placing a stamp on it. "It isn't that they either believe or not believe. They don't even listen. That is to say, they wouldn't listen if the problem should arise."

There was a long silence. Then Bernardo asked: "Who are *they?* And what problem do you mean exactly?"

"Who are *they?*" the mother said. "Her father, for instance. Vincenzo." She pointed to Caterina with her thumb.

Caterina now spoke in a tone of forced patience, as if having once more to explain the obvious: "Father has said many times that when he was with Massimina, his fever would go. I don't know whether you remember that he always had those fevers. And he goes on saying that, even now that she is dead. It calms his head, he says. One day he also said that *the vision makes him feel better.* There is a particular disease, which Odo and my father invented, but which actually exists—they gave it a name, *la mattana*—a special variety of derangement of the mind. Sometimes they used to refer to it also as brain nausea."

"Moscato tried everything against that thing," the mother said. There was a new prolonged silence. "Now suppose," the mother resumed, "that some day Debaldè, and perhaps Gervasutti and his brother, who is military chaplain, should come with that doctor you call a fish, who is so friendly with them, and suppose they should ask Vincenzo . . . " The mother stopped, as if things were already too obvious for her to continue.

(2 4 0)

"To offer testimony," Caterina explained with slight impatience, "to ascertain the recovery . . ."

"Well, then?" Bernardo asked.

"Then, even if he felt perfectly recovered, Father would answer, 'No comment.'" Caterina seemed rather happy to show that she was up to date with the fashionable language of press conferences.

The mother said: "In Italy they ruin everything to give themselves importance, to do things with great pomp. Dr. Debaldè, titles, ceremonies, speeches. It's worse than with the journalists, because with them at least you know that even if they make a big fuss for a week or two, in the end everybody understands that it was all fake; and then, some journalists are very nice; there was that boy Tranquillo here, who became very friendly with your father and who was such a good, unhappy boy."

"When I arrived in Italy I should have come here immediately," Bernardo said, "to stay with you."

There was a new exchange of looks between the two women, but this time they seemed to feel less threatened. In fact, the mother said invitingly: "You can come back and visit us any time you want. There are all sorts of airplanes now, aren't there?"

CHAPTER NINE

✳

It was rather cold in Rome, and as Clement Blumenfeld and Dora were getting out of Bernardo's car, which they had appropriated in Venice, he realized that his camel-hair overcoat and colorful scarf would be inappropriate in church; he accused himself of naïveté for having dressed like that, and he was going to escape, with an almost desperate sense of abjection.

Meanwhile Dora was meeting her Ovidio, who had been waiting for her near the church, with his arms and his smile wide open. Both Ovidio and Dora firmly maintained that the idea had been to wait for Genziana at the exit after the ceremony, and not to go in and attend the Requiem Mass for the Senator. Clement was undecided; he felt very curious about the spectacle in the church, as about practically anything; as usual, the battle between his curiosity and his timidity was beginning. He advanced to the main entrance and felt sure that somebody there wanted to stop him almost as if an entrance card had been requested. Then, out of stubbornness and, even more, out of extreme nervousness, he started acting, and entered the church saying to the ushers: "I represent Dr. Debaldè."

Once he was in, he kept himself apart, near a side door.

From a distance he recognized a leftist senator and a former prime minister, and also, from the back, the two Horst daughters, Lauretta and Genziana. Then suddenly, at the idea of waiting for Genziana and meeting her, he was overwhelmed by anxiety and a feeling of absurdity; before the Elevation he went outside, determined to leave.

As soon as he was out in the square he realized that his only desire was to meet Genziana Horst and talk to her. The mist had faded, the sun was out. This was a rather new section of town; on the opposite side of the square Clement saw a portico with shops and a bar, and the façade of a neon-lit hotel spotted with dampness. There were now other people besides Dora and Ovidio. Ovidio had given his friends false hopes, telling them that he would also bring Tranquillo Massenti; both Massenti and Quarto Martelli, he had said, felt very awkward in front of Genziana and preferred to meet her in a group. However, Massenti was not there. Quarto Martelli was with Tito Solmi, who followed Ovidio's talk with intense participation. Ovidio-Tito-Quarto formed a trio; during Dora's absence in Venice they had embroidered on the theme of her entrance into Ovidio's life, discussing all of its possible developments.

Dora had perceived this warm interest around her; she savored her state of quiet well-being. She liked Ovidio, so ruddy-faced and so latently strong, with his mountaineer's accent and his promptness to help—a quality which, far from making him squalidly servile, rather confirmed his strength. Besides, Dora guessed that before discovering in him a possibly exceptional degree of capacity in the love game, she might have to help him relax a certain timidity; this gave her a reassuring feeling of tenderness and, at the same time, of power. She had observed herself naked in the mirror: "There is a definitely domestic touch about me," she had told herself, "with my little round face and my hair parted in the middle; and I don't look in the least aggressive." She observed the correct size of her breasts, her large hips. "Legs—somewhat tube-shaped; feet—a bit flat." But all that gave an air of pleasant solidity to her walk. "Real contact with the soil. And I have a wonderful skin; he will like me. It will be as if he went to bed with a woman who is already his family, a conventional fiancée, who nevertheless already knows all about how to make love. Ovidio is lucky."

The Senator's funeral had been strictly private, in accordance with his expressed wish. This Mass for relatives and old friends had nothing official about it. Therefore, coming out into the square in the sun, Genziana and her group looked like ordinary Sunday churchgoers. They took leave of the few senatorial personages, treating them like old family friends. Rodolfo Piglioli-Spada was the first to part from the senatorial group, and having caught sight of his distant cousin, Quarto Martelli, he went toward him with outstretched arms. As they came close, Quarto bent over Rodolfo, and they embraced and kissed each other on both cheeks. Piglioli-Spada whispered reassuringly: "There wasn't really anybody at the funeral, you know, not even the most intimate, and today also as you can see . . . " His eyes followed the senatorial characters in the distance, then they turned to Clement nearby; he offered his hand: "Piglioli-Spada," he introduced himself, and when Clement did the same, Piglioli-Spada said vivaciously: "Oh, I know who you are." His eyes brightened with desire to talk. But his wife came near him, followed by Genziana; Quarto kissed both women, and was trying to tell Genziana something when Clement, with the sudden intrusiveness of the shy, interrupted them. Quarto introduced him.

Genziana said, without looking at him: "We know each other."

In the background, Tito Solmi had taken charge, and was organizing introductions and greetings.

"No," Clement said, speaking in quick jerks, "but my brother-in-law, Bernardo Partibon, told me to look for you, to apologize."

"For what?" Genziana spoke in her usual tone, but in a slightly softer version: "Think how curious"—and at this point she looked him straight in the eyes—"exactly today your brother-in-law Bernardo and I, according to the initial plans, would have finished our weekend at their house." She pointed to the Piglioli-Spadas. "You know my sister, don't you?" She did not wait for an answer. "It feels like a year ago. How is Bernardo? But what is the matter with you?"

"Nothing." Clement was staring at her with such stupefied admiration that it looked like terror.

"It is I who should apologize, but I haven't been well, yesterday and today. And it seems that tomorrow Harry Berger is coming, he's in Paris already. No, carissimo"—she raised her voice and her neck toward Piglioli-Spada—"you go, I'll walk, it's only a few steps."

She took leave of her sister and her brother-in-law with quick kisses.

Dora and the trio followed the Piglioli-Spadas toward their car; Clement saw himself isolated with Genziana in the middle of the square as in empty space.

He had imagined her taller; actually she was a little shorter than he. He had always imagined her in the full bloom of youth, bright and proud; now he could see the very light wrinkles around her famous, splendid eyes; then under her eyes the two bluish diagonal lines, strongly marked. But she had said that she had not been well. She looked as if she had just got out of bed, combed her hair, and quickly put on that unadorned black tailored suit she was wearing. She was thinner and more fragile than he had

(245)

thought, but in breathing she raised her chest with the proper strong rhythm. Before he could think about it, Clement was saying, in a whisper: "What can I do for you?"

But he was not sure that she had heard. Genziana had turned her head to one side, she raised a hand and moved her fingers in the air to catch the attention of the distant trio: "Good-bye! Good—bye!" she called out; she lowered her hand again immediately and offered it to Clement with determination: "Arrivederci, carissimo, thank you," she said with a quick hard smile, as if Clement's behavior troubled her and she wanted to bring him down to something more conventional.

"I'll accompany you. Where are you going?"

"No, really, I live around here, and I'm going to bed immediately. But why don't you give me a ring?"

She had already moved away from him but she turned around and smiled: "Really, do call me." She waved her hand walking away, slightly stooped, pressing her bag against her stomach like a muff.

There followed hours of Sunday emptiness accompanied by heavy talk and food. Around four in the afternoon they had finished eating—Dora, Clement, and the trio—in Piazza del Popolo. Every now and then, either Ovidio or Tito would get up and go out of the restaurant to have a look at the nearby café; they would come back with long faces, saying: "No Tranquillo." Dora and Ovidio were holding hands under the table and laughing a lot; they were now creating the irradiation which, at the time of the Solmi reception and the visit to Perineschi, had been produced by the masculine trio. Quarto and, even more, Tito studied the pair with possessive curiosity, both to protect them and to capture their secrets. Occasionally the pair would announce that they had decided to go to a movie, and the other two members of the trio would object: "Wait, Ovidio—Massenti is supposed to come." Then Clement would say: "No, he's not coming," and he would go back to his isolated thoughts. The trio observed him with some uneasiness. He would get up to make long telephone calls in English; when he returned from the telephone, Dora would ask: "Corinne?" or "Phoebe?" but Clement simply shrugged. Finally the pair got up—the cinema decision was final. They were unshakable. Quarto and Tito followed them with their eyes while they walked out into the square and passed by the large church cupolas, holding each other tightly.

At any rate, it was too late to stay on in a restaurant, so the three men also got up and went out. Tito went once more to have a look at the nearby café, but he came back shaking his head at the other two, who were waiting near his Oldsmobile.

"Many times Massenti changes cafés," Clement said. "Did you try his house?" He gave the telephone number from memory.

"He isn't there. The Swedish girl isn't there either."

Before getting into his Oldsmobile with Quarto, Tito tried in vain to offer Clement a lift; he held Clement's hand a long while in his own, questioning him with his benevolent, round eyes, as if imploring to do something for him. "We'll meet again soon anyway, won't we? And lots of luck."

Clement stared at him with apprehension.

"For your show, of course," Tito said, laughing. They patted him on the shoulder, they shook him by the arm, as if to wake him up.

"Thank you, thank you," Clement said, as if anxious to convince them that he was sincere.

Tito made a last attempt: "Why don't you come with

us?" offering it like a totally new suggestion.

"No, please," Clement said, and he was off.

He had no hesitations; he moved rapidly, jumping around to avoid the automobiles over the uneven cobbled pavement, and he threw himself toward the sumptuous portal which was the entrance to the square; he went out into Piazzale Flaminio and turned to the right walking up along the Muro Torto, gaining speed. He had had an excellent athletic training; he could lose himself in his own thoughts and let his body move by itself, increasingly responsive, charging energy. The high irregular wall, the trees, and the smell of damp grass helped him get into the right rhythm as in a country walk. Tito Solmi's good wishes had frightened him; he had realized that there were moments when the thought of the show disappeared from his mind completely as something unreal, while in other moments it presented itself as a threat and a nightmare; between the imminent public presentation and his work of many years, no rapport could ever be established. He continued to walk rapidly up that road, close to the wall; keeping outside that kind of bastion was like remaining anonymous, safe from traffic jams, from people and words, from the cafés where one encountered the mediators and the judges. When he reached the summit, he kept out of Porta Pinciana, and followed Corso d'Italia until he got to an important crossing; he went over to the other side and into Via Po on his left.

He walked along palaces built in the early years of the century, along their solid foundations punctuated by the blind, iron-barred windows of the basements, or occasionally along an urban garden preserved behind a cast-iron gate, or an open portal that revealed, like a theater, the small marble atrium with steps in the background flanked by little columns, and the faint globe of the lamp hanging in the middle. Clement knew the old Rome well—popular, princely, and churchly—but he was attracted by these high streets, halfway between antiquity and neon light, with elements of the South American hotel style and of the fake Renaissance palace. A timid and avidly curious stranger, he could go on for months studying a person from a distance; and he knew that Senator Horst had lived on this street, that in one of these palaces the child Genziana had lost her mother. There had been nights when he had pored over the telephone book, reading names and addresses and imagining the lives of people behind façades like these; in the night he would go out to contemplate them, animating them with a fantastic, ghostly life in the light of street lamps. Some long rows of windows worthy of official and governmental palaces, each with its regular, triangular tympanum, had reminded him of rows of *carabinieri,* some, more ornate, wearing a parade uniform, and others, more sober, an everyday one. Those were the types of windows that on days of national celebrations were flanked by candlelike lights; behind such a row of windows, the Senator had spent, among thousands of books, his scholarly widower's evenings. Lauretta had left him, to go and marry that jockey character, dried up by the sun; Genziana had left him to go and live as a career woman, very well known in the important circles, spreading conceit and courtesy, hardness and grace. Genziana—in the last few hours that was what it had all been about. Clement was full of reluctance and courage, and of premonitions. He took a side road, looked for a tobacco shop, a public telephone. Since the moment when she had left him that morning, he had rested with the thought of calling her only after a few days; now he put the token into the slot and dialed the number.

It was busy; he decided he wouldn't call any more. But he tried a second time. Her voice answered immediately. Clement gave his name.

"I beg your pardon? Oh, yes, of course, carissimo. Tell me."

"Are you a little better?"

"Thank you. How kind of you to call." There was a prolonged silence. "Hello?"

"I don't know whether you go out these days. If you can, I would very much like, please, to have dinner with you."

"When?"

"Tonight?"

"Look, I don't know, but why don't we . . . Would you like to come up here and keep me company for a while?" Genziana's voice was weak and inexpressive in reciting these formulas.

"Certainly."

"If you come up now, would you do me a favor? See if you can find a pharmacy and get me . . . wait a minute, let me read." She gave him the name of the medicine and she hung up almost immediately: "Thank you, I'll see you in a short while."

Clement's immediate worry was to remember where he had left his car, or rather, Bernardo's car. He had left it in the church square where he, Dora, and the trio had all got into Tito Solmi's Oldsmobile. He took a taxi to that square and found the car, now all by itself. Although he was close to Genziana's house, he crossed a large section of the city to go by his own house a moment. There he changed very quickly, putting on a fresh shirt, a dark suit and overcoat. On his way to Genziana's he found a pharmacy and bought the medicine.

The door of Genziana's apartment, of light-brown wood framed in marble, was opened for him by a nurselike maid with glasses and wearing a white robe, who greeted him in a Lombard accent and as though she knew him. She brought him immediately into the room where Genziana was, wearing the same black skirt she had worn earlier, and a gray sweater which outlined her chest favorably; on top of this sweater she wore a kind of cassock, also gray, light, with red borders. Dressed like that, she made the living room look rather like a workroom; in fact, Clement noticed in a corner an unpainted wooden table, with slanting top and a lamp with movable arm screwed onto the edge. Genziana took the medicine box from his hand as if it had been flowers to place in a vase immediately, and she thanked him, mumbling that they would settle their accounts later. "It's very kind of you to have come here," she said. Then, brightening up for the first time and smiling with a kind of cheerful tenderness: "You've changed your clothes," she said, "you're all dressed up." From that moment she started to study his every gesture.

She made him sit while she went on talking: "Think, how wonderful. Harry Berger called, he won't arrive in Rome until a week from tomorrow. Chet Marshall is here already, in fact he called a moment ago; do you know him?"

"Yes. And my sister wrote his book; well, anyway, ghost-wrote, with a friend of hers."

"How curious. I really think this is rather curious. Chet wanted to come here but I asked him to leave me alone. Whereas I told you to come and see me; I hope you forgive me. Americans, especially when they want to help, are so demanding."

"I am an American."

"Well—no. I spent a very restful evening with your brother-in-law, Bernardo, we talked a lot about you. Now you tell me. I saw some of your sculptures."

Clement looked at her as if he had been beaten. Then, pointing his finger at her: "Don't you have to take the medicine?" Genziana still held the box in her hand, playing with it. "Wait, give me . . ."

"There's nothing more annoying than cellophane."

"How many tablets?" Clement asked while in one instant he broke the cellophane, opened the box, pulled out the bottle, unscrewed the top, pulled out the cotton.

"Two. You have very beautiful hands."

Clement poured two tablets into Genziana's palm, replaced the top, put the bottle on the table. They looked at each other as if surprised. They studied each other's faces. Then Clement said in a low, tender voice: "Where is the water? You need a glass of water." He was already getting up. "I'll go."

She followed him with her look, smiling as if she had decided to humor him. Clement came back from the kitchen with a glass of water, followed by the white-robed maid, who looked at Genziana questioningly. Genziana asked her to bring the liquor cart closer and to get some ice; meanwhile, under Clement's watchful look, she swallowed the two tablets, one at a time, with ceremony, each followed by the proper amount of water.

By now they smiled at each other continuously; they didn't notice the maid, who came in with the ice bucket, put it on the table, and went out. The still life of bottles and glasses was nicely set in front of them, but Genziana said: "You know what? I'd rather drink wine."

"Tell me where it is. I'll go. What wine?"

"Lambrusco, don't you think?" She examined Clement from head to foot, taking in each detail of his appearance as if she wanted to think them over later on. "But listen, you're all dressed up to go out to dinner. I won't go out, obviously. I should have told you." For a moment she seemed lost. "I sincerely apologize."

"Not at all. We'll stay here. I'll cook," Clement said. Genziana watched him incredulously, again as if she decided to let him play. "It's true, you know," he insisted, encouraged by her doubts. "I'm very good. You can dismiss that nurse of yours and just sit quietly, I'll do everything. I know how to do things." He moved his eyes around as if looking for convincing arguments: "For instance," he said, "I know how to repair a radio, a light switch."

"Really?" Genziana seemed ready to let him do what he wanted, a bit awed.

Enrico Fassola and Bernardo Partibon met at the Corniano station and left for Venice together. On the train, talking ramblingly and with gusto, their spirits rose, so that when they arrived in Venice Enrico decided: "Come to our house, in fact you could come and live there. I'm going to London. At this time of year Mother goes to Corniano for a while, you can stay there alone with Ortensia. At any rate, I will tell Mother that we are coming now." He looked for a telephone booth, Bernardo went to wait for him outside the station, near the Grand Canal; when Enrico joined him, he found a gondola ready, into which Bernardo invited him ceremoniously.

On their way home in the gondola, they were silent a long while, their faces half wrapped in scarfs, while the gondola was carrying them forward, with its rhythmic jolts, vigorous yet flexible, surmounting the strenuous waves produced by motorization. All wrapped up and silent, the two men occasionally glanced at the parade of palaces in a mist which was like a silver smoke lying over the water and the stones.

Enrico broke the silence: "You had better know. Mother told me that your sister Maria is visiting her."

Without raising his head, his chin pressed to his chest, Bernardo produced a moan.

"And that's not all. Later on . . ."

"I bet you Clare and her mother will go there too."

Enrico nodded. They were now in front of the Rezzonico

palace. There were two of the canal steamers used as water buses, getting in each other's way. One of them found the pontoon station occupied by the other. Also, one of the large public-service motorboats was threatening them. There were sudden stops, backward slidings. A rowboat, heavy with a cargo of fruit, planted across the canal, suspended between the clashing patterns of waves, aroused furious honkings and uproar. It was as rough as the sea. "Well, at any rate," Enrico said, his voice broken by a wave which first made the arched and cutting prow of the gondola point to the sky, then brought it down again, quick as an elevator, along with the whole boat, whose bottom beat the hard water like the chest of a diver, "at any rate, Mother said that she expected them too."

"So this is it?" Bernardo said. "Enrico? This is it?"

In the smash of another wave, like a shipwrecked voyager asking a companion the very last questions, Enrico cried: "Don't you want to see them at all? Neither your sister nor your wife? What are they to you? What relationships are there?"

"Excellent," Bernardo cried. He wrapped himself up again in his overcoat, and stayed there until they had passed the Accademia, Santa Maria del Giglio, coming to the richest section of the Grand Canal, close to where it opened up into the lagoon and the sea wind blew more freely; then, with his huge head and big neck unexpectedly emerging out of his coat collar and colorful scarf, Bernardo raised his arm, pointing to the dogal architecture with a vast circular gesture: "Here I could very well buy myself a palazzo!" he cried. "And also a Palladian villa somewhere around Corniano! I have made a fortune! I have means!" Then, crouching again in his coat: "I'm sorry for Clement, who had his heart set on this. The family summit meeting."

They caught sight of a feminine figure, majestic but

quick, behind one of the mezzanine windows. "That's Maria," Bernardo exclaimed, laughing.

She herself came to open the door of the apartment; there was no trace of Ortensia. Her eyes lingered for only one moment on her enormous brother; she said to herself: "Here we are." She pulled him into the house with her embrace; here she held him comfortably in her strong arms, stamping long substantial kisses on his cheeks. In her youth Maria's principal characteristic, besides her green frightened eyes and her flushed cheeks, had been her fine, aristocratic slenderness; she had looked like an adolescent doe; now twenty years had passed, and she was a country lady, a matron. Her eyes were still very large, but self-assured and opaque; the red skin of her face was rough.

"Where is Mother?" Enrico asked while they were leaving their overcoats and scarfs in the vestibule.

"She's in the living room. I came to open the door because I was in a hurry to see Dino."

"How is everything, Maria?" Bernardo asked in a perfectly natural tone.

"Quite all right, Dino," she answered in the same way; but they were exchanging very attentive looks, joyous and frightened.

Enrico pointed to the living room door: "I'm going to talk to Mother a minute . . ."

Bernardo had already taken Maria by the wrist and was pulling her in the opposite direction. From there one entered into a wide corridor. Brother and sister started talking in whispers.

"Where are you taking me?" she asked, and the question, echoed in time from thirty years earlier, meant between the lines: "Are you taking me to the bathroom?" When Bernardo had had secret or reproachful things to tell her, he used to take her to the bathroom.

"Do you remember these?" Bernardo asked, pointing to some heads of angels and lions carved in wood, hanging on the white walls of the corridor. "They were in the house of the Venice Partibons at San Tomà."

"Only God knows how you can remember that."

Then immediately Bernardo whispered, like the interrogator dropping the crucial question into his talk with feigned casualness: "Why did you avoid me in Rome?"

Maria replied at once: "Rather, why did you run after me? Or was it curiosity about what had happened with my daughter—you too, like the journalists?"

Caught unaware by that direct manner, Bernardo replied: "Why did you avoid me? Had you forgotten me?"

Still talking in a whisper, Maria broke fully into the theme: "In case you are interested, Dino, when I was twelve or thirteen years old you were the most important man in my life. But what does that have to do with it now? All these years, and you come back, fresh as a rosebud, as if time didn't exist for you . . ."

"Of course it doesn't exist, Maria, with the kind of remembrances we have."

"Oh, yes, time exists all right, Dino . . . " She took him by the hand, reasonable, sedately middle-aged: "You have made a nice rich life for yourself in America, so why do you come here? To torment yourself, Dino. Why are you so interested in tormenting yourself? And why do you want my help in this?"

"I looked for you almost to distraction, Maria."

"Perhaps that's true, and it's all the more reason why . . . We are all here caught in our own stories, and you come, with your complications, with your bulk"—she raised and lowered her eyes looking at him from head to foot—"and the least you can do is create confusion for yourself. Not for somebody like me, but for yourself, Dino."

"Of course not for you, we know that very well, Maria. Of course!" He took her by both wrists and fixed his eyes deeply in hers: "You believe in the passing of time, and you think that you've changed an awful lot, Maria. On the contrary, you are absolutely the same as you were, with exactly the same way of thinking, with your own system, all quite clear-cut, and you expect the others to . . ."

"That's where you are wrong, Dino, I stay by myself and I don't want to create confusion for anybody and least of all for you. Come now, Fausta and Enrico are anxious to see us together."

In the living room, Fausta, very small, flew toward Bernardo with outstretched arms, and raising a hand to the back of his head she made him bend down, and whispered into the vast fleshy shell of his ear: "Your wife and your mother-in-law. You may expect them too, any minute."

"I know that," Bernardo said, raising himself; and as if to encourage Fausta, he took her by the hand and made her sit near him on a small eighteenth-century sofa. Maria and Enrico sat in front of them, symmetrically, in armchairs.

In the presence of the others, brother and sister became unconsciously stagey, they assumed the theatrical tone of the Venetian living room; yet the whispers they had exchanged in the corridor had left glimmers in their eyes.

Enrico asked Bernardo: "Did you discover why she avoided you?"

With a benevolent, pontifical gesture Bernardo transmitted the question to his sister: "Well? Why? Tell me all."

"You don't even want me to look at you comfortably. Anyway, you haven't changed much, you look miraculously young. Well, then"—she lowered her head, weighing each word, looking at her hands in her lap— "why didn't I answer your messages, for what reason didn't I come forward?" She raised her head: "That is your question, isn't it? I consider it more correct to put it in those terms, Dino, than to say that I was avoiding you?"

"All right, Maria, you put it in those terms."

"Good. Then, Dino, the reason is that at some point *I withdrew from the whole thing.*" She remained silent for a long while.

"You don't suppose you could explain yourself a little better, Maria?"

"I could try but it isn't at all easy. And besides, why should I torment myself with answering you?" She turned to the others: "A man comes back suddenly after twenty years—and what years! He has lost all—what do you call them—all contacts. Hasn't he? And yet *he has claims.*"

Bernardo felt the techniques of his relationship to Maria as a child coming back spontaneously to him, including those used to intimidate her. "Wrong way to pose the problem, Maria," he discarded hurriedly. "No claims. And never lost contact."

Enrico inserted, turning to Maria: "There has been a war. He has won it and we lost it. And his desire is to have lost it with us. You call that *claims?*"

Bernardo blocked him with an almost terrified look. But the women did not even hear, Enrico's remark seemed not to concern them.

Turning back to his sister, Bernardo spoke more calmly, with a sober voice: "Besides, I read. I do an incredible amount of reading."

"What do you read?"

"Everything."

"What? The newspapers?"

"Everything, Maria. Including the little prayer cards you send around when somebody dies."

"Besides," Fausta arbitrated, "his mother wrote to him, she kept him very well informed. Enrico too, for that matter, during the war."

"No, not Mother," Bernardo said. "Caterina, if anybody. Whom I have found again now. Always a good-looking woman: beautiful large face, a little like a lioness." He turned to his sister abruptly: "Through the years, Maria, I have tried as far as possible to keep your sorrows company with my thoughts, and if at some point I lost you, who is to blame? Come, come, who is to blame?"

Fausta and Enrico followed his talk with amusement and surprise.

"It isn't even quite clear what you are talking about," Maria murmured.

"Who is to blame?" Bernardo resumed. "And now, Maria, at this moment, here in Venice—in Venice, Maria, where twenty-five years ago, and more, you were at the convent and we were both paupers, and I went to school, where I was despised by ninety-nine point ninety-nine percent of my schoolmates, so that my most beautiful and enchanting moments were the few times I met you and took you to St. Mark's Square to have ice cream—now, Maria, if I try, not to get definitive answers, which is always impossible, but at least to pose questions, patterns, vague sketches of questions—whom do I find, Maria, to ask questions about you? De-bal-dè, Maria. Not Mother, since you never go to see her, not Father, whom you wouldn't go to see even if he were alive . . ."

"Whereas you did go, didn't you? At least for Easter and Christmastime, these last twenty years, didn't you, Dino?"

"Superficial and ineffective irony. The only possibility

(259)

you have is to admit that *I am the real pivot of the family.* And if I'm not there, then there is Clement."

"There is who?"

"Clement. Clem."

"What does he have to do with the . . . with the Partibons? With us?"

"You see?" Bernardo pointed his finger at her. "You see that you don't understand anything at all? What do you believe families are? Granting, for the sake of argument, that the family makes any sense as an institution, what do you believe it is?" He prolonged his pause, consciously at the center of general tension. He added: "At Corniano I lived over again all that was indispensable, including Father's death. And I have mentally compiled all possible last wills and testaments."

"At least you haven't changed," Maria said in an effectively sober tone, which gave her again central position in the debate, "you talk and you don't even listen to what you are saying, since you know it's nonsense."

Now brother and sister were studying each other with lively eyes and persistent smiles. They were permeated with the deep delight of seeing each other, of talking. If possible, they would have preferred to talk holding each other's hands tight, touching each other.

Then Bernardo set things in motion again: he sighed, and threw himself farther back on the little sofa, dislocating its joints and producing fearful squeaks.

"*You* talk to me about your little girl, then," he said, "you give me your version."

"Not I," Maria said somberly. Then, more sibilantly: "Go to your informers, the jour-na-li-s-ts, the damned lee-ch-es. And listen, Fausta," she asked pointedly, "could you give me an aspirin? Talking to Dino gives me a headache."

Enrico got up. "I'll get you one." Simultaneously, the

doorbell rang. "This must be Nicole and Clare," Enrico said.

Then Maria looked at her brother with an intimate, triumphant, feline, and affectionate smile; she said: "Your various families, Dino, are attacking you from all sides."

"That's the way it should be," Bernardo roared, raising himself and therefore almost touching the ceiling with his head. "I am the center."

Genziana's Lambrusco wine and the food prepared by Clement had brought both of them to a state of lively relaxation, of excited languor. Since childhood Genziana had not had dinner so early. "No," she said, lying on the sofa, "I'll show you the sketches for the *Caligula* costumes tomorrow, in fact you can help me with your advice."

Clement, seated on the carpet near her, held her hand, raising it occasionally to his cheek. "It has been important that we met this morning, hasn't it?"

"It's the seventh time you've asked that. Of course. Important."

"Since then every moment has been important, new, hasn't it?"

"Important, new."

"And when I called you over the telephone it seemed perfectly natural?"

"The most natural thing in the world."

"Next time perhaps I'll make you *pasta e fagioli.*"

"Tomorrow, if you want."

"Tomorrow. We'll see each other every day."

"I hope so."

"You do? You hope so too?"

"Of course."

"Good. Good." Then Clement asked: "Even if I talk about myself I don't bore you?"

"Not for a second."

"If I talk to you about Ilse?"

"If anything, I could be a little jealous."

"Oh, no, no, no. However, I or somebody else would have been the same to you; you needed a certain thing, certain company."

"No, no, it's you, my dear."

"Good. Good. Even when I talk to you about what concerns me it doesn't bother you?"

"I've already told you, I adore everything. I really like everything very much. And listen, your show doesn't make you feel a lump in the stomach any more, does it?"

"No."

"Good. I'm rather proud for having . . ."

"I never talk about it with anybody, not even Bernardo. He helps me a lot, but we never talk about it. In fact, we don't know how to talk about *art*, neither he nor I, unfortunately."

"Why unfortunately?"

"I don't know. I'm thinking of people who talk and really get around, you know? Agents, critics. So, they are the people who really count. Much more important than artists. They walk through cocktail parties greeting everybody; except me, of course. But Bernardo is a rather unusual man. He showed me how to live. It isn't that I have learned. He has never had any interests except perfectly naïve ones."

"Really?" Now Genziana was closing and opening her eyes. Clement realized she was listening only half-heartedly, therefore he went on.

"I even doubt he has ever liked making money, and yet he has made a lot, partly because he has an incredible eye; Bernardo should be seen at the auctions."

"Really?" Genziana asked vaguely.

"We never talk about what I am doing, we don't know

how to express ideas. Some American girls are very good at that. But it is true perhaps, that those are all family questions. All that one does. Do you understand?"

"Well, yes," Genziana mumbled, her eyes shut. "Your mother is the Seal, isn't she? Santa Monica. Go on talking to me."

Clement went on in a whisper: "What right does one have to publicize his private affairs, I'm asking you; the question of art is not well put; in fact every *action,* every *gesture,* becomes wrong the moment you talk about it. Only the absolutely indefinable is worth-while. Absolutely indescribable, Genziana. The most difficult art is literature: putting things into words is a desperate task. I know little about it even though I've read enough. I know by heart whole scenes in *Faust* and in Shakespeare. I know several languages. I write long diaries which I will show you some day, Genziana. I will tell you everything." He observed her and he delicately stopped to caress her hand; he placed it on her lap, he rose and left her, whispering: "Quiet, deep, *nourishing* breathing. My dear. My dear."

With extreme precaution he left the house on tiptoe. A high wind was dragging rapid clouds under a changing moon. Everything, even the white blank blocks of houses, even Bernardo's worn car with its seasoned woods and its red leather seemed to him new and very significant. He absolutely did not want to see anybody. He drove very fast to the section of town from which he had called Genziana; there he stopped the car and left it, to wander on foot, observing, studying, as if to reconstruct a complicated series of actions; meanwhile he continued to talk to her in a whisper: "Yes, it seems that once as a sculptor I used vaguely to do the breakers at Santa Monica mingled with portraits of our mother as a seal. If our mother had told us: 'Children, come here,' taking us both together, Ilse on one side and me

(2 6 3)

on the other, and if she had allowed us to tell her, laughing with love: 'You are a seal,' perhaps it would have been a good start. The seal, a mammal—I have studied her a lot. Clumsy and very agile at the same time, as for example Bernardo is too. Rhythm, and total anarchy. Like the sea itself, for that matter. Gestures reinvented each time."

He went to the same place from which he had called Genziana. He lifted the receiver. He put his finger on the different holes that made up her number, but without turning the dial. He smiled and had tears in his eyes. "At last," he said. "At last."

Flames mobile as quicksilver, the reflections of water on the stuccoed ceiling of her mezzanine: Fausta Fassola had often compared them to the very breath of conversation, always varied and always alike. They were like the motion of the earth turning on its axis, while then the breathing of the sea tide, which determined the great systole and diastole of Venice, was like the wider motion of the earth around the sun. She had been sunk various times in these vague thoughts, while she followed Bernardo and his relatives with half an ear, during the late afternoon. The mercurial flames on the ceiling disappeared, evening descended, Murano glass chandeliers were lit, and in the room made more golden and intimate, the coming and going of words continued.

"With a saint in the family," Bernardo was saying, "you Flanagans would be divided between the social-prestige aspects of the thing and a certain sense of fear, and embarrassment. Am I right? There is no important princely family without cardinals, popes. But a saint?" He challenged wife and mother-in-law with his eyes.

"What a way to talk."

"Let him talk, Nicole," Fausta and Enrico said.

"He talks like Clement," Clare said.

"All right, I talk like Clement," Bernardo agreed affably. And, turning to his mother-in-law: "Your husband, dear Stew, had an aunt who was a nun. Clement has met her, of course; he knows everybody, he is well informed, precise. This nun lived in Arizona."

"What of it?"

"I don't know, it just came to my mind."

"It came to your mind," Maria said, "but you yourself don't know what it is. Like all of you. You see things come to your mind, and you don't know what they are; you don't know what you are talking about. Like the journalists."

"There you go again. I told you I have known only one, a man called Tranquillo Massenti, who was a person of the highest caliber."

"At Corniano, he used to drink two bottles of grappa and a case of wine every day," Maria said.

"If I must tell you the whole truth, Maria," Nicole intervened, "I came to Europe with the feeling that if there was *something,* this *something* should be blocked. And I am perfectly convinced that on this point I have complete support from Fausta here, and from Enrico, who after all are the grandmother and the uncle of that little girl who died."

"And whose daughter was she? The cat's?" Maria said with sudden wild lamentation.

"Certainly, Maria, but you know how it is," Nicole continued without changing register, "how rumors get around. When Cecilia Ghezzi-Walther came to see us in America, she spoke about a movement that was afoot to bring about the eventual beatification of your child—all fabrications, but then, Cecilia is notoriously one of the two or three most ignorant women in Europe; at any rate, my program instinctively was one only: as far as possible the thing ought to be blocked."

(265)

Maria did not seem to listen to her. "Wretched little journalists," she went on, "small despicable people . . . People without hope."

"What about that man Debaldè?"

"He's our friend," Enrico said cheerfully, "he comes rather often to lunch at Mother's."

"Ugo Debaldè," Maria said, "in spite of appearances, is a disorganized, impulsive man. Italians, my friends, are lazy people, people who want everything but give nothing, who do not want to follow the rules and wait, wait. Hope," she concluded, head lowered, hands in her lap, "is a hard, deep thing."

"All in all, Maria," Bernardo said, stretching out on that little eighteenth-century sofa and producing for the hundredth time those fearful squeaks, "you have not changed at all, and you have always been a happy girl. Always keeping to yourself, with that inner smile. Is it true, however, that sometimes you used to beat your child?"

"You keep quiet," Maria said, brightening up with a sarcastic smile and looking at her brother with a curiously voracious expression, "You who have always been a bully. Do you remember when you used to slap me in the face, as a child; and now, Dino, you have an expression as though you were able to do it all over again."

"I loved you enormously, Maria."

"God knows what you mean when you say love."

Nicole cut in: "I'll explain." Her blue-green, attentive, and calculating eyes were already directed at Bernardo, as if she had decided to aim at him now. "He is a nostalgic sentimentalist. A hypocrite, too, because he is far from admitting it. Since we have known him, we have always understood that as far as he is concerned we do not exist." Bernardo made all sort of faces, ostentatiously expressing

(266)

surprise and incomprehension; therefore Nicole pursued with gusto: "His real affections had remained here; more exactly, at Corniano. This trip to Europe has been a whole system of escapes and disappearances, one after the other: he disappears from California and re-emerges in the gambling houses of Las Vegas; he disappears from the West, and turns up in New York to disappear from there in the most . . ."

"Stop it, Mother," Clare murmured.

" . . . in the most insane fashion. Then, there are rumors that he is in Rome. He disappears from there too; he is in Venice; he disappears; and then we are at the real center of everything—Corniano." She looked around as if having just completed a flashing demonstration or a legerdemain trick.

"At Corniano I was sick; Mother cured me."

Somewhat unexpectedly, Nicole's voice became harsh and complaining: "Why do you oppose your mother to me? To humiliate me?" But her eyes remained clear and scrutinizing.

"That's enough, Mother," Clare murmured.

"Now really, Bernardo," Nicole went on, uttering her words with a kind of sensual delight: "Really. Do you know what you look like to me now? You look like a *big bottle full of Corniano up to its neck*. The second I set foot in this room and saw you I understood everything, in a flash. I know you, Bernardo. I see through you." She had a guttural little outburst of laughter; she observed Bernardo avidly.

"How silly of me, not to look for you earlier," Bernardo said. "I always forget that talking to you is such fun." Then, in an extremely low voice, as if exhaling the words in a quick whisper: "Why did you write to my mother? Don't you know that she doesn't answer letters?"

"Whom should one write to? Clement is one of your associates, even a conspirator; Cecilia Ghezzi-Walther herself, *your former traveling companion,* says that you have escaped from Rome. Who is there to . . ."

"Do you know why I see the Ghezzi-Walthers? Do you know the nature of our relationship?"

"Let's not go into that."

"Business, Nicole, *business.*"

Enrico inserted: "Firmino Ghezzi-Walther told me that you are the very man he was looking for; he repeated that to me several times."

"Here in Italy," Bernardo said, turning to Enrico over the women's heads, "as you know better than I do, things are in full progress." He returned to the ladies: "I foresee investments in works of art as a form of tax evasion, just to give a frivolous and easily understandable example. But global developments are looming on the horizon. Ghezzi-Walther factories will dot the earth. Village-factories, installed ready-made, in Africa, in Lichtenstein, in Florida. I and a Bulgarian architect, if we want, will be able to do everything for him, from general planning, supermarket, church, concert hall, to the last decorative tesserae in the toilets."

"I don't know what, but something must have gone to his head," Nicole said.

"Perhaps he is delirious, but there is no doubt that he is making a very great deal of money," Clare warned.

"You follow me, don't you? Financially, even if not matrimonially? Come, come, come! Cards on the table. Clare? Nicole?"

Nicole said: "All right. Let's put the cards on the table: we could have sued you for divorce—desertion."

Bernardo's voice again became a quick whisper: "And I could have sued Clare for . . ." He raised his voice again:

"But we don't want to discuss things at that level, do we? Let's see what Maria thinks about it."

The sister confined herself to a choked laugh, with her mouth shut.

Nicole said slowly: "Your great delight, your supreme joy, Bernardo, is when you can throw your success, your power, in our faces."

Again Bernardo lowered his voice to a breath; he said quickly: "My life is a complete failure."

This time Nicole studied him a long while in silence, sighing. When she spoke she had a lump in her throat: "You have always mocked us, after all. The poor immigrant, et cetera, et cetera. For years I reproached myself for having treated you badly. Big liar. You would put on the act of admiring a painting, or the furniture in a house, to pull us into a trap; you knew we would express admiration too, if you did, but then you would throw the mask away and start jeering at us. You would leave us stranded. You despised our circle of friends. We were willing to learn." Her chin was trembling. "And now, there you are, choke-full of Corniano, and you oppose your mother to us. Tell the truth. I am tired. What have we done to you? You are like one who believes he has been subjected to an indignity and you want to revenge yourself on me. But I am tired. You used to be so gentle. You were our support. In fact, you see, here we are. We ran after you."

"That's bad! That's very bad! I'm a wretched kind of support! And I have never been gentle, never! Gentle? Ah, ah! I am full of dark things; there are moments when I could kill . . ."

Clare looked at him, bright with admiration. "Don't go on, Mother," she murmured.

"This is it," the mother pressed on. "It's the scene he has been wanting for years. And he starts it right here in Ven-

(269)

ice, where I was born and raised." She curled her lips with bitterness, but her cautious eye was questioningly aimed at Bernardo.

"What are you discussing? I should like to bring a little order, and at any rate, dinner is almost ready," Fausta said.

"Keep quiet," Maria told her, "I want to see this."

Bernardo's forefinger was pointed at Nicole: "Wonderful! Precisely! You, a Venetian! And then you go to America, and instead of looking for people that really exist, you surround yourself with unreal characters! You let them build you up as the vivacious, temperamental Italian! You had real possibilities, and you became a bit actress! Who has ever despised your friends? No—simply *unreal*. Stew. *I say, Stew.*"

"Leave him alone," Clare said, "he is my father."

Now Bernardo's finger turned to his wife: "He is your father, and yet," he accused, "it was none other than he who organized the nightmare of our wedding. With the bishop and all of his unreal friends and the little smiles. Some father! And then, after the nightmare was over, everybody back to base: the friends back to their villas, the bride and bridegroom back to the alcove, the Negro butlers and the Negro maids back to their ghettos, everything fine, everything gentle and correct. Isn't it? And I, caught in the middle. You should have thrown me out—dangerous individual, capable of shooting!"

"Platitudes," Clare whispered.

"Why didn't you shoot?" Nicole said. Her voice was firm, like her face—down which, however, she allowed two tears to roll. "It's clear, anyway, that deep inside you detest us and wish we were dead."

"Nicole!" Fausta cried with a hollow voice, more fascinated than frightened.

Nicole had discovered the effectiveness of a calm tone:

(2 7 0)

"You are a monster, Bernardo. When I think that you had brought so much joy into our lives. So much imagination. Perhaps your sickness burst out as you returned to Europe, to Corniano—the crisis of a disease which already was . . ." She shook her head; then she lowered it, and became grave and solemn: "But we shall always love you. Come here. Come close to me a moment."

With something between a sigh and a roar, Bernardo got up and went to sit on the arm of her chair; she took his hand, she brought it around her shoulders making a stole of his arm while Bernardo extended his other hand, palm up, toward Clare, who immediately placed a handkerchief in it. Making a ball of the handkerchief, Bernardo pressed it on Nicole's eyes several times, then he dried her cheeks very carefully.

"And how did you find your mother?" Nicole asked.

"Extremely alert. And then, she at least has the good taste of not thanking, if by chance she receives something. In fact, of not even realizing it. And of treating me like a stranger."

"Is that what you want, Bernardo? What do you want? What have you decided?"

"Ah! What have I decided!" Bernardo freed himself and jumped to his feet. He started walking up and down the room. Every now and then he would produce a wild laugh. At each passage, he would brush the chandelier with his head; his bulk produced infinite reverberations of fluid shadows in all directions, on the walls, on the ceiling.

Nicole was following those motions, her mouth open. Finally she said: "No. I can't take it. I'm tired. You are insane." And she resumed: "What have you decided? Are you coming back to America with us? Are you going to be associated with Firmino Ghezzi-Walther in Italy? What are you going to do?"

(271)

"Let's not talk about me," Bernardo answered, "let's talk about you." He sat between his wife and his mother-in-law. He settled himself comfortably. He coughed. "I'll arrange things for you," he said. "I'll give you a lot. I'll do things for you. I'll perform such actions that the bigots—that's the word—the bigots, *if they ever heard about my actions*, would say: 'Oh!'" He shrilled in a falsetto voice: "'Oh! That man Bernardo, what a soul, what a heart!' But instead, let this be clear"—and he looked at them one by one, weighing his words, calling also Fausta and Enrico to witness—"let it be absolutely clear that a decision of this sort is of no use either to me or to you. It does not confirm anything. It should be considered outside of any feeling of family piety. Giving, in my case, is less of a gesture than not giving. But the very concept of family relationship has nothing to do with this—it does not exist—and this is the last time we'll talk about the whole matter."

"He is insane; his sickness at Corniano has deranged his mind."

"Oh, no"—Bernardo reacted immediately—"my dear, if I say something, that's it. You must all believe me. In fact, you must obey me. I am the one whose words carry weight, of course."

Nicole pointed her finger at him: "Mad laughter," she denounced. "And by the way, I don't even understand you very well."

"My support, Nicole. The opening of accounts at the bank. The registering of property in the name of your daughter, which means you and your daughter. Written pledges. *Written* means *silence*: we shall never talk about this again. We are not relatives, and the very concept, as I said . . . Or if you wish, you may put it this way: I am in charge. I am the father of the family. I hold power. And as head of the clan, if I wish I can declare it nonexistent. So

(2 7 2)

there you are, you see." Then he pointed to Maria and lowered his voice: "And no one escapes me," he said, "wherever each of you may be. So I also decree that the only authorized source of information on Maria and her little daughter shall always be my mother, period."

"My foot," Maria said.

"There goes Maria, already escaping you," Clare said.

"I have loved Maria; it is up to her to preserve or to destroy that moment."

"He is insane, he is raving, you know," Nichole insisted, "and then he talks like that to confuse us, to torture us." She appealed to Maria, then to Clare.

But Clare was staring at Bernardo, magnetized: "He has loved me too," she whispered.

Bernardo laid one of his huge hands on the soft hands of his wife, who held them crossed in her lap. He shook them a couple of times, smiling.

"Now I understand," Clare said, "it was for this that I came to Venice. For this show."

With genuine curiosity, Bernardo asked her: "Why did you go with that little Belgian? It is he, isn't it?"

On Ortensia's face, as she stood at the door, Fausta recognized the well-known symptoms of desperate impatience. She got up, to make it clear that the conversation could be continued at the table. They all followed her toward the dining room, except Bernardo, who lingered in the living room, and opened a window.

He leaned over it to breathe the already nocturnal air, a humid wind which came in gusts from the lagoon and made all kinds of light vibrate as they mixed in the water like on a dark palette: boats' lamps, neon lights, windows of palaces, moon. The salty odor of the wind mixed with that of broiled fish and lemon from the dining room, from the kitchen. Then Nicole appeared behind him; feeling cold, she had gone and put on her fur coat. Now she was wearing mink and newly applied make-up. For Bernardo, Nicole mingled with his memories—of ladies in fur coats during his years of wretched poverty and solitary school: Countess Boschinetti; and also Mrs. Cerega, the mother of the boy who, when Bernardo implored him to resume violence, had defined him *a cannibal from the jungle, in fact a creature living in trees, an orang-utan.* Nicole took his arm and whispered: "Aren't you coming to dinner, Bernardo?" and then: "You are a lion, but besides roaring, you also purr." Finally, anxiously: "You won't abandon us, will you? You will never abandon us?" He allowed the soft, withered hand of the lady to take refuge in his own: "No," he replied, "but you must let me stay alone." Nicole smiled and said raucously, warmly: "Come now, you beast," and she pulled him by the arm, to make their entrance into the dining room. They had reserved the head of the table for him.

The conversation stopped when they entered. They let them sit in silence. Nicole asked: "What is it? Why are you all so quiet?"

Maria shrugged and broke the silence: "They were talking about that other daughter of yours; it seems she is coming to Italy too."

"Now let's not create new complications. Every nervous system has its limits."

Nicole's and Clare's eyes, almost identical, met across the table. Clare said: "I thought we would hold a complete summit meeting." She sighed. "In the last years, one has heard Ilse referred to as a whore, while earlier, when she was a child, it was fashionable to say that she was a kleptomaniac. Where do we stand now?"

"Every nervous system has its limits," Nicole repeated.

CHAPTER TEN

✻

Bernardo came down to Rome with a charge of energy he had never known before in his life. He had persuaded his relatives not to come to Rome for the opening of Clement's exhibition; they should come on the second or third day, if at all. Actually, he did not want to have them in Rome either now or later; he would meet them again in Paris around wintertime, or else in Connecticut in the spring. He had had indirect news that the American art scholar of Belgian origin with whom Clare had been connected, was now in Paris for a year on a scholarship; he guessed that Clare would take leave of him in France between late fall and Christmas, and come back with the new year into full possession of a fresh, radiant American country home.

Clare had never frontally accused Bernardo of betrayals, abandonment, and negligence, let alone mental cruelty. When Nicole hinted that Bernardo and Clare should subject themselves to psychoanalysis in order to present themselves to each other later, clarified, and free for a new life, Clare had reacted with courteous smiles, as if she had been listening to a rather poor joke. There was, however, a well-rooted form of alliance between Bernardo and Clare, comprehensible only to the two of them; the mother counted on it, although she did not understand its terms.

Bernardo took a suite in a hotel overlooking the Villa Borghese gardens. He let all telephone calls come through, he answered all sorts of solicitations and telegrams with vivacity. He spoke for hours with the Ghezzi-Walthers in Milan. He received a long visit from Umberto Boschinetti, his old schoolmate and later his agent; he decided to deprive him of much of his power; he realized, leafing through the artichoke of that personality, that he had always sensed in it a central core, which was, rather than normally dishonest, grotesque.

He maintained contact with Rita McKillop, a vivacious Northern Italian from Bergamo, well scrubbed, with ample bosom, separated years earlier from a Canadian wartime husband; she ran the little gallery where Clement's work was to be shown. Of Clement himself, she said: "Disappeared. Everybody knows he is always with Genziana Horst, but nobody ever sees them."

On his arrival in Rome, Bernardo had also received the same bulletin from Dora and the trio. For even better reasons, he had gone to a hotel, leaving the apartment at Clement's disposal. In fact, after calling the apartment and not finding his brother-in-law there, he had told Mrs. McKillop with satisfaction: "That's Rome for you. Ideal city for this sort of thing. Right format. Possibility of meeting as in St. Mark's Square, and then all you have to do if you don't want to meet anybody is to deviate one inch from the established routes."

Mrs. McKillop had said: "Clement is making a mistake, not staying in circulation."

"I don't know whether I agree with you, and at any rate I'm sure he is right in staying with Miss Horst. I have met her, and she is not just a beautiful woman."

"I know her very well; a *falsa magra*. Her father died a few days ago."

(276)

"Clement as an artist has capacities for understanding, and for giving help, vastly superior to the average," Bernardo said, "and I am happy—as a matter of fact I'm rather proud—that the two of them have . . ."

The woman looked at him with blank eyes. She never completely understood Bernardo but she liked to maintain contact with him, to arrange for presentations of American artists in Rome, or of Italian ones in America. Bernardo, in turn, held her in high esteem. He saw her rarely and briefly, each time with intense pleasure. She was a woman who loved her profession. Dora and the trio had qualified her for him as frigid; Ovidio had taken the occasion for a long dissertation on career women and frigid women; Bernardo had lost the thread of Ovidio's talk almost immediately; Ovidio managed to talk with the tidiness and precision of a printed article, and that was the reason why Bernardo found him very confused. The only one in that group of friends that Bernardo had found completely lucid, was Tranquillo Massenti; but Massenti was always extremely difficult to track down.

Clement called Bernardo over the telephone the morning of the very day the show was going to open. Whenever the two brothers-in-law met or simply talked after an absence they started to laugh, by way of introduction. They did not exchange any relevant news. Bernardo knew that in Dora's milieu there had been much talk about his sickness at Corniano; now Clement confirmed to him that everybody had found that story quite funny. "Dora is always with Ovidio," Clement said, and Bernardo replied: "Really?" overlooking the fact that he had seen the couple various times. Bernardo and Clement felt that there was always something unreal in news, in data; their tendency, therefore, was never to exchange any information, and if they received any, to forget about it. One day, in the right mood and with nothing to do, Bernardo would report to Clement on the family conclave, the Venetian summit meeting, altering it for comic effects. Now, toward the end of their telephone conversation, Clement mentioned his lady companion for the first time: "Genziana and I will not come to the opening of the show," and Bernardo reacted to that announcement by saying parenthetically: "Is that so? Good, good." They talked about other subjects, and just before hanging up Bernardo said: "I'll go by the gallery later on with the others, and if I hear anything funny I'll try to remember it."

Bernardo knew that at the right hour Dora and the trio would appear to pick him up at the hotel in Tito Solmi's capacious car, in which there would probably also be Rodolfo Piglioli-Spada. Since the Senator's death, Piglioli-Spada had started coming to town, independently of his wife, attaching himself to Tito Solmi's group. Tito liked to make him talk, and maintained that somebody like Perineschi should convince him to write. Tito was the connective tissue of an association which had had its origin the evening of the reception at the Solmis'; within the group, one could clearly single out the couple destined to epoch-making isolation from the rest, namely, Dora-Ovidio. Bernardo and the others could follow the ascending diagram-line of Dora's love in her mellowing eyes and hips.

Now the girl did not look at herself in the mirror alone, but with Ovidio at her side. They devised all possible forms of conjunction. Already the first time, when they had preferred Ovidio's apartment to a Sunday cinema, they had lingered in bed through the long afternoon hours, first in the light from the windows, then in the twilight and into the evening, making discoveries, praising each other. In her relationship to Ovidio, Dora had assumed at once the position of a guide. It was very sweet to him to let her make deci-

(278)

sions. Since that very first time, he had given her a key to his apartment, so the next day he could dial his own telephone number from the University or from the newspaper, and announce his return in the evening like a husband. Dora herself, in those first few days, had liked to go into his apartment during his absence, to follow the traces of his life alone, to take possession of things, and perhaps on his return to be ready for love, wearing a light gown, her "somewhat tube-shaped" legs looking very smooth and childish, her "somewhat flat" feet naked on the floor, and a pervasive sense of recent bath and talcum massage; in other words, she was not offering him the *cinq à sept* alcove scene, with herself a voluptuous and alluring mistress, but a happy smile on her experienced lips, domesticity and tenderness in her attentive eyes. "Never mind what I did before I knew you," she had told him, "that was so long ago. With you it's all different, this is a new era." Actually they had agreed that since that first Sunday every day had counted at least as a month. She would receive him at the door of his apartment. She would sink her short fingers into his thick soft red hair. She would caress his large face, and kiss "one freckle at a time," then she would take his coat off, pull off his tie, unbutton his shirt and resume, on his chest, her systematic kissing, at once delicate and upsetting. "With you," she would go on, "everything is different. Some of the things I do with you I had done only in my imagination; at twelve I already knew everything, in my imagination. This is the right hour in our lives, Ovidio. It's like noon. You don't know how lucky we are. From the first moment I saw you, I decided I would come with you, and listen to what I am saying: even if we didn't want to get married, I would come anyway."

She would go and lie on the bed; from there she would stretch her arms out, uttering tender and rather maternal Venetian endearments. When she had him near her she would pull his hair, his ears, she would torture him with tickling; then she would slowly allow full play to her abilities one by one, speaking freely of what they were doing; in supreme moments, while with the motion of her hips she accompanied and regulated the growth of pleasure, she continued to keep her dark eyes fixed on his clear ones, smiling, consciously proud.

Later, at the restaurant with the rest of the group, even their choice of foods was followed by everybody with attention. For a while the couple would jokingly give themselves the air of dieticians and health addicts, with the bloody steak, with the fish eaten practically raw. The others would look at them with suspicion. Then suddenly they would deviate toward dishes among the heaviest and most damaging, throwing themselves on them without restraint, arousing warm envy.

Bernardo, urged several times over the telephone in his room, finally came down and found them in the hotel bar, all four of them, Dora and the trio, gathered around Rodolfo Piglioli-Spada.

"Exclude from your line of thinking," Piglioli-Spada was saying with nasal monotony, "the by now fixed entities like the Roman monuments or Venice, and try and define with simple schematic formulas the rest of the nation, the active and operative part; well, you will follow me, I hope, if I distinguish in the national pattern three types of civilization: (a) Balkan-African; (b) Vatican; (c) Lombard-American. Don't be surprised if I provide the terminology so offhandedly; actually I have been ruminating these matters a number of years, in the country."

"Trash," Ovidio said.

"Trash, isn't it?" Quarto Martelli asked, reassured, brightening up.

They discovered Bernardo and they all got up; Dora raised her arms to throw them around his neck and kissed him on the cheek, whispering: "Clem has really disappeared and there is no news of Ilse's arrival."

"We, however, shall have to go to this show," Bernardo said. "They tell me it will be even worse than a cocktail party." Cocktail parties destroyed him both physically and morally.

The dialogue between Genziana Horst and Clement Blumenfeld was made, rather than of information, of mutual confirmations. "You too, don't you?" and every time they would laugh. Only rarely now, Clement would let some uncertainty transpire: "You needed this, I or somebody else would have been the same." He did it for the pleasure of listening to Genziana's simple, practical replies: "Then let's put the cards on the table. I have caught you and I intend to tighten the knot more and more; I want to have the right to come to you if ever I need help."

"That's it, you needed the thing, not the particular individual."

"No, it's you, it's you. Or let us say: I didn't know that something like this existed."

"Are you sure?"

"Very sure." They would laugh, discovering and savoring their laughter as it grew within them.

They had been alone for three days at the Piglioli-Spadas' country house, where they had arrived one day in the early afternoon; until evening they had taken long walks in the pine grove in the rain. They had retired early, she to her room, he to the room with the Russian canopied bed. Toward midnight Clement had come out into the corridor on hearing the squeak of steps on the old wood at the far end; a neat blade of light was cutting the floor. He went

(2 8 1)

to the door, left ajar, knocked on it, trembling with confusion and nostalgia, as if he had abandoned Genziana long ago in an unknown place and had now found her again: her lively voice made him laugh with joy.

"Carissimo, are you awake too? I'm trying Lauretta's room; the bed is divine."

They had both fallen asleep on it, hardly touching each other, equally exhausted, and finding immediate rest. She had awakened first; between sleep and the light of dawn, Clement had heard the water cascade from the bathroom. He went there; every object looked absolutely new, unexpected, in the early-morning glimmer, its light spreading in the vapor of hot water like the sun in the early-dawn mist. In the sparkling porcelain and the water in the enormous bathtub, the body of Genziana had revealed itself to him; with his hand under water he had explored it all while their eyes met searchingly, in silence; they heard nothing but their own breathing and the swishing of the water. "Give me that," Genziana had said, pointing to the red bathrobe. He had wrapped her in it, drying her; from her body arose a vapor of soap and cologne; he held her tight, they touched each other with open lips. She had a childish smile; the beautiful, proud Genziana, followed at a distance for years, was now a figure out of earlier times; she had whispered: "Funny how last night we fell asleep." In the room she had taken off her bathrobe, going back to the bed and inviting him: "Come, my love, but remember—I am not at all good at this, you know."

Now they were going back to Rome and Genziana was driving with great calm and ability. She liked to drive and he liked to look at her. Every moment and everything they saw—pine grove, path cut in the fields, gate closed on a wild garden, country inn with trellis and hens pecking the ground—everything gave a sense of absolute novelty, arousing attention and gratitude. "No, it is absolutely *you*," Genziana resumed in her normal tone, a little hard. "Let us say, first, that I find you very handsome, I adore your face. And then I adore you also because you are well organized, punctual at appointments, you know everybody and you dress in the right way; you are precise and practical, you remember things, you can orient yourself immediately . . ."

They had decided to come back from the country, not for the opening of the show, but for Ilse's possible arrival. "That's how she is," Clement was saying, "she won't wire the exact hour. She won't even call from the airport. She will just come to my studio and sit down, entering the conversation as if she had been with us all the time."

"I can see Ilse's style very well; I adore her."

"We'll go to my place, perhaps stay there till next Monday, how would you like that? Bernardo is at the hotel, the apartment is all right."

"But of course. Everything is perfect. I am just thinking of what all movements used to be for me; they were important problems, even a trip to Cortina or Venice, or even weekends at Laura and Rodolfo's. Now with you it doesn't matter at all where I am, everything is so simple."

"It's because I organize things."

Genziana suddenly stopped the car on the roadside, close to a large abandoned field drenched with water. "Come near me, stay here a moment." Her entire leg was in close contact with his, pressed against him from the hip to the ankle. He moved his hand over her face in a slow, strong caress; then he took her face between thumb and forefinger, pulling it closer, losing himself in contemplation of those large, questioning, submissive eyes.

"You know, I don't take tranquilizers any more," Genziana said. With her lips parted, she breathed on his face, from the eyes to the cheeks, to the lips, without touching him yet. "I adore your face," she whispered quickly, and chose the moment when their lips joined; they almost set their teeth into each other suddenly, and they remained joined in a tight, violent knot until their breath failed. They freed themselves, flushed and panting. Genziana started the motor, resumed her silent driving.

"If Bernardo arranges a show for me in America," Clement said, "you and I will go there together."

"More than once, in America, I was alone, in the evening. I would watch television, in my hotel room, or at a friend's house where I was staying."

"We'll go there together this time."

"There was a television program with stories about gangsters, all of them very slimy and with Italian names."

"That one is wonderful; Ilse thinks it's one of the great comic spectacles."

"Does Ilse like living there?"

"She works all the time. America is extraordinary; here you can't explain it, though."

"Of course."

As often between them there was a long silence, of which they savored every moment.

"Really, I must say that I don't care at all to go to my exhibition."

"They'll probably say awful things about it."

"When I think how impressed I used to be by experts, agents, et cetera. Now they are like castrato voices; or even like a film without sound track." He kissed Genziana on the cheek.

"Perhaps that's a danger."

"I have never been able to talk with them. A few days ago I was with Tranquillo Massenti in a bar, and there were . . ." Clement was silent a long while.

(2 8 4)

"Well?" But Clement did not speak.

"How is Tranquillo? He hasn't called me lately. Every now and then he calls me."

"He writes. He drinks. He is well. There were three people with him, among them that man Paleona who sometimes writes for *Roma Sabato;* and they talked a lot. Do you know what they talked about? They talked about how one can use, in a work, pieces of some material, the stuff itself. To give you an idea—bits of a real cannon in a sculpture, or a piece of rope, just any old rope, sewing a slash made in the canvas itself." He fell silent again.

"Go on."

"Well, then I think, why not put for example a dead bird there, or a squirrel? Supreme work of art: the artist himself, dead, nailed there."

"The ultimate self-portrait." Genziana turned her eyes away from the road a moment, glanced at Clement as for a quick control. They both smiled, reassured. Then, with her look fixed on the road, frowning, Genziana said: "Perhaps you and I won't work any more, nothing but this will matter to us any more."

Clement said immediately: "No. Both you and I have been alone so long. Now we deserve this, it cannot damage us. You think so too, don't you?"

"Of course. Yes, yes, of course." Again she glanced at him a moment, then they both laughed. "I am still clumsy," she said. "I am always a little afraid to unbalance myself."

"Much less than you used to be, though?"

"Much, much less."

"I am used to it, because I knew you from a distance."

Genziana frowned; she had taken after his habit of lowering the head and pondering the words, even the words they most often repeated between them. In spite of that pensive air, she looked younger, her eyes were full of attention and curiosity. If she spoke in her usual manner, it was only to translate into a known language the new events that were happening to her: "How *extraordinary* all this, how *right,* but you must always *tell* me, you know, carissimo . . . " She liked to undress in his presence; his most intimate kisses had appeared to her the most natural and gentle acts in the world. She looked for ways of abandoning herself to him more and more completely; one of her only worries had been that of not giving him pleasure. But it soon vanished; she was soon sure of herself, and asking for confirmation became rather a game: "Am I really a good mistress?" she said, without anxiety or incredulity.

When Bernardo's group arrived, the small gallery was already crowded. Bernardo kept himself between Ovidio and Dora; Ovidio recognized and identified people known to him. Moving meant bumping into people and into sculptures. The multifarious voices melted into a vast, deafening hum. The place seemed basically refractory to the possibility of communication between people. Ovidio, relatively more experienced, tried to isolate voices or people of note. No one tried to see the sculptures. Every now and then a phrase would emerge neatly over the rest.

"Things that have already been done, on the whole much better, by the Futurists forty years ago . . . "

"He's already finished before beginning . . . "

The two phrases were traceable to a slender blond man with a huge Adam's apple, and to a vivacious fat one with a mustache. Ovidio turned abruptly in the direction of those two voices but halfway he met Rodolfo Piglioli-Spada's intensely attentive look; Piglioli-Spada shook his head with electric quickness, and with his finger raised he whispered warningly: "Don't worry, they are all talking about a different show, not this one. A painter's show. Is there a painter called Mariano Folchi? I presume you can confirm that for me."

With a conspiratorial air he pointed his finger toward Tito Solmi, who as a well-informed extrovert had placed himself immediately between the two speakers, explaining to the slender blond one: "Mariano, with the start he had, could have remained at the center of general attention and just let people pet him while he went on purring."

"Exactly," the fat speaker with the mustache pressed on cheerfully. "But the trouble with Mariano is that he started talking, explaining his paintings, all of the problems, so everybody was bored and was left speechless. No one bothers about him any more."

Ovidio pointed out to Dora and Bernardo some of the people he knew, identifying them diligently: Pietro Alano, author, and in charge of a fiction series at one of the major publishers; Poldo Sappugi, who was "a classic example of what I call a 'fashionist.'" At a brief but not easily surmountable distance, he pointed to Angelo Paleona. "I must try and talk to Perineschi myself, otherwise perhaps Paleona is going to write something in *Roma Sabato*, and God knows what . . ."

Paleona was turning his heavy look slowly around: evaluating potential interlocutors. From these he did not seek conversation, but openings for his own brilliant lines. He launched this one: "I am told this man Blumenfeld is an excellent dancer," and tried to open a passage for himself in the crowd.

Bernardo, seeing him at close range, took him by the arm: "Say that again. I'm interested."

Paleona looked at the unknown man without either seeing him or hearing him; his eyes, surveying the field beyond Bernardo, took in Pietro Alano and Poldo Sappugi, friends; he raised his elbow to shake off Bernardo and moved toward the two men. He still had to get by Mrs. McKillop, and two unknown girls, who were talking to each other.

"Perhaps in America they will sell."

"I wouldn't mind having an object like this in my house."

"I wouldn't."

"Wouldn't you?"

"Wouldn't I what?"

Having finally reached Alano and Sappugi, Paleona pointed his bulging eyes in the direction of Alano, and shot again: "I am told this man Blumenfeld is an excellent dancer."

Alano did not listen, but he laughed, thus permitting Paleona, who was watching him like a runner at the start of a race waiting for the flag to be lowered, finally to underline his own phrase, letting off a long hard laugh. Poldo Sappugi's face remained absolutely still. From his towering height Bernardo Partibon, with his forefinger raised almost to touch the ceiling, was making signals toward Paleona: "This time I heard you," he cried, sounding a little inebriated, "and as far as that goes, his dancing is in the championship class."

Paleona, reabsorbed in himself, did not listen; but Sappugi registered Bernardo's words and smiled.

Sappugi's smile was echoed by a ravenlike brunette with a sharp face and disorderly hair, who seemed to hold Sappugi under continuous and uneasy surveillance.

"That's Petrucci," Ovidio explained to his friends, "and I call Sappugi a fashionist, which means 'one who is attuned to fashions.'" He smiled but no one reacted to his words. Dora did not follow his talk, but her hand was joined to his with tender, hidden force. "Except that Sappugi has discovered a wonderful formula," Ovidio went on, dreaming of future winters when he would explain Rome to Dora, and the history of Italy and of the world, "that is to say, he depends on fashions inasmuch as he lies in wait for them in order to demolish them."

"What fashions?" Dora asked. They had got out of bed an hour earlier and each still felt wrapped within the other as in a warm breath.

"Of any kind—novels, film directors," Ovidio explained into empty space. He greeted Sappugi with a gesture of the hand and a smile. Sappugi had a still, clean face, the face of a well-bred boy, but with mountaineer cheekbones—a face, Ovidio noticed, which would have been positively irritating if it had been expressive; as it was, it almost gave him the look of a *simpatico* village simpleton. Ovidio knew him well enough and had once or twice contributed to spreading "Poldo's latest remark." Now he could almost have sworn that Poldo was following a line of thought of this kind: in the present moment and milieu, an American like Clement B. Blumenfeld, and a sculptor to boot, was so obviously unacceptable that a minimum of novelty could be found only in abandoning oneself to the whimsical capriciousness of favorable comment. Costanza Petrucci, with her mobile eyes sparkling through her uncombed black hair, clearly understood all that; she knew Clement Blumenfeld, whom she had even visited in his studio; she liked him physically, and she planned to devote to him one of the weekly columns she wrote for *Roma Sabato,* entitled "Secret" and signed "The Initiate." Spurred by attraction toward her remembrance of the physical Clement and by silent authorization of the arbiter Sappugi, she already formed in her mind possible headlines: "Sculptor Sees World in a Mountain of Melted Wax"—too long; perhaps: "Anticipates Martian Mineralogy"—more intriguing.

Partibon closed his eyes and tightened his lips, perceiving an impending attack of his disease; there already was the suspension of reality, the vast, initial sense of failing. Normal reactions and dimensions were replaced by the void; there followed the vain search for other usable reactions and dimensions; only indecipherable messages came from that direction. This time he felt as though he were listening visually, or seeing with his ears: the voices around him became the images of certain tall and narrow gravestones with very minute inscriptions in incomprehensible alphabets, which he remembered having seen as a child in the house of the Venice Partibons at San Tomà, in old engravings illustrating burial customs of the ancient Egyptians or Assyrians; along with that vision there even came perceptibly to his nostrils an odor of damp old earth, as from a ready-to-use, wide-open grave. He leaned on Dora, and seeing her raise her black, round, and happy eyes toward him, he managed to laugh: "Dora, I warn you, I don't feel well at all," he said, and she replied, laughing too and brightening up: "In fact you look strange. Come and sit in the next room."

She kept close to him without taking her eyes away from him while they moved to the inside room of the gallery; Bernardo sat at the desk, leaning heavily on his arm. He saw the telephone near him and it immediately seemed to him a sinister object. He realized that he had never really observed a telephone in his life. Then he started to complain in a low voice.

"There is no relationship. My fault. What have I done," he said with a murmur that was almost only a trembling of his thick lips. Dora was standing near him; Ovidio and Piglioli-Spada appeared at the door of the little room and stood there; all followed Bernardo's movements intensely. "I knew him when he was a little boy, on the beach at Santa Monica."

"Of course, I know that, dear," Dora said, putting a hand

on his shoulder, pressing her fingers strongly into it, pinching the cloth of the jacket as if she wanted to tear a piece off; there was a light veil of tears in her eyes, and she watched Bernardo with an expression of affection and of helpfulness so lively that it looked cheerful. "What's happening to you now? How do you feel?" She felt his forehead, she caressed his hair with gestures that managed to be concerned and pleasurable at the same time.

"I have nothing but remorse," Bernardo murmured.

He automatically lifted the telephone receiver and dialed the number of Clement's apartment. With the receiver pressed to his ear, he raised his eyes toward Dora and repeated: "Nothing but remorse." Her brief outburst of laughter came out like a sob. At the fourth ring of the telephone, Genziana answered.

"Bernardo Partibon! Carissimo! Of course I recognized the voice immediately. Unfortunately, you know, Clement is not here; this is what happened: some totally unknown person, some lawyer I think, or some engineer who had been on the same plane as Ilse, the twin, you know, but of course you know her—well, this engineer, or lawyer perhaps, called to say that they had stopped her, they hadn't let her in."

"In where?"

"In Italy. This man evidently was an ordinary passenger who could enter; so she asked him to transmit the message . . ."

"I understand, I understand."

"Do you understand? Ilse had already landed, she was at the Rome airport, but in a way she was still abroad. You tell me if one could imagine anything more peculiar even if one invented it." Bernardo recognized Genziana's society tone; yet, as she went on he felt she was tense, feverish. "Clement called I don't know how many numbers, at the airport, everywhere, but without any results, so he seemed literally insane, and I must admit that the whole thing did make one insane with annoyance, it's a rather atrocious situation, I find. Don't you find?"

There was a long silence. Then Bernardo asked: "Insane in what way?"

"Well, he seemed all changed, I must say; with this message from Ilse and the fact that he was unable to communicate with her, he seemed to stiffen. I stayed here to wait in case there were phone calls. After all, I understand how much Clement needs her; he has often talked to me about her; they are like one person, even if they are far apart; she must be quite extraordinary . . . " There was a long pause. "Are you listening?"

Bernardo was rambling: "I knew them when they were little. I knew him before I knew her. At Santa Monica. For a period they kept her in Europe."

"You talked to me about them the first time, don't you remember?"

The little boy on the beach at Santa Monica had made long speeches with intensity, demandingly, knowingly; speaking of the twin, he had assumed an air of pride: "Ilse is courageous. We are not identical twins; she is very beautiful. She has been very very sick but now she is very very well; she can stay under water for hours." Or he would also say things like: "She is clean, fresh, she smells good; it's a pleasure to be near her."

Genziana recalled: "A detail has stuck in my mind, of the boy who looked into gynecology treatises to see how twins are placed . . . you told me that. It seems like ages ago, and it's only been days. One lives in such a hurry; or perhaps it isn't the hurry, I don't know what it is. Hello? Are you there? Listen, carissimo, I did all I could . . . "

"What do you mean? Where was Clement going?"

"He left in a hurry. He was going to the airport, obviously, although they stopped her without letting her come into Italy, I imagine they'll keep her in a sort of quarantine; at any rate, Clement told me he would call from the airport; in fact, perhaps we had better hang up, otherwise he may find the line busy; as soon as I know something I'll call you at the gallery. How is the show going?"

"I don't know; what can I know?"

After he had finished talking, all the others surrounded Bernardo; they had grasped the general trend of the situation, the event: Ilse stopped at the airport border; they appeared as if desperately euphoric, moving with agitation in empty space. "We've got to do something at once," Dora said with little conviction. "We must move the authorities." They did not listen to her. On her own she tried to reach her brother Enrico at the Foreign Office, but a subaltern, Dr. Geloso, told her that he was not in his office.

After ruminating for a long while in silence, Ovidio spoke a little didactically: "We must not let our destiny be shaped by imbecilic misunderstandings and absurd bureaucracies."

Piglioli-Spada listened to the phrase and took it in avidly. "Opposition is difficult," he replied with his calm, precise voice, "very difficult. Wait and see how they'll fix him up, the poor boy, as an artist too, unless he has the good luck of passing totally unobserved."

"What do you mean? What does this have to do with it?" Ovidio asked aggressively, but it was public-debate aggressiveness, a panel tone.

"My dear Professor Semenzato, everything is reducible to the tritest patterns, isn't it?" Piglioli-Spada paused, questioned everybody with his look, and went on: "Visas, permits, you can or you cannot go through; in the last analysis —nationalism. Stop me if I talk nonsense. As far as I am

concerned, all that has even remotely to do with nationalism may produce either comic or tragic results; serious results, never."

Monotonous, nasal, small among the others, he had
forced their attention as if hypnotizing them. Ovidio murmured only: "Well, of course, if you put things on
that . . ." They realized that the voices from the showroom
were much more sparse; evidently many visitors had already
gone, the opening was becoming a closing. Mrs. McKillop
appeared at the door with nothing to do; Tito and Piglioli-
Spada told her about Ilse's story. "Maybe there is some
drug business involved," the woman suggested, just to make
her own contribution, lowering her eyes on her full breasts,
with a kind of courteous timidity.

"Wait a minute, what was the name of that lawyer I
knew well at the American embassy?" Tito asked, vital,
efficient.

"Leave lawyers alone for the moment," Bernardo said,
standing up authoritatively all of a sudden. "You could do
me a favor"—and he took Tito by the arm, lowering his
voice—"let me have your famous Oldsmobile for this evening."

"Of course, let's go wherever you want, you direct us,"
Tito agreed immediately; he assumed a somewhat military
air, he looked around as if at enlisted men. Clement had kept
Bernardo's car. As usual there was a problem of cars. Bernardo took Dora by the hand. The telephone rang.

Still holding Dora with one hand, Bernardo with the
other brought the receiver slowly up to his ear: "Here I am,
dear, tell me." He listened to Genziana's talk, punctuating it
by saying frequently: "I see, I see," while the others looked
at him, holding their breath.

"It's rather painful," Genziana was telling him, "that
Clement should go all the way to the airport, you can imag-

ine him, alone there, walking madly around, on the opposite side from hers, lost in those buildings, worse than the desert, because at least in the desert one can communicate by radio, can't one? She did the right thing, I find. Clement wouldn't have been able to see her anyway. In her shoes, I too would have left again immediately, for any other country, wouldn't you have done the same? I suppose she went to London, or to Geneva, there is always an airplane for a destination like that; and that would seem the most logical thing to do, don't you think?" But her voice trembled and she had a lump in her throat. "Don't you think? Do you hear me?"

"Yes, yes, I hear you, why shouldn't I hear you? And where is he now?"

"Imagine: he was coming back into town from the airport and he was going to Perineschi's."

"To do what?"

But Bernardo didn't even listen to the answer, there was no need for it. Already as a little boy at Santa Monica, Clement would send long letters on all sorts of subjects to the local newspapers; at that time he had said things like: "The newspapers must talk about this. I'll set the thing in motion. I'll make a big case of this." Fragments of some of the letters had been published rarely and without results.

"Perineschi was not in his office; however, he has an efficient secretary—you know he has this American pose—so they tracked him down and he let Clement know that he would be happy to see him at his house, and that's where Clement is going. All things considered, I don't see the purpose of that; Perineschi is a small fatuous bourgeois, and I imagine that he may be rather excited by the story of the American girl blocked at the entrance into Italy; last year he wanted to have Tranquillo do a piece on the Beddoes scandal at the Lido, you know?"

(295)

"Listen, pay attention to me; you wait there, at your house," Bernardo said, "Dora and I will come and pick you up." He hung up almost without waiting for a reply. He raised his finger toward Tito: "Your Oldsmobile." He was still holding Dora's hand in his left.

Dora and Ovidio exchanged a look: that was sufficient; they immediately felt isolated from the rest, much more self-possessed, calm, and capable of facing situations. "Yes, the two of them had better go, we'll wait for them at the Tuscan restaurant. Meanwhile we'll take my little car, and perhaps on our way we'll try and see if . . ."

"Exactly," Tito said, "we'll try to find Massenti too, and we'll all stay together and discuss with him what we should do."

The steep cobbled street where Perineschi lived was terminated at the bottom by a high narrow arch, beyond which lay a small stagelike square, slanting and asymmetrical. Bernardo, with Dora and Genziana, drove Tito Solmi's car down the street while all three attentively examined the automobiles parked on the side; Bernardo's was not there. Other agitated cars, their lights blinking, formed a thickening line behind them, honking and croaking in various tones, a kind of maddened metallic poultry yard; finally, in spite of the funnel-like narrowness of the street, a waspish car passed them with a falsetto roar, two more cars followed it, hurtling forward with doubled ferocity, their motors loosened, through the arch. Bernardo descended slowly, and instead of going through the arch he stopped the car by the side that was contiguous to an ancient tower; meanwhile, other delayed cars passed by with reproachful honkings. "I like to drive fast too, but if it's impossible I resign myself and keep quiet," Bernardo said. "I live and let live." He switched the motor off and extended his arm on the back of the seat behind Genziana's shoulders, his eyes passing several times from her to Dora, seated behind; he sighed with satisfaction and smiled.

"Wonderful," Dora said, "Clement hasn't come yet." She looked at Genziana: "That's much better, isn't it? So we stop him before he goes up to Perineschi's and then we'll all stay together. What's the matter with you? Why are you cringing like that?"

"If it hadn't been for this I would have stayed at home. I'm afraid it is my usual bronchitis." There was no Clement to hold her tight, kiss her, bring her the medicine; for the first time in several days, Clement had been away from her longer than an hour.

"Do you want Bernardo to take you back home?" Dora suggested. "I'll stay here, I'll walk up and down in front of Perineschi's door, like a gendarme." The door was a few steps above the spot where they had stopped; they surveyed it, as they did the cars rushing down the street.

"Not at all, let's all wait for him here," Genziana said. She had imagined she would receive him with a happily detached air, to make him understand that she could live very well even without him; now the very fact of having been able to conceive such an idea increased her pain. "I am never well, I am no good," she said.

"Don't be silly," Dora said, opening the back door of the car and getting out. "Come with me"—and she opened the front door to let Genziana follow her—"there is a little bar down here and we'll get something hot to drink."

"Good," Bernardo said, "I'll stay here on duty."

The two women walked through the arch into the little square; with each step they lifted their feet on the wet cobbled pavement like long-legged birds in a marsh; they evaded a skidding car; they came to the little bar, in a narrow medieval street that opened into a major traffic road;

Dora authoritatively ordered two orange-and-rum toddies, piping hot. She drank rapidly; her face glowed. It wasn't only the temperature and the alcohol that made her brighten up, it was also the almost unbearable sweetness of the orange. She sighed: "Wonderful stuff." Genziana, instead, drank slowly, looking suspiciously at the little glass in its small metal basket, as if questioning it before taking each sip. At the end she laughed drily, put the empty glass down, and turning to contemplate her companion so happy and overheated, she murmured: "Dora, you are really something."

Dora grasped her hand with a kind of sob of joy: "I'm happy to be with you," she said. "And now, when Clement comes too, we'll go eat at that Tuscan place I know he likes."

Genziana looked at her, trying to understand.

"Between Clement and me," Dora went on, "there is really a lot of genuine tenderness, and I think I know him better than most people do. Now I'm enormously happy that you and he . . ."

Genziana nearly stammered, as if feeling the ground or attempting a game she did not know: "I too, Dora, am very happy that you and that professor, Ovidio Semenzato . . ." She realized that her tone gave an impression of hardness. "I have known him for a long time, he was a great friend of . . ."

"Of Tranquillo Massenti, of course. Clement too . . ."

"Yes, Clement too . . . " But mentioned like that, in that company, Clement sounded to her like somebody else. She looked at Dora with a streak of suspicion.

Dora took her hand again: "I am very fond of you, Genziana; it has taken me years to understand that, and to be able to say it to you; you used to frighten me. Even that evening when we met at the Solmis', I was still a little afraid of you. I have always admired you, though; like everybody, for that matter."

"I assure you there is very little to admire," Genziana said weakly.

Dora insisted on paying. Outside the bar, they walked arm in arm until they reached the car again; it seemed as if Dora was supporting Genziana.

They found Bernardo seated in the car with his eyes closed. "I have been paying attention," he told them immediately as he heard them, "nobody has come." He wore his beatific smile.

They got into the car, both women squeezing in front with Bernardo; Dora, the smallest, in the middle. They were all silent for a long while, close to one another.

At some point Dora suggested cheerfully: "Why don't we all go up to Perineschi's?"

Genziana looked at her with apprehension.

"You used to write for *Roma Sabato* once, didn't you?" Dora said to her cheerfully. And to Bernardo: "She used to write a fashion column, Genziana was a columnist; that's how you started, didn't you? It was the time when you used to see Tranquillo Massenti a lot."

"Massenti and I were rather good friends; even now he calls me," Genziana said, her teeth clenched. "But look," she cried, jumping up, "wasn't that Clement?" She had seen him in a quick apparition, framed by the arch.

She threw herself out of the car, raising her arms to make signs, but he had already disappeared. A car had rushed down the street and was passing through the arch.

Evidently he had walked from the side of the Imperial Forums, perhaps he had left his car near Piazza Venezia. On that side, there was a sort of wooden balcony suspended above ancient Roman ruins, sparse and well-ordered in their vast square concavities; traversing the balcony, Clem-

ent had come to the little square via a corner passage with
the idea of turning left and going to Perineschi's through
the arch; but before he could pass through the arch a car
had come toward him from above. In the car's lights, Genziana had seen him, beyond the arch, disappear like a deer
or a hare frightened and blinded jumping across the asphalt
track from one piece of night forest to another. Dora too
got out of the car, remained standing near her friend.

Another automobile rolled down the street shortly after-
ward. Almost immediately Clement reappeared, framed by
the arch. When Genziana cried: "Watch out, wait," she understood that she could not be heard. The same with Dora,
when she said: "Move, what are you doing," rather in a
tone of surprise, of discovery, than of warning. Already the
car was passing under the arch and they heard the squeal of
the brakes and the tires, but there was never any doubt that
Clement had been hit. After the car had passed, Clement's
silhouette had disappeared from the arch framing it. Bernardo ordered the two women: "You stay where you are,"
and shut the door they had left open; he checked in the mirror to see whether any car was coming down behind him, he
started the motor, he passed under the arch. Out in the little
square, much farther to the left than he had expected, he
saw Clement thrown on the ground, face down, his right
arm stretched out on the cobbled pavement, his head hidden by his shoulder; for a moment Bernardo had a vision
that he had been beheaded.

There were these two separate images: the car which had
run over Clement; and his body, now lying on the ground.
Not connecting these two images was the only way to go on
moving, living, for the moment.

More or less at the point where Dora's little bar was,
Bernardo reached the automobile which had hit Clement
and was about to ram it, but the driver stopped as soon as

he found a place to park. Bernardo pulled up behind him. The man got out of his car with a face already terror-struck and questioning; standing in front of Bernardo he put his hand in his pocket as if to pull out some identification papers; he didn't manage to do that, perhaps because he had none or because his hand was trembling too violently. With his powerful fist Bernardo struck him in the forehead; or rather than strike him, it was as if he tried to grab him by the brow in order to pull and tear off his whole face, like a mask. But almost immediately he released the man and stood still, staring at him, panting, stupefied.

The man had a closely shaved head, bony and Gothic, from which only those wide blank eyes now emerged, in an effort, which they knew to be vain, to enlist other people's pity. Bernardo took him by the arm, and the man seemed relieved in assuming immediately the position and the behavior of a person under arrest. Then, perhaps with the intention of describing himself as a citizen with a spotless record, he said with a kind of languid monotony: "I am an accountant. Leandro Carducci is my name. I was up here at the Ministry of Defense." Bernardo, as if he were dealing with the victim of an accident, and were telling him: "Now we'll go to the emergency ward," mumbled reassuringly: "Now you will be arrested. You'll tell everything to the police." The man nodded, perhaps he didn't hear the exact words but was reassured by the fact that somebody would talk to him, would have dealings with him. "It isn't a hit-and-run case," Bernardo mumbled. Actually, it was clear that the man hadn't made even the slightest attempt to escape; and right at the moment a formal observation of that kind seemed somehow reassuring. At all events, there was an order, a rule. However, Bernardo felt his body traversed by an almost epileptic tremor while a violent impulse to retch rose from his stomach.

In the square they found a little crowd already assembled. Soon there were also two policemen, one of whom set himself to keep traffic moving with technical motions of his arms. The other policeman was creating a breathing space for Clement within the circle of stooping observers. This little group seemed already settled, still, not even very curious, against the background of an ancient historical palace with its immense door open on the majestic atrium with Roman statues in Olympic attitudes. Among the other observers, nobody was doing anything. There was no doctor among them. Bernardo elbowed his way through the little circle of people and came to Clement lying on the ground.

Now the two women, Dora and Genziana, were there too, Dora kneeling down and Genziana standing behind her. Dora was looking at Clement, who lay motionless as if already dead; she seemed to be talking to him. Then she raised her eyes toward Bernardo—dark, intense eyes, in which he thought he saw concentrated the whole scene in its desperate and irremediable precision. "Thank God she is here," Bernardo said to himself rapidly, without looking for the meaning of his thought.

Actually Dora was in a state of calm that went even beyond heart-rending pain and fear. She felt as if she were living in the past. What was happening at the moment had the same substance as what had happened a while ago, or years earlier.

One knew only this: that Clement had planned to come back with Ilse and take her to Genziana, to whom only the day before he had said: "She will stay with us, you and I will be a little bit like a family for Ilse." Instead, he had returned alone through dead pieces of architecture toward the house of a journalist for an absurd, useless protest, when suddenly Genziana had revealed herself to him, framed within that arch. It seemed clear that Clement, blinded and stopped, nailed under that arch, during those few seconds, was confronted by two alternatives—whether to reach Genziana or to avoid mortal danger—and that in the decisive instant he must have chosen the first. Infinitely dividing and subdividing those few seconds, one would have to get to a central core, impossible for the others to reach, something of which he alone, Clement, could have had a distant glimmer—act of love, refuge, peace—and he had walked toward it.

Dora was following his painful breathing, but it already seemed to her like something external, mechanical, not perpetrated by him—something that went on a while longer by itself, before being extinguished. "He is not suffering," she murmured, reassuring herself. She had always experienced this feeling in front of Clement, although it was now intensified to a supreme point—the feeling that he was alone and that no one could help him. One could only feel pity, love; this was more than ever possible now; it was useless, but it was all.

Fifteen years earlier Massimo Fassola had died testing a difficult airplane on Lake Garda. It was a rainy night, and Dora and her mother had left together for the place of the accident. But they knew that they would find nothing: the charred remains, dispersed, nothing really recoverable.

Dora now let large slow tears run down her cheeks. Two years earlier, once only, she and Clement had loved each other, one afternoon, very pleasantly; he had been her last man before Ovidio. She had never really thought about it again; now it seemed that the recollection was useful to give her strength. Clement was there, in front of her; with his corduroy pants and his tweed jacket, stretched out as in sleep, his long arm on the cobbled pavement and his cheek pressed on his shoulder. It seemed as if in that position he had found refuge from a desperate headache, later subdued by the total loss of feeling. There were orders not to touch him until the ambulance came. But Dora raised her face streaked with tears toward Genziana standing rigidly behind her, and told her, as in a sweet, gentle invitation: "Come, Genziana, come closer, kiss him."

Genziana seemed to be smiling, leaning her head backward. But soon Dora realized that her friend was fainting. Bernardo was immediately near her, holding her before she fell. She came to herself almost immediately, opened her eyes and said: "I have a tablet in my bag."

Now there were other officials too, preparing to write a report on the accident. Bernardo, questioned, pointed to the guilty driver and punctuated his answers with the phrase: "They'll arrest him immediately, I imagine, I hope," and the man nodded every time. Actually, this too was nothing but a useless attempt to give form to the events. Bernardo could very well have ceased bothering, for the rest of his life, with that bony-headed, terrified prisoner.

The ambulance had arrived. Everyone followed the delicate operations intently. Rigid on the stretcher, Clement was carried through the back door into the large white automobile. By now he belonged to a different world, a different set of facts. Bernardo approved Dora's suggestion that the two women go up to Perineschi's apartment, since after all it was the most logical place; from there they would call a taxi as soon as Genziana felt strong enough to go back to her own house. Bernardo would follow Clement to the hospital. Dora exchanged an understanding look with Bernardo.

Clement died during the trip in the ambulance. Bernardo lost sight of the ambulance, then in his confusion he took several wrong turns. Naturally, his visit to the hospital was useless and only much later could he go and see Clement at the morgue. He called Genziana's apartment, hoping that

(3 0 4)

Dora would be with her. The maid answered and said that Genziana had been away for several days.

Bernardo assumed that the two women were still at Perineschi's and he went there without calling. He found Perineschi alone and feverishly nervous.

"They were all here till a moment ago," he said. The trio too, and Piglioli-Spada, had finally gone up to his place. "A very curious little man," Perineschi said of Piglioli-Spada. "Solmi wants me to have him write for my magazine." Bernardo looked at him with dopey eyes; his ears were popping; he felt as if he were under water. Perineschi offered him a drink. They both drank a double whiskey, straight. Perineschi's hands were trembling. "How was it? What was it? I didn't hear anything at all, yet it was right under here. What happened later? Where did he die? Was it very quick?" He put his questions imperiously, his mobile blue eyes anxiously piercing empty space. Bernardo did not answer; he let Perineschi talk: "He hit the pavement with his head, didn't he? That's what the little Fassola girl was saying. Brain trouble? Concussion?" He said the last word in English; he recalled Bernardo was "Americanized." "They were very close friends, weren't they? Genziana Horst too, wasn't she? She used to work for me."

Bernardo noticed that Perineschi had a nervous tic: its effect was that of a short frenetic frown, a kind of agitated caricature of pensiveness, while the look in his eyes remained intense but absent. "He lasted a half-hour at the most, didn't he?" For a moment his voice became strangely sorrowful, a kind of enraged lament: "Imagine, the information that he was dead came to me from Massenti. He called, and I had to communicate it to the others here. I don't know how Massenti gets to know things immediately. He thought I knew more than he did, on how it really happened, considering that it was practically under my window, but I didn't hear anything. I think I remember that Massenti once wanted to do a journalistic inquiry on automobile accidents. He will never do it. Oddly enough, he still has to write that piece on Genziana Horst's father for me. She used to work for me. Where are you going now, Partibon?"

Bernardo got up without answering, went to the telephone, called Clement's apartment. Dora answered. She said that they had all been sitting there, in Clement's studio, but now only she and the trio remained. Piglioli-Spada had returned to the country, where perhaps Genziana would join him to stay several days. Genziana had preferred to take the few things she had left at Clement's and return for the moment alone to her apartment. Dora's voice was like a quiet lament evoking distant events. "She kept repeating that she had to be alone, put some order in her mind. Listen, Bernardo, you and I will have to call Venice. Come here. Perhaps we can see Genziana later on, neither she nor anybody else will sleep anyhow. A few days ago, her father; and now, Clement. The two most important men in her life, perhaps. There were moments when she seemed to be paralyzed, you know, but in between she looked rather normal."

Genziana moved around her apartment a long while, as if to rearrange things, to resume contacts and habits after returning from a long trip. She felt as if she were sleeping; more exactly, as if she were going through one of those brief moments of dream stolen from her most severe insomnias. She doubted that she could continue to live like that, but at any rate she would try and stay alone a few hours; then she would call Dora and Bernardo, also in order to go with them to see Clement at the morgue the next morning. The idea of this duty to be performed was obsessive and tranquilizing at the same time: she was looking for rules, for the things one should do in such cases. Harry Berger was expected the following Monday for certain; one had to receive him, go to him with some projects and ideas. With the passing of hours and days she had no longer thought of showing her costume sketches to Clement. She didn't remember when she had done them. In the drawer, under the sketches, she found a package of old correspondence held in a large envelope made of transparent plastic material. It contained Italian and American letters, contracts, documents of dealings either suspended or forgotten. She had never been well organized, she thought; in all that she did there was always something accidental and improvised, but she couldn't do any better, using, as it was, all the energy she had had, with her feelings of failure, with her splitting headaches.

The maid brought her hot bouillon and some tranquilizers; Genziana told her to go to sleep. She started reading newspaper clippings that Lauretta had sent her: funereal announcements and obituaries of the Senator, their father. To a large extent they must be the result of Rodolfo Piglioli-Spada's activity with the newspapers: perhaps that was the reason Rodolfo had often come to town in the last few days. Now leaving for the country again, her brother-in-law had asked Genziana only in passing to go with him; actually it was clear that he wanted to be alone with his wife for a while, to discuss Genziana with her and prepare for her arrival in the proper manner. Genziana realized that her relationship with her sister and her brother-in-law had always been pleasant and without importance.

Dora and Bernardo called; they had talked with Venice. First they had called Fausta Fassola and told her what had happened, seeking her advice as to the best way to break the news to Nicole. Then there had been a call from Clare;

she had talked with Bernardo in English, Dora said, asking precise and punctilious questions on the accident: how, when, and whether the culprit had been sent to jail. Dora said that she and Bernardo had endured a sense of physical effort in the attempt to make Clement's death appear as a tangible fact to his half sister Clare; it had almost been as though the telephone wires had not had enough energy to carry the vision to the North, to Venice. Clement's mother, Clare related, had several times repeated the phrase: "He's always driven too fast," and even when the accident had been explained to her in greater detail she had held on to that phrase, weeping considerably, until she had collapsed. In fact, there was some talk of a heart attack. Tullio Moscato, the old doctor of the Venice Partibons, was examining her and had already suggested moving her to a private hospital.

"You should go to Venice too," Genziana said. "I'll stay here, I'll take care of everything."

"Of what?"

"Did his mother say anything? Will they come here, or do they perhaps want to have him transported to Venice? Or to America? I know so little about these things." Then Genziana added: "At some point, I don't know why, I had thought of the English cemetery, which is rather beautiful, it looks a little like a garden, but God knows how many formalities there would . . . " She maintained her typical tone more than ever, in fact she seemed entirely detached from what she was saying. Then she seemed to be shivering, her teeth were chattering.

"Genziana? Shall we come there? Shall we come and pick you up?"

But it was evident that she wanted to remain alone, at least for a few hours. She hinted at the possibility of going to the Piglioli-Spadas', but when Bernardo offered to accompany her she rejected the idea; she said she would try to sleep a little.

Instead, she continued to move around the apartment, as if animated by an impulse to organize things, which pushed her in many directions toward the void. At her work desk she bent her head, hiding it in her crossed arms. A moment later somebody was turning the doorknob; Clement was entering the room, behind her back. She jumped up abruptly, she wasn't sure she had really been dreaming, she rather felt that from now on she would never perceive any difference between being awake and being asleep.

It was already dawn when she started preparing her little suitcase. Usually when she went to the Piglioli-Spadas' she did not carry anything. She left at their house whatever was sufficient for the weekend; but this time somebody, she did not remember who, had told her that she would have to stay there a longer period of time, and it was as if this unidentified authority were now guiding her acts, which she performed smiling. From the medicine cabinet she took some creams and a box of new American toothbrushes; she also found a bottle of barbiturates, intact, and with a smile she put it in the suitcase.

Although it was cold she had no difficulty in starting the motor, as she had feared. She got out of the city through the same streets that she and Bernardo had taken one night; they were empty, and in the light of dawn everything revealed itself to her in unusually bright, definite shapes.

When she arrived at the pine grove she evoked the night when she had passed through it with Bernardo; she could have quoted their conversation word for word. She had a feeling of extreme lucidity. Her mind contained a few isolated facts and she was left alone with them; there was an air of leave-taking, of dismantling, not at all sad.

Then a phrase formed in her mind, but she could not

quite place it in time: "At least someone must be equal to the challenge." Repeating it several times, it seemed to her that it must be a phrase of her father's. She drove confidently, although the road was damp and slippery. She listened to dogs barking; those were the dogs that went alone on expeditions along the sea; perhaps they belonged to her sister's house.

She pressed the accelerator and the car skidded, got out of hand for an instant. From the moment she had awakened at her work desk, if ever she had slept, she had not lost that quiet smile. Then a memory came to her, of the only case in her life in which she had had to be operated on and subjected to total anesthesia. Before then she had always thought she was so self-possessed that nothing could tear her away from consciousness; on the contrary, at the very first anesthetic injection she had discovered, immediately and totally, the new force, powerfully sweet and inevitable, to which she could abandon herself.

The barking of the dogs was now much nearer. Again she lost control of the car. Again that phrase came to her, *at least someone must be equal to the challenge,* and this time she said it aloud while she made a very violent turn to the right.

She accompanied her act with a lively motion of her hips and she had an image of herself as a child: of a time when, after a few hours on skis, suddenly she had felt that kind of inner jolt and had discovered herself capable of motions that were absolutely free, weightless.

Hours later, Laura and Rodolfo Piglioli-Spada tried to call several numbers in Rome. No one answered at Quarto Martelli's apartment, where Tito Solmi was a guest. Bernardo was not at his hotel, nor was he at the apartment. Ovidio was not traceable; nor were the Fassolas, Dora and

Enrico. In the end, Piglioli-Spada called Perineschi.

Perineschi received Piglioli-Spada's words with the un-comprehending tone of a man still turbid with sleep; then mechanically he asked questions about details, and listened to answers; these finally awakened him completely and made him break into sobs.

According to the most reliable reconstruction of the ac-cident, that morning at dawn on the road toward the Pig-lioli-Spadas', Genziana had fainted behind the wheel. When they found her, nobody knew what to do. Should they move her? Or call some authority? Recognizing her, peasants had finally taken her, probably in their arms, to the little deserted chapel. It was impossible to reconstruct an exact sequence of events from so many fragments of talk; it was certain, however, that in the chapel, before anyone went to wake up Laura and Rodolfo, the young woman had been laid out in a sarcophagus posture on the floor, in the fullness of her calm splendor, by a maid now stunned, and capable of re-peating only: "So beautiful, so beautiful."

This disorderly news was given by Rodolfo in increas-ingly reticent form. He realized he preferred to cut it short, also because Perineschi, from the distant reading of his magazine and from a recent meeting, had aroused in him an instinctive though unjustified feeling of mistrust.

CHAPTER ELEVEN

Tranquillo Massenti:

Rome, October —Senator Mario Horst, who died last week
at the Senate library, had named his daughter "Genziana"
because that flower reminded him of the alps of his youth.
The Senator's mother had sung lyrics written by a little poet
named Müller, and set to music by Schubert; of the *Win-
terreise* she had not favored the sadder and more nightmarish pieces, like the two final ones, but had preferred the
simpler and nostalgic ones like the *Lindenbaum* or *Auf dem
Flusse*. The Senator's favorite Italian poet had remained
Abbé Zanella; I myself have seen dried flowers crushed between the pages of that poet's work in the Senator's library.
A good mountain climber as a boy, he had remained a great
walker.

Perhaps he would have preferred to become a professor
of natural science, but he turned to politics because he was
an Austrian citizen of Italian feelings; he fought the First
World War, at twenty, on the Italian side, so that if the
adversaries had caught him he would have been sent not
to a prisoners' camp but to the gallows, and his widow
would have received the bill for the rope. Well, that is your

cultural background, Perineschi, but I shall not continue to write this article for you. I was going to proceed: *The Senator spoke very little about all that; his conduct in that war was to him a question of plain good manners.* Obviously this is not it. At any rate *Roma Sabato* would not be interested in a character of this sort, perhaps invented by myself who have loved his daughter, now dead. In fact, I wanted to tell you that I am tendering my resignation. I am abandoning newspaper work altogether in order to write my three novels. Pietrino Alano is enthusiastic about my plan and promises acceptance in his fiction series; so there will soon be talk of Tranquillo Massenti's trilogy; my hero will be a young man, Gianluigi Albini, who has decided to accept the favorable cultural conjuncture. Part One: From the newspaper, Albini has gone on to the public relations office of a huge pharmaceutical concern to edit their monthly artistic bulletin in color. Part Two: He is in the movie industry as a writer. Part Three: Attempts at independent production, consequent ruin, return to newspaper work, marriage. "There are times," you told me one evening, sitting at a café in front of a newspaper stand, where fresh copies of your magazine were hanging like laundry, "when I look at those headlines, those articles, and suddenly I have a kind of revelation: phrases become combinations of meaningless words, the words, in turn, empty combinations of letters; finally, if you observe them carefully the letters themselves are abstract, arbitrary forms." Such feelings are like daily bread to me, so I could only mumble: "It's undoubtedly a revelation, Peri," but luckily, Tito Solmi was with us, ready to step in: "Go to Leo Gerolami. He is marvelous in cases like that. Nervous cases, not at all uncommon. He'll get you out of that kind of mess. Go to Leo." Did you go to Leo? At any rate, now you are well, you believe in your country and in your magazine. Your error is to go on wanting articles from me, full of facts and with cultural background—from me, a drinker! One night I was under the influence (as I shall be, if I go on like this, within about twenty minutes) and at some point I told myself suddenly: *Everything is wrong therefore everything is right,* but after that moment I was never able to recapture what I meant. Since words are not understandable anyway, now I shall arrange words into novels rather than into articles. I'll acquire fame, I'll appear photographed in *Roma Sabato* rather than write in it. Novels, like for example Silvio Perucchini's *The Idiosyncrasies,* or *The Substitution* by Pietrino himself, even if everybody speaks more or less unfavorably about them, do exist, have weight, are *a thing.* After all, even the proposition *favorably or unfavorably doesn't matter, provided people talk about it* is *passé* inasmuch as nobody realizes any more whether *a thing* is talked about favorably or unfavorably; same with people, we don't know whether we are friends or enemies. But, wait a minute. Our last telephone conversation. Last straw. From I don't know what sources of energy, whose depletion should have brought me to cardiac collapse, I drew the false statement: "Yes, I had heard that a while ago myself." No, Perineschi; you were giving me the announcement; you were telling me that Genziana had finished without explanations. Slight (after all) disappointment on your part: "So, you had heard it already?" And then: "What an incredible thing, a few days after her father's death. You knew that sculptor Blumenfeld rather well, didn't you?" Perhaps you were slipping between the lines the suggestion of a treble obituary? Clement Blumenfeld—American, Venetian, what was he? Sculptor, boy with complexes, exiled intellectual? The girls used to say: "He has very sweet eyes, and the only face that can decently support a classical profile," but to us he always looked a little frightened and stand-offish. At some point he and

Genziana disappeared; the thing was not understood and there was no time to appropriate it and discuss it. A matter of hours rather than of days. I went to see him at the morgue immediately. There I saw Bernardo Partibon arrive, whose father happened to die in my presence, and I slipped away, pressing myself like a shadow against the walls. It wasn't the right moment. Partibon came back from Venice the other night, or perhaps it was last night, and he looked for me *because in Rome I am the only person whose conversation he understands,* and for hours we told each other everything. But let's go back to Blumenfeld. Yes, Perineschi, I always arrive at the morgue before you do. Generally I know everything long before you do, Peri. Coming back from the morgue that night, I tried to get into a telephone booth and call Genziana, but my hands literally did not react. Tito Solmi and Quarto Martelli found me later in that café—with mirrors and Empire furniture—which in the last long days we have made fashionable, and I left them there a moment ago—Ovidio too, good Ovidio. Well, I was at an unusual café, at an unusual hour, holding an unusual drink (rum) in my clenched fist, when I saw them both at once, reflected and multiplied by the mirrors. They were excited at having hunted me down, their faces were adequately solemn and sorrowful but they also oozed curiosity; there was *a thing* in the air. Question in their eyes: What should one do now with Genziana? Have you looked for her? Have you seen her? Not seen, for weeks, for months, I call her, however, every now and then, but my hands now happen to be . . . I seem to remember that Tito Solmi did most of the talking. The friend of intellectuals & artists. Tito's ideal in life was to have become a criminal lawyer and to have many intellectuals & artists commit *crimes passionnels* and request his services for the defense. "Apparently they were planning to go to America together.

(3 1 5)

It has been an important love for Genziana; she is in a complete state of shock; Ovidio knows a lot from Dora Fassola. Clement didn't even appear at the opening of his show, they lived in a world of their own. Dora knows a lot. What will you do?" In less than two hours they had come to problems like: who should get Genziana now, and whether Genziana erotically was the clitoris or the vagina type; all of this wanting to help her, being her friends. They requested my participation, they said every now and then: "Admit, you must admit." We spoke fluently a language we no longer understood. I allowed myself to be involved, Quarto and I made a pact, with Tito acting as witness: since Genziana had remained a widow, Quarto and I as old friends would look for her and persuade her to love us both; the one of the two who would first make her reach an erotic climax would marry her. The rum which I was and am still drinking is not Bacardi, it is of the dark dense variety; I also brought some bottles of it with me here to the house. When the news about Clement was followed (a matter of hours) by yours, Perineschi, concerning Genziana, I was still under the influence, and I went back to the Empire-style café without telling Ingrid anything. My very severe headache has not deserted me a single minute. Fortunately Ingrid has abandoned the attempt to talk to me. I hardly ever come home and when I am here we only look at each other. I have continuous extrasystoles but on the whole I am not unwell physically, except for my head.

Rome, October —At the time when he was serving as Undersecretary for Foreign Affairs, Senator Mario Horst spoke to me rather at length one morning at Palazzo Chigi; he, bilingual even in his name, a man born and raised in a multicolored and supranational empire, spoke to me about Europe. Nonsense. All that is destined for your magazine, Perineschi, is automatically transformed into nonsense. One day in Venice, in order to make us realize that it was out of the question for us to be able to write about Maria Gervasutti, née Partibon, Dr. Debaldè asked: "Is there anything in your life that is equivalent to what the faith has been, since childhood, in hers? Just tell me this." Then, benevolently: "You feel a little disqualified to talk about her, don't you?" Somebody, perhaps myself, said to him: "Some subjects may perhaps even be important, but when you touch them, Dr. Debaldè, they automatically become tripe." After your announcement, Martelli and Solmi sat near me in my Empire-style den like Job's (so to speak) friends, who come to contemplate him in his mourning and desolation, waiting politely for him to open his mouth first. A curious situation, because in this case Quarto was in mourning too. Usual mediator, Tito Solmi. We remained in ritual silence a long while; then I started, not to say splendid lines of poetry like Job, but to sob. All three of us were rather astonished, observing this phenomenon: this weeping I was doing for everybody, this force which from the inside of my body was agitating me. "I'm playing with the idea of going back to Padua to live," Quarto said. And questioning us with his eyes: "I haven't even called Laura and Rodolfo. Nothing." Perhaps days had passed when he said this. We met every day among those mirrors; they must still be there. At some point Ovidio came, having emerged a few days (hours?) earlier from the bed of Dora Fassola, who had now left for Venice with Bernardo Partibon; Bernardo is now back in Rome but they don't know it. I know it because I am the *only person whom he understands in Rome.* Our Ovidio oozed pure biological bliss in spite of sorrow on his face; bringing him to talk about himself and her (Dora) was the simplest thing: "I'm a countryside Venetian. Dora is a Venice Venetian. I felt from the first moment that ours was the right thing. It gives a meaning to everything."

Then he said also: "That evening at the Solmis'. So much has happened since. Do you remember," he told me, "that you were supposed to come too?" Tito Solmi inserted a piece of news on the good fortune of one of his cousins: "Duilio announced to me yesterday that Harry Berger is taking him, he will be one of the set designers for *Caligula*." Ovidio said: "I am so happy." I said: "She was supposed to be in it as costume designer, or, as she used to say, wardrobe mistress." Tito was saying: "Duilio's mother and father, Aurora and Orlando, are a bit perplexed but, after all, proud." Some time ago I had already started forming a general pattern of the situation in my mind. It had all begun from a kind of peak, which no one or perhaps only Ovidio had recognized as such on the spot, the evening at the Solmis' in which I had not participated; from that peak, various streams had descended; Ovidio, Dora, Duilio, after all Tito and Quarto too, had taken good streams. But one must talk about the others too. I asked: "Who has seen her dead?" Tito said: "It's the third time you've asked the same question. I forbid you"—he was energetic, persuasive, with a Bologna accent—"I forbid you to let yourself go in that manner." I asked: "Has anybody seen her dead?" I appealed to Ovidio: "After Clement died Martelli and I made a kind of pact, the first of us to . . . We had decided to compete for her, as it were. But we loved her, it was one of our ways of loving her." Tito inserted: "I'll take you to Leo. How long have you gone without sleep? Let Leo examine you. Try a couple of weeks' sleep therapy perhaps, but try *something*. And if that's what you wanted, I could have taken you all in my car to see her." I said: "Of course your car would have been large enough for everybody." Then he said something bizarre: "Perineschi has talked to me about you, he understands you, he trusts you and your work more than ever." I replied: "You know that I am supposed to write my novels now." He brightened up: "Bravo. That seems to me a very vital thing." I said: "And they will be very successful, you'll see." Meanwhile Quarto Martelli was saying apologetically: "Rodolfo Piglioli-Spada, who is the younger brother of Ambassador Piglioli-Spada, is, among other things, a distant cousin of ours, but I never managed to talk to him and I don't understand him very well when *he* talks." I recall lines of dialogue but God knows when they were uttered. Seated at that café for entire days. I left them there a moment ago to come here. Did I? So I thought. For that matter, our days and our conversations have always been like that, backward and forward. I don't remember what day it is, but I do have a reputation for knowing how to compose sentences, hold the banner of syntax raised high, even when I am under the influence. Or under water. Or in sleep. In fact, better in sleep. "I sleep badly because my head goes on making up sentences. Has Leo Gerolami ever had such a case? We need a medicine to decompose sentences. In fact, to forget the vocabulary. That would fix us all up." Mediating, Tito said: "You talk, Ovidio, tell us." He looked at me with his round shiny eyes, he invited me to listen, warmly recommending Ovidio to me: "He knows a lot, through Dora. And he has seen Clement's famous twin, Ilse." I said, or mumbled: "I saw her too. I went to the airport with a photographer even . . . " At that time I was still a journalist. But I had the impression that they didn't believe me. "And then last night, or perhaps it was the night before last, Bernardo Partibon talked to me a lot about her . . . " They believed me even less. For that matter, I too preferred to hear Ovidio talk, I sensed Ovidio as the new event among us. Quarto Martelli was asking: "Wasn't there some scandal last year on the Lido? There was even a rumor that they kicked her out of Italy because she was the mistress of her twin brother." Ovidio, with the tone of the safe fiancé and of the university instructor very close to a Chair of Modern History: "Ilse was not responsible for anything, but she *wanted* to be. Very American in that: loyalty, sticking to one's friends. They were arresting and expelling her friends from Italy, so for example when they asked her about her civil and professional status, she declared: 'I am an abortionist.' She started yelling, in the midst of Viale Santa Maria Elisabetta, protesting against everything, death penalty, erotophobia, positions of responsibility and leadership being held by virgin men full of complexes, so finally they included her in the raid, so to speak." *Tout se tient*—everything is connected. Do you remember, Peri, that you wanted to send me to Venice to do a piece on the Beddoes scandal, orgy, strip tease? Through Beddoes we remount to Clement and from there to Genziana to the Senator to Bernardo Partibon to the Solmis to Maria Partibon to Dr. Debaldè, and so on and so on; any road you take you always have the possibility of the Total Vision, the Final Revelation, the Big Article. Only I can't do the article for you, I have gone over to fiction. But Ovidio knows a lot: "Clement Blumenfeld's sculptures. I like them enormously. Cascades of new matter from new planets. Very beautiful, cheerful things. They seem to be moving in all directions; they are perfectly still, but if you look at them it's your eyes that make them move. Although he denied it, he was apparently trying to represent objects free from the force of gravity, fluctuating in space." Tito, at home in the art world: "Pity. He wasn't really in touch. And now he is dead and we shall never know whether he was important as a sculptor." Ovidio affects a global look: "Bernardo Partibon will handle them on the American market. Bernardo, a new Partibon I hadn't known, a countryside Venetian like myself. My Dora is very fond of him. When we are married, we shall go to America to see him. He was a relative of

Clement too. Relative means very little. It's the type, the quality, the stuff they are made of. Supranational beings." Tito cocks his ear: "Meaning what?" Ovidio, good Padua teacher, teacheth: "Americans, but then also Europeans. Aren't they? Clement was a romantic. A European of the early nineteenth century. One evening in his studio he was mentioning the people *who talk about you the next day*. Think, he was saying, if the next day, while they talk about you, they heard a report: he is dead. It's just a little gimmick. You should always keep this in mind before you start talking. Then you would say: he was true, he was genuine, he was right. You always have to listen to friends as if they were to die the next day. A romantic; I remember him as a kind of Jacopo Ortis. *Oh, if men always kept death at their side they wouldn't be such cowardly serfs.*" Tito, deeply moved, encouraging: "Bravo, what a wonderful phrase. You should write things like that. And what about the twin?" he asks with a leer. "Didn't you say you saw the twin?" I keep quiet but Ovidio teacheth: "Enrico Fassola has set the authorities in motion to let her enter Italy. Which means passing through one of those gates near a glass cage, a kind of box office; you pass, and you are in Italy." He smiled; he briefly gathered the vision within himself: "A small girl, self-assured in her motions, attractive. She talks continuously. She told us that in America she was very friendly with a man sentenced to death. A man sentenced to death by due process of law; there was nothing more to be done, in spite of committees, and of the opposition in principle to the death penalty on the part of the governor of the state himself. All these very influential people, all agreeing on the horror of the thing and the advisability of avoiding it. Meanwhile, the action was going on, it was carried out. We don't do what we are doing. It's one of Bernardo Partibon's phrases, who, in turn, was quoting somebody in Los Angeles." With a forcedly casual air, Tito asks: "And did she witness the execution?" Ovidio says: "No, at the time when the man was entering the gas chamber, and during the twelve minutes, if I remember correctly, that it took for him to die, Ilse was drinking her café au lait; she realized that it was exactly the time, and she went on drinking her café au lait. She didn't complain at all that they wouldn't let her into Italy, that is, beyond that box office, and she left immediately again for Israel. Bouncing up and down the Mediterranean; Enrico managed to have the news about poor Clement reach her somehow through our embassy, then he eased things up here. But now Enrico is very much occupied, he is leaving for London. At the office he is never in his office. That's another quote from Bernardo; we never are where we are. Enrico has asked me to take Ilse under my protection while he was informing Dora in Venice, but there was very little to protect, she must have her own circle of people here in Rome; she has disappeared. Besides talking over the telephone with Dora in Venice, I also talked with Bernardo and he told me to let Ilse do what she wants: 'You see, her mother is here too,' he said. I ask him whether that meant that Ilse too will go to Venice, and he said, 'Not necessarily, not necessarily.'" I say in a very low voice: "But she went there, in fact exactly to the scene of the crime, on the Lido," but after all I don't even particularly want them to listen to me. Ovidio by now has everything under control: "Ilse's mother is, of course, Bernardo's mother-in-law. Little by little I must get to know everything, the true nature of the relationship between them; they are very important families and very much ramified, and I myself, marrying my Dora, will be part of them." I tell him: "It pleases me to see you so well oriented. You are where you are and you do what you are doing." My observation encourages him: "When Bernardo goes back to

America, I'll take things into my hands a little. The family as an institution is very much underestimated in our milieu; in fact, it is mistreated. Instead, why not try?" Tito and I are hanging on his words. Quarto moans to himself: "At some point I would have married Genziana." Ovidio is still on Bernardo: "I have known Bernardo only a short time but I already feel about him as about an older brother; I say older because he is so large and big but we must be more or less the same age. We are of the same stock. With Dora, we shall go to America to visit him. As far as I could gather, in some cities of Texas and California he has created some real little phases of taste. There are those who say that American culture is irremediably bidimensional, but I see there also magnificent developments in depth. One must operate in one's limited milieu: a sector, *a thing*." I say automatically: "Consider my case now, with the novels." He proceeds: "I was also thinking of poor Clement Blumenfeld. He had started on the right foot. This increases one's sorrow at his horribly premature end." Enviable Ovidio, he sheds normal tears, lustral waters. "After all—" he smiles with admiring participation—"I have the impression that Bernardo Partibon in Venice will take advantage of this rather crucial moment in the history of his family, or let us say, his families, to bring order, to organize a general settlement. His trip to Italy acquires a precise significance; it is being referred to as a family summit meeting. He is there on the Grand Canal among the women of his family . . . " Ovidio goes on while I whisper inaudibly: "He has been very much alone, and he isn't there any longer. He came back to Rome and for a whole night he told me everything. Clement is dead and I am substituting for him as Bernardo's biographer." Enough. By now I speak in silence. I have the moment of perfect focus before crumbling. The optimum of lucidity, the peak, before I redescend by the dark side of the mountain. Et cetera, et cetera. If I talk they don't hear me. They don't know what they are missing. Sentences and paragraphs form into rings within me. One should have a weightless style. Writing is, by definition, impossible. But you, Massenti, have got your syntax, you are a syntaxist.

He has remained for hours, days, in that mezzanine where the Fassolas have fixed him up, looking from the window over the chic-est bend of the Grand Canal, he just arrived from Rome, where he has given Clement, with his own hands as it were, a presumably temporary burial. In spite of his declared desire for isolation, especially from his mother-in-law, his wife has come to visit him.

"With Nicole one communicates only when one is in a good mood," Bernardo tells Clare. "If we talked now, in the end she would admit that after all she is also experiencing a sense of relief these days. A part of her life is extinguished, in which she never really believed, and which she prefers to forget. Herbert Blumenfeld is as good as dead. She may be frightened by the idea that of the twins only Ilse remains. But didn't she consider her dead too?"

"On the contrary, *she has asked* about her. The most recent call from the private hospital is: *Bring Ilse to me*. Embracing her. Having her at her bedside for words of reconciliation and forgiveness. The theme, now, is death; her mind has taken that direction. It's her hobby. The idea of everyone's being buried in Venice some day. There isn't only the question of death, there is also that of knowing how to commemorate the dead properly. Some people prepare the commemorations beforehand, including their own. You undoubtedly know, Bernie, how enormously successful the cemetery industry is. It's surprising how much your mother-in-law, Nicole, knows on the subject, how much she has already prepared in her mind. I say *your mother-in-law* because she includes all of you, she would like you all, some day, buried in Venice. For a person like her, when somebody dies, beyond heart rending and heart collapse, it is also as if a new administration were being inaugurated: other problems, other interests, another *way of life*. And she sees everything clearly, she has those green, steady eyes, made of limpid glass. Actually, you are wrong: Clement and Ilse's father is not dead at all: he still has the card of his death up his sleeve. Some false rumors have been spread, by Cecilia Ghezzi-Walther, I believe (but then Cecilia specializes in unreliable, useless gossip), to the effect that he, Herbert, had sent Ilse to Israel to buy him a little piece of land. No. He is still attached to Venice; one has no idea what Venice can do to some people who are maniacally attached to it. And Nicole, your mother-in-law, is, for him, Venice."

Bernardo has contemplated his wife a long while, thunderstruck: "I like you. What a head! What lucidity! In this moment I am happy I have arranged such a nice financial settlement for you."

Clare, feeling she has gained several points, does not behave like a person on a visit but almost like the mistress of the house. She starts moving about, studying ways to make the place more comfortable. Finally: "Look, I understand very well what you are doing for us. Mother understands it too, but she doesn't mention any details, and anyway, she is in a state of shock now. But I'm talking about it. You are bankrupting yourself. What with help to your mother, and your other commitments, you are giving us all that you possess. Let me talk for a minute."

"It's no use. I know very well what you want, you want to stick labels on actions, medals: love, generosity, goodness . . . But you and your mother should have understood . . ."

(325)

"Mother has nothing to do with this. If you should tell me now: 'Don't see her any more,' I would do it. My desire is to stay here with you. And if you want, I accept even the fact that you deny me the explanation of your gestures, including your latest. However, remember that I find them perfectly consistent with your character, with your way . . ."

"Why do you do this to me, Clare? Why don't you keep quiet?"

"Your way of living and of seeing things, Bernie, which has never changed and never will. . . "

"Every day, Clare, it changes every day. Every morning, one starts all over again. Of course!"

Clare shakes her head before such stubbornness, but she has a genuine veil of tears in her eyes while she contemplates Bernardo, her husband. Gentle but vigorous, she extends her arms; she squeezes him tight: "Your goodness will never change; your goodness is like a vice."

Then he holds her in his arms too, caressing her face, with a kind of affectionate exasperation: "Clare, Clare, if you understand so many things, you could also have understood that it was an order—keeping silent, letting me stay alone. There is no point in making up fantasies about staying here together, or whatever . . . I am not staying here, I never stay anywhere, Clare. I'll take some of Clement's things away with me, I'll go away with his things . . . I start all over again every time, it's the only way, I'm not saying it's the only way to save oneself or even to respect oneself or even to manage not to despise oneself too much, I say simply this, without any qualifications: *it's the only way.* You can give it any meaning you want, you can say that all of the Partibons have always been insane—why don't you try to work on that, for example?"

(*3 2 6*)

Clare is defeated, or at least she has lost one round; she accepts the result with sportsmanship. She smiles with all of her sweetness and all of her strength. The fact remains that Bernardo is *her favorite man in life;* and probably the main reason for her next, tenderly imperious motion is that she doesn't want to go away without performing an act of homage, and, at the same time, of dominion; and leaving a token of remembrance.

She is a beautiful woman with a classical profile, with perfect, well-groomed skin; she speaks well, she reads a lot with her clear, steady eyes; she understands painting, silver. She has never been with a man without feeling pleasure. She is now crouched on the floor at his feet. She puts a hand under his jacket, she feels that strong side, she goes down to the muscles of his leg. Then she moves toward the center, she opens and starts caressing, kissing, soft, sweet, experienced. As she is engaged in these operations she maintains a solemn expression on her face. Bernardo's deep, convulsed sighs become a rattle: "It's absolutely incredible," he whispers in a broken voice. Meanwhile, with the movements of her shoulders, Clare is easing the descent of Bernardo's hand into her décolletage; then she stops, gets up and says: "Finish undressing me, and let's go to bed."

Later his sister too has come to see him—Maria. They like each other still, they find each other irresistible. She is the girl who has been closest to him during childhood and very early youth. He would have liked to protect her, order her about, guide her. She has been taken away from him by something which, in the language of Odo Partibon, her father—a marvelous, toothless old man, with a powerful voice—has been vaguely referred to as *religion.* Now for practically the first time since his return the two of them are alone, full of mutual curiosities. They devour each other with their eyes, and even she, who had been evasive and distant, wants to know what effects some of the vicissitudes of her past life have had on her brother far away.

"When did you hear about it, and how?" she asks. "That I had been *seduced,* left *pregnant,*" she stresses them as if they were foreign words, "by one who died before doing his *duty?*"

Letters from Caterina Visnadello, and from Enrico himself, and even from Umberto Boschinetti . . . Seduced, pregnant, violated: all terms which, once uttered, immediately appeared irrelevant, because the alleged physical and social outrage was, actually, the sign of Massimo's adoration, of a Fassola, of one belonging to a clan then among the most powerful in Italy; of this boy, who in appearance was brutally physical according to the affectations of the times, and who had probably been, instead, just a bunch of nerves and uncertainties. And finally, to negate the trite story of seduction, there was above all Maria herself—the outraged, the violated, who was, on the contrary, a temperate and majestic woman, firmly set in her powers and in her secrets, who carried her dead child in the palm of her hand like a scepter.

At some point Bernardo has told her: "I was so close to you, I loved you as a child. Now, what could I do, in front of you, if not laugh? Massimina's story—has it, or has it not been a fabrication of some individuals, of some newspapers?"

She shuts herself up, she lowers her very long eyelashes toward her cheeks. "Call it whatever you want. The sure thing is that there hasn't been a single word from me."

"Why didn't you publish some serious denials?"

A pause. "No, my dear, you won't get anything out of me."

Bernardo's hand grasps hers, squeezes it, goes up to her

forearm, shakes it: "I would like you to explain it to me, at least something, a hint . . . "

"I would read stories of childhoods, of heroic lives, and realize that I was thinking: That's she, that's the way she was. Well, then, my dear, I thought, one must go ahead, push on, say certain things clearly. Proceed with clarity, with hardness perhaps. That's what *I* used to tell myself. I say, I used to. Then I withdrew."

"When, Maria? When the leeches got hold of the thing?"

Maria shakes her head. "We'll talk about it. Perhaps. I feel like telling you now: even if I didn't believe in it, I would believe in it anyway. It's not an explanation. Always, even as a child, you wanted to understand, to ask. You are confused, aren't you? You are very confused, Dino, aren't you? I'm sorry I cannot really help you at all."

"Nobody has ever helped me; you don't imagine *you* can, do you, with that kind of talk?"

"If you find yourself alone, it's because you want it, Dino."

On her leaving, they have embraced each other solidly, Maria shedding a tear. "Let's write each other," they have said, with smiles, with intense sighing; they have seen, wide open between them, a long perspective of endless struggle. "From now on, let's keep in touch." They have kissed each other again, embracing tightly.

It was time that they left him alone. In fact, for hours (days?) Bernardo has been leaning out of the window looking at the Grand Canal or, re-entering the house, he has been looking over all those rooms full of very complicated memories and of infinite family histories deposited behind the doors, in the furniture, in the shadows. Centuries ago, the façades of Grand Canal palaces, for instance, were frescoed; now everything inside or out has the same patina, really recognizable only to those who have grown up with

(3 2 9)

it; the amalgam between the inside and the outside is provided by the quicksilver of water reflected on the ceilings. Once upon a time even boats were of many different colors; now, being black and shiny, they produce a reflection and silvery sparkle like all the rest. Among the furniture in the mezzanine, there emerge the two chairs once belonging to the Venice Partibons, standing there, light and yet solidly planted on their legs, like Fausta and Dora. Graceful and solid furniture. Decorative and necessary curves. From the old house of the Venice Partibons, dismantled at the dawn of the Second World War, there have also turned up here fragments of a wooden sculptured ceiling, hit by bombs during the First (War), mainly representing heads of angels and of lions, now hanging on the white walls of a corridor. The heraldic lion of the Venetian fatherland appears in various poses, but with similar expressions on his noble, stately face. During those hours (days) in the deserted house, Partibon and the lions have exchanged frequent looks. Observed since childhood in the historical house of the Partibons at San Tomà, those lions had always attracted him for the capacity that they had, in the expression on their faces, of mingling domestic conviviality with haughty detachment. Already at that time Bernardo had visited them with intense participation and friendliness, studying them, alive as they were to him against the background of that house which, for that matter, had kindled in him the first sparks of taste for art. His eyes ran over those frowning foreheads, those wide flat noses, like mantelpieces. He contemplated and loved those solemn, self-absorbed faces, he descended with his eyes along those ageless whiskers. With the ears of the imagination he heard self-controlled roars, deep and powerful purrings. At the base, like a thread hanging over the chin, was the thin closed mouth, on which his

(3 3 0)

slightly near-sighted eyes had always perceived a formal, inaccessible, stubborn, and desperate smile.

After having recognized and saluted them there, from the lions he would go back to the window; feeling calmer, he would take a quick look at his situation. Clare had been right, the dissolution of his American fortune was complete. Smiling, Bernardo thought of that as he looked at the Grand Canal on his right, opening into the Venetian lagoon, toward the autumnal Lido, the ports, the lighthouses, the Orient. He had had vague and fantastic dealings with Ghezzi-Walther. He had made no commitments. Crossing the ocean would be for him like emigrating again, for the first time. This at the present moment is B.P.'s desire, if he has any. Emigrating in solitude. Trusting his own strength. Seeing what can happen to him, what he can yet do.

In the history of Ilse Blumenfeld's trip to Europe, the tragic and the stupid elements are subtly interwoven: but she is also a working girl on a two-week holiday. She is on the Lido, off-season. From here she calls Bernardo: "In fact it's very beautiful, you feel like you are in the country. I detest the summer on the Lido, with bathing and people all broiled, but now it's very beautiful. Right behind the sea you realize that the Venetian countryside creeps in, the green, the orchards." She has also visited the proprietor of the establishment where the scandal had taken place the previous year. Ecstatically happy to see her again, that young man, muscular and hospitable, Sergio Vianello by name, has evoked the painter Beddoes, the Pauling girl, the little Tahitians, as if referring to a golden age now remote. Ilse has rarely stopped talking. Her way of announcing herself to Bernardo has been: "Listen . . . look, I'll come and see you . . . but you are alone, aren't you?"

"I am alone."

Here is Bernardo receiving her as if he were the owner of the place. "You can hardly fit in here, with these low ceilings," she says, being half his size and therefore much better proportioned to the rooms. They realize they don't know each other very well. But then immediately they feel they do. This is Clement's twin. They are not at all identical twins. *Ilse is courageous, very beautiful, now she is very well, she can stay under water for hours.* She sits down; as a drink she accepts wine; she lights a cigarette but it's clear that ordinarily she doesn't smoke. She asks for news.

"As soon as your mother is a little better," Bernardo announces, "she and Clare will go and pay a visit to Clem in Rome, then they will leave for Paris. From that point on, it's their business. At any rate they are nicely fixed up, even if they want to go to America later on, to Nicole's old house in Connecticut."

Ilse hasn't paid much attention. Bernardo feels he should transmit the famous message; "Look," he says, "your mother has repeatedly expressed a wish to see you."

"I know that. But why? Can you explain?"

"Clare has certain theories about Nicole's wanting collective burials here in Venice on San Michele Island, but obviously, above all, your mother has pulled an old weapon out of her Venetian lady's storehouse. It's the moment when Venetian ladies shift from the dialect to official Italian. Relating to her friends the tearful scenes of which she has been the protagonist, she will say: *At that point I was moved, I gave free vent to my emotion.* It reminds you of fur-wrapped ladies at funerals, charitable ladies, committees. Now this sort of thing is rather on the decline here; it flourishes in America, the only country, as Mr. Piglioli-Spada brilliantly pointed out, which can still permit itself sentiments and traditions."

"Listen," Ilse said, "I haven't the vaguest idea what you

(332)

are talking about, but I want to tell you that I am not going to the Countess and to Clare. Curiously enough, Clare rather liked me. Once she told me all about the way you make love. She is a little idiotic, of course, but she is better than many others."

"Come, let's go to the window a while and look at the canal." He puts his large hand on her head, he pushes her gently. She follows obediently and points her large clear eyes, not on the palaces across the canal or on the opening toward Saint Mark's Basin, but on the green-silver water with its veil of fog, on a big puffing motorboat, on a huge slow barge carrying cases of bottles. "Remind me I have some stuff that Larry gave me for you. Both he and the Peach are very, very well." She never changes her tone: "When you were in Venice as a boy, did you know Elena Partibon well?"

"When she was a child."

"And of course you knew Manuela . . ."

"Of course."

"The Partibon women are rather extraordinary, I admire them, they always find the thing that persuades them to survive."

"You too, don't you? What is it that persuades you?"

Ilse keeps silent a long while, it is her longest pause since California. Then: "What captures you in the end is words. Cataracts of words. Talk talk talk, trying to define something that will never be defined, that will forever remain uncertain, and therefore open, available for new cataracts of words to gush over it. I was saying this the other day to Donato Plea, who is a friend of yours. In the milieu where I have lived, people talk a lot. The extreme case is Venice, the Venetian tone. At some point it may very well happen that *you want to die,* I've wanted it sometimes with the greatest sincerity, really with a beatific sense of peace, the

(333)

peace you find at the bottom of the sea; perhaps that's why I'm so good at swimming under water. Well, but then, you are brought up to the air again from that silence, you get captured in a net of words. It isn't that you start consciously to talk, you realize you are already talking, perhaps with somebody you've seen for the first time in your life, just met at a party, and you end up spending even days and nights together, mainly talking. And always you keep thinking that the ideal perhaps would be to achieve silence, but on the other hand, the ideal then is death, the absolute cessation of any desire to be in the game. But then a new round starts, and it isn't that you realize you want to play it, it's that you are there anyway, playing, getting into the picture, claiming recognition: everybody excited, caught in the situation. Actually, of course, you don't even understand what it is all about, since you have only words to understand, which is something obviously insufficient, but that's precisely why the flow of words continues, which means that existence perpetuates itself because it has this huge basic insufficiency—or you could call it despair, couldn't you?" She catches her breath and resumes, raising her voice: "Of course silence would be better, but where can you find it, except in dying or in never being born? Perhaps that's what the child Clement remembered nostalgically, silence, close to somebody . . . And look, we used to talk about these things in the family, with the utmost clarity. Of course! The famous 'morbid attachment.' " Suddenly she raises her voice, she utters a lacerating cry as if they wanted to hit her and she defended herself: "I loved the way he moved, the way I saw him grow up, the few times they let us be together; he made me proud; I wanted him to be good at school."

Bernardo has lowered his huge head, he shakes it up and down, his eyes staring into empty space, like an old man.

"And now," she continues, "the whole family, the reconciliation at the grave of the poor boy; the twin also, they take pity on her too; Bernardo, you know that pity is useless. Or, let me say, it would be useless even if it were respectable. It isn't even that. It is egotism, personal satisfaction. I limit myself to my own experience, of course. And I'm telling you, soaking in the treacle of compassion for your neighbor means nothing. Feeling pity means nothing. Helping does. Or rather, it would, if it were possible. Listen . . . look," she says, struck by some idea, talking with urgency, coming very close to him, in fact throwing herself, head forward, against Bernardo's chest, "do me a favor, squeeze me, but really with all of the strength you have. You or somebody else, it doesn't matter, hold me tight for a while, as tight as you can, and for God's sake don't talk." They seek each other, their eyes shut. With his hands, with his lips, Bernardo discovers that face, that small body shaking violently, pressed against him, that reality, Ilse, those tears.

Understandably, Ovidio's source is still Dora, whose serene, rosy-cheeked wisdom we are all willing to admire. "From Dora I know everything. Bernardo himself, after all, trusts the wisdom of women. They do usually stage the final scenes, especially in Venice, as in Goldoni's plays. I am aware of that, I know the types. Don't believe that I marry my Dora blindly; I know that under her feminine tenderness and soft talk there is a Venetian fiber. Think for a moment of that city," he teacheth, "of that very precious work of art laid on the treacherous softness of the lagoon. Think of the mad titanic work there is behind such an achievement. Curious," he goes on, "that Venice should have been taken for a symbol of decadence; there is nothing more vital, and in my own life, Dora is the sign of that vitality, God bless her." I insert: "Besides, in Venice now Dr. Debaldè also does a lot," but I don't even manage to smile, and for that matter the style of my contributions is a bit passé. I add: "You are right, I envy you; perhaps if Genziana had been born in Venice she would have saved herself." Ovidio resumes dreamily: "The fiber of those women. Think of Dora's mother. Did you know that she was the mistress of an uncle of Bernardo's, the famous Marco, in the years around 1915? Ageless women." He is accustomed to debates, to panels, so now he catches the thread I had left dangling in the air: "Dr. Debaldè. He wants to institute regional Caritas awards, he is an opportunistic climber restrained only by confessional necessities." The rather involved definition produces an unexpected cry from Q. Martelli: "You are wrong, my friend. He is very nicely fixed up, while we are forever going to be nothing but vagabonds. He is healthy; we are neurotic. He doesn't screw; we consume ourselves inside of women. He always does things he likes, *while we hardly ever do*. That man will bury us all." Ovidio, perfectly calm, with a Padua accent: "Damn it, don't you realize that there will never be a significant relationship between Debaldè and another human being? And for significant relationships one has to pay; they require stamina. So much so that one *must* limit oneself: a family, a . . . *a thing;* otherwise . . ." I suggest: "Take for instance Bernardo Partibon," and Ovidio immediately accepts my candidate: "Bernardo, in fact," he raises his forefinger, "is a giant of strength and yet he is always sick, as he told me himself; *but now he has caught on.*" Tito's eyes move from Ovidio to me, from me to Ovidio, as if he were following the ball at a tennis match; his eyes shine, clearly he would like to have a tape recorder to register everything and play it back later, at home, in Bologna. "Dora and Bernardo are very close, she admires him no

(336)

end, and she is right. Bernardo is a man who practices pure, secular goodness." Tito triumphantly: "What do you mean?" Ovidio simply: "To begin with, doing good without boasting about it, in fact without letting anybody know." Tito immediately: "An evangelical character." The unpredictable Quarto intervenes: "Evangelical, my foot. Do you know Umberto Boschinetti? I know him because we go hunting together. Now, Bernardo one day recently treated him like dirt, and shortly after that occasion Boschinetti was reminiscing to me about Bernardo at school in Venice. He was, by the way, exactly as big as he is now. Well, to summarize, some of his schoolmates, apparently inspired also by their mothers, had decided to treat him absolutely and completely as though he were an orang-utan, that's how barbaric and violent he was. He didn't love anybody except his sister, and it seems that he and his schoolmates had bloody fights a couple of times a week because they accused him of incest." I confine myself to a moan but Ovidio goes on: "Boschinetti is not acceptable as a source," he declares, "he is a figure belonging to the world of farce." Quarto shrugs mockingly: "The evangelical element," and Tito's eyes become questioning, he has lost the thread, the score. Ovidio shakes his head, his fine red and freckled face opens up in a smile: "You are a bunch of idiots. What does evangelical mean? I'll tell you something: a so-called Christian action cannot be given that epithet any more because too many people have misused the label. Instead, one should act without any expectation of a reward. Without medals. Without beatifications. Without hope." Now I am very sure that nobody listens to me, and I whisper: *"Without even the reward of knowing whether what you've done is good or evil."* Ovidio goes on: "I am reconstructing from things that Dora told me, and of course my sweet darling has her own limited way of expressing herself. Clement was

(337)

the only one who knew Bernardo well. We shall have to get hold of Clement's diaries, he used to keep thick diaries, he wrote like a maniac." He points his finger at me: "You had the right view when you were doing your articles on Maria Partibon and her dead child, your intuition of Maria's character was exemplary; only, perhaps it was too difficult for Perineschi's magazine." I say: "I don't write for Peri any more, in fact I don't write for any magazine at all." He goes on teaching me: "Perhaps for the sake of publicity Peri would have allowed you to go the whole way with your idea of blessedness achieved through political pull, this story of an attempt to set the machine in motion, starting from the *vox populi,* to create a movement toward the beatification trial, all of this through favoritism, influence. The whole thing should have been conducted at the level of paradox but in a convinced and precise style, somewhat in the manner of Swift. Dora was telling me about an idea of Clement's, who suggested it to Dr. Debaldè, about miraculous recoveries obtained at the level of mental diseases. In other words, religious authorities, who in these matters are extremely prudent in accepting the verdict of science, should use psychiatrists as experts rather than ordinary physicians. It would be fascinating work. Actually, why don't you conduct journalistic inquiries any longer?" Come to think of it, we were supposed to do one together, on the women as victims. I say defensively: "You told me yourself that, for example, women now settle everything in the end, as in Goldoni's plays. Time is running fast, Italy is in a ferment, problems are too quickly outdated." He smiles sweetly, because Dora comes to his mind: "One thing I find very moving in Dora is her total absence of a historical sense. For the wife of a history professor that's not bad at all. But that's the way they win. In fact, women are the true protagonists of history and we are only its arid teachers." Tito

(338)

shines: "What a beautiful phrase!" Ovidio amplifies: "And that's because history is made *for* them and not *by* them; and *it does not interest them.*" Tito incites him: "What were you saying a few nights ago about career women?" Ovidio corrects him: "Rather than about career women, we were talking in particular about frigid ones. I was saying a very simple thing, namely, that many men live in terror of being or of becoming impotent, while women, even if frigid, organize their lives accordingly and pursue other forms of satisfaction." Quarto has doubts: "They pursue what?" Ovidio, lucidly: "Power, which to them is either social or sentimental." Quarto shakes his head: "At any rate, your Dora is not like that." By now Ovidio has a fixation about Venice: "No. There is the Venetian fiber there. Born and raised in that city," he teacheth, "that strong, terrible city badly sheltered against winter cold, frozen canals, fogs and humidity and atrocious discomforts, where you have to go on foot through the net of narrow streets, whose intricacy takes your breath away and dismays visitors. For centuries, with insufficient heating, on the mud, through extremely arduous architectural and structural organizations, they have created trade, galleys, arts, amusements. It's a hard, hard city, of stone, with floods every year, not in marshy lands, but in the most splendid center of the city, with submerged caves, which were once upon a time storerooms for Oriental spices or crypts of churches. And frost, fog in your bones, and at the other end, summers when the stone is incandescent even during the night . . . " At this point he excites me too: "Bravo," I cry, "and the indestructible spirit of Dora passes through all of this, which is also the Partibon spirit that Bernardo carries within himself as he wanders through the world, for instance through Texas and now perhaps also through other continents . . . " I don't know what I am saying, but Ovidio is exultant and he pushes on:

"Dora says that Bernardo should be seen at auctions. Zeus's nod, which makes the art market tremble." I resume and I develop the idea with the stubbornness of the half inebriated: "The hardness of Venice, the indissoluble mixture of fantasy and calculation, of solidity and folly. Stone, stone, and within the huge stone palaces, little eighteenth-century boudoirs, deceptively fragile like the women, and inside those, astonishing sexual events, go to it, push on, screw on, isn't that it, Ovidio? Isn't that it, Ovidio?" *And now I am sinking.* Meanwhile Tito's mediating voice rises again, attentive, demanding: "And what did you mean," he asks Ovidio, "when you said that Bernardo now has got the idea? What idea?" Ovidio, very lucidly: "Bernardo too refuses to be a dissociated man. Every life must regulate itself along its own pattern, within which it has a minimum of sense and coherence. Cultivate one's own garden. We can't, each of us, always take upon us the burden of universal questions." I yell: "Bravo! This is Bernardo all right: he, formerly the universal sufferer, the 'Weltschmerzler,' has got the idea, his particular, nourishing, tasteful idea, and he returns to his own Clare, decorative, important wife, very tolerable mother-in-law, a villa in Connecticut, friends, connections, habits, security, the serene suburban dwellings, rustic and city elements mixed, the old moccasins, sailing across the Sound, the solidity of indoor plumbing, comfort and wilderness mixed; I was there and I got the picture. The richness and the thickness of carpets, of milk. I understand B.P. He is right. His career is a success story, his biography a triumph. Voltaire would kiss him on the forehead. He has found a way to be applauded by the right and by the left. Only dissociated men could speak evil of him." And now I crouch on the sea bottom. This is the Bernardo image that convinces them, *but it has been invented by me. Nothing is true. He won't go back to his wife. He hasn't caught on. He hasn't a penny left. All he wants to do is emigrate like the first time and start all over again every morning.* I don't know how much time has passed, I see them as through water; hours, days later, they say with distant, grave voices: "Let's go to her, and bring flowers. Perhaps, before that, we can also go to him, who has stayed on here in the city. Where is he buried?" They seem to ask me and I seem to reply: "What does it matter where he is buried? The dead don't stay there, my friends, they go with solitary people like themselves, who carry them inside, around the world." Tito is all agog: "Also this thing you are saying is very beautiful. We can all fit in the car, we go tomorrow morning early to the grave." I won't. I have to write. But I am submerged. However, I can also compose under water. I am subaqueous. They are supranational. Rome, October —One morning in the Chigi palace he talked to me about Europe. They are all supranational. I am under the influence. Go to Leo. Always first at the morgue. If men would always keep death at their side. Ilse was very friendly with an executed man. Debaldè will bury us all. Seeing her, dead. A way we had of loving her. Ovidio, I envy Ovidio. Lustral waters on the funereal mound. I would have married her. The family is underestimated in our milieu. The alps of youth. *Falsa magra;* wardrobe mistress in *Caligula*. Duilio is settled, Ovidio is settled; Bernardo, Enrico, Tito, Quarto, settled. The women no longer victims have settled everybody. But you sleep, Genziana, and if you sleep, I want only to stay and look at you; then you'll wake up and we'll talk if you feel like it. Go now, carissimo, you know that I have never been able to rest with somebody near me.

Rome, Beverly Hills, Crans sur Sierre, 1953–1963

About the Author

P. M. PASINETTI was born and grew up in Venice, where his father was a prominent physician and his mother belonged to the Ciardi family of painters. He attended school in Venice and took a degree at Padua; later he went to Oxford and Berlin to learn the languages. In 1935–37 he came for the first time to the United States, where his first published fiction appeared in *The Southern Review*. Mr. Pasinetti has since contributed to various literary reviews in this country, and since the age of eighteen has written pieces for magazines and newspapers in Italy, where he has also worked editorially on a literary and film review and done occasional work on screenplays (for film directors Franco Rossi and M. Antonioni). His first book, three novelettes, was published by Mondadori in 1942.

Mr. Pasinetti first thought of teaching as a means of moving from his native country. After lectureships at Gottingen and Stockholm (where he spent most of the war years) he returned to the United States in 1946, taught briefly at Bennington and received a doctorate at Yale; his dissertation won the John Addison Porter Prize for 1949. He has since been associated with U.C.L.A., where he holds a professorship, lectures in World Literature and is a co-editor of *The Italian Quarterly*. He has been appointed to the University's Institute for Creative Arts for 1964–65 and is at present in Venice working on a third novel. His first, *Venetian Red*, was published by Random House in 1960 and became a considerable international success. Mr. Pasinetti's own Italian draft of *The Smile on the Face of the Lion* was published in Milan by Bompiani in 1964; the Italian title: *La Confusione*.